Frank Muir was born in 1920. He left school at fourteen, on the death of his father, to train with a firm of carbon-paper manufacturers. After the war, in which he served as a photographer in the RAF, he started writing for BBC radio, where he soon teamed up with Denis Norden, a partnership that was to last for over twenty-five years. *Take It From Here* was immediately successful and they were hailed as Britain's best comedy writers for radio and subsequently television. In 1956 they began the literary quiz programme *My Word* which was described by the BBC as 'the most popular radio programme in the world', and followed it in 1967 with the equally successful *My Music*.

In 1967 Muir and Norden decided to work separately. Muir spent three years running BBC television comedy, and a further three years doing the same for London Weekend Television. Among his many successful books are *The Frank Muir Book* and *The Oxford Book of Humorous Prose*. He was elected Rector of the University of St Andrews 1977–9, and holds honorary degrees from both the Universities of St Andrews and Kent. In 1980 he was appointed a CBE.

THE
WALPOLE ORANGE

A ROMANCE

Frank Muir

CORGI BOOKS

THE WALPOLE ORANGE
A CORGI BOOK 0 552 14137 2

Originally published in Great Britain by Bantam Press,
a division of Transworld Publishers Ltd

PRINTING HISTORY
Bantam Press edition published 1993
Corgi edition published 1994
Corgi edition reprinted 1995

Set in 10/12 Linotype Plantin by
Chippendale Type Ltd, Otley, West Yorkshire.

Corgi Books are published by Transworld Publishers Ltd,
61–63 Uxbridge Road, Ealing, London W5 5SA,
in Australia by Transworld Publishers (Australia) Pty Ltd,
15–25 Helles Avenue, Moorebank, NSW 2170,
and in New Zealand by Transworld Publishers (NZ) Ltd,
3 William Pickering Drive, Albany, Auckland.

Printed and bound in Great Britain by
Cox & Wyman Ltd, Reading, Berkshire

For my grandchildren,
Abigail and Isobel

CONTENTS

CHAPTER ONE

TWO LETTERS

William looked at his young, small wife across the breakfast table and thought how lovely she was. It was a particularly good moment to look at Milly because she had just decapitated her boiled egg with a neat horizontal swipe and was opening a letter with the eggy knife when a shaft of West Kensington sunshine came in through the kitchen window and backlit her. She began reading her letter.

With her head bowed, the sun shining through her cornflake-coloured hair, slender in her crumpled nightie, eyes still puffy from sleep, she seemed to William to be wondrously fragile, vulnerable.

'Well, bugger me to Bermondsey and back,' she said.

William sighed. He rarely swore and even the mild expletives which he did use had to be forced from him by some emotional shock, such as when he first met Milly's rather grand parents, nervously put soda water in his gin instead of tonic and took a deep swig; or when he dropped a hot cast-iron frying-pan, with omelette, into a sink full of virtually all their wedding-present crockery.

His first experience of Milly's casually devastating way of expressing herself in moments of stress happened during their wedding reception when a lumpish bridesmaid stood on Milly's wedding dress and tore it away from one shoulder. The bridesmaid's mother, who was within earshot of Milly, went a mottled colour and backed into a flower arrangement. William was now a little more used to Milly's outbursts and understood that they were a symptom of some crisis.

'Got egg on your letter?' he asked, without much hope.

'It's Catriona!' said his wife.

Physically, Catriona was the key member of Milly's Baroque String Trio, the most sexy-looking; always pushed to the front by Milly when the trio was being interviewed for a booking by a heterosexual Festival organizer or hotel conference manager.

'The great over-uddered cow!'

William thought that, in fairness, over-uddered was pitching it a bit strong. Catriona was of normal build mostly but she did have an important, impressively proportioned, Edwardian one-piece bosom. When she was dressed formally at recitals and turned sideways on, elderly gentlemen in the audience breathed heavily.

'What's Catriona done?'

'Done a bunk!'

'Oh, Milly, how rotten. Does she give a reason?'

'I'm just getting to that bit.' She glared down at the letter. William thought her face showed the kind of ferocious disbelief with which Goneril must have taken the news that her difficult old father King Lear had decided to retire and move in with her.

'How *could* she!'

William waited. He knew by experience that this was the best thing to do when Milly had the swears. While he was waiting he cut a strip of bread and butter, wrapped it round his boiled egg to save his fingers from the agonizing heat which only an intact boiled egg can retain and very gently tapped the egg on the table, rotating it skilfully a little at a time until the whole shell was a mass of tiny cracks, like the crazed surface of an old porcelain plate. Then with the nail of his forefinger he painstakingly picked off the tiny flakes of shell one at a time.

It usually took him about four and a half minutes, or six if the egg was one of those portly ones over which the pulpy cardboard egg-box would not close properly. Milly went on reading her letter and seething.

'Sex-mad, of course,' she muttered. 'She was peculiar as a child, drawing in the naughty bits on her dolls sort of thing. Well,' tapping the letter, 'she's now a self-confessed pyromaniac.'

'Nymphomaniac,' said William, 'unless her love-making sets her lovers alight.' His boiled egg was now naked in its thin caul. He eased it into its cup, dug out a spoonful and gave his wife his full attention. 'Just what has Catriona been up to?'

'Listen to this.' Milly read loudly: ' "Desperately sorry darling but it's bye-bye Baroque Trio for me. Met Trev at the Rudolf Steiner Hall last Thursday at the Stravinsky thingy. Trev is truly beautiful. A bit too much hair around the bald bit on top but a neat bum and he's a musician. Plays lead guitar in a group. Well, most groups actually because he is a session musician for a recording studio and sits in for all the pop musicians who can't really play their guitars. His daddy bought a disused tram factory in the Toxteth area of Liverpool where he manufactures organic farmhouse cheese and health-shop yoghurt and is v.rich, though of course with granny's money that is not a factor with me. Trev is a mighty man 'neath duvet and it's true love for ever this time, Mill. On Tuesday we are flying off to Bolivia (I think it's Bolivia) where me and Trev and a soul-singer I've never heard of are going to save something. Mahogany trees or children or whatever. I'll write." Oh, William, with Catriona gone my lovely trio is now just a trio!'

'I thought your trio *was* a trio.'

'It's complicated. They were called trios but composers liked the fuller sound of two violins so baroque trio sonatas were often written for harpsichord, cello, and two violins. And now I've only got Estelle's violin, which means a thinner noise. And visually, too, Estelle, pretty girl that she is, is no Catriona in shape.'

'You have a problem,' said William. 'Even in the soft light of the Ritz at teatime, Lovely-but-Thin Estelle's hardly what Arab princes are going to charter Concorde to fly over and ogle.'

'So what's left?' wailed Milly. 'Six reasonable legs, particularly Pippa's sexy knees and feet, but not a bold titty among the three of us. Oh, soddy-soddy-soddy!'

William was about to protest that Milly was beautifully formed in all directions and indeed he knew that Lovely-but-Thin Estelle had a figure like a roll of kitchen foil, but she was a very beautiful girl in all other ways, and that the loss of Catriona did not mean that the all-girl trio (quartet) would never be booked again. But warning bells tinkled. This was a serious crisis for Milly and any comment he made would almost certainly only exacerbate things. William thought he understood his wife quite well. That is to say he reckoned he understood about 30 per cent of her character and qualities which, looking around, seemed to him an above-average husbandly achievement.

The four girls in Milly's original Baroque String Trio (quartet) were Milly (harpsichord), the Hon. Pippa (cello), Catriona (violin), and Estelle (violin). William got on well enough with Lovely-but-Thin Estelle and top-heavy Catriona but found the tubby Hon. Pippa (of the sexy knees and feet) a curiously shy girl who seemed to prefer her cello to people. Rather frightening. But she was a good cellist. And Catriona and Estelle were very good violinists and Milly really was a most promising harpsichordist.

Milly's group had met and formed when they shared a bedroom at their dour and damp boarding school in Sussex and discovered they were all mad about classical

12

music. Irksome disciplines such as restricting photographs of ponies and Labradors to five per animal per girl, posters of Gary Glitter restricted to one per room and a complete ban on Sunday-lunch pork crackling being wrapped in a hanky and stored up knicker legs for chewing during Sunday-afternoon letter-writing, had been imposed with vigilance. The only opportunity the four small music-lovers had to express individuality was in the privacy of their pale pink bedroom where they developed an innocent but inventive use of foul language.

Sex education had yet to arrive and embarrass everybody so the girls did not know exactly what the words they were using meant but they knew that they were taboo words which no lady or gentleman would utter and that was good enough for them. The swears, as they called them, were initiated one evening by Milly when she locked the bedroom door, turned to the others and snorted: 'Those two Irish nuns confiscated my chocolate cake before I'd even eaten it – well, sod 'em and begorrah!'

'Who's your letter from?' asked Milly in a small, ordinary voice. 'Hope yours is better news than mine.'

'Ah' said William. 'I'll look.' He laid the envelope flat on the table face down, produced his Swiss Army penknife and carefully slit along the top edge of the envelope. He then swivelled the envelope round and slit along the first narrow side, then the other narrow side, then he slid the knife blade under the envelope top and opened it up like the lid of a suitcase. He always opened his morning letters this way because when he was a schoolboy he had carelessly ripped open an envelope and torn in half a birthday cheque for five pounds from his rich aunt.

As he extricated the letter he heard a slight sound and guessed that Milly was crying. He listened more carefully. Could be laughter but he reckoned it was crying all right. He did not look up because he had a feeling that Milly wanted to have a private cry. Oddly enough, Milly appeared to be crying when they first met. At the time William was running a very temporary second-hand bookshop in Lewes, Sussex, an ex-fried-fish takeaway driven into liquidation by hygiene bye-laws which a quick-footed local entrepreneur had rented on a very short lease and hired William to manage. The shop, smelling faintly of haddock, was filled with stacks of grubby second-hand, out-of-print and incomplete volumes which the entrepreneur had clearly either bought by weight or stolen.

William saw this pale, thin young woman sitting on the floor between piles of books, head bowed, shoulders heaving. He thought she had probably hit the sad bit in *Black Beauty*. But then she looked up and he saw that her eyes were filled with tears of laughter which she was trying to suppress as un-bookshop-like merriment. Not trusting herself to speak, she handed William the book, which was open at a photograph.

William glanced first at the title page. It read:

MARRIED LOVE-MAKING
What Every Bride-to-be should Brace Herself to Endure

By A Lady. 1912.

(Photographs by H. Meredith Punt ARPS, Frith St W1)
(3/6d: Post Free, in plain wrapper)

The greyish photograph showed a sizeable bride in a bullet-proof corset seated at her dressing-table brushing rather a lot of hair. Behind her a thin man with very shiny black hair, a worried expression and no trousers was removing his stiff collar from his back collar-stud with evident difficulty. He was wearing sock suspenders.

The totally unerotic effect of the photograph caught William on the hop and he laughed and laughed in an uncontrollable, honking, way.

Eventually he managed to gasp, 'I thought you were reading *Black Beauty*!' Which set the two of them off again. He sat down beside her on the floor and they talked.

'My name's Milly,' she said. 'I play the harpsichord and will be leaving the Royal College this year and I want to form a Baroque String Trio with my three best friends and I'm terrified.'

'Milly as in Millicent?'

'As in Millamant. My father played the female lead, Millamant, in a wig when his school dramatic society did *The Way of the World*, during which he discovered that he enjoyed being applauded more than anything else in life. Which is why, I suppose, he named me after Millamant. In shops they say, "Filament? Could you spell it, luv?"'

'Your father an actor?'

'No, an MP. It wasn't a very good wig. The school couldn't afford to hire one, it was donated by a bald parent who decided to come out. A photograph of father wearing the wig was in the school magazine. He didn't look like Millamant at all to me, more like a young Rod Stewart at a Glasgow gig.'

'Should I have heard of your father?'

'He's Sir Garnett Bracewell, Ex-Chairman of the Investment Manager and Stockbrokers Association, Ex-Chairman of the Tory Backbenchers 1894 Committee or something. I've never really known him. He sits on about fifty committees and boards of directors and is never home. If we do meet he doesn't like the way I've done my hair and can't understand why I'm not still aged twelve. Mother doesn't mind his being away all the time. Means she can get on with her projects.'

15

'Charities?'

'My mother's contribution to world happiness is making enough money to buy silk suits in Rome and start thinking about organizing herself a toyboy. I'm exaggerating a bit – sorry. She makes quite a bit of money setting up these awful agencies. Agencies for anything saleable: second-hand wrapping paper; memorabilia of the Sex Pistols; young butlers for gracious homes in Florida; refilled throwaway ballpoint pens; first-night tickets to see Pavarotti in concert at the Birmingham Exhibition Centre. I don't see a lot of her, well I'm a bit of an embarrassment because I haven't got a career or a husband or anything for her to boast about. She's all right, of course. Well, I suppose. So's father. I suppose. It's just that we don't – we don't get along too smoothly. All three of us. Or any two of us for that matter.'

Darkness fell as they talked on but they didn't notice. After some thought, William kissed her gently and she clung very tightly to his arm. It was an unbelievably short time in which to fall in love but they managed it.

Milly got on with her private cry and her egg. She was undismayed by her little manifestations of all-is-not-well-with-me, which to William and most men meant the end of the world, like being sick or fainting or crying in public, and Milly was quite enjoying her cry.

She stirred her egg with her knife. I did so love William at first, she thought. Instead of those pink, shiny, overweight young dealers in copper futures whom her mother kept manoeuvring in her path, she had found William. Calm, reliable, decent, lots of humour.

'What's his name? What does he *do*, darling? Is he PLU – People Like Us?' A caring mother's anxious questions tumbled out.

'His name is William Grundwick and at the moment he's

got a job in a Railway Lost Property Office but it's only a temporary . . . '

'*William*?' shrieked her mother. 'You'd be Milly and Willy! Just wait until I tell your father about this!'

'I wouldn't bother,' said Milly. 'He won't remember who I am.'

'Of course he will, silly. But he does have rather a lot on his mind. He's very fond of you in his own funny old way. But what's this – this William's – background? Grundwick? Get the *Who's Who*.'

'They're not in it. Grundwick is not the family name. It's Anson.'

'I suppose it was changed in the hope that a rich aunt named Grundwick would leave him money.'

'That's right. He was her favourite nephew and the legend in the family was that her jobbing-builder husband had left her a row of houses in Carshalton.'

'How gullible can you get!'

'But it was true. His aunt paid for William's education and left him a tiny freehold house in Peel Street. He lets the upper half as a flat so he's got a bit of money coming in. Quite enough for us to get by on.'

Her mother slumped into the sofa, all her plans of a brilliant, society marriage for her problem daughter shattered. The notice in *The Times* announcing 'The engagement of Millamant Bracewell to the Hon. Adrian Constable-Devereux-DeWitt'; the four-page spread with photographs in *Hello!* magazine – 'The bride's mother, the ever-youthful and soignée Lady Bracewell, enjoying a joke in the tack-room with the Lord Lieutenant' – all now dreams down the drain.

She arranged her skirt into more attractive folds and said: 'You won't make this stupid marriage work, you know. You'll fail as you always fail at everything.'

Milly gulped, but as she went through this every time

she tried to do anything at all, she was bitterly used to it. When she told her mother she wanted to go on from school to the Royal College of Music and become a professional harpsichordist, her mother almost hit her with a bottle of Campari.

'Oh, Millamant!' she said. 'After all that I, and to a certain extent your father, have done for you; expensive convent education, holidays in the better parts of Spain, and that damned pony. And all you want to be is a musician! Playing *music*! Nobody in our family – or even in your father's as far as I know – has ever been mixed up in that sort of thing. There's no money in it, you know.'

Milly tried to explain her idea of the musician friends from school staying together and getting jobs playing in hotels and at conferences as a well-dressed and very feminine trio but her mother just snorted and said, 'Huh!'

Perhaps her mother had been right all along, thought Milly, still stirring her now tepid egg. She had been so happy with William to begin with. Trying to furnish the ground floor of William's tiny house in Peel Street from local junk shops. Their first bed was a stained and ancient futon they bought from a barrow in the North End Road. William said it was like trying to get a good night's sleep on a Jiffybag.

So they moved wildly up-market and bought a second-hand sofa bed, one of the early models made before the designers had got the hang of the problem. The discomfort and danger to the spine of sitting on it as a sofa was only surpassed by the agony of trying to sleep on it as a bed. There was no instruction book so they had a Jacques Tati-like struggle every night trying to open the thing up. Fingers were trapped in moving metal bits. Springs fell off and would not go back on. One side of the bed would unwrap peacefully and lie flat whilst the other side would put up a fight and stick half-open pointing towards the ceiling. When they did get to bed William said it was like trying to sleep on a wrought-iron gate which had been struck by lightning.

But they were happy together. She and William had approached love-making with innocence and trepidation and found that they were both rather good at it. Even on the sofa bed. William was unselfish and physically reliable and Milly proved to be endlessly inventive, notably in the preliminary warming-up activities. Whose most sensitive, central place was to be worked upon first by the other became such a delightful decision to make that Milly took to sliding up to William at parties or in the car and whispering in his ear, 'My place or yours?' It was their code. After which, pleasure apportioned, they would wilfully drift home, savouring the anticipation, only to find themselves steadily accelerating as passion welled.

Milly reflected that she had not said the code words to William for quite a while now. Well, his new job had awkward hours and she was deeply concerned with the Trio's rehearsal schedules, indeed its survival. William's ritualistic destructuring of his boiled egg and his obsessive method of opening his letters, endearing when she was getting to know him, had become just a little bit irritating. And his transparent devotion to her, which had been so comforting at first, had somehow taken away a little of the excitement.

Milly pondered whether her lessening passion might have been caused by the difference in their ages. She was now just twenty-three. In four years' time William would be thirty. Really getting on. And yet. When William had taken a temporary job in Leicester teaching some sad children to swim, she missed him dreadfully, egg and envelope-opening and all. Perhaps because she had got used to being married, to being one of two. So she went to her great-uncle, the distinguished Judge of Appeal Lord

Sidmonton, and asked him to help her find William a job in London.

As it happened this came as a godsend to Uncle Sid, as she called him: His Lordship was the Master of one of London's oldest gentlemen's clubs, the Walpole, and the Club was in urgent need of a Club Secretary. The previous Secretary, Flight-Lieutenant Giles Dundas-McHugh, RAF (retd) was caught by a member making athletic love to a New Zealand waitress on the billiard table. Of course the House Committee had no option but to dismiss the Secretary. Not only because he was wearing studded golf shoes at the time and the billiard table had only recently been re-covered – the cost of repairing the gashes could have been deducted down through the years from his salary – but because New Zealand girls working their way round Europe were strong, sunny, popular waitresses and for the Secretary to risk losing one through being overwhelmed by a wave of lust was judged to be behaviour not in the members' best interests.

Being a club secretary was a job notorious for long hours, pressure from the committee, abuse from members and poor pay. But after a few weeks William, to his surprise, grew to like it.

'Oh *damn*!' cried William suddenly and very loudly. Milly came out of her sad reverie with a bump to see William staring at his letter.

'What's the matter?' asked Milly. 'Damn' was an unusually strong word for William to use at any time let alone at breakfast. 'Is it from Uncle Sid? Has the committee decided to do something barmy for the birthday treat?' The Walpole Club was about to celebrate its two hundred and fiftieth birthday and what form the celebration should take had been under hot debate amongst members for months. 'What excitement have they plumped for? Actor-members reading from their autobiographies? Talk on the

Golden Age of Great Estates by the Duke of Whatsit? Do show me.' She held out her hand.

William hastily crammed the letter into his inside coat pocket. 'I'm terribly sorry, darling,' he said, 'I can't say what's in it.'

'Is it from Uncle Sid?'

'I can't say.'

'Then who is it from?'

'I can't say. It's from – it's from a friend. No, not really a friend, let's say somebody I know. I really am most sorry, Milly, but I'm not able to tell you anything more than that.'

'You won't even tell me who your damned letter's *from*?' asked Milly. 'Me?' William felt awful.

'Look, I fervently wish I wasn't in this position – but there it is. I can only ask you, well, to trust me.' He realized immediately that this was for some reason the wrong thing to have said. Milly just sat there looking chilly and un-Millyish. He glanced at his watch. 'Must get moving, it's going to be quite a day,' he said and tried to give Milly the usual casual peck on the cheek on his way past her, but she turned her head and the kiss landed on the back of her neck.

Now what? thought Milly miserably, as William went. Is he having a ding-dong at the Club? Is it Mrs Hardcastle the young accountant? Uncle Sid says she's dazzlingly beautiful. Oh shitty-shitty-bang-bang!

In the hallway William took out the letter from Lord Sidmonton and read it through again swiftly to double-check that this home-wrecking degree of security was essential. The brief letter, written in Uncle Sid's own hand, was explicit.

'Dear William,' it began. 'This letter has to be most secret. Its contents must not be revealed or discussed or even hinted at to anybody. Not even, I am so sorry about this, to Milly. Secrecy is absolutely vital on such a sensitive issue as this and I cannot overestimate its importance, particularly to your good self as you will, of course, be responsible for the entire thing. You and I, as Master and Secretary, must meet as soon as possible to consider the implications of the Events Committee's decision, which is I am afraid, according to Club rules, irrevocable.

'I have to tell you that the unanimous decision of the Events Committee, and I can see no legal retreat from it, is that the Club's two hundredth and fiftieth birthday be celebrated with an orgy.'

CHAPTER TWO

THE WALPOLE CLUB

William, his thoughts chasing one another in a confused and miserable stream, dragged his bicycle from under the stairs, trundled it down the stone steps into Peel Street and cycled off to the Club.

The bike was no modern feather-weight job with nobbly tyres and forty-eight gears. It had belonged to his father who, every working day, rain or shine, had ridden it slowly and steadily the six miles from his home to the Public Library where he was Borough Librarian.

The ancient sit-up-and-beg machine was a dull black with nickel-plated, pre-chromium handlebars and a Sturmey-Archer 3-speed gear-change clamped to the crossbar. The second-gear position had been broken for years and disconnected the pedals, so any change from top-gear to bottom gear, or from bottom to top, had to be made with a practised lunge of the lever and hardly ever worked. The bike weighed about half a ton.

Originally, the machine had sported a headlamp worked by fumes from wet carbide but this had been replaced between the wars by a dynamo, one of the first bicycle dynamos marketed. It was about the size of a teapot and when clicked into service against the tyre put such a load on the front wheel that William had to stand on the pedals and heave to keep the bike moving and upright.

But it was all worth it. The bike was so robust that only a very foolish cabby indeed would try to edge his taxi close to William and force him into the kerb. The old bike's handlebars, of good pre-war steel, were bereft of rubber grips and could be relied upon to score a deep and expensive furrow along the side of any aggressive vehicle. And cycling was the cheapest and probably the quickest way of getting from Peel Street to the Walpole Club in St James's. Taxis were definitely out. Not only could he not afford them but no cabby knew where the Walpole Club was.

William did a skilful slow-bicycle-race weave, alternately pedalling and braking between the BMWs and buses and Volvos and vans motionless in Kensington Church Street. He tacked towards Kensington High Street because it was downhill practically all the way from there to St James's: the heavy old bike was the devil to pedal uphill even when the slope was only about one in a thousand but it dearly loved going downhill and would immediately accelerate into a kind of fast, lumbering canter, like an old war-horse hearing a bugle.

That morning William's mind was fixed on more serious matters than avoiding being run over. He had left Milly at home worried and upset and he was facing a difficult and delicate job of work. He went through undamaged because the traffic in Kensington High Street was locked in a motionless mass, most of it with engines switched off and radios switched on to cheery local radio telling them to avoid Kensington High Street at all costs.

The Walpole Club was off St James's Street, where members of the grand clubs like White's and Brooks's and Boodle's once used to enjoy themselves sitting in their bow-windows gazing down upon the common people walking to work in the rain. William pedalled along Piccadilly, turned right at Fortnum's, sailed round St James's Square and along Pall Mall and then pedalled strongly to get up St James's Street. A left turn into a quiet road and then a short run beneath a brick archway and through a mews brought him to a tiny cul-de-sac dwarfed by the Walpole Club's massive dark stone frontage. The cul-de-sac was named Petherbridge Court and as this was far too long a name for its size it was not to be found on any London street map.

William steered round to the back of the Club and taking advantage of one of the perks of being Club Secretary, humped his bike down the area steps and padlocked it to a huge steel bin of kitchen waste. Whisking off his cycle-clips, he climbed back up the iron staircase and made his way round to the Club's front door.

When William's nose came to within eighteen inches of the massive door it swung open swiftly as though operated by an electronic eye. Inside, saluting with the fine flourish which he had invented and of which he was rightly proud, stood the enormous Sergeant Chidding, probably the most loyal and devoted servant the Club had ever had; willing, uncomplaining, kindly and, as William had to admit to Milly, as dim as a nun's nightlight.

Chidding had never been a sergeant, it was only a courtesy title, but he had been in the army during the war as a Lance Corporal in some odd, forgotten unit which had something to do with mules. Senior military members of the Club and even a distinguished war historian, fascinated, had tried to interrogate Sergeant Chidding at various times as to what his unit was supposed to accomplish with mules in the Second World War, but the sergeant could never understand their questions.

'Morning, Chidders,' said William cheerfully.

'*SAH!*' roared the sergeant, and the glass windows of his cubby-hole rattled. 'Now you've arrived, Mr Secretary, let our day's work commence!' Sergeant Chidding made his amusing little welcoming speech every morning when opening the door to William.

'I must talk to the Master urgently. Is he up yet?' The

judge usually slept in one of the Club bedrooms when he was on an Appeal, which he was reputed to be at the moment. Sergeant Chidding's brow corrugated. His eyes glazed with mental effort.

'The Master,' said William loudly and carefully. 'Lord Sidmonton. Is he up yet?'

'Up where?' asked the sergeant cautiously.

'Excuse me, Mr Seckertree, sir,' said a smooth, whiney voice behind William. 'I think I might be of some assistance in regard to this one.'

William sighed. It was the Club's under-porter and telephone operator, Stanley Tozer. However much William tried to be liberal-minded, Christian, tolerant of all God's creatures, Tozer defeated him. William found Stanley Tozer to be at all times a pain in the sphincter.

Tozer sidled round William and stood in front of the sergeant. William thought it significant that Chidders, as the porter was affectionately addressed by members, wore his ancient plum-coloured club livery with dignity whereas the under-porter, addressed by members without any affection at all as Tozer, looked like an understudy in the chorus of *White Horse Inn* wearing the borrowed costume of a fatter, taller baritone.

'G'mornin', Mr Seckertree, sir,' said Tozer with probably the most insincere smile outside the catering industry. 'Madam well, I trust?'

'Thank you, yes,' said William.

'And the kiddies?'

William ground his teeth. The Unspeakable Tozer had been told repeatedly that there were as yet no children.

'Growing pains, I shouldn't wonder,' said Tozer. 'Most kiddies get 'em, take it from me. Nothing to worry about. Now, sir, in reference to your enquiry about the whereabouts of the Master. Is it a matter of some urgency in a manner of speaking as you might say and that?'

'Yes,' said William. 'I want to see to him as soon as possible.'

'Then, Mr Seckertree, sir, I am able to help information-wise, viz, the Master ain't here. He didn't sleep here last night as per he was supposed to because I heard a press gentleman in the bar say that the Master had adjourned his case for two days. But then I heard Mrs Baxter, head waitress, inform the coffee-room manager that the Master would definitely be in after lunch today because a Club crisis had arose.'

It dawned upon William that Mr Tozer's information came entirely from listening in to other people's conversation.

'Rest assured, Mr Seckertree, sir,' said Mr Tozer, 'that as soon as the Master sets foot in the Club you will be informed by my good self. Whether you're having your lunch or in your office or on the toilet, I'll come and fetch you.'

William felt a sudden and desperate need to escape from Mr Tozer. He swiftly turned on his heel and strode back out of the front door. He gave Tozer a couple of minutes to return to his telephone exchange downstairs and then rapped discreetly on the great door. It swung open instantly.

'*SAH!*' roared Sergeant Chidding, and glass rattled again. 'Now you've arrived, Mr Secretary, let our day's work commence!'

For a fleeting moment William was tempted to go out and come in again to see whether Sergeant Chidding was good for a third display of welcome but decided that he had wasted enough time. He began his Monday morning stroll through his fiefdom.

William particularly enjoyed the Walpole in the mornings when the old building was still dozing and not yet quite awake. Standing in the morning-room he savoured the feel of the place. The furniture was very old but still comfortable. The Club décor, the wallpaper, pictures, were dignified and sombrely agreeable. As somebody once said, 'The atmosphere is like that of a Duke's house – with the Duke lying dead upstairs.'

The great curtains were still drawn across in the dining-room and it was dark and smelled of cigar smoke and cold chops. Overhead he could hear the surging whine of a vacuum cleaner as Mrs Addington went at the library carpet with vigour, punctuated at intervals by a bump or a splintering crack as the vacuum cleaner was driven into a late eighteenth-century Davenport or took the leg off a Hepplewhite chair.

One of the first things William did when he moved in was to read up on the Club's past. In the library he found the official history, an enormous volume penned by a member, Bartholomew Usher, MD, retired physician, in 1872. Dr Usher's prose style was so soporific that a paragraph read aloud would have put a swallow to sleep in mid-flight, but William thought the information was probably accurate enough.

It seems that like many of the early clubs, social, literary and political, the Walpole was founded in the middle of the eighteenth century. It started as a political club, a gathering of rich and noble Whig landowners who were staunch admirers of their late Prime Minister Sir Robert Walpole, reputed to have studied his gamekeeper's reports each morning before applying himself to the less interesting task of running the nation.

Originally, the noblemen and gentlemen assembled once a week in a tavern whose keeper let them have a private room upstairs without charge so long as they drank themselves senseless. As heavy drinking was the *raison d'être* of the Club the arrangement worked well enough until the turn of the century.

In the early 1800s middle-class values intruded and the tavern-keepers ceased being toss-pots and poets and began to turn businessmen. By then, getting beastly drunk was less popular a hobby even with Dukes and so the profit per square yard of an upstairs room no longer warranted the tavern-keeper providing the room free. So he began charging a reasonable rental to new customers such as the burgeoning nonconformist religious clubs; he found that this gave him an even bigger profit although most of the religious clubmen did not drink at all, even in moments of zeal and fervency.

So in the early nineteenth century, clubs had to look for premises of their own. One thing which most of Sir Robert Walpole's admirers did not lack was money. Most were rich and many immensely rich landowners, though some of them became immensely poor suddenly on the wrong turn of a card or throw of dice.

Rich noblemen bet wildly on anything, ate and drank prodigiously and spent fortunes keeping whores. In the Club they behaved arrogantly and abominably because they were aristocrats and reckoned themselves above having to behave like gentlemen. As Henry James later remarked, 'There are bad manners everywhere, but an aristocracy is bad manners organized.'

Money, to noble members, was ample compensation for appalling behaviour. At luncheon one day the Duke of Sheffield threw a waiter out of the first-floor window. The Club porter hurried up and informed the Duke that the waiter was lying moaning on the pavement outside with a broken leg.

'Put him on the bill,' said the Duke.

As the century progressed the social pattern changed; the madness of heavy gambling abated somewhat and Dukes tended to live in their Dukeries and only attend their St James's clubs when they had to come to London to buy new guns or boots. But the restrictions on admitting into membership only aristocratic friends, or relations, was applied so strictly at the Walpole that during the year 1822 the noble committee blackballed the entire list of applicants; at the end of the year the Club had fifteen members, eleven of them over seventy.

But the Walpole survived, by gradually relaxing the traditional aristocratic loathing of new members and allowing in some clubbable men who were in professions formerly hopelessly beyond the pale as far as the nobility was concerned, for example, 'filthy pen-pushers with dirty fingers' (Lord Tennyson, Anthony Trollope), 'greasy Levantine Jews' (the Governor of the Bank of England, the Chairman of the Stock Exchange), 'vulgar clowns and face-pullers' (Charles Kean, William Macready) and 'untrustworthy, venal liars' (the Solicitor-General and the Master of the Rolls).

The freehold of a small plot of land in Petherbridge Court occupied by wobbly lodging-houses was negotiated with help from the immensely influential Marquess of Westminster, the rickety houses and taverns were pulled down and the Walpole Club arose in their place, a substantial stone-faced mansion with four floors and a noble façade in the fashionable neo-classical style of pillars and rustication and Venetian windows, impossible to view properly because the street was too narrow. The architect, a Mr Anabona, immediately disappeared from Britain and architectural history.

William, walking through the coffee-room with his mind preoccupied with the task ahead, was suddenly stopped in his tracks by the realization of a great and horrible truth: he had no idea what exactly an orgy *was*. He hurried up the grand staircase towards his office at the top of the building to look up 'orgy' in his encyclopedia.

The stairs were designed to be wide enough to carry four

clubmen abreast, however unsteady on their feet, from the billiard-room on the third floor down to the ground-floor lavatories. These facilities were ice-cold even in summer but were spacious; the wash-basins, some without plugs, held small pieces of cracked soap and a useful assortment of ancient and none too clean hairbrushes and combs and on the wall was a newly installed automatic roller-towel machine.

Members could weigh themselves on a mahogany and brass sit-upon weighing scale, of the kind used years ago by small, beady-eyed men on Brighton pier dressed as jockeys who bet sixpence they could guess a punter's weight within two ounces. The Walpole's weighing machine went out of use in 1932 when a temporarily unhinged member of the House of Lords, in wine, took all the weights off the balance arm, staggered upstairs with them and tried to murder a political opponent by bombing him down the stairwell. The modern concern with bulging stomachs caused new weights to be bought and the machine was made serviceable again.

William enjoyed the non-twentieth-century other-worldliness of the Walpole. On the tiny table at the bend of the stairs stood a cabinet displaying a monogrammed silver snuffbox squashed flat by a musket ball at the battle of Malplaquet. Or so it said in beautiful brown writing on a card.

There was a snaffle which had once had the honour of snaffling the great eighteenth-century racehorse Eclipse. Or so it said on the card. And a pair of handcuffs used by the suffragette wife of a member to chain herself to the Club railings. She nearly starved to death as nobody at all passed by, but her name was printed in the *Morning Post* and her husband, a colossal bore, had to resign from the Walpole, so some good came from it all.

Beside the handcuffs was a single china false tooth on an ancient dark brown, vulcanized-rubber dental plate which an old member had probably removed for comfort and then forgotten. Soon after he became Secretary, William propped a card against it reading 'Property of Her late Majesty, Queen Victoria. *Not to be used as a bottle-opener.*' Nobody noticed.

Higher up, opposite the billiard-room, there was a gap where two bannister supports were missing. It seems, according to Dr Usher's book, and William felt the good doctor would not lie to him, that in the old days new Club members were not welcome although their subscriptions were. One evening a new member stopped the old but burly Duke of Rattray on the stairs and asked him where he might find the library.

'And who the devil are you?' snapped the Duke.

'A newly elected member, sir.'

'Oh, are you!' said the Duke and with a tremendous uppercut knocked the new member downstairs. Unhappily the new member was a war hero from the Peninsular campaign and had a wooden leg which caught in the bannisters and broke off two of the supports. When the House Committee asked the Duke to pay for repairs to the staircase he resigned in protest at the Club's insolence in demanding money from a Duke. His subscription was, at the time, fourteen years in arrears.

As William hurried higher up the staircase, now leading only to the attic rooms which housed the accountancy department and William's office, it became dramatically less grand; the stairs, a third of their previous width, were clad in coconut matting and rose steeply. The comforting wallpaper ceased and serviceable dark green and beige gloss paint took over.

As William's face rose above landing-level he glanced anxiously at the accountant's door, which he had to pass to get to his own office. The door was usually wide open and presented a problem. How to close the door and slip past it without being seen and talked to by the Club's accountant, the beautiful but disturbingly scented (and believed to be predatory) Mrs Hardcastle? He should have remembered to take an umbrella up with him. Not that he owned an umbrella but he could have asked Sergeant Chidding to find him one.

A week or two earlier William had borrowed a member's umbrella from the downstairs cloakroom and it had done the job well. He had lain prone on the landing, hooked the edge of the door with the brolly handle and slowly and smoothly closed the door. He had then got up and strolled safely past Mrs Hardcastle to the haven of his own office.

But he failed to return the member's brolly to the cloakroom. A day later a card appeared on the notice board:

I would be grateful if the nobleman who stole my umbrella from whence it has always been left, beneath hook No.3 on the west wall of the cloakroom, would kindly return it. I say 'nobleman' because I understand this to be a club for noblemen and gentlemen; as no gentleman would steal another gentleman's umbrella it follows that the member responsible must be a nobleman.

Next day there was a new card pinned to the board, written in a vigorous hand:

Noblemen do not steal umbrellas because noblemen do not use umbrellas. Only 'gentlemen' such as city clerks, golfers and Japanese policemen use the beastly things which resemble dead bats. Noblemen are able to shoot deer over moors in heavy snow and fish icy rivers in driving rain because the British aristocracy happens to be, by and large, waterproof.

William discovered the vital umbrella under his desk, quickly slipped it back beneath hook Number 3 and that was that. But now he had no umbrella and he was prone on the landing with no means of getting past Mrs Hardcastle's open door unseen.

He wriggled out of his jacket and tried casting it like a gladiator's cloak in the hope of it settling over the doorknob but it was too difficult and a mouth-organ flew out of the top pocket of his jacket and hit the wall with a dangerously loud clatter. William, breathing heavily, lay still for a moment getting his breath back and wondering what a mouth-organ was doing in his jacket pocket. He did not own a mouth-organ.

A sudden wave of common sense surged over him as he lay there face down on the landing, jacket off, reaching out to pick up a mystery mouth-organ.

Why am I doing this? Why cannot I walk past the open door, wave cheerfully to Mrs Hardcastle and so reach the safety of my office? Because, he thought grimly. Because Mrs Hardcastle is a beautiful woman. Really beautiful. And desirable. I acknowledge this honestly. But as it happens I do not desire her. I desire my wife. My admiration for Mrs Hardcastle's physical attractions is completely objective. But I find her flirtatious attentions so embarrassing that I will crawl along the landing floor and shut her door with an umbrella rather than face her. But no, today I will be courageous. I will get up now and walk briskly past Mrs Hardcastle's open door and establish a sensible precedent.

Hardly had he even begun to rise up than a waft of subtle oriental scent drifted across his nostrils and his toes tingled.

'Good morning, dear Mr Secretary,' said the soft and lilting voice of Mrs Hardcastle as she reached the head of the stairs and stood above him. 'And how are you this goodly British morning?'

William could think of nothing better to do for the time being than just lie there on the coconut matting. Clearly the traffic had delayed Mrs Hardcastle way past her usual time of arrival. Out of the corner of his eye he noted the mauve-sandalled foot and the edge of the sari which this morning was the near-transparent gold and green number.

He rose to a kneeling position and hammered on the floor with the mystery mouth-organ. 'Carpet worn but floorboards good for another ten years,' he announced loudly and authoritatively to nobody. He leapt lightly to his feet and pocketed the mouth-organ. 'New carpet next year though. Oh, hello, Mrs Hardcastle, didn't see you there for a moment! Excuse me – must get on.' He squeezed past her on the narrow landing. It was like squeezing past warm Turkish Delight.

In his office he sat down for a moment breathing heavily then took down Vol.18 of his encyclopedia, OOSPERM – OVOVIVIPAROUS and flicked swiftly through the pages to ORGY.

The information he needed so badly read in its entirety:

> **orgy** a modern philological blunder as the Greek *orgia*, adopted by the Romans, existed only in the neuter plural. Metaphorically, it was the post-Homeric word for studies which involved training, such as philosophy.

William closed the volume and put it back in its place. It was going to be one of those days.

CHAPTER THREE

OSBERT GORE-BELLAMY

After William left for work, Milly, with considerable restraint, did not treat the crockery like a Greek restaurateur in party mood but gently put the breakfast dishes into the dishwasher, amazed yet again at how many bits and pieces it took for two people to have an egg and a cup of coffee.

Although her tears had stopped she was still feeling down and decided that making some music might help. She went to her little workroom where she kept her harpsichord and had a go at a Scarlatti sonata. It made her wish for once that she had taken up the piano instead. The trouble with playing a harpsichord when in murderous mood was that bashing the keys made very little difference to the volume of sound, whereas hard thumping on a piano produced a violent and satisfying noise.

So she played the Scarlatti as sensitively as she could and felt much better. Then the Hon. Pippa came struggling through the hall with her cello. Milly heard the cello case bang against her hall-stand, a splendid Victorian creation of fretwork, curvy mirrors and hooks for coats and hats and umbrellas which she had bought for £1.50 (buyer collects). Milly remembered she had agreed that Pippa could come and rehearse. Pippa lived in a flat next to a couple of tone-deaf, litigation-prone political researchers.

'Hi!' said Milly warmly to her old friend, smiling at her brightly.

'My God, you look horrible!' said the Hon. Pippa. 'Red-eyed and dismal.'

'Not at my best this morning, one way and another,' said Milly, handing Pippa the letter from Catriona.

Pippa read the letter through carefully.

'Oh, shit,' she said, 'and we've got the IBM Conference audition on Tuesday. May boils and coitus interruptus plague her.' She handed the letter back to Milly. 'Catriona really can be seriously stupid. My guess is she might well come back to us. Trev sounds a bit impermanent to me.' She sat down on a chair in the kitchen, took out her bow and sawed away at a worn lump of rosin.

'But that's not all that's troubling you,' said Pippa. 'It's William, isn't it?'

Milly gaped.

'You're just guessing!'

'I've sensed it for months. Something's wrong between the two of you. You've gone off him a bit, haven't you?'

'Oh, really!' said Milly. It was astonishing how her little friend with her pale oval face and huge eyes like something out of the Small Mammal House, clad in extreme patches of colour which made her look as if she was wearing a stained-glass window, could read Milly so acutely.

'You are stark, raving barmy,' Pippa went on, chattily. 'Your William is pretty terrific all ways up and if you lose him it will be wholly your own stupid fault.' She plucked a string on the cello and tightened its peg a fraction. 'Can you Larry Adler me an A?' she said.

'I seem to have lost our mouth-organ,' said Milly. 'Must have put it somewhere.'

Pippa gripped the cello with her knees and leant her chin on the whorl. 'You do know your William is a good lad, don't you?' she asked.

'Well, yes. Of course. I married him, didn't I?'

'But do you know the lad you married? Really know him?'

'Pippa, I'm his wife. I've seen him happy and worried and dancing round the bedroom half-pissed wearing only a silly grin and a corn-plaster. How much more should I know?'

'Oh, my dear, a great deal more.'

Milly was getting nettled. 'It's a bit much, you claiming to be an expert on William. I can't think why. You never talk to him unless you have to. When he comes in the room you turn away.'

Pippa gently drew her bow across a string. When the note had died down she said: 'That's because I'm sort of in love with William. I can't trust myself to talk to him in case I do a Judy Garland; you know, that old record where she gushes all over Clark Gable.'

'Oh Pippa!' said Milly.

'I've been sort of in love with the man ever since you brought him down that wet day to the Brixton concert and introduced him to us.'

Milly ran over to Pippa and embraced her as tightly as she could to comfort her. As Pippa was sitting at her cello this meant Milly pressing Pippa's head against her tummy. Pippa moved Milly's arm half an inch so that she could breathe. Milly's cheeks were moist. Pippa began to sniffle.

'Seriously,' said Pippa, 'you don't have to worry about me and William. It's all in the mind. Not in my dreams it isn't, they're a bit pornographic, but in reality. William's my fantasy Mr Wonderful. I would never, ever, do anything about it because you're my oldest friend and anyway I would destroy my lovely little fantasy. But O Mill, to me he's verging on the perfect!'

'I think,' said Milly, 'that William's perfection might well be the problem; he's so totally capable that he doesn't really need me. He seems to have all sorts of friends he can call on and there is nothing I can contribute, which makes it all a bit pointless. After only a couple of years.'

Pippa played a snatch of Bach from memory, faltered and put the bow down.

Milly went on, 'And then this morning a letter came for him which upset him. He went all secretive and wouldn't tell me who it was from or what was in it. I'm sure he's got involved with some woman and she's putting on the pressure. Oh, Pippa, what do I do?'

'Find out what it's all about. If he won't tell you what's happening then you're entitled to discover it for yourself.'

'You mean pry? Follow him? That sort of thing?'

'Yes. William's behaviour sounds a bit out of character to me. You've nothing to lose by finding out what's troubling him. And perhaps you can help him.'

'You're right, of course. Thanks, Pippa. At least it'll give me something positive to do. Meanwhile, have you got a nubile young lad in mind or are you settling for a randy-William dream after a take-away curry supper?'

'The only man I've met recently at all interesting to look at turned out to be a Free Thinker.'

'What's that?'

'Well, he thought he was so beautiful that everything he needed should be provided for him free. By me.'

'Whatever became of that strange boyfriend of yours, Osbert somebody hyphen somebody? Wanted desperately to be editor of *The Times*? Short, fat and going bald? We were all terribly afraid you were going to marry him.'

'Osbert Gore-Bellamy? Oh, dear, oh, dear! He was so much older than me I suppose I was flattered. He really just wanted to have a father-in-law with a title. Turned out to be a copper-bottomed, hundred per cent, snobbish, over-ambitious swine. And what a groper. In a taxi it was like sitting next to a randy octopus. In the end we did not, as they say, have it off, 'cos I was much too innocent to realize what he was trying to do. That man, Milly, was the one really shame-making episode in my otherwise blameless, that is to say dull, life.'

'What became of him?'

'He went into down-market journalism and is now gossip columnist of the crummiest tabloid newspaper in the world, the *Grass*.'

'That thing?' cried Milly.

'He's covered up the awkward fact that he went to Marlborough College and claims he was educated at Swindon Comprehensive. Now he talks like David Bellamy whom he puts it about is his uncle. *Private Eye* calls him "Britain's fattest dispenser of legal porn, O Gor-Blimey."'

'Wasn't he involved in that fruity newspaper trial that my uncle Sid presided over?'

'That's right. And what a deeply nasty bit of intrusion into a public figure's private grief that case was,' said Pippa. 'There was lying, attempts to bribe the police and Osbert wired up a baby with a radio mike so that the *Grass* could record the mother revealing things to her husband during the midnight feed.'

'The case caused a terrific stink at the time, I remember that,' said Milly.

'I should say so!' said Pippa. 'Your Uncle Sid gave O Gor-Blimey a tremendous wigging from the Bench, called him a boil on the bottom of British journalism. Osbert Gor-Blimey will never forgive your great-uncle. Never. I know the sod. He'll find some way to get his revenge, and like all gossip columnists I bet he's got paid spies planted everywhere. Your Uncle Sid had better watch his back.'

Stanley Tozer locked himself into his tiny room in the basement, picked up the receiver from the small hi-tec phone exchange it was his job to look after and dialled a number. The machine chirruped. A voice said 'GRASS Newspaper Group.'

'I wan speag termist Gawbellme,' said Tozer.

'You what?'

Tozer put down the slice of cold game pie he had snatched whilst passing through the kitchen and spat the piece he was chewing in the direction of the waste-paper basket. It missed.

'I want to speak to Mr Gore-Bellamy, your Gossip Editor,' he said. 'Tell him it's Mr Tozer, ringing urgently and importantly from the Walpole Club, London, on a matter of important urgency.'

In a few moments the gossip columnist was on the line.

'Gore-Bellamy, 'ere. What you got, Tozer?'

'Listen. Something secret's building up here and Lord Sidmonton's in it up to his neck.'

'What sort of thing?'

'I dunno, I told you – it's secret. I've a feeling it's something to do with the Club's forthcoming two hundred and fiftieth birthday celebration. How about fifty quid?'

'You what? You ain't told me nothing yet.'

'You said you'd pay for anything about Lord Sidmonton.'

'Nothing ain't anything. When you really get me some serious dirt on the Judge, that'll be another matter. That's worth a grand.'

'A what?'

'A thousand quid.' The columnist heard a dull thud, then silence, then some scraping noises. Then the hoarse voice of a dangerously over-excited Mr Tozer came back on the line.

'I'm your man, guv. I'll comb every waste-paper basket, secrete myself in cupboards, listen-in on every telephone call till I achieve your behest. And besides the Master and the snooty bloody Secretary, there'll be many other posh people and social parasites for you to publicly besmirch in your rag in a manner of speaking that is and that. Believe me, sir, the sword of Dammocockles is dangling over the heads of those toffee-nosed swine in the bar upstairs.'

CHAPTER FOUR

UNCLE SID

'Well, Stanley, here's another fine mess you've got us into,' said Lord Justice Sidmonton, flicking the end of his tie towards William.

William looked at him coldly. It was a rotten impersonation of Oliver Hardy because Lord Sidmonton was a small, wiry man about a third of the volume and weight of Olly, and his face was not round and fat but lean and bony with small eyes. He looked like a cross between Laurence Sterne and an unreliable elf. What is more he could not do an American accent.

William felt aggrieved. They were in William's office and the Master, who had turned down William's request to provide the office with a spare chair, had commandeered William's chair leaving William to perch uncomfortably on a small part of the word-processor table which had a sharp, plastic edge and just accommodated part of one buttock.

The judge had turned up for their urgent meeting at precisely the wrong moment for William. One of the concessions which made the Secretary's job tolerable was his freedom to drink in the bar and eat in the dining-room with the members, and the new chef was excellent. William, after an unenjoyable morning making notes of his thoughts on the orgy problem, was in the dining-room about to detach a superb grilled sole from its bones when Mr Tozer appeared at his elbow and in a loud stage whisper that could be heard clearly above the thunderous roar of members' small talk said, 'The Master's 'ere, sir. I've shoved him in your office pro rata so you can discuss the Club's big problem in private.'

Heads swivelled round and members stared.

'*What* big problem?' asked William, furious. 'There isn't a problem, you idiot!'

Mr Tozer laid a forefinger along the side of his nose in conspiratorial fashion. 'If you say there's no problem then there ain't, even if there is, as the proverb has it. But not to worry, sir, you can trust my jurisprudence.'

William leapt up and raced up the staircase to his office hoping to shake off Tozer whom he could hear thudding up behind him wheezing like an old seal. William shot into his office, saw the judge sitting in his chair and motioned to him not to speak, then snatched the door open again. Mr Tozer was standing outside, sideways, ear against where the door would have been.

'Faxing,' said Mr Tozer. 'Photocopying. Suchlike similar. There's a little shop round the corner. Secret information you don't want nobody to know about, just pass it out to me and I'll run round the corner and get it copied and you can lock it up. Play safe, I always maintain, sir, if you're on something dodgy.'

William gritted his teeth. 'Your work is manning the phone exchange downstairs. Why don't you get down and man it!'

So what with being wrenched away from his Dover sole and having to cope with Tozer's peculiar behaviour, William was not in the mood for Uncle Sid's Oliver Hardy impressions.

'We're not in a fine mess,' he said. 'At least, not yet we aren't. And I didn't get us into it in the first place.'

'Feathers a bit ruffled?' said Uncle Sid blandly. 'I was quoting a well-known comical line of Laurel and Hardy's because there's nothing like a bit of simple-minded fun when a crisis looms. As Voltaire put it, "The superfluous is very necessary." '

'Well, we've got a crisis looming all right, and superfluous at that,' said William. 'It ill behoves me to comment on club members, sir, but the Events Committee must be raving bonkers; eighty centimes to the franc; brain disadvantaged; nine candidates for a footnote in *The Lancet* as prime examples of senile decrepitude!'

'Do I detect a hint of criticism in your tone?' said the judge, wondering whether to do his funny Oliver Hardy tie flick again but wisely deciding not to.

'How *could* eight venerable committee members plus, if you please, Canon Prout as Chairman, decide that this ancient Club should mark its two hundred and fiftieth birthday with an . . . '

'HUBBER-DUBBER-DUBBER-DUBBER-*DUB*!' said Uncle Sid swiftly.

William was stunned into silence.

'Security,' said Uncle Sid. 'You were about to use a word which simply must not be spoken in the Club or anywhere from now on until after the event. We will use a code word for our chosen celebration and I suggest that we use the word "Orange".'

'Ah,' said William. 'Right. Orange.'

'Listen!' said Uncle Sid very quietly. 'Can you hear a faint hum coming from the telephone?'

They listened.

'No,' said William.

'Well, there was a few moments ago,' said Uncle Sid. They peered closely at the handset. Somebody had propped it up at one end clear of the little metal buttons.

'You're right,' said William. 'It's been on all the while we've been talking.'

He lifted the handset and saw a lump of something under it. He picked it off, examined it and sniffed it.

'It's cold game pie,' said William.

'Now who could have put that there?' said Uncle Sid, now much concerned and looking quite frightened.

'Tozer!' said William. 'It must be Tozer, I just know he's up to something. He's recently changed his act from being humbly poisonous to being transparently sinister. Today he's been creeping around like a police informer in an early Italian film about the brothels of Napoli.'

'Sack him,' said Uncle Sid. 'And the sooner the better.'

'Point is,' said William. '*Why* is he spying? What's he doing it for? Money, presumably, but whose? I think we'd better suffer Tozer for the time being so we can keep an eye on him. I now see the point of your letter emphasizing the security problem of this little nightmare. Can't you just pull rank with the Events Committee and get the Orange cancelled for legal reasons?'

'It seems not. Not yet, anyway, until we know what is actually going to happen. I had a word this morning with Sir Gerald Norman, our QC, and in his opinion, and I have to agree with him, there might well be nothing illegal in it at all. The law is not normally concerned with drunkenness or fornication or displays of wild licentiousness on private property so long as the revellers don't break any bye-laws or upset the peace.'

'The whole thing is so extraordinary,' said William. 'I mean, how Canon Erasmus Prout as Chairman could have even considered the Club holding an Orange, let alone sign the minute? He's a conventional, unkinky sort of cleric from what I've seen of him. Terminally dull, but
. . .'

'He's also extremely unpopular with the more raffish members, and he is short-sighted and vain.'

William got up to stretch his legs, wincing. The sharp edge of the table had left a rather painful red weal on his behind, a condition known to dinghy sailors as 'gunwale

46

bottom'. 'What's the canon's eyesight and vanity got to do with it?'

'Everything,' said Uncle Sid.

'You know more about this than you're letting on,' said William, grimly, now firmly aggrieved.

'I know *all* about it,' said Uncle Sid. 'I spent the whole morning contacting the Events Committee one by one and impressing upon them the need for absolute secrecy. And I managed to piece together why they chose to hold an Orange.'

'Bloody-mindedness?'

'No, it seems it was a joke.'

'A joke?!'

'A caper. The committee's idea of a bit of fun at the unpopular canon's expense.'

'A bit of *fun*?'

'Let me fill you in. You're a young man and almost all the members here are twice your age if not thrice. The Events Committee is traditionally, and ironically, made up of those loyal and devoted clubmen of great age whom we call "limpets". Canon Prout is only sixty-two but most of the committee are debauched seventy year olds. The point is, although their joints might creak their minds are still flexible. Making the highly respectable Canon Erasmus Prout responsible for setting up a Club org . . . Orange, is an example of our old members' sense of fun.'

'From where I stand it's an example of nothing except perhaps senile folly.'

'The leading light of the wheeze seems to have been our sprightly old actor friend, Brandreth Jacques, MBE.'

'I might have guessed Brandy Jack would be in there somewhere.'

'He's in most of these schemes that add a little brightness to Club life. One time half a dozen aged limpets were dozing over their tea and anchovy toast in the library

47

and old Brandy Jack suddenly sat up and said "This is a terribly dreary afternoon – let's all exchange dentures." '

'But how on earth did they get Canon Prout's agreement? Put him to the torture?'

'The plan was in fact quite simple. Canon Prout wanted a short meeting so Brandy Jack offered to form a sub-committee with the Chairman, Lord Wick, and two others to suggest a suitable form of birthday celebration which might be agreeable to the rest of the committee. It would then be minuted and all the canon had to do was to sign it.'

'Surely the canon read it through before he put his name to it?' said William.

'This is the really cunning part of the plan. They got Sir Archibald Alloway to write out the minute.'

'Sir Archie? Our Sporting Baronet? But his writing's almost totally illegible. Can hardly write his own name on a cheque. Ah. I see light. You said that Canon Prout is short-sighted?'

'I did. And what else did I say he was?'

'Vain. In which case he would not admit his eyesight was failing by wearing spectacles.'

'Exactly. Before the meeting, the wicked old men changed all four light bulbs in the committee room to 40 watts apiece and announced that to save time the Chairman of the Events Committee, Lord Wick, would read the minute out aloud. Which he did. It said that the birthday celebration was at planning stage yet but it would all be organized by the Secretary who will blah-blah-blah . . . '

'Thanks very much,' said William.

'Then Lord Wick said that it stated at the top of the minute the most important point, namely the theme of the evening. And he pointed out to the canon the undecipherable scrawl which was the Sporting Baronet's attempt at writing the words THE ORGY. "The light in here is oddly dim this evening." said the canon – "*What* does it say is to be the theme of our celebration?" "THEOLOGY," said wee Lord Wick. "Sign here, padre." '

William sat back on to the painful edge of the computer table, sunk in wonder at the seemingly bottomless cunning of the ancient club limpets when in playful mood. 'And you say Sir Gerald Norman QC insists that the committee has acted lawfully?' he asked wonderingly.

'Yes,' said Lord Sidmonton. 'Mind you, Gerald's on the committee.'

William had had no previous experience of dealing with these unpredictable, irrational, unreliable old villains and he suddenly had a surge of panic. 'I don't really know why you chose me for the Secretary's job, sir, I really don't. I have a feeling that I am being heaped with responsibilities beyond my abilities,' he said.

'I didn't choose you,' said Uncle Sid. 'My lady wife, Parthenope, did. When Milly brought you to the Hall for tea, Parthenope thought you looked honest enough and harmless. Remarkable praise from her.'

'I understand that it's my function to organize this bizarre carnival,' said William, glaring at Lord Sidmonton as if to defy him to interrupt. 'I've given some thought to the really frightening problems facing us – or rather me,' William went on, 'and this is how I propose to set about it. Our biggest problem is preventing the tabloids getting to hear about our— er— Orange. You've nobbled the committee so we can move on to the problem of muzzling the rank and file. The problem here is that by no means are all of them limpets and oldies; there are youngish journalists and media people who might not be able, professionally, to keep their mouths shut, so they have to be prevented from attending the big night.'

'How?' said Uncle Sid. 'What are you going to do?'

'I thought I'd put a notice on the board saying there'll be a small surprise birthday celebration dinner in the dining-room, members only, no guests, details to be arranged, and as space is limited members must apply immediately.'

'They'll all apply,' said Uncle Sid.

'Yes, but we can hand-pick those members we can trust.'

'It'd better damn well work,' said Uncle Sid. 'Now, can't waste time gossiping with you. The chef is keeping me a grilled sole. By God, he's a good chef is young Anton; best thing you've done so far, finding him. Can't think why you don't eat in the dining-room more often. Get on with all the arrangements and keep me informed. And don't discuss the Orange with *anybody* outside the Club.'

He made for the door.

'But Milly? It's simply not fair on her that . . . ' said William.

'Least of all Milly,' said Lord Sidmonton sharply. 'If she blabbed to her father or her mother our Orange would be the chatter of every semi-smart dinner party in Greater London.'

'Milly doesn't blab!' said William. 'I really do think I should be allowed . . . '

But His Lordship had gone.

William moved his aching behind to his own chair, warm from Lord Sidmonton, and consoled himself with the thought that he at least had one asset in putting together the birthday evening: the services of Brandy Jack.

The spry figure of old Brandreth Jacques, MBE, graced the Club every Friday and had done so for a great many years. He always said his weekly walk to the Walpole was the only regular exercise he had ever taken in his life, apart from making love to seemingly all the leading ladies of his day and most of the lesser ladies, too, according to his fund of elegantly erotic and increasingly lengthy anecdotes.

He propped up the far right end of the bar at half-past one and had a small whisky. He never accepted a drink from others, nor bought one. Always dressed in the same ancient but well-cut check suit, wing collar, floppy spotted bow-tie, he looked like a raffish version of Max Beerbohm. But when it came to compèring a club concert or introducing a distinguished guest speaker after a dinner, he came into his own. The old back straightened, the rheumy eyes gleamed and a man with real ability to entertain exercised his gift and gave a great deal of pleasure to those present.

William's happy thoughts were disturbed by a gentle knock at the door. 'Come in,' he shouted cheerfully.

A wave of scent, elusive, exotic, with a lot of musk in it, came in through the door followed by Mrs Hardcastle. She turned and locked the door behind her.

'Ah,' said William.

'You don't mind? We must be most private.'

William leapt to his feet. 'Must go!' he cried. 'Meeting!'

Her big brown eyes seemed to grow bigger, and glow. 'Please, Willy,' she said. A finger, light as a petal, touched his wrist. 'I need you. Urgently,' said Mrs Hardcastle softly. 'Now.'

CHAPTER FIVE

MRS HARDCASTLE

'There is a member behind with his subscription,' Mrs Hardcastle said.

William's breathing rapidly returned to normal. 'That's what you needed me for?' he said. 'Urgently? To tell me that a member owes the Club money?'

'What did you think I needed you for?' asked Mrs Hardcastle, in wide-eyed innocence. She sat on the edge of his desk. William noticed, and she noticed that he noticed, that any movement she made caused bits of her to wobble.

'Mrs Hardcastle,' said William bravely, if a little hoarsely, 'there is a kind of office behaviour, frowned upon by the law as a matter of fact, which is known as sexual harassment . . . ' Which was as far as he got. Mrs Hardcastle broke up into laughter. Delightful laughter, thought William miserably, like the tinkling of many bells.

'Oh, Willy, Willy, Willy!' cried Mrs Hardcastle. 'You are so *serious*! I am only playing small games!'

'Well, I'm not sure that you should play these sort of games. Your intentions might be misunderstood.'

'Now Willy, listen to me. You are kind and nice, and shy and funny, did you know that? I like you very much but not for your body. When I need a body I have the body of my husband, Mr Hardcastle. When Malcolm is not away installing word processors, which he is doing much too often for my wishes, he is at home being a dutiful husband, if you see what I am suggesting.'

'But, Mrs Hardcastle . . . ' began William.

'Call me Belkis,' she said. 'It is more friendly. And we are friends as well as office comrades, is that not truly so?'

'Belkis,' William repeated dully and dutifully. He had a feeling that Belkis had already gained the high ground in this encounter.

'Belkis was the name of the Queen of Sheba,' said Mrs Hardcastle. 'It means "more beautiful than the houris of paradise".'

'Oh, dear,' said William.

'Houris were young girls of exceptional beauty,' said Mrs Hardcastle reprovingly. 'They were not naughty whores. You must not be misled by the nearness of the two words.'

'Sorry,' said William. 'But Belkis, you must admit you've been coming at me a bit strong. I mean – leading me on. All that fluttering of eyelids, and pouting and, well, body language.'

'Willy, Willy, you are so wonderfully English! Just because I am young and pretty – and I know I am these things because my husband Mr Hardcastle always tells me so when we are in congress – you conclude I must be a sex-lunatic. But I am just having fun flirting. If you are a liberated woman and pretty you *must* flirt. It is using what God has given you to spread a little harmless pleasure. Is that sinful?'

'It's unusual behaviour for an accountant,' said William.

'Then let me put it to you another road,' said Mrs Hardcastle. 'I have one of those trick minds for figures; I have many diplomas and a small degree and I wanted this job. But do you think the Master hired me because I add up figures rapidly and do cube roots in my head? Or was it, do you think, because I made him a little curtsey of supplication and gave him a special smile?'

'Pax,' said William and held out his hand. 'Which means, in this case, Belkis, you win.'

'Pax to you, too, Willy,' she said. She took his hand, pulled him towards her and kissed him lightly on the lips. 'That is my last piece of sexual harassment,' she said.

William's experience of being kissed by beautiful young women was limited but he enjoyed being kissed by Belkis who was full of innocent young passion clearly inadequately assuaged by her not-always-home-when-he-was-most-needed Malcolm. But William did find that compared with Milly, Belkis's kiss was just a touch leathery.

'Now, we must go back to our muttons,' said Belkis, ruffling through her notebook. 'This member who is in debt to the Club.'

'Can't we leave it until later?' said William. 'Thing is, I've got rather a lot to get through this afternoon. It's all go at the moment.'

'Poor Willy,' said Belkis, sympathetically. 'It can't be easy having to organize an orgy.'

'*What*!' shouted William, leaping up and banging his knee against the edge of the desk. 'Ow! What did you say?'

'Can't be easy arranging an orgy.'

'You mustn't say that word!'

'You just asked me to repeat it.'

'I know I did but that wasn't what I meant. I meant how do you know about the— er— ?'

'The orgy?'

'Belkis, listen!' said William frantically. 'That word is totally banned in the Club. The Master says we must say "Orange" instead.'

Belkis went off into peals of laughter. This time the tinkle of many bells had lost their charm.

'It's not funny!' said William, quite sharply for him.

'Oh, yes it is!' said Belkis. 'Orange! "We all looked at naughty films then stripped off and had an Orange!" Oh, Willy, it's not the same!'

'Who told you about the Club Orange?'

Belkis began to titter again.

'STOP IT! This really is serious,' said William in such a commanding voice that Belkis went silent mid-titter. 'However lunatic the decision to hold an Orange in the Club, I have to go ahead and organize it,' he said. 'And I don't even know what's supposed to happen at an Orange. And if the newspapers get hold of the story there'll be a very nasty scandal. Many of our members are judges, politicians, clergy: even if they have nothing to do with the party their careers will be ruined simply because they're members of the Club.'

'Sorry,' said Belkis. 'I didn't realize that part of it.'

'How did you come to hear about it?'

'Last week a member of the Events Committee told me; it was the big American gentleman, Mr Sol Fish, who laughs very much and very loudly.'

'I know him well,' sighed William.

'I remember Mr Fish's words exactly,' said Belkis. 'He said to me, "Keep this under your bra, lamb-chop—" '

'Good Lord! Do all members talk to you like that?'

'No, only Mr Sol Fish. He said, "Keep this under your bra, lamb-chop, but Brandy Jack's planning a great little scam for the Club's birthday – we're going to vote through a motion that we hold a—" and then he said the forbidden O-word.'

'Orange,' said William.

Belkis tittered and then stopped herself. 'Yes,' she said. 'Mr Fish wanted to know whether the Events Committee fund would finance it.'

'And would it?'

'First, I must know what is planned to happen.'

'So must I,' said William. 'Look, do you really need me over this membership problem? If not I must start talking to chef about suitable Orange food.'

'Sorry, Willy, but my problem calls for Secretary action. Fact is, the Club rules are very strict on subscriptions.'

'Not surprising,' said William. 'The old Dukes hardly bothered to pay at all. Like paying their tailor, wasn't done.'

'Well, it's done these days, my goodness. The rules state that if any member is more than a year behind in paying his sub he must be warned twice by registered post. If after three months he still has not paid, he ceases to be a member.'

'Quite right!' said William cheerfully. 'Out with the bilkers!'

'It's the Secretary's job to inform the member that he has ceased to be a member. I will give you his address so that you can send your letter or speak up to him face to face.'

Mrs Hardcastle found the right page in her notebook.

'He has always lived in his chambers in Albany, Set J4. That is where I sent his two recorded-delivery letters. But he did not reply.'

'Perhaps he's moved,' said William, feet up on the desk, half his mind on what the modern orgy-goer might expect to be given to eat.

'I think not. Both recorded deliveries were signed for.'

'Has he run up a bar bill?'

'Oh no. He pays cash, the barman says. Counts it out carefully from a funny little leather purse like a sow's ear.'

'Anything known about his general behaviour?'

Belkis consulted her book. 'A gentleman of the old school but a bit of a bottom-patter say the dining-room waitresses. He is much liked.'

'But nevertheless, a non-payer of his dues,' said William, removing his feet from the desk and standing up. 'And who *is* he, this miscreant whose sword I have to break over my knee before I throw him out of the Walpole?' he asked.

Belkis handed him the notebook and pointed at the page-heading.

William sat down again. Very heavily. 'Oh, hell!' he said.

It was Brandy Jack.

The sun was high and hot by mid-afternoon but William neither noticed it nor enjoyed it. Albany, where Brandy Jack lived, was just a short walk from the Walpole Club so William did not need to unchain his bike.

He preferred appointments which were to the left along Piccadilly. In good weather he often ate a sandwich in solitude in Green Park rather than tangle with problem members in the Club dining-room, in which case his agreeable habit was to turn into the side door of the Ritz hotel, have a pee in high luxury and then walk through the foyer and out of the front door into Piccadilly. After months of doing this the side-door doorman saluted him as an old Ritz customer under the impression that William was on his way to his usual table in the dining-room, and the front-hall porter was even more obsequious being under the impression that William had descended from his suite for his usual pre-luncheon stroll.

Unfortunately Albany was to the right along Piccadilly so a Ritz pee was not on. William turned into Jermyn Street and had to make do with walking in through the back entrance of Fortnum's and out through the front door into Piccadilly. But he was able to stop at the food counter and buy a brace of smoked trout in their skins, a rare treat of which Milly was particularly fond. It was, William thought, at least something cheerful to have achieved on this day of unpredictable drama.

He crossed Piccadilly clutching his bag of smoked trout, walked smartly up the little road which led to Albany, across the forecourt and through the open front door of the eighteenth-century conglomerate of the most prestigious and expensive sets of chambers in London, one-time home of J.B. Priestley, Terence Rattigan, Graham Greene, the Rt Hon. Edward Heath, *et al*.

Almost immediately William entered the entrance hall a porter was at his elbow. 'May I help you, sir?' he said, eyeing the fishy parcel without pleasure.

William took out the card on which he had written Brandy Jack's address. 'I wonder if I can have a word with Mr Brandreth Jacques,' said William. 'Set J4. He should have got back from lunch at the Walpole Club by now. I'm the Club Secretary there.'

'I'm afraid there's some mistake, sir,' the porter said. 'There's no such set of rooms as J4. They don't exist. What's more, there's nobody named Brandreth Jacques living in Albany.'

CHAPTER SIX

BRANDY JACK

'A word, sir? If I may?'

William found they had been joined by a more authentic version of Sergeant Chidding, a large figure of great presence clad in the mid-brown, scarlet-trimmed morning coat of Albany livery, complete with a most impressive black beaver top hat with gilt band and gilt cockade. A modest few medal ribbons, like bright rectangular blossoms, made a brave show on his chest.

'Thank you, Albert,' he said cheerfully. Albert, who was not splendidly clad, went back down the long corridor to carry on attending to the Albany gardens. 'Head-porter, sir,' said the splendid figure. 'George Dymchurch.'

'Ah, right,' said William. 'Hello, Mr Dymchurch.'

'I gather you are interested in contacting Mr Brandreth Jacques, the distinguished actor?'

'That's right,' said William. 'I'm Secretary of the Walpole Club. Mr Jacques has always told us that he lived here, we've always written to him here and his replies have always come from here. But it seems he doesn't live here. Or perhaps he once lived here but no longer does. It's all rather odd.'

Mr Dymchurch took a long, deep breath. 'He never *has* lived here, sir,' he said. 'May I suggest we move to that little room on the left, we can talk there.' They went and William sat.

Mr Dymchurch removed his top hat with the dignity

of a large British ambassador attending a small and unimportant foreign state funeral, cradled it in the crook of his arm and sat down on the edge of his chair, back straight as a ramrod, knees apart.

'Do you know where I can find Mr Jacques?' William said.

Mr Dymchurch did not answer immediately. He seemed to William like a man unfamiliar with personal emotions having suddenly to struggle with one.

'The thing really, when you come down to it, sir,' said Mr Dymchurch, 'the nitty-gritty of it, as you might say, is do you bring Mr Jacques good news or the bad sort?'

'Oh, good news,' said William. 'Starts dodgy but there'll be a happy ending. Don't know quite how yet. Somehow. But first I've got to find him.'

'Message understood, sir. Well, Mr Jacques puts it about that he lives in Albany and with his gentlemanly bearing and natty suiting he looks the sort of gent who lives in Albany. But in actual point of fact he lives in a couple of rooms above a dry-cleaners in Walthamstow.'

'Well, well, Walthamstow, eh?' said William pointlessly. He had some mental adjustments to make quickly.

'Fourteen A Linden Road, sir. Two streets down on the right off the High Street. He's lived there for years. With his Philly.'

'Where does Albany come in, then?'

'It's what you might call an accommodation address, sir. Mr Jacques is no longer as famous as he used to be but he still has a bit of his old style. When he had no money left and no more work coming in, he and Philly took the two rooms in Walthamstow on their pensions but he's always loved to pretend and he pretended he lived in Albany. Harmless thing to do, sir. Hurt nobody. All letters addressed to Set J4 were passed to me. I readdressed them to Walthamstow. Likewise I posted his letters as though they were written here. None of the other staff knew.'

'Why did you do it?' said William. 'You could have lost your job.'

'It was my older brother, Arfer, wasn't it? I always wanted to be a soldier but Arfer had his heart set on the theatre. Years ago Mr Jacques was a big star on Shaftesbury Avenue playing sly butlers and silly aristocrats – and very good he was too, sir.'

'I saw him in a film or two but never on the stage,' said William.

'My brother Arfer was in a play with him. Well, behind him really. Arfer was a stage-hand. One matinée the scenery fell on him. He broke his arm in one of those complicated fractures which don't never seem to heal. He was off work for years. Well, Mr Jacques went round to see Arfer's wife, told her not to worry and paid for everything. Gave them something to live on until Arfer was in work again. Now, sir, if you were me, would you have objected to readdressing a few envelopes for Mr Jacques?'

'No,' said William. 'No, I wouldn't. Well, now, how do I get to Walthamstow?'

'I'd take the tube to Leyton and a bus from there to Walthamstow High Street. Don't do anything to hurt him, sir, please. They don't make gentlemen like old Mr Jacques no more. Nowadays, if you'll pardon my French, they're all too bloody sensible.'

Walthamstow High Street on a warm summer afternoon had more than a touch of an oriental market about it, William decided. As he walked down looking for Linden Road, spicy smells drifted out of the doorways of shops selling cooked bits of things. Stalls by the side of the road offered strange-shaped vegetables, herbal cures, odd bits of carpet. There was a surprising number of small, dark shops which seemed to sell everything, their stock spilling out onto the pavement and all of it apparently second-hand; saucepans, dusty television sets, baby clothes, guitars.

Linden Road was where Mr Dymchurch had said it was, second turning on the right. It was much quieter than the High Street with only an odd shop or so, a mini-cab office, a steamed-up café, a newsagent selling *TV Times*, *Penthouse*, the *Sun*, the *Grass*, and bars of chocolate, and on the right, sure enough, a dry-cleaners.

William crossed the road. Above the dry-cleaner's doorway was 'No. 14' in stuck-on plastic lettering. Next to it a postcard was drawing-pinned stating that 'No. 14A' was round the side and up the ladder and please knock because bell is out of order. William went round the side of the shop and found the ladder, actually a shaky wooden staircase. He climbed carefully up it and knocked on the door at the top.

After a brief wait the door was opened, seemingly by nobody.

'Well, come in, don't hang about, I'm in the middle of ironing!' said an angry voice. William, who stood six feet, looked down and there, standing close to him and intruding on his private space, stood a small, elderly figure like a belligerent gnome, hair corrugated and turning from ginger to white where it neared the ears.

William closed the front door and followed the ginger gnome into a tiny, neat room. There was an ironing-board in the middle of the room and on the board was a pair of trousers in a familiar houndstooth check. As worn by Mr Brandreth Jacques, MBE.

'I'll put the kettle on in a mo. Don't hurry me,' said the gnome.

He went over to the gas cooker, which was in between the sink and a rusty-edged refrigerator, grabbed an oven-glove, picked an old-fashioned flat-iron off the gas ring and spat on it. An explosive 'splat' told William that he had arrived at a bad moment for the ironing.

'I'd like a word with Mr Brandreth Jacques,' said William, feeling like a detective-constable in a bad telly play.

'I didn't think you'd come to see *me*,' said the gnome, making strange passes in the air with the nearly red-hot iron. 'Well, you're out of luck. He's gone to the pictures, back about seven. It's Monday, see, matinée, cut-price for OAPs. He's gone to see his old colleague Laurence Olivier being terrible in an early film called *Moscow Nights*. Watching Larry being bad gives Branny a nice warm feeling. He'll most probably see the film round twice.'

'My name is Grundwick,' said William, 'I'm from the Walpole Club. Secretary, actually,' said William.

'Mr Nemesis,' said the gnome, cooling his flat-iron by swinging it dangerously round and round in a circle like a Scot at the Braemar Games about to throw the hammer. 'I've been expecting you. Come to give Mr Jacques the big elbow, right? Non-payment of subscription, right?'

He spat on the iron again and this time it made a satisfactory 'chuff' and he spread a Views-of-Windsor-Castle teacloth on the trousers, took a swig from a bottle of water and squirted a fine spray through his teeth on to the cloth. He then glided the hot iron across the damp cloth, intently, expertly.

'My name's Phil,' he said. 'Branny calls me his Philly.'

William again had to make some rapid mental adjustments.

'Just a guess,' said William, 'but were you once his dresser?'

'Forty-two years on September the tenth,' said Phil, lifting the steaming cloth and inspecting the trousers closely.

'Still am his dresser, really,' he said. 'This is the only

decent suit he's got. I get him into it for his Friday lunch up the Walpole, then when he comes back I go over it for gravy then give it a press and put it away for next Friday. Which is what I'm doing at this moment of time, as the yankee-doodles say. Not that there'll *be* a next Friday I suppose, now you've turned up.' He bashed steam out of the trousers with the back of a clothes-brush and hung the trousers over the kitchen chair.

'He's eighty-two,' said little Phil. 'The Walpole is his last link with the life he once led; witty chat and whisky I used to call it to annoy him, but it was more than that. He was respected in that world. And loved.'

Branny's Phil sat down on the kitchen chair. 'Playing a part,' he said. 'That's what he's been doing all his life, playing the role of Brandreth Jacques, the rich, debonair womanizer. The 'orrible truth is he's never saved a penny in his life, he's only debonair because I look after his one suit and if he got stuck in a lift with a pretty girl he'd faint.'

'If he hasn't worked much for years,' said William, 'how on earth has he been able so far to pay the six hundred quid a year subscription to the Club?'

'Living's cheap here,' said the little dresser. 'We rent the flat for next to nothing because we're no trouble to the old lady who owns it, I keep it clean and neat and we pay up on time. Neither of us eats much so I can make our two pensions go a long way.'

'But to save up six hundred quid a year . . . '

'Well, I'll tell you. Part-time jobs can pay well round these parts. I do a bit of shelf-stacking at the supermarkets and I do an early-morning spell at the petrol pumps. Bit of nightwatchman duty guarding the big boutique on the High Street, Madame Fifine, that's Ben Moses, nice bloke, keeps getting broken into. And there's good money in hospital work. General cleaner and porter at weekends and nights and over Christmas, work nobody else wants to do. Bit mucky at times but on triple overtime, what's it matter?'

'So at your age you work long, anti-social hours to pay for old Branny's club?'

'And bloody glad to do so. When you're a person like me, or him for that matter, you've got no young family to take care of you when you're old, you've outlived most of your friends and the one thing you dread is ending up all by yourself in some lonely, crummy room. Well, I'm dead lucky, aren't I? I've got Branny to share the rest of my life with. I've always said that I only wanted two things when I was old; some of me own teeth and somebody to look after, and see?' he grinned. 'I've ended up with four of one and one of the other!'

'But on top of the annual sub you presumably had to find some money to pay for his Friday trips to the Walpole?'

'Not much. He travelled up by tube and bus on his Twirlie.'

'His what?'

'Twirlie. His OAP free-travel pass. They're known as "twirlies" because transport's only free after nine thirty in the morning when the rush hour's over. But all the old dodgers try to get on before then and the driver has to hand their card back and say to 'em, "Sorry mate – too early!" At the Club Branny only ever had one small whisky and the cheapest thing on the menu. No coffee. He didn't go to eat and drink. He went to be Brandreth Jacques again for an hour or so. It's those Club Fridays that've kept the old luv going.'

'So what happened to the money you'd saved up to pay this year's sub?'

'There's a neighbour along the road who's got into trouble. Old friend of ours, runs the mini-cab service, messed up his VAT and you know what they're like. He's in a bad way because he's got a wife and four daughters and he's an illegal immigrant. That's where Branny's sub went. You know Branny by now, he lent this man the whole lot, didn't he? You'd better tell the Club there's no hope of Branny getting his money back for a few years, if at all.'

'As a matter of fact,' said William slowly, feeling his way, 'that is not a problem. I didn't come here as Mr Nemesis, I came to tell you that in certain cases a member's subscription can be waived at the House Committee's discretion, and this year they've elected to waive Mr Jacques's current unpaid sub.'

'No, no, no!' said the dresser. 'He wouldn't countenance it for one moment. He won't take charity.'

'It's not charity,' said William. 'It's a special fund. Set up to recognize the contribution made to the Club's well-being by a popular member of over ten years' standing. And this year they've chosen Brandy Jack. It's as simple as that.' William was pleased how plausible his complicated, ad-libbed lie sounded. The little dresser was breathing rather heavily and looking down at his shoes.

'Don't believe it,' he said. 'Amazing bits of good luck like this don't happen.'

William rose. 'Must get back,' he said. 'I've got some arrangements to make. Then I'll come down again and have a chat with him. Right by you?'

'You're the gaffer!' said Phil, happily.

'One more thing,' said William, waving his Fortnum's bag. 'Can you do me a favour? I was given a couple of smoked trout and my wife and I only eat fresh fish. We hate anything smoked. Can I leave them for you and Branny?'

'Yes, please!' said little Phil. 'This really is our lovely day!'

He took the Fortnum's bag and held the door open for William.

William gave a wave and began the perilous descent of the staircase.

'One last thing, sir!' called little Phil down the stairs after him. 'I've never been proud, sir, it's a sin anyway, what I mean is, thanks very much indeed for the smoked trout. But it's only quarter-past four. If you hurry you can catch Fortnum's before they close and get another couple for your supper.'

William, clutching his bag of replacement smoked trout, climbed up the Club stairs to his office, mind awhirl with a new problem. How was he going to find funds to pay Brandy Jack's subscription? It was now unthinkable to him that the hard-earned, fragile happiness of the little *ménage à deux* in Walthamstow should be destroyed.

He burst into his office and Belkis was sitting on his window-ledge in her sari, the late afternoon sunshine shining through the muslin and silk and silhouetting her stunning figure.

'Unless you move out of the sunshine,' said William, 'I shall either report you to the Ethical Committee of the Institute of Chartered Accountants or leap on you.'

'Oh, no, not to leap, if you please!' said Belkis, moving rapidly away from the window. 'Mr Hardcastle is back this evening from two weeks in Newcastle under Lyme. We have a little party always when he returns home. I have chilled champagne waiting in the refrigerator and we have a drinky. Then I take all my clothes off and dance in the naked for Malcolm. That is nice, isn't it? Think of me this evening.'

'Oh, I will! I will!' said William with fervent honesty. 'What-erm-er-time will you be performing your dance? Midnight?'

'Oh, no. About ten-past six, during the early evening news on BBC1.'

William shook his head in wonderment.

'Now, Willy, look happy, please. I have really cheering-up information for you. Guess what I have uncovered in the files?'

'A fund for paying the subs of hard-up members?'

'There was one last century but senior members used it all up paying their relations' subs so the committee said, "No more!" '

'What's the good news then?'

'This afternoon I found another old fund in the archives dating from much earlier days, and I think nobody knows about this one. It was called the Fines Fund. In the eighteenth century they used to fine members who had something nice happen to them, like getting married or winning a rich horse-race. The fine would have been to counteract their good luck and help them avoid the Evil Eye; I know lots about the Evil Eye.'

'How do we get at the fund?'

'We can't, it's capital and we'd be stealing. But there is the interest. The fund is just a few hundred pounds but it was invested two hundred years ago and the interest runs into many thousands of pounds. Many thousands indeed, Willy.'

'Good Lord. But wouldn't using the interest be stealing?'

'I do not think so. The minutes say quite clearly that the interest must be used for encouraging Club conviviality.'

'Belkis, you are quite wonderful!'

'My Malcolm will be telling me that, too,' said Belkis, 'this evening during the early evening news. Oh, Willy, keeping Mr Brandreth Jacques in the Club is beyond argument promoting Club conviviality. And with his subscription paid you will have, for certain, your Orange compère!'

William looked up in surprise. 'Good heavens, so I will!' he said. 'D'you know, I'd forgotten all about the Orange.'

CHAPTER SEVEN

A MEANINGFUL POSTCARD

That evening things were understandably a little strained between William and Milly. They both behaved creditably but neither could be frank with the other so they were artificially normal, like two people at breakfast with crippling hangovers pretending to be jolly. Matters were not helped that night when William was feeding his trousers into his trouser press and Milly, already in bed, caught a glimpse of his bare bottom.

'What's that weal on your bum?' she asked.

'Nothing, really,' said William. 'I sat too long on the edge of the plastic table in my office, that's all.'

Milly thought it a hopeless excuse. If where he was sitting was raising a painful weal why didn't he stand up? Anyway, why wasn't he sitting in his own chair? A tingle of alarm ran through her. What, or indeed who, had inflicted the weal? Had her relationship with William grown so cool that he had been driven to seek the services of 'Miss Payne, Correction of Naughty Boys a Speciality'?

No, not William, Milly decided, common sense momentarily taking over from panic; pain had never been William's pleasure. She remembered a particularly steamy session with him on the sofa bed when they had simultaneously reached, as it were, point of lay, when an errant length of steel bar sprang free from the bed mechanism and caught William a violent slap on the behind. William screeched like a seagull with its foot caught and he and

Milly had to give up love-making and go back to reading their books.

Still worrying slightly, Milly turned over on her side, put her light out and was asleep before William had finished emptying his trouser pockets onto his bedside table.

The following days turned out to be busy for William. He had only weeks in which to organize the Orange and all he had for certainty so far was Brandy Jack. And ever-present and bothersome, like a small wart on the working surface of the thumb, was the problem of what the Unspeakable Tozer was up to.

The next morning, as William was almost at the top of the stairs on the way to getting some desk-work done, he saw the lower half of Tozer disappearing into the door next to his office. This gave William cause to pause; the door next to William's office into which Mr Tozer had disappeared led not to a room but to a cupboard where stationery was stored. William decided to take countermeasures.

Affecting nonchalance, he sauntered, humming casually but noisily, into his office, banged the door shut, tiptoed over to his desk, opened the drawer where he kept his little portable radio, tuned in Radio 4 and adjusted the sound and tuning so that the voices which emerged were loud but unclear. He tiptoed back to the door, opened it silently, tiptoed along the landing to the stationery cupboard and suddenly flung the door open.

Mr Tozer was in the cupboard, sitting on a stack of boxes of A4 paper. He had cleared a space between two shelves on the wall next to William's office and, head inserted sideways between the shelves, had his ear pressed to the bottom of a beer glass which he was holding against the wall. He was clearly listening intently to the muffled voices in William's office.

'And what do you think you're doing?' asked William.

Tozer jerked away from the wall hitting his head

painfully against the edge of the upper shelf, William was pleased to note.

'Mice,' said Mr Tozer.

'What mice?' asked William.

'Any mice, really, sir,' said Mr Tozer. 'It's the best way to catch 'em. You wait 'til one runs up the wall and then, quick as lightning, ram a glass over it. Then slide a postcard in between the glass and the wall and you've got 'im. Then you empty him down the toilet. It's humane you see, sir.'

William peered. 'But there isn't a mouse in the glass,' he said.

Mr Tozer peered too, 'Nor is there!' he said, visibly mystified. 'I must have missed 'im.'

'What is more, during the time I've been Secretary of this Club I have never seen a mouse on the premises, nor has a sighting of one been reported to me. Mice were professionally eliminated some years ago and have never returned.'

'Did I say mice? I meant cockroaches,' said Tozer. 'That's what I meant, sir, cockroaches. All the old buildings round here are infested with the nasty black things, sir. Infested. It's a disgrace to the Royal Borough of St James's. I followed one up the stairs just now and when it ran up the wall, I pounced!'

'There isn't a cockroach in the glass either,' said William.

'What?' said Tozer. 'I don't believe it!' He peered carefully. 'You're right, sir,' he said. 'You're not wrong you're right! Well, I never! The clever little devil must have tunnelled his way out under the edge of the glass and . . . '

'No, Mr Tozer,' said William. 'There never was a cockroach, was there? Nor a mouse. You were trying to listen to me through the wall, weren't you?'

Mr Tozer looked startled for just a moment then a quirky, totally unconvincing little smile appeared. 'You've caught me out fair and square there, Guv! As the Duke of Wellington said when his wife accused him of chopping down the cherry tree with their son up it, "I cannot tell you a porky." Truth is, sir, on my day off last week I was watching *Blue Peter* on the telly and they showed us how to listen through a wall with the help of an empty yoghurt pot. So I thought I'd give it a try. Bit of childlike fun, that's all.'

'Rubbish,' said William. 'You've been spying on me.'

Mr Tozer staggered back a pace, visibly aghast at the vile accusation. '*Me*, sir?' he said. 'Me spy on *you*? Never, sir! Not while there's body left in my breath!'

'Anyway, does it work?' asked William casually. 'Listening through the wall with a glass?'

'Nah, not really, you can't make out the words. A stethoscope's better but where would I get . . . Oh, dear!'

'Oh, dear, indeed, Mr Tozer. That's all I need to know, thank you. Off you go back to your work. For the time being. And return the glass to the bar, if you please, to be thoroughly washed. Better still, disinfected.'

'Sir,' said Tozer almost inaudibly, shuffling off with his thin shoulders sloping miserably down like those of a hock bottle, the image of a faithful employee wrongly accused of disloyalty.

William went back to his office to get on with his own work. Tuesday was his day for replying to the week's niggles entered by members in the massive Suggestions Book. This was one of the formal duties most enjoyed by Club Secretaries, the point being that they tried to make their replies as succinct and laconic as possible.

William once playfully suggested to Uncle Sid that he should inaugurate an annual inter-club contest with a cash prize going to the Secretary whose answers were the most gnomic. Lord Sidmonton, who as it happened was in a bad mood having been ticked off during breakfast by

Parthenope for slopping vintage brandy over her side of the eiderdown, told William not to be so mercenary.

William sighed, opened the book and began. Luckily, as he had so much else more urgent on his mind, many dedicated suggestion-writers were still away on holiday and there were only a few entries.

The first came from a limpet, Henderson Brougham Esq., an angular retired senior civil servant who wrote in a neat, vicious hand. Like a disgruntled phone-in addict, he turned up nearly every week complaining about some trifle not worth complaining about:

> *Yesterday there appeared yet another totally illegible entry. It was written by Sir Archibald Alloway, 17th baronet, if 'written' is the right word to use in regard to anything penned by Sir Archibald. I know that Sir Archibald is culpable because he is the only Club member whose signature is totally illegible. His message in the book was, as usual, also totally illegible. So can he not be persuaded to stop these pointless scribblings? This book already contains fourteen of Sir Archibald's illegible entries which have wasted expensive paper and cost the Club money which would have been better spent on oiling the hinges of the second lavatory seat on the left past the weighing scales.*

H. Grantley Brougham, CBE

> *For many older members Sir Archibald's handwriting is a source of Club pride. Oil will be arranged.*

W.G.

The next entry came from Harry del Guido, a startlingly successful young advertising executive whose annual expenditure in the bar and dining-room, according to Belkis, paid for the new lift:

> *Club food has improved enormously over the past months except for one item: bread. The toast is passable, but eating one of the Club's soft rolls is like biting into a lump of extruded plastic packing material. No taste and it does not diminish when chewed but packs itself tightly round the teeth like plumber's tow. Our dreadful club rolls simply cannot be justified when London streets today are aromatic with automatic bakeries and warm, fresh croissants are for sale on Waterloo station.*
>
> Harry Guido

> *Agreed. Will discuss with chef at once. Many thanks.*
>
> W.G.

Captain (retd) 'Slim' Blisworth asked to be called 'Slim' not because of his build, which was portly, but after General Slim whom he had narrowly missed meeting in the Far East during the war. Slim Blisworth had been something murky in Indonesia for most of his life, a hanging judge or Chief of Secret Police were the favourite Club theories, and his face had that golden-syrup colour which most British faces seemed to acquire after years enduring the hot shadows of tropic verandahs and enormous pink gins. He did not just give his order for food in the dining-room but barked a sharp command for it. The waitresses loathed him:

> *I find the reading-matter in the morning-room too namby-pamby for a simple soldier's taste; daily papers and weeklies stuffed with things like*

*books and politics and the theatre. As if everybody
goes to the theatre these days or is interested in
books. Do you think the committee would consider
dropping either the boring* Times *or the dreary*
Daily Telegraph *in favour of a more stimulating
and lively paper, e.g., the* Sun?

Slim Blisworth

No.
W.G.

The last entry was taut with restrained fury. Its author
was Arthur Branston, a mauve-faced Mayfair wine-merchant.
William thought his contribution was more moderate than
usual but still agreeably hispid:

*I write in utter dismay and disgust. In the dining-room
at luncheon on Friday I saw our Master, Lord
Sidmonton, at a side-table with a guest. The guest
ate his wild mushroom purée and then produced a
BRIEFCASE! Are Club rules to be mocked? Are the
Goths taking over? Briefcases and business talk have
always been totally banned from the Walpole's social
rooms. Did the Master recoil from this flagrant breach
of club manners? He did not. He tucked into his Bœuf
en Croute and continued talking, no doubt about
profits, to his squalid businessman guest. I demand a
stringent enquiry into this lamentable breach of our
Club's most cherished rule and also the immediate
resignation of the Master and, of course, the Secretary.*

Arthur L. K. Branston

*I have made enquiries. The guest did not
produce a briefcase but a handbag, an article
much carried by gentlemen in Italy but, for*

good reasons perhaps, less frequently in this
country. No business matters were mentioned.
The Master was taking his guest to the opera
that evening and they were mostly discussing
Monteverdi and Gluck. The Master's
guest was the Italian Ambassador.

W.G.

Another little job jobbed thought William cheerfully to himself as he closed the heavy book. But on consideration not jobbed all that well. Only one reply was really gnomic and the last reply was almost longer than the complaint. A good thing perhaps that Uncle Sid put the kybosh on the idea of setting up The Great Suggestions Book Handicap?

Never mind, on, on. What to tackle next? Confer with chef Anton on Orange food? Seek historical information on Roman Oranges from an academic member? Go back to Walthamstow and tactfully break the good news to Brandy Jack about his subscription then discuss a programme for the Orange with him? Find out from Belkis how much money she could make available for the Orange? William felt in his hip pocket for the postcard on which, yesterday, he had jotted down his notes.

The pocket was empty.

'I found this postcard by William's side of the bed,' said Milly, holding it up. 'He must have dropped it when he was getting dressed.'

'What does it say?' asked Pippa.

'Seems to be a rough *aide-mémoire*,' said Milly. 'The writing's madly William-in-a-hurry. I haven't really deciphered it yet.'

The others fell silent and watched Milly concentrating, brow furrowed, an occasionally muttered reaction escaping such as 'Good God!', 'No!', 'What does *that* mean!'

They were taking an enforced break in their rehearsal for the IBM Conference audition on Thursday. As usual their rehearsal room was an empty space temporarily owned by Estelle's father, Bradfield, a jolly man all three girls called 'Papa', who also acted as the trio's agent; he qualified for this honour because he was the owner of a damaged fax machine which he had accepted in lieu of part-rent on one of his properties. It sent out fax messages which never seemed to arrive anywhere, and although it would not print out, there was a microphone somewhere in the machine's insides and when somebody sent it a fax, Bradfield could shout at the sender through a small hole in the machine and it became a useful second telephone.

Bradfield was a big, burly man, built more along the lines of Fats Waller than Harry Belafonte. He usually greeted the girls with a grin which managed to reveal all thirty-eight of his teeth. Milly loved him.

Bradfield had begun his career as a property developer back home in Barbados when his family land, a few acres of terminally unproductive scrub, was so important to a hotel chain wanting to build that they paid him a good deal of money for it. In Barbados Bradfield was rich. Even when he moved to England with his silent, holy wife and young daughter Estelle he was extremely well off, although he became slightly less well off after each business venture. Papa was more a man of vision than of business acumen and he was only too happy to let the Trio rehearse free in whatever premises reflected his most recent error of judgement.

What Milly particularly loved about him was his curious reversal of normal reactions. When a property deal came off and profit resulted, he became moody and scratchy. But when, as more often happened, a deal fell through and he lost money, he reeled about with laughter.

In the past year the Trio had rehearsed in the remains of

Estelle's father's Pizza Parlour, which the previous owner had prudently set on fire just before quarter-day; a Chapel of Rest at the back of an undertakers whose proprietor had developed a painful allergy to flowers; an ex-massage parlour in Stoke Newington, which the leaseholder could no longer afford to run when his working ladies found that on reaching retirement age a little earning was a dangerous thing and it was more profitable for them to give up the part-time massage game and draw their full pensions; a ground-floor flat in Pimlico (the most glamorous of their rehearsal rooms) previously operated by Lady de Boot, a friend of Milly's mother, as a collection centre for cast-off Mayfair clothing destined for Africa which she washed carefully and wore, or mended and sold to friends; and a BBC recording studio for small orchestras beneath which, rather unexpectedly, had been built a minor but busy branch line of the Inner Circle, with a train every few minutes.

The ex-studio was by far the most suitable of the bunch, small and warm, but it did mean that the Trio had an enforced break from rehearsal every five minutes.

'What do you make of this, then?' asked Milly, about to read aloud from the postcard.

'Quickly or we'll cop the next train,' said Estelle.

But Milly took too long deciphering William's handwriting. A distant rumbling grew louder and the building began to shake. Their rickety music-stands trembled and Pippa's fell over. Spectral wind seemed to blow through the room before a heavy silence descended.

'Sod this for a game of soldiers,' said the Hon. Pippa on her hands and lovely knees, gathering up sheets of music.

'No, listen,' said Milly. 'William had a red mark on his bot last night. He said it was from sitting on a hard edge in the office but listen to what he's written: "Must sort

78

out Orange food but weather v. hot and got back to office whacked." Could mean he visited one of those stony-faced ladies who advertise offering correction.'

Estelle burst into peals of laughter.

'William?' said Pippa. 'The only correction your William will ever need is a dab of Tipp-Ex, and that's not very sexy!'

'Depends where you dab it,' said Estelle.

'You're sex-mad,' said Milly, getting a little exasperated.

'How can I be?' said Estelle reasonably. 'I haven't had any yet.'

'What do you think the following little lot refers to?' said Milly. She peered down at William's postcard and read out, ' "Arrange rendezvous – 14A Linden Road, Walthamstow, Thursday after work—" then he's drawn a doodle of a bosomy girl in what looks like a sari – I suppose that's the office siren, Mrs Hardcastle. It goes on: "Get rid of old dresser so just Brandy. Take anti-Tozer precautions. Put fish in fridge." '

'Great stuff!' said Thin Estelle.

'I think this is all getting a bit silly,' said Pippa.

'It was your idea,' said Milly. 'Follow him, find out what he's up to, you said. Well, that's what I've been trying to do and I feel cheap and shabby and altogether deep-down rotten.'

'You've no need to be,' said Pippa. 'Not yet. You've no proof of hanky-panky. I mean, a few dubious lines on a postcard can mean anything or nothing. My guess is they mean absolutely nothing at all.'

'But what about that bit about taking "anti-Tozer precautions"?' asked Estelle. 'What's a Tozer? A toe job? What precautions are you supposed to take for that? For safe toe jobs make sure he wears a sock?'

'Tozer's a creepy porter at the Club,' said Milly. 'William's always loathed him.'

'He says he's got some brandy so it looks like William's setting up a real fun party. I wonder what he plans to do with the fish?' said Estelle, still enjoying her sexual musings. 'Could be a goldfish, of course and we all know what you can do with that, but he doesn't say. Could be any fish. "How about a little playtime, Mrs Hardcastle? I've brought the kipper! Sorry it's straight from the fridge but you could warm it up by . . ."'

'Oh, Estelle, do shut up,' said Milly. 'The fish was last night's supper, smoked trout, and very good.'

'Thing is,' said Pippa, 'we know William is planning a rendezvous with somebody. The postcard doesn't say who it is he's meeting but we know where the meeting is and it's next Thursday. I think we should be there and find out what's going on.'

'Oh, no!' cried Milly. 'That really would be spying!'

'I just want to have old William cleared of all this silly mystery,' said Pippa, quite calm and determined. 'That postcard does read badly, Milly, I admit. But there must be an innocent explanation and the sensible thing is to find out what that is.'

'We can't spy on William next Thursday,' said Milly suddenly. 'It's the night of our IBM audition.'

'Oh, my Gawd!' said Estelle, hand to mouth. 'I forgot to tell you, the IBM audition's cancelled.'

'What?' shouted the others.

'Oh, Estelle,' said Milly.

'What happened was, Papa sent the IBM Conference man one of our publicity photographs, that one where Catriona looks like Cleopatra on heat, and it seems that this IBM man is very straightlaced, won't whistle in the presence of ladies or eat gravy on Sundays and that and he's cancelled us.'

'That's what you might call ironic,' said Pippa, 'considering that Catriona wouldn't have been there anyway!'

Milly's shoulders drooped. 'What a bloody mess everything's becoming,' she said. 'Men . . . Music . . . '

'No, you've got to cheer up, Milly,' said Estelle. 'Listen to me, now. Good old Papa's got us a replacement booking for two weeks' time. A real live booking not an audition and know what it is? A dinner at the Guildhall, London. White tie and tails, the Prime Minister is making a speech, it'll be televised! It is a big function on behalf of English Heritage! We'll be famous!'

'What's the catch?' said Pippa. 'With respect there always seems to be one with good old Papa. For instance, what do they want us to play?'

'Oh, yes, well – as it's English Heritage, you know, country houses and Olde Englishe rubbishe, they want us to play Elizabethan music.'

'But we don't play Elizabethan music, you know that. The Tudors weren't that hot on string trios.'

'Doesn't matter,' said Estelle, grinning happily. 'The great thing about a Guildhall gig is that we shall be stuck high up on that tiny balcony and the chatter and bashing about of crockery during dinner is so deafening that nobody'll hear a note we play. We can practise our Scarlatti and Handel all evening and nobody'll even notice.'

'How do you know all this?' asked Pippa.

'One of the London Brass Ensemble trumpeters told me. He's often there for the fanfares and he's lovely. Huge, sexy boy named Foster.'

'There you go again,' said Milly. 'Man-mad.'

'A trumpeter's kiss is a maiden's bliss,' said Estelle shyly.

'Again, what's the catch?' said Pippa. 'Like, for instance, what fee has Papa negotiated for us?'

'Well . . . ' said Estelle. 'Actually, Papa told English Heritage that we'd be happy to contribute our talents for nothing. For Great Britain and the publicity.'

'I do not believe this!' said Pippa. 'What publicity does our wise old business manager think we're going to attract stuck halfway up a wall and inaudible? Enough publicity to pay for dry-cleaning our best dresses after being bombarded with profiteroles last Saturday at Roddy Forbes-Jellinek's wedding? Enough to pay for repairing the Citroën 2CV which we need to transport the harpsichord and cello? – the entire exhaust system died of old age and fell off yesterday when I was driving round Hyde Park Corner.'

'Looking on the bright side . . . ' said Estelle.

'There isn't one,' said the Hon. Pippa.

'Actually, there is half a one,' said Milly. 'Now Thursday evening is free I can go to Walthamstow and try to find out who William is meeting.'

'We'd better all go,' said Pippa firmly.

'Now, I know you think I'm thick . . . ' said Estelle.

'Unfortunately not in the right places,' said Pippa.

' . . . but, listen,' went on Estelle. 'I know just the thing Milly needs for spying in Walthamstow and moreover I know where I can get hold of one.'

'One what?' asked Milly.

'"Baby Beautiful Electronic Supa-Sitta",' said Estelle. Milly and Pippa looked at each other.

'Papa won a contract to import them from Japan and sell them to baby shops. He'd be a millionaire by now but when he negotiated the contract he got the value of the yen wrong so he owes *them* money. But Papa's got about a hundred unwanted Electronic Supa-Sittas in a cupboard in his flat and I can easily pinch one.'

'Just a thought,' said Pippa, 'but what the hell is a Baby Beautiful Electronic Supa-Sitta? A po which gets Radio 1?'

'It's a sort of electronic gadget you put by the cot which lets you know when your baby's crying.'

'Listen all,' said Pippa. 'We'll get into number 14A Linden Road somehow and leave the thing where it can pick up conversation. I'll do a reconnaissance to Walthamstow tomorrow and get the lie of the land and we'll all meet on Thursday about five in the evening. Does that make sense?'

'You sound like Just William briefing the Outlaws,' said Milly. 'But it makes good sense. Meanwhile Estelle had better borrow or steal a silencer for the 2CV or they'll hear us coming before we get to Hackney Marshes.'

Pippa took the tube and bus to make her recce and found Linden Road, Walthamstow, without much trouble. She strolled casually past No. 14 and noted the wooden staircase leading up to 14A.

On Thursday the Trio met at Milly's and set off for Walthamstow in the 2CV. Estelle's father had arranged for the silencer to be repaired so the exhaust no longer sounded like the Honourable Artillery Company celebrating the Queen Mother's birthday.

They parked the car and had a cup of tea in the steamed-up café opposite No. 14, taking it in turns to wipe a bit of the window clear with a face tissue so that they could monitor any movement.

Estelle was clutching a large cardboard box on which was a brightly coloured picture of a black-haired baby in a cot howling its head off in the direction of a 4-inch high, plastic Mickey Mouse: outside the door stood an oriental couple grinning happily and clutching a matching Minnie Mouse.

'Look!' said Pippa sharply.

Milly quickly demisted a patch of window and the three girls saw two old men carefully descending the wooden ladder from No. 14A. The smaller, ginger-haired one was clutching envelopes. They strolled slowly up Linden Road, in no hurry on the warm evening, on their way to the postbox.

'*Now!*' said Pippa.

'Suppose they turn round?' cried Estelle.

'They don't know us from Adam,' Pippa pointed out.

'Eve,' said Estelle.

Milly left money for their teas at the urn and they strolled nonchalantly across the road to the dry-cleaners and through the side gate to the foot of the wooden stairs.

'I'll take the Supa-Sitta up,' said Estelle.

'Do you know where to plug it in?' asked Pippa in a hoarse and quite unnecessary stage whisper: the girls were beginning to succumb to the drama of their faintly illegal operation.

'You don't plug it in,' said Estelle. 'It works for a whole day on four AA batteries. It says here on the box, see? – Oh, shit!'

Milly grabbed the box and read out, 'Batteries not included.'

'Oh, Estelle!' Pippa shouted, security yielding to exasperation.

'That newsagent down the road'll have batteries,' said Milly. 'They always do. I'll run.'

'Hurry!' yelled Pippa. 'The men might be back any moment!'

Milly sprinted off at a most impressive speed for a harpsichordist, wrestling money out of her handbag as she ran.

Estelle took the two plastic figures out of the box and opened up the battery compartments ready for a relay-race-style hand-over of the AAs when Milly returned.

'The men are coming back!' hissed Pippa who was keeping watch round the corner of the building. '*Come on, Milly!*'

Milly skidded to a halt, gulping air, batteries out-stretched. Estelle grabbed them and with a violinist's adroit fingers stuffed them swiftly into place.

'I'll run up and plant the Supa-Sitta,' she said. 'You go off to the café and I'll join you when the coast's clear. Wish me luck.'

The three clasped hands, like the canoeists in *Cockleshell Heroes* before they paddled off to attach limpet mines to the German fleet. The girls had seen the film about forty times at the Sunday evening film-show in the school gym, or over fifty times if you include half-showings when the projector broke down and a nun played the recorder instead.

The old men were already quite close when Milly and Pippa crossed the road, so to make sure they would not be recognized later the girls pretended they were returning from the internment of a loved one and hurried over to the café covering their faces with their hankies and sobbing piteously.

They collected their teas and made for their window seats, wiping a bit of the window clear and peering out anxiously. No sign of Estelle so she had presumably made it to the flat safely and was busy planting the Supa-Sitta.

The two old men were now almost up to No. 14 and were both talking at the same time but, as Pippa pointed out to Milly, they were not chatting but arguing. The arguers reached the dry-cleaners and Milly's heart was in her mouth but the old men, still arguing, walked past the house and up the road.

A minute or two later Estelle appeared cautiously on the wooden balcony, peered down the road to make sure the coast was clear and then danced across to the café.

'Did it!' she said triumphantly, crashing into a chair next to Pippa, her face even more beautiful as it glowed with the excitement of it all. 'It's a really tiny flat. I parked the microphone thing out of sight under an armchair! Just in the nick of time, too – look, the men are outside the house now!'

'Estelle . . . ' said Milly.

'We'll be able to hear everything that's said in the flat. Clear as a bell!'

'Estelle . . . ' said Milly again.

'They don't know it but their flat has been bugged. By me! Aren't I a clever little bugger?'

'Estelle,' said Milly. 'Where's the loudspeaker?'

'The what?' asked Estelle.

'Oh, no!' wailed Pippa.

Milly produced the box the Supa-Sitta came in. 'Look at the picture, Estelle. The thing has two parts. A microphone and a loudspeaker. The instructions say, quite clearly, "Position the transmitter – the one shaped like Mickey Mouse – near the cot and take the loudspeaker – the one shaped like Minnie Mouse, with you into your own room. You will then hear every noise your baby makes."'

'Oh,' said Estelle. 'I left them clamped together under the armchair.

'If I live to be a hundred,' said Pippa, 'I will never understand how you achieved an O level.'

'It was mainly Sister Ho's doing,' said Estelle in a small, contrite voice. 'She felt sorry for me because she too was a member of an ethnic minority.'

'Minority? She was *Chinese*!'

'Heads down!' said Milly. 'The men are coming in.'

The café was the old-fashioned sort with high-backed, pew-like seats which gave some privacy. The girls crouched over their table as though inspecting the plastic for knot-holes. They heard vague scrapes and clinks as the old men settled themselves in the next booth and tried their tea.

'Gnat's pee,' said the beautifully modulated voice of Brandreth Jacques, MBE.

'And who's bleedin' fault is that?' came the

unmodulated, irascible voice of Philly. 'You never take no notice whatwhomsoever of anything I tell you, do you? I said before you set out for Tescos, that nice Secretary from the Walpole Club is coming this evening, I said, and we're out of tea. So get a packet of Earl Grey, I said. Didn't I say that? Get some Earl Grey. And what do you bring back? Dar-bloody-jeeling. You know I never drink Indian tea, it turns my liver into an old boot, but you bring back Dar-bloody-jeeling. Which is why, thanks to your lordship, we're sitting here drinking gnat's pee.'

'Tescos had run out of Earl Grey,' said Brandy Jack, mildly.

'You'd better give our young friend Nescaff,' said the old dresser. 'I'll leave the Nes out on a tray. All you need do is boil the water. Do you feel capable of that?'

'Dear old Philly,' said Brandy Jack affectionately. 'Full of wind and piss today, aren't we?'

'Well, you make my blood boil sometimes. And another thing. You bloody well behave yourself when the Secretary arrives. None of your loose language. How well do you know him?'

'Young William? Meet him in the bar, sometimes. Sit next to him at lunch so as to avoid the lawyers. I like him. But why does he want to see me this evening? Going to sue me for my subscription?'

The three girls were listening so intently that their ears were almost bleeding.

'Well, I'll tell you, Branny, so as you won't get into one of your moods and go all boiled shirt. I'm not supposed to say anything but it won't do no harm: young William is coming all the way down here to tell you the good news that you are still a member of the Walpole Club for at least another year.'

'Had a whip-round in the bar to pay the poor old sod's sub, did they?'

'No, they bloody didn't. Our young friend's discovered a special fund. He's a thoroughly decent young chap who's gone to a hell of a lot of trouble, mostly in his own time, to keep you in the Club. He's done it because, God knows why, he likes you for what you are, not for what you used to be. So, luvvy, either you make him a nice cup of Nes this evening and accept what he's done for you with charm and gratitude or I'll bash your face in.'

There was the clinking of cup on saucer.

'It's not really quite gnat's pee,' came the voice of Brandy Jack in the thoughtful tones of a wine-taster rolling burgundy around his tongue and breathing in. 'More like an infusion of coffee-flavoured, cremated ferret.'

'Well, at least you now know the truth about William's suspicious assignation,' whispered the Hon. Pippa to Milly.

'What a swiz,' sighed Estelle. 'I was looking forward to sounds of unbridled lust coming from 14A.'

Milly just sat there thinking. Eventually she said to Pippa, 'I'm very glad we came.'

CHAPTER EIGHT

THE ORANGE BEGINS TO TAKE SHAPE

Milly was friendlier than she had been for some days when William arrived home in Peel Street. It was after midnight and he went straight to bed where Milly was lying half-asleep. They chatted idly and dozily for a minute and then Milly kissed him good night gently and sweetly. He urged himself a little closer, yawned and let his arm accidentally fall across her. She snuggled up to him.

Does this mean we're back as we once were? wondered William. Had Milly's strange remoteness evaporated as swiftly as it had arrived and normal love-making would now be resumed in Peel Street? It might have meant that if William had not suddenly had to get up and have another pee.

He fought against it but he was topped up to bursting point with a peculiar sequence of drinks which he had been obliged to endure throughout the evening and go he had to.

William had begun the evening in the Club bar downing a tall can of rather a lot of export lager to give himself courage and he arrived at the Walthamstow flat just after eight o'clock. Brandy Jack was clearly expecting company as he was a little riot of colour standing at the top of the wooden stairs in the late evening sunshine wearing a canary-yellow sports shirt, a bright blue cravat and a pair of baggy russet sailcloth trousers. He looked, thought William, as though he might at any moment bring the curtain down on Act II with an emotional rendering of *Pedro the Fisherman*.

Brandy Jack looked with keen pleasure at the bottle of wine William was bearing. Just as William was leaving the Club it had occurred to him that it would be civil to take along some wine so he signed for a bottle in the bar. He was allowed such freedoms so long as they were in the course of duty.

The wine was an ordinary and rather sharp-edged claret which had been sold to the Club by the mauve-faced wine-merchant when he had been, briefly and expensively, chairman of the Club wine committee. The claret bore one of those presumptuous names which had about nine hyphens in it and incorporated so many deeply un-English place-names such as *Thorigny-sur-Oreuse* and *St Médard-en-lailes* that even when a British bibber did manage to remember the name of the wine he couldn't pronounce it. The trade had to sell it off cheaply.

Not that Brandy Jack cared. He accepted the bottle with a charming murmur of pleasure, ushered William into the tiny kitchen/living-room, opened the bottle skilfully and swiftly and filled two huge mugs, handing one to William. William's mug celebrated the head of Sir Ralph Richardson as Falstaff. Brandy Jack's mug depicted his deeply envied ex-colleague Sir Laurence Olivier as Hamlet. A hole had been drilled through Hamlet's pottery nose and a piece of string threaded through it from which dangled what was clearly the back-door key.

'Cheers, dear heart!' cried Brandy Jack, lifting his mug in salute to William and gulping down about a third of a pint of the chilly claret. William took a cautious sip. The wine was edgy and unfriendly.

William was amazed how calmly Brandy Jack took his own sudden appearance at the Walthamstow flat, which completely blew Brandy Jack's cover-story of living like a gentleman in Albany. William supposed that Philly had done a good job of briefing the old actor. He could hear mouselike noises coming from behind the bedroom door and guessed that Philly was creeping about in the bedroom trying to hear what was going on.

'Like the flat?' asked Branny, taking another huge swig of wine and then grandly swinging his mug round the tiny, untidy room as if it was the salon at Blenheim Palace. A little wine slopped out of the mug and wet one of William's socks.

Brandy Jack carefully tilted the bottle and topped up Sir Laurence Olivier. 'Bit on the *bijou* side as the estate agent chaps used to say but quite big enough for Philly and me. Philly's been my man-servant for many years. Beyond it really but won't leave me, loyal old dear that he is. He's a bit barmy but no trouble.'

William noticed that the noises coming from behind the door, though still muffled, were getting louder. They sounded like an ancient cat fighting an attack of asthma.

'I always wanted to retire to Walthamstow,' Branny was saying, chattily. 'It's not the West End, thank God, but it's not boring old Essex either. Sort of halfway, and it's easy to get to the Walpole Club from here. You know,' he went on with a sudden burst of boyishness, 'I had a little jape going at the Club and pretended I had a set of rooms in Albany!'

'You didn't!' said William.

'I did! *And* they believed me! Could you imagine me living in a noisy apartment in the middle of Piccadilly? No, old love, after a long career in the excitement of theatre in Shaftesbury Avenue and under the arc-lights and pressures of Hollywood it was the peace and quiet of old Walthamstow for me.'

He tried to refill William's mug but William moved Sir Ralph away in time so Brandy Jack refilled Sir Laurence

Olivier again and dropped the now empty bottle into a bucket under the sink. 'Chin-chin,' he said, and drank deeply.

William gazed down into his mug. The wine seemed to be eating away the glazing. 'The thing is,' William said, 'I came to tell you that the Club will pay your subscription for the next five years. There's a fund for doing this and it's your turn to benefit from it.'

'Philly told me,' said Brandy Jack quietly, not looking at William. 'Don't know what to say. I really am deeply grateful.'

'Now we must talk about the Club Orange,' William said.

'The what? Oh, yes, the celebration that Dares Not Speak its Name. The Master warned me about security and all of us calling it the Orange.'

Visibly cheering up, he twisted a kitchen chair round and sat astride it. 'Fire away, dear heart. What seems to be your problem?'

'Well, to begin with,' said William, 'what, to your way of thinking, constitutes an orgy?'

'Oooh, naughty!' said Brandy Jack. 'You said the word!'

'We can say it here in your flat,' said William. 'We mustn't bandy it about in the Club, that's all. Now come on, what do you think should happen at an orgy?'

'Damned if I know!' said Brandy Jack, cheerfully. 'I'm not an expert on Ancient Greece!'

'But the whole thing was your idea!' said William, getting a bit exasperated. 'You must have had some orgy-like events in mind?'

'Nary a one!' said the little old actor. 'Fact is, old dear, I think up the grand concepts and leave it to others to work out the details. In the past I've suggested plots for plays to writers, put old Hitchcock on to a couple of useful notions for thrillers, persuaded one bright young composer to have a go at rock musicals but I've never meddled in the actual product. I'm an ideas' man, old love, not a worker at the coal-face.'

The sheer irresponsibility of Brandy Jack's attitude William found breathtaking. 'But you must have *some* idea of what you want to happen?' he persisted.

'Lots to drink, to begin with . . . Good God!' Brandy Jack suddenly shot to his feet. 'I nearly forgot!' He grabbed William's half-empty mug, rushed to the cooker and switched off the kettle which was on the way to boiling itself dry. He vaguely rinsed both mugs under the tap, wiped them with a much-holed, greyish cloth, filled them from the kettle and made his way back to William, carefully balancing the mugs which were now filled to the brim with scalding-hot water.

William gripped Sir Ralph Richardson and politely thanked Brandy Jack who waved acknowledgement and took a deep pull from Sir Laurence Olivier. The heavy key dangling from Sir Laurence's nose swung down and bounced playfully against Brandy Jack's Adam's Apple.

William tried a sip. He vaguely remembered that drinking hot water was supposed to be medically beneficial, flushing out the kidneys or somewhere, and supposed that Brandy Jack and Philly made a habit of an evening swig as a health measure. It was not a drink to which it was easy to take objection as it tasted of nothing at all except heat. He dutifully sipped on.

'Tell you what,' said Brandy Jack, brows knitted, 'why don't you have a word with some of the other members of the Events Committee? You may have to shout because they're probably a bit Mutt and Jeff but you might get some orgy ideas from them. For instance, Sir Archibald with the hopeless handwriting. He was in Cairo during the war and went to all sorts of wild parties, or so he says.' He gestured at William's mug. 'Coffee all right?' he asked. 'It's only Nes, I'm afraid. Not too strong for you at this time of night?'

'No, no,' said William. 'I can honestly say it's not too strong.'

'And then there's the Chairman, the little fellow, Lord Wick. He's as evil an old fool as I am. What's more there's much more to old Wick than you'd ever guess by looking at him . . . Good Grief!' Brandy Jack peered into his mug and then peered into William's. 'I forgot to put the coffee in! It's plain hot water! Philly'll have my guts for garters! Why didn't you say?'

He bore William's mug off to the cooker and filled it with more steaming hot water from the kettle. He picked up the jar of Nescafé and a spoon and began rhythmically spooning instant coffee into Sir Ralph. 'As far as my participation is concerned, can I assume that I'll be persuaded to compère the evening? Whatever show you eventually decide to put on will need some sort of introduction.'

William nodded. He was counting the spoonfuls of instant coffee going into his mug. The total so far was eight and Brandy Jack's spooning hand was showing no signs of slowing up. William went over to the old actor, gently prised open his fingers and rescued Sir Ralph. Brandy Jack did not even notice. His mind was on a higher plane.

'I'll need a good microphone, of course,' he was saying. 'I presume that we'll be holding the orgy in the main dining-room? It's our biggest and best room and we can put a podium in the south bay window so that I am not only heard but clearly seen. You will have to arrange for the tables and chairs to be removed for that evening and stored somewhere. The revellers will recline on masses of hired cushions or *chaises-longues* or sit on the floor on rugs.

Chin-chin, old love!' he said, holding up his mug of hot water in salute.

'Cheers,' said William, taking a exploratory swallow. His hot, dark liquid looked like Brown Windsor soup but had the viscosity of marine varnish and tasted like neat Camp coffee essence. He persevered and found that small sips were less emetic than big ones. It was not comforting to realize that there was probably enough caffeine in Sir Ralph to stimulate a moderate-sized African male elephant into musk. William quietly parked his mug underneath his armchair.

The old actor was getting into the part of the visionary producer, striding, none too steadily, to and fro in the tiny room, waving his mug of boiling water and bestowing advice in his beautifully modulated but now rather over-loud voice.

'Food is fearfully important!' he boomed. 'Memorable food, d'ye see, unusual and exciting food. Also lots of fruit to dress the set. Y'know, bunches of grapes all over the place, pineapples, mangos, oysters . . . '

'Oysters?'

'Fruit of the sea, ain't they? Point is, old love, I adore oysters but I can't afford them these days and that's what an orgy really is, isn't it? A little holiday from being poor and bored and boring? Have some more coffee.' He bent down to retrieve William's mug from beneath the armchair but came up instead holding two large plastic mice. Seemingly stuck together.

'It's Mickey Mouse,' said William. 'And Minnie! What on earth . . . ?'

'Philly!' hissed Brandy Jack in a confidential stage whisper which rattled the windows. 'He's gone round the twist at last! Look – toys!   At his age.'

William, who had suddenly seen from his watch that he would not get home unless he left immediately, seized the moment of excitement to make his escape. He jumped up. Brandy Jack was examining the plastic mice with distaste.

'Bloody old fool,' he said. 'What's he thinking of? It was my birthday two months ago. And he knows I've got a thing about mice. I hate all sleek, twitchy things. Ugh!' He tossed the mice towards William who caught them and guessed by their weight that they were more than just plastic toys. He turned them over and instructions embossed on the sole of Mickey's foot told him that the mice were a listening device to tell parents when their baby was crying.

Tozer! thought William gleefully. I can bug him! 'Must go,' he said to Brandy Jack, slipping the mice into his pocket. 'Last bus! Terrific coffee, thanks so much. Bye!' He skipped down the wooden staircase before Brandy Jack could stop him and made his escape.

Home in Peel Street, back from the loo after his third pee and lying wide awake next to the now sleeping figure of his wife, mind racing from caffeine poisoning, he realized that the evening with Brandy Jack had been fruitful. Brandy Jack had given him an inkling of the logistical problems of mounting the Orange like organizing the hire of microphone equipment and considering very carefully what food to lay on. Plus, of course, the urgent problem of finding out just what Tozer's little game was. Yes, it had been a useful evening indeed. Yet at the back of his mind William had the feeling that he was missing something important; something which Brandy Jack had said.

The night was hot and Milly lay next to him with nothing on. William bent over her and kissed her lightly on the shoulder. She was a bit tacky. He watched her as she stirred slightly in her sleep and began gently to snore. He decided that his Milly was probably the only person in the world who snored with charm. He kissed the breast nearest to him with deep pleasure and settled down to try to get to sleep.

Both Milly and William had so much to do the following day that they got up earlier than usual and had their breakfast while they dressed, a useful trick for busy mornings which they had devised when newly-wed, consisting mainly of having coffee in a mug rather than a cup and saucer and mashing the boiled egg onto a portable slice of toast.

Milly and her Baroque Trio were due to rehearse at a new place provided by Estelle's papa because Pippa had dug her sexy toes in and refused to rehearse any more in a room with tube trains running busily beneath it.

At one wild moment in the middle of a sleepless night, Milly had even wondered whether Catriona's voluptuous charms might not be replaced by Pippa playing her cello, *pizzicato*, with her sexy toes. But wiser counsels prevailed. Not because Pippa would have objected but because the choice of *pizzicato* pieces written for a cello played by foot was probably limited.

Their new rehearsal studio was a handsome empty shop which Estelle's papa said was 'just off the West End'. It was in Leatherhead High Street. Inspired by the fortunes made by bright young women who founded chains of specialist shops selling only socks, or ties, or healthy soap smelling of rhubarb, Estelle's papa cautiously opened the shop in Leatherhead which he was confident would be the first of a chain of four hundred or so retail outlets.

He called it The Bum Shop.

Estelle's papa's brilliantly original idea was that The Bum Shop would sell only products associated with that particular part of the human body; and as he explained confidently to Estelle, everybody had one. There would be wittily colourful Y-fronts and knickers, ergonomically designed office chairs, vintage loo-paper with mottoes on each sheet, shooting-sticks with wide seats for ample Home Counties matrons, inflatable cushions for air travellers required to sit down in Heathrow Departure Lounges, soothing, anti-pile, pink bullets known to Harley Street as 'shoverupskis' and so on.

The Leatherhead Bum Shop opened on a Monday to considerable free publicity from Surrey local radio. Normally the overworked journalists who chattered away all day on the local radio stations had precious little local raw material to work upon and when a shop opened in their bailiwick called The Bum Shop it was like manna dropping from heaven onto their word processors beneath. By the following Wednesday the radio-listening citizens of Greater Surrey were so sick of feeble puns and saucy little innuendoes about The Bum Shop that they steered well clear of the place. On the following Friday the shop had only one customer, a lady of great age who had friends coming to tea unexpectedly and misread the shop's name as The Bun Shop.

Estelle's papa was only too happy to let the girls use the now empty Bum Shop as a rehearsal room. The music lent the premises a touch of tone, useful as papa was trying to lease the shop to a mildly corrupt company which marketed boring greetings cards by hinting that all profits went to charity, which they certainly did not.

The girls had an enjoyable rehearsal. The drive to Leatherhead, in the Trio's convoy, which consisted of the 2CV with Milly and harpsichord, and Pippa's elderly Maxi with Estelle, Pippa and cello, was much longer than their previous drive to the studio in Liverpool Street, but prettier. And their music was coming together hearteningly well; growing confidence was giving their playing an agreeable lightness of touch, which was new.

'I miss Catriona, but only slightly,' said Pippa, when they were having a rest.

'Oh, I forgot to tell you. I've heard from her!' said Milly, rummaging in her handbag. 'A card came this morning.'

'That's quick!' said Estelle. 'From Bolivia?'

'No, Heathrow,' said Milly, waving a colour postcard of Concorde and a lot of blue sky.

'She sent it before they took off. And they didn't fly to Bolivia, either. I quote,' Milly read from the card, 'Trev has had a change of heart. We're going to Los Angeles, not Bolivia. Trev has a friend there, Tarquin Cohen, who believes that inanimate objects have rights just like people and has founded a sect. Trev thinks we should join and make campaigning for inanimate objects our reason for existing. Isn't life wonderful? Love to all, Cat.'

The girls sat in silence for a while.

'She shouldn't be allowed out on her own,' said Estelle. 'That's what my mother used to say about me back home when I was a kid. She didn't like the way I used to slip away from the village and go for long walks along the beach, just idly picking up pretty shells and boys and things.'

'I don't think Trev sounds barmy,' said Pippa thoughtfully. 'Not *barmy* barmy. Just sort of pop-music thick. It's not as though he's after her money.'

'Or her virtue,' said Estelle. 'That went years ago, lucky thing. Our first year at the College. Ah, memories! Bernard and his reed-instrument. Had a go at all four of us but only Catriona had the strength of character to close her eyes to that awful black hair growing on his shoulder-blades and yield herself to bliss.'

The girls sat in silence for a while longer.

'I used to think of him as our Sex-oftenist,' said the Thin-but-Lovely Estelle dreamily.

'Back to Bach,' said Milly.

William cycled to the Club more briskly that morning, anxious to get events moving, so he was something like an hour earlier than usual padlocking his bike to the kitchen-waste bin.

Nevertheless, when his nose came to within eighteen inches of the massive oak front door it was whisked open as though made of balsa wood and he was greeted by the reassuring bulk of Sergeant Chidding.

'SAH!' bellowed the sergeant, saluting vigorously. 'Now you've arrived, Mr Secretary, let our day's work commence.'

William glanced about him. There was no sign of Mr Tozer.

'A word in private, Chidders?' said William, nodding towards the sergeant's glass cubicle.

'Private?' said Chidders, baffled for a moment. 'Oh, I follow your reasoning. Private. This way, sir,' said Chidders, waving William respectfully towards his cubby-hole like a floorwalker at Harrods urging a sheikh towards the gold bathroom fittings.

'This is very secret, Chidders,' said William quietly. 'I need your help on a security problem of great importance to the Club. I know I can trust you.'

The sergeant's eyes bulged slightly with emotion. 'I need hardly reiterate, sir, that you can count on me to the ends of the earth.'

'It concerns Mr Tozer.'

'Say no more,' said the sergeant. 'Right little sod. Beg pardon, sir, but you know what I'm hinting at. And shifty with it. I wouldn't trust him as far as I could throw my own grandmother.'

'Point is,' said William, 'we think that Mr Tozer is passing secret information about the Club to somebody outside and I want to find out who that somebody is.'

'Leave him to me, sir. I'll punch him until he talks. I'll hit him on the nose and then bring me knee up.'

'No, no!' said William. 'We just have to stop him passing on secrets, that's all.'

'I tell you what,' said Chidders. 'How about if I kill him? That should do the trick. I'll hit him again and again with a shovel until he passes away and I'll hide the body in the kitchen-waste bin where you park your bike.' He looked expectantly at William for the go-ahead.

'I can't say how much I appreciate your desire to help,' said William, 'but I have a simpler plan.'

'Oh, right, sir,' said Chidders, a disappointed man.

'I think Tozer might well be telephoning somebody outside and I propose that we find out who it is by tapping Tozer's phone.'

'You mean tap it with a hammer or suchlike thus putting it out of action? By the way, may I ask what particular information might Tozer be passing on, sir, so's I'll know?'

'It's to do with our top secret birthday party in a couple of weeks' time.'

'You mean the orgy?'

Despair gripped William. How could he possibly maintain any kind of security in this hive of gossip? 'That O-word must not be spoken on these premises!' he said. 'And who told you what form the party was going to take?'

'Ted, the maintenance man, sir. You know old Ted? Only got half a right ear from being out East doing his National Service? A coupla days ago he was changing the light bulbs in the committee room – somebody had put in 40-watt bulbs – and he found some papers on the table saying that the Club was going to hold an . . . was going to hold a thingummy. So he reported the matter to me.'

'Oh, my God! Who else do you think he's told?'

'Probably nobody, sir. He's not a chatty man, isn't Ted. His gammy ear's probably got something to do with it. Gwen-on-coffee says that when he takes her to the pictures they usually end up at his place and he hardly says two words in a row even when they're in the throes of hows-your-father. Mind you, Gwen likes a bit of silence. She says it makes a change from her husband rabbitting on about VAT and Leyton Orient.'

William gave a profound sigh. On, on. 'Can we get into Tozer's room now without being caught?' he asked.

'Oh, yes, he won't be in for another half hour at least,' said Chidders. 'Idle little swine. Last in, first out. This way if you please, sir, mind your nut.'

He led William down a narrow steep stairway and into a small room, more like the large broom cupboard it once had been than a telephone exchange. The modern electronic switchboard was just a small, grey box with lots of buttons and a handset. It stood on a table with telephone directories, a pad with phone numbers written on it, a ballpoint pen and a screwed-up copy of the previous day's *Grass*. Also on the table was a half-filled ashtray marked *Do Not Remove from Billiard Room* and a plate containing crumbs and an elderly wedge of pie.

William looked round carefully and took Mickey Mouse from his jacket pocket.

Above the table was a shelf holding a clutter of personal items; a mug with dried tea in it, a stack of much-thumbed copies of *Penthouse*, a woollen pullover with a hole in it, a heavy torch marked *Property of the Walpole Club* and an empty cigarette packet. William put Mickey on the shelf and carefully arranged items round him so that he was not visible but should be able to pick up sounds unimpaired.

'Back we go,' he said and they climbed back up to Chidders's cubby-hole. There William took Minnie Mouse out of his other jacket pocket and set it down on the shelf which did Chidders for a desk.

Chidders was fascinated. 'It's a little mousey!' he said with delight. He tentatively stretched out an enormous forefinger and gently stroked Minnie. She fell over.

'Well, it's more than a mouse,' said William, righting Minnie. 'It is, in fact, a loudspeaker. And inside Mickey in Mr Tozer's room is a transmitter.'

Sergeant Chidding shook his head in wonder at the giant steps that modern science was taking. 'What will they think of next,' he said, stroking Minnie's ear. She fell to the floor.

William picked her up and set her in position in front of Chidders. 'Listen very carefully,' said William. 'I am relying on you utterly.'

Chidders nodded wisely.

'When both Mickey and Minnie are switched on,' William said very slowly and distinctly, 'Mickey will hear everything that's said by Mr Tozer in his room and whatever he says will come out of Minnie here.'

'Minnie here,' said Chidders.

William ploughed on. 'I want you to keep a pencil and paper handy and make a note of everything Mr Tozer says on the telephone. I particularly want to know who he rings up. Got that?'

'Who he rings up.' The sergeant's brows were corrugated with the effort of remembering everything he had to do. 'Loudspeaker, eh?' he said. He picked Minnie up and examined her closely, holding her very gently and turning her over. 'Oh, yes, I can see the little speaker!' he said excitedly. 'It's up her jacksy!'

William gently took Minnie from the sergeant and put her back on the shelf. 'We'd better try it out,' he said. 'I'll nip downstairs and say something into Mickey and you tell me whether it comes through to you loud and clear. Right?'

'I'll go, sir, don't you bother,' said Chidders.

'But if you go downstairs you won't be able to hear this end, will you? I must be sure that you can hear what Tozer says.'

Chidders considered this carefully. 'I could shout?' he said.

'Dear Chidders,' said William with infinite patience, and slowly, 'you stay here. Stay . . . here. Right?'

'Right as rain, sir.'

'And make a note of any words which come out of Minnie.'

'Out of Minnie,' said Chidders. He picked up the pencil and held it poised above his note-pad expectantly, like a secretary awaiting dictation.

William nipped down the stairs and into Tozer's room. It occurred to him that he should be a bit scientific about the test and it should test Chidders's powers of reportage as well as the system's technical efficiency so he thought for a moment and then murmured, quite quietly, from the middle of the room: 'This is a test transmission. I am speaking quite quietly from the middle of the room. My number is 071-982-6519. I am now speaking more loudly. I wish to speak to Clarence Fitz-Montague, please. He lives in Sri Lanka and is Bratislavian. I AM NOW TALKING LOUDLY. HURRAH FOR LEYTON ORIENT, 12 NIL AGAINST MANCHESTER UNITED, YOU'LL NEVER WALK ALONE. End of test transmission.'

Feeling rather smug with his virtuoso performance, William nipped back up the stairs and into Chidding's cubby-hole.

It was empty. The pencil lay on the unused note-pad. There was no Chidding.

'Sorry, sir!' came the sergeant's voice as he bustled into view from the depths of the Club. 'Old Mr Treadgold turned up with a suitcase so I carried it to his room for him. All clear now, sir,' he said, picking up the pencil and looking expectantly at William. 'Begin when you like. I'm ready and able.'

Up in his own room William considered the state of play. The tapping of Tozer was set up but depended wholly on the reliability of Chidders. Organization of the Orange was moving forward but painfully slowly and security in the Club was about as watertight as a shrimping-net.

His next move was to take Brandy Jack's advice and see what ideas he could coax from the Events Committee, but they would probably not turn up in the Club until bar opening time, half-past twelve, and it was only nine o'clock. So for solace he turned to writing up the Suggestions Book, with the faint hope that a wise old limpet might emerge from the pages and prove helpful.

The first writer could by no means be termed a 'wise old' anything. He was a fragile retired solicitor with almost transparent ears who lived permanently in the Club, venturing forth into the real world only for two hours on alternate Wednesday afternoons when he visited a lady in Swiss Cottage. His entry in the book read:

I am deeply concerned that the Club should not subscribe in any way to the financial support of Chief M'Boo, dictator of the tiny state in South Africa renamed Bawataland after the coup of 1961 but previously known as New Bournemouth. My aunt and her lady companion lived in New Bournemouth very happily for a number of years, just the two of them and a devoted staff of forty-two. The ladies became a helpful and valued part of their village community, planting a number of ground nuts and providing accommodation for an elderly horse. But they lost everything in the coup of '61. Their estate was compulsorily purchased by Chief M'Boo's minions at merely double what they had paid

*for it, a fraction of its worth, and, heartbroken,
they now eke out their last lonely years in a
suite at the Royal Palace Hotel, Nairobi. My
enquiries have revealed that Bawataland's
economic prosperity comes from growing Kiwi
fruit. It is vital, therefore, to ensure that no
Bawataland Kiwi fruit crosses the threshold
of the Walpole Club. It is not an easy fruit to
differentiate; labels reading 'Grown in New
Zealand' are easily dabbed on by communist
sympathizers, but one method is to slice a
suspicious specimen in half; Kiwi fruit grown
in Bawataland have a star which in a good light
faintly resembles the Star of David. Would the
Secretary please confirm that this Club does
not buy fruit from Bawataland?*

*P.S. General Sir Horace Haversham-Greeley
promised to counter-sign this request but
unhappily he was arrested on Tuesday. His wife
was too distressed to explain as to why.*

H. Thornton Hicks-Bewdly

> *Happy to confirm that none of our
> fruit comes from Bawataland but from
> Thos. Whipple and Son Ltd.(Est.1929),
> wholesale fruiterers off Chiswick High
> Street.*

W.G.

The second entry for William to deal with was character-
istically briefer. It was from the American ex-Persian-
carpet dealer and Bob Hope of the Events Committee,
Mr Sol Fish. Mr Fish wrote:

*Ever since I learned in Summer Camp how to make
a fire by rubbing two boy scouts together I have been
fascinated by English coal fires. Not everybody thinks
likewise. Take my wife, Hannah. Please! Like most
women she would rather have a huge log fire like
as in Olde Russia, 'Throw another peasant on the
fire, Rasputin honey, it's cold enough to freeze the
rowlocks off a brass ikon.' Trouble with good old
British coal fires like Momma used to make, let's
face it – or rather don't let's face it – is that your
nose burns while the back of your neck gets frostbite.
They simply don't damn well work, particularly the
almost heatless coal fire in the Club smoking-room.
Before another winter freezes my assets, could the
smoking-room please have central heating installed
instead of the present coal non-fire?*

Sol Fish

> *The smoking-room has central heating. The
> coal fire, which is in fact gas and a fake, is
> mainly decorative and an error of judgement.
> Your solution would seem to be to sit further
> away from the cold non-fire and closer to a hot
> radiator.*

W.G.

The writer of the third entry was, at last, helpful to
William. He was a youngish publisher, Jeremy Pugh, a
cheerful thin man with wispy hair and one of those old-
gold-coloured corduroy jackets worn almost exclusively
by French university lecturers, Dr Jonathan Miller and
youngish English publishers. Jeremy Pugh wrote:

*Why should the Club's birthday celebrations be
limited to just one event, the special party in the*

107

*dining-room which only about eighty members will
be able to attend? Surely we should organize more
vaguely eighteenth-century events in which more could
participate? Off the top of my head I would suggest
hiring a Thames steamer and sailing to Greenwich
for a whitebait supper; hiring the whole of the Dress
Circle for the performance of a suitable play (The Old
Vic has just revived* Polly, *the anti-Walpole satire);
taking a party to a greyhound-racing stadium, drinking
and betting heavily on the dogs with the silliest names.
And so on. I will happily submit more detailed
proposals if this would be helpful.* ·

Jeremy Pugh

Yes, please. It would be most helpful.

W.G.

William put the Suggestions Book back on its shelf with
a small but positive glow of elation, an emotion which had
been foreign to him for far too long.

Jeremy Pugh's idea was not only a good way of
broadening the range of the Club's birthday fun but it took
some of the heat off the Orange, which would now be just
one element in the celebrations rather than the entire thing.
With a lighter step he strolled along to Mrs Hardcastle's
office, knocked on the door and went in.

'Good morning, dear Belkis,' he chirruped happily.
'Now I've arrived let the day's work commence!' Mrs
Hardcastle, William noticed, was wearing one of the
more frothy items from her collection of mind-numbing
air-cooled saris, the dusty pink number with pearls placed
impractically here and there. She smiled sleepily.

'Good morning, Willy.' She flicked her head and her
glossy black hair floated back from her forehead.

William grinned.

'You're always like this after your Malcolm returns home, did you know that?' William said.

'Like what?' said Belkis, widening her huge and beautiful brown eyes.

'All soft and limp and – well, un-mathematical. What happens to the ice-cold logical brain, I wonder, during these passionate homecomings of Malcolm. One of these days it might melt into ordinariness.'

'Oh, Willy, you are skittish this morning. If you are worried that I can no longer think figures then try me.'

'OK. How much money can you make available to finance the Orange?'

'Well, apart from dipping into our reserves, which the birthday would very much justify, I have discovered three ancient funds which we are entitled to call upon plus, of course, our current bank account which is healthy.'

'But how much in all, would you say. Rough guess?'

'Five to ten thousand pounds?'

William whistled softly and sat down on the window-sill. 'What a lovely sunny day this is turning out to be,' he said. 'So at least we have no financial worries.'

'One small, teensy point, Willy. If you are going to mount a cabaret entertainment at dinner, please do consider using my Malcolm. He is a very clever impressionist.'

'Is nothing beyond him, one wonders?'

'No, he really is gifted. He can impersonate the voices of all the film stars, well, mainly John Wayne. And the Prime Minister. And he can do Mr Jeremy Beadle the TV humorist.'

'I'm tempted to say that it's about time somebody . . . '

'Please keep Malcolm in mind to do a turn, that's all I request.'

'Yes, of course, I will,' said William.

'And now something really important, Willy. In all you have told me about your plans for the Orange you have not mentioned what I think is going to be your most difficult problem. And I wonder to myself whether you realize yourself what a knobbly problem it is which you face up with.'

'Where to put the dining-room furniture for the evening?' said William. 'No problem as it will be staying put. And I'll be having a word with the police about parking.'

'I think perhaps you are a little unworldly for your task. I will have to choose the words I say with care or I will upset you no end.'

Her long, thin fingers twisted a piece of her sari then carefully smoothed it out again. 'The point which I make is this. The basic purpose of every orgy always has been for a group of gentlemen to meet and make sexual sport with a group of willing ladies, all together.'

The sun went in for William. He knew Belkis was right. He had realized all along what went on at your average, everyday orgy but had thrust it to the back of his mind in the vague hope that a turn of Club circumstances would provide an escape route.

'So your knobbly problem is, dear Willy, from where are you going to find sporting ladies willing to frolic with elderly gentlemen on the Club's dining-room floor?'

CHAPTER NINE

A WEE LAIRD IS SEMI-HELPFUL

Routine club secretarial duties occupied most of the rest of William's morning. The problem of supplying sporting ladies for the Orange hovered over his head like a seasick albatross but his spirits were elevated slightly by some entries in the Suggestions Book.

During his coffee break William took the book down because he remembered that a week or so before there had been an exchange featuring Lord Wick, Chairman of the Events Committee, warmly recommended, for what that was worth, by Brandy Jack.

The exchange did indeed begin with an entry from Duncan Iain Percy Drummond Angus Wick, 24th Earl of Wick, the tiny club limpet who owned a great deal of the north-east of Scotland.

Unlike most contributors to the Suggestions Book, Lord Wick wrote neither in anger nor in sorrow but from a modest anxiety to rid himself of a personal predicament:

I cannot master the new roller-towel machine in the downstairs lavatory. In my limited experience these machines work best when the loop of towelling is not snatched but pulled downwards firmly and steadily. This seems to operate a ratchet affair inside the machine which permits a length of clean towelling to be pulled out, about twelve to fourteen inches normally. During the

*pulling action the device should emit a metallic
'Zzzzzzzzzzzzzzzzzzzzzzzzzzoink' but from last
Tuesday, even with a steady and firm unsnatched
pull, it has not gone 'Zzzzzzzzzzzzzzzzzzzzzzzzoink'
but 'Zonk' and has released merely an inch of
clean towel. The result is that since last Tuesday
I have had to sit down to meals with a wet
chin. I would be most grateful if the machine
could be adjusted to behave itself.*

Wick

*The machine is leased and an urgent repair has
been requested.*

W.G.

As was usual when any suggestion in the book was even
faintly lavatorial, waggish entries accumulated rapidly,
beginning in this instance with one from Giles Adams QC,
a huge, jolly barrister with an ear-splitting laugh:

*Whilst sympathizing with my fellow Walpolean
in his struggle with the towel machine I am
fascinated as to why he finds it necessary to
wash his chin before eating. Hands, always.
Feet, under certain circumstances, possibly.
But chin? Is it perhaps an ancient Scottish
custom dating back to the days when the Laird
wore a beard and politesse required him, when
lunching in company, to lave the neeps, crumbs
of shortbread, blobs of cold porridge and other
scraps of semi-edible Scottish pabulum from
his beard before sitting down to carve the
haggis?*

Giles Adams

Lord Wick replied swiftly in his neat handwriting:

*I always wash my hands and face before eating, a
routine which I am sure Mr Adams was made to
follow when a child. Unfortunately Mr Adams is now
almost grown-up and has the freedom to live down to
his own personal standards of hygiene.*

Wick

This promising feud was sadly nipped in the bud by
a practical suggestion from a member experienced in
defeating machines:

*Lord Wick is clearly not an Old Wykehamist or
he would know how to get more towel per pull.
The technique we used at Winchester College to
cheat the Post Office's stamp machine and pocket
the money given to us by our parents to stamp our
letters home was to put a penny in and wait for a
penny stamp to emerge. This stamp was then grasped
firmly between finger and thumb and another penny
inserted. When the machinery was again in motion
and another stamp on the roll began to emerge,
the first stamp was given a swift and steady pull.
If the pull was rightly gauged a stream of stamps
could be extracted before the locking mechanism
re-engaged. Our champion puller at Winchester
was Romsey S.J.R. On one occasion Romsey
extracted forty-two penny stamps with one heave.
In later years Romsey became completely deaf and
Liberal MP for, I think, Daventry.*

Geoffrey, Bishop of Ickney and Mott

This description of a technique for minor villainy had
an immediately stimulating effect on that most dangerous

sector of the Walpole membership, the seventy to eighty year olds.

A couple of days later a note was left on William's desk. It was from S. Talbot Beresford BA, one-time editor of *The Country Lady*, with which is incorporated *The Domestic Servants Register*:

Dear Sec.,
Sorry to bother you because I am sure you are up to your eyebrows in whatever Club Secs do to while away their day but there has been a development in the Lord Wick v towel-machine affaire which I think you should act upon rapidly. Yesterday a few of us, well, nine of us as a matter of actual fact, had a convivial luncheon (the dry red wine from Chile is a real find) after which we discussed the Bishop's brilliant idea for bilking stamp machines and at Lord Wick's suggestion decided to put it to the test on our recalcitrant towel machine. We trooped off to the downstairs bog although not all of us arrived. Sir Fingal O'Connor fell over and we had to pick him up and put him in the laundry cupboard and old George Fetters RA, the painter chap, was so tired he fell asleep on the weighing-machine. Do you know he is only 8 stone 4? Point is, the Bishop's trick worked. Once Lord Wick had got the hang of the right kind of pull he heaved towel out by the yard. It was such good sport that we all had a good pull together which resulted in the ratchet breaking and the whole of the rest of the towel reeling out over the floor. I have never seen so much towel in my life. It seemed incredible that so long a piece of towelling could be fitted into such a small machine. The washroom was filled with great coils of endless clean white towelling and for

some anxious minutes we completely lost wee Lord
Wick. I decided that the towel had somehow to
be got back into the machine before the pre-dinner
washroom rush so I fetched Sergeant Chidding and
requested him to stuff the towelling back as best
he could. He found a shovel and urged the towel
back into its slot bit by bit with the forward edge
of the blade. But there was no room in the tangled
bowels of the machine to accommodate the last
few yards and Chidders had willy-nilly to push his
shovel with considerable force, which resulted in
it becoming fast lodged in the slot. In the ensuing
attempt to wrench his shovel free, the sergeant tore
the machine off the wall together with many tiles
and a great deal of plaster, all of which fell upon
the wash-basin beneath, breaking it. Will you
kindly deal with the debris and have the machine
operational and the basin replaced asap.

Simeon Beresford MC BA

William had immediately sprung into action and cleaned
up the debris himself; the waiters and the rest of the junior
male staff had disappeared, having some kind of seventh
sense for sniffing out any threat of physical exertion,
much as a herd of young antelopes is able to scent from
afar a predatory cheetah. William never found out where
the junior male staff hid but suspected they crammed
themselves, as in a game of sardines, into the lady guests'
tiny powder room which was unused in the daytime.

William then telephoned the towel-machine company's
West London Area Customer Care and Problem Facilities
Manager, a spectacularly dim but cheerful Australian girl
named Charlene. William resolutely flirted with her on
the phone and then set about persuading her to arrange a
replacement towel machine at no expense to the Club. This

was not easy because of Charlene's difficulty in writing down the name of the Club.

'No,' said William. 'Not the Ripple Club, Charlene, it's the Walpole Club. No, listen – not the Wheel-pull, no, nor the Wipe-all Club, no. It's the WALpole, W.A.L.P.O.L.E. What? W for Whitney Huston, A for Abba, L for Little Richard, P for Elvis Presley, O for Roy Orbison – yes, that's right! You've got it! The Walpole Club!'

But Charlene proved to be far from dim when it came to contracts. Her pert, innocent little voice took on a steely edge when she pointed out to William that there was a clause in the leasing contract which absolved the company from any liabilities whatever if the company's machines were in any way subject to abnormal treatment or were vandalized.

William switched his male charm on to turbo but it did not seem to be working that morning so he settled with Charlene for a surcharge on the leasing payments in return for a replacement machine within a week.

The wash-basin was more of a problem because it had to match the remaining wash-basins and they were Edwardian and unfashionably huge. It was Sergeant Chidding who again came to the rescue.

'I got one of them basins you can have,' he said. 'The previous Club Secretary-but-eight give it me. Mr Penge, he was at the time. Got jail for naughty-naughty with a lance-bombardier in the Jermyn Street Turkish baths but there you go. Mr Penge had claimed one too many bombed wash-basins on the Club's war-damage compensation and he give me the extra one for nothing in exchange for a five-pound note. Myself and my Gwen have had it as a birdbath ever since. Modern birds are dirty beasts, you know. Don't wash their feathers and private parts like the old-time birds used to, so I'll gladly replace the basin to its rightful venue tomorrow, if I can borrow Gwen's brother's van and a bag of cement.'

Which he did.

William was impressed with Lord Wick's dry, imperturbable style and decided to seek him out as a potential ally. As usual when going to meet a member he did not really know, William nipped down to the library and consulted *Who's Who*. Lord Wick's entry ran:

Duncan Iain Percy Drummond Angus Wick, 24th Earl of Wick; landowner; *b* Thurso, 5 Feb 1915, *s* of late Angus Drummond Percy Iain Duncan Wick, 23rd Earl, and late Lady Flora Wick (*née* Cromarty); *m* 1948 Nicole-Madeleine Bonamour; five *s* four *d*; *educ*. Eton, Balliol (MA); served with Scots Guards in Crete (DSO). *Publications*: The Crete Inheritance, 1950; Greek Theatre and Hoi Polloi, 1962; A Feast of Orgies, 1968. *Address*: Wick Castle, Highland. *Club*: Walpole.

The words *A Feast of Orgies* leapt out at William and he could not help registering his surge of joy. Lord Wick, Chairman of the Events Committee, was an expert on orgies. William uttered a high, rather girlish Indian whoop, as whooped by quiz show contestants on television when told they had won a Dream-of-a-Lifetime Luxury Weekend for two at Lowestoft.

'Well, *really*!' came a quavery voice from inside an armchair.

'I'm so sorry,' William said, moving round to the front of the speaking armchair. Lying well down in it was a small elderly gentleman, knitting. 'I'm the Secretary, sir,' said William in a near-whisper.

'I know that,' said the small gentleman. 'My ears may be about to drop off but my eyes are still quite reliable.'

'Sorry for the noise but I've had a bit of luck and I'm a mite over-excited. You see, sir . . . ' His voice tailed off as he saw the gentleman put the empty knitting needle between his teeth and begin counting the stitches on the other needle with his thumb-nail.

'Eighty-eight,' he muttered round the needle in his mouth. 'Three too many stitches, would you believe it. What a damn waste. All that effort . . . ' He counted three stitches carefully with a quivering thumb and slid them off the needle, muttering ancient Highland imprecations to himself.

'Lord Wick!' said William, light dawning.

The small gentleman looked up. 'Of course!' he said. 'Who else in his right mind would spend a sunny morning in the library knitting? Not that Madeleine will appreciate my industry. Takes everything for granted, never even a kindly nod of appreciation. But one soldiers on.'

'Your wife, sir?'

'My *what*? No, no, Madeleine's my dog. Retriever. Bloody great golden retriever, not one of those nervy, yappy lap-dogs in a red collar. A very fine lady is Madeleine. A kind of soft beige in colour like one of the old original Smith's Potato Crisps. Remember them? More golden in those days. Different potatoes, I suppose. Madeleine and I've been together for twelve years and now her kidneys are on the blink. Pees everywhere. Even while she's walking she pees. Up the stairs, over all the carpets. I clear up after her, of course. Unless my wife has stayed up in Scotland then I don't bother all that much. What does the odd carpet matter when your father's left you a copper or two and your old dog's feeling rotten?'

He dug his second needle in and began knitting again, slowly and evenly. He held it up for William to see.

'It's a sort of pair of woolly canine knickers, d'ye see?' he said. 'Old Madeleine wouldn't wear a bought hygienic contraption so I designed this. It fits neatly round her rear and I shove in six folded sheets of the *Daily Mirror*. Works a treat. This is the third pair I've knitted for her so that she'll always have a dry pair standing by. Do you think I'm off my chump?'

'No,' said William.

'Thing is,' said Lord Wick, 'I can't just do nothing. Can't sit around all day reading novels, swapping small talk with other bores. Wish I could but I'm a bit lacking in social skills so instead I have to do something. Make something, if possible. Are you sure you don't think I'm goofy?'

'Quite sure.'

'I ask again because only the other week in Wick Castle I found myself in the kitchen, my mind a blank. I said to my dear wife, "What am I doing in the kitchen? What did I come in here for?" And she said, "You're not in the kitchen, you're in the boiler-room."'

William thought a moment. 'I think you knew perfectly well you were in the boiler-room,' he said. 'My guess is that you were in one of your skittish moods.'

Lord Wick also thought for a moment. 'Quite right,' he said. 'Good thinking for an Englishman.'

'I need your help, sir,' said William. 'It's about the Club's birthday celebration.'

'You mean the orgy.'

William looked round quickly but the two of them were alone in the library.

'Why are you twitching?' asked His Lordship, pushing his spectacles onto his forehead and peering round the room. 'Has the Master been getting at you not to say the dreaded word? He's been at me and the rest of the committee. Foolish fellow. I don't know about the law being "a ass and a idiot" but many lawyers seem to be. The Master is a strong man in his own court of law but outside the court he bends to the will of his wife, Parthenope, the terror of the Home Counties. That man is gradually losing his nerve.'

'But surely it could be very dangerous for all our distinguished members if our secret got out.'

'Not necessarily. Depends what goes on.'

'Ah,' said William. 'I'm glad you brought that up. I can't get any sense at all out of Brandy Jack and he thought the whole thing up.'

'No, he didn't,' said Lord Wick. 'I did.'

'But he told me . . . '

'In his whole life the only really good idea Brandy Jack has dreamed up is Brandreth Jacques, rich actor and Don Juan. An excellent invention which he plays to perfection.'

'But did you really take the trouble to plan the whole complicated change-all-the-light-bulbs-to-40-watts scheme? Just to embarrass Canon Prout?'

'Well, it was something to do. Can't just sit around, you know, otherwise you grow old and drop off the twig. It was great fun to plan and it worked beautifully, did it not? The dreadful Canon Prout hasn't been seen in the Club since!'

'If you don't mind me asking, sir, what do you have against Canon Prout to go to these lengths?'

Little Lord Wick slowly took off his specs, hurred on them, polished them on his tie and put them back on his forehead. 'He kicked my dog,' he said.

A silence fell.

Mr Tozer sidled in with the midday edition of the *Evening Standard* and some magazines and began to arrange them on a table, glancing occasionally across at William and Lord Wick. He was clearly lingering. William caught his eye and motioned him to leave them. Mr Tozer sidled out, his ears not actually flapping but seeming to.

'The canon didn't do a run-up and wallop her like a striker taking a penalty kick,' said Lord Wick. 'She was just in his way, that's all. Lying on the steps outside in the sunshine. Rather than be bothered to walk round her, he kicked her hard on the rear leg to shift her. Probably didn't mean to hurt her but he did, and she yelped. I was trying to get a cab and saw it happen. "That dog almost tripped me up," he said to me angrily and stalked off, red-faced. Well,' Lord Wick said and smiled happily, 'the deplorable Canon Prout's name will now live for ever in Club anecdotage!'

'May I ask you to look at it from another point of view?' said William. 'You enjoyed yourself exacting revenge on the kicker of dogs but in the course of this you've committed the Club to mounting an orgy. Or "Orange" as we are all supposed to call it but I, seemingly, am the only person in the Club who bothers to. I have only a matter of days to put the thing on and I must know what sort of evening you all expect. What is it you want an orgy to be? What do you want to happen? You simply must help me.'

'Don't ask *me*!' said His Lordship cheerfully. 'Not my line of country at all.'

William looked at him incredulously. 'But I looked you up in *Who's Who* and it's there in black and white! You've written a book about orgies, for Heaven's sake!'

Lord Wick put down his knitting and stared at William. 'Have I?' he said. He sank into thought. 'Must have been during the war,' he said eventually. 'Yes, I remember now. We were captured in Crete and for something to do I researched and wrote some things. They had a very fine library in the house where we were kept and they let us use it. Yes, I did a thing about Cretan history and then a thing about Greek theatre. Got to do something, d'you see? Got to make something. It's the way to keep going.'

'And then you wrote a book about orgies,' said William.

'Don't remember that one,' said His Lordship.

'It was the last book you wrote and it wasn't published until years later.'

'Book on orgies? No. Doesn't ring a bell.'

William almost hit him.

'Mind you, I could have written it after the war when I got home,' said Lord Wick. 'Wasn't much at Wick Castle to keep me occupied. You can't wander round fifty square miles of grouse moors with a pair of secateurs, now can you? I got married and made a few babies and that was very much all right, but a history of orgies? You surprise me.'

'But it's in your entry in *Who's Who*!' said William, in a kind of desperation. 'You called the book *A Feast of Orgies*.'

'That rings a bell,' said Lord Wick, affably. 'A far-off bell, but a definite tinkle. *A Feast of Orgies*. Yes. A publisher with a silly beard came and gave me a hundred and fifty pounds for it. He wrote later and told me he'd sold eighty-two copies and lost money on it. Damn fool.'

'Please,' said William. 'Please, Lord Wick, this really is vitally important! Please tell me what your research turned up about the ancient world orgies. What was their purpose? What happened at them? Who went to them?'

'Well . . . ' said His Lordship, ' . . . no, it's all gone. Too long ago.'

'Can't you remember *anything*?'

'I do remember the bearded publisher wore a brocade waistcoat. Rare in those days. Louche London fellows usually went in for camel-hair waistcoats but this bearded fellow wore a brocade waistcoat if you please. What a sight. Picking his way through brambles he looked like a male pheasant walking on hot coals.' His Lordship smiled at the pleasant memory.

William felt like bursting into tears. He had seemed so near getting at the truth about orgies but it was still as far away as ever. Then he had a thought. 'Sir, you must have kept an archive copy of your book,' he said. 'Please may I see it? I'll happily go up to Wick Castle if you keep it there. Or anywhere.'

'Why should I have kept a copy?' asked Lord Wick, puzzled. 'The fun was in writing it, not reading the damn thing. The fellow in the pansy waistcoat gave me some free copies and I kept them for a while and then a rather odd second-hand bookseller came up from London and bought a whole vanload of books I was trying to get rid of. I needed the space to make cheese. Did I tell you my eldest boy is going seriously into cheese? It's whisky-flavoured cheese for the Japanese market.'

But William's sprits were soaring. 'Could you let me know the bookseller's name, sir?' he said.

'Can't remember it,' said Lord Wick. 'I think it began with an F, but I do remember that he's got a shop in that alley which runs between Charing Cross Road and St Martin's Lane.'

'Burghley Court?' asked William.

'That's the place. Run along and see whether he's got any copies left. All of 'em I should imagine! Good luck!'

But William had already gone. For once he was so keen to get there that he took a taxi on petty cash.

Burghley Court was by tradition a mecca for collectors of second-hand books. There were seven or eight cluttered bookshops strung along the narrow alley, together with a vandalized phone box, the exit door for the gallery of a theatre in St Martin's Lane, a dozen or so pigeons strolling perkily in the sunshine and a shop with its window painted black and a sign above it saying, with confident simplicity, ADULTS.

William made a quick recce of the bookshops. Most of them specialized in books and prints on ballet, or on railway engines, or the occult and had names like 'Fan

Fare' and 'The Fabulous'. Only one shop name, Simon Books, did not begin with an F so William, with growing wisdom, made for that one. The shop was, as were they all, unbelievably untidy. This one was piled from floor to ceiling, along the shelves and up the stairs, with dusty second-hand books of all descriptions. The door gave an old-fashioned 'ping' as William went in and a man, presumably Mr Simon in person, emerged from an inner room.

The piles of dusty books reminded William of the bookshop he ran where he first met Milly but Mr Simon was better dressed than William ever was. He was a small, neat man with a small, neat face, a neat tweed suit and polished shoes. He looked to William like a smart young gynaecologist.

'Can I help you find something? Or shall I just leave you to delve?' said the gynaecologist.

'I'm looking for something special,' said William.

'You've come to the wrong place for *that*!' said Mr Simon, sharply. 'You want ADULTS up the alley. Teddy Pierce-Whittingham and Mave have got the whole gamut of special publications there – hetero, S and M . . . '

'I mean, I know what I'm looking for,' said William quickly. 'Do you remember buying a batch of books from Lord Wick of Wick Castle, Scotland?'

'Oh, yeeeees. I went up to the Highlands on a trawl, if you'll forgive the expression, and bought a load of stuff dead cheap from his lordship. COLINNNNN!' he shouted suddenly and piercingly.

A youth appeared from the back room chewing on a slice of cold pizza. He was hairy with a skin texture like gently simmering porridge. He wore designer-torn jeans and a T-shirt reading RELEASE POPE MICHELANGELO CONTI – HE IS INNOCENT.

'Colin, that stuff we bought from the Earl of Wick?'

Colin waved William towards a packing-case. William picked out at random a few examples of the books which Lord Wick provided for unwelcome guests: *Hiawatha, rendered into Latin*, F.W.Newman, 1862, *Our Debt and Duty to the Soil, the Poetry and Philosophy of Sewage Utilization*, E.D.Girdlestone, 1878, *Little Elsie's Book of Bible Animals*, 1878, *Hindustani Self-Taught by the Natural Method*, E.Marlborough, 1908.

'There was another book,' he said. 'Written by Lord Wick himself. *A Feast of Orgies*. That's the one I'm looking for.'

'Think there's one left,' said the youth, plunging his arm into the packing-case of books and stirring it round as though it was a bran tub of surprises. 'They sold well so the price went up from £1.50 to £25. Well, it's always a saleable subject, isn't it?' With a thin grin of triumph he produced a quite large volume. 'Cheers, mate,' he said, handing it to William.

William breathed a prayer of heartfelt gratitude and opened the book. At first glance it seemed to be a collection of lists, with a lot of italics. There were pages devoted to extraordinary banquets described in the *Satyricon*, and to Vitellius's invention of dishes such as 'Shield of Minerva' which was parrot-fish livers, pheasant and peacock brains, flamingo tongues and the insides of lampreys. There was a cautionary note in the Preface that recipes from Ancient Rome and Greece gave the ingredients but did not bother with quantities.

Heart sinking, William flicked through more pages: 'Inside the pig were stuffed roast thrushes, ducks and warblers, pease purée poured over eggs, oysters and scallops . . .'

Lord Wick's *A Feast of Orgies* was a cookery book.

CHAPTER TEN

A MATTER OF SOME DELICACY

The bookshop owner had popped round the corner to the Salisbury for a sherry with the owner of the ballet bookshop so William had to settle on a price for Lord Wick's book with Colin, who as soon as William refused to pay the asking price of £25 began scratching his chest and continued to do so unnervingly during the negotiation.

William resolutely looked away, kept his nerve and bought the book for £4.50. He took a taxi back because time was getting on and he wanted to catch a couple of Events Committee members in the bar before they went into lunch.

In the taxi he skip-read parts of Lord Wick's tome but it was not a comfortable experience. William always felt queasy when he tried to read in a moving vehicle and reading about patrician Romans at dinner crunching up stewed dormice was so disquieting that he had to breathe deeply and look out of the cab window at the horizon to reach the Club *stomach intacta*.

On the desk in his office was a file of papers left by the young publisher, Jeremy Pugh, with facts about his suggested Club Birthday outings. The trip to the theatre was seemingly not on. The revival of the eighteenth-century musical *Polly* was being so successful that there was no hope of booking the entire Circle or indeed booking enough seats for a reasonable number of members.

But the whitebait feast at Greenwich was a practical

possibility. The riverside restaurant would make a large room available and a pleasure boat capable of carrying a hundred passengers could be hired for the evening. It had a bar on both decks and left Westminster Pier at 6.30 p.m., returning at 11.30 p.m. The only snag was that to tie-up a minute over midnight would cost an arm and a leg in overtime. An evening's greyhound racing was also on. A party of fifty members could be bussed to the stadium, dine in the glass-fronted restaurant overlooking the track, place bets and watch their money being lost in great comfort.

Mr Pugh pointed out that bookings had to be made as soon as possible and he had provided notice-board sheets to be signed by members wanting to book a place, the whitebait trip was for a maximum of a hundred names and greyhound racing for fifty.

William had already made out a chart for members who wanted to attend the Orange itself, in the dining-room – a hundred spaces, members only, no ladies, no guests – and he went downstairs with all three sheets and pinned them on the main Club notice-board in the entrance hall. He decided a drink would be in order next.

The usual wall of sound hit him as he went into the bar. Quite a bit of the noise was coming from a mix of television pundits and newspaper columnists who had congregated as usual at one end of the bar, talking stimulatingly but loudly and drinking rounds of champagne out of small silver tankards. William had never got on with silver tankards. He had a recurring fear that he would one day bang his teeth with the metal edge and they would shatter like porcelain, as in a Tom and Jerry cartoon.

In the middle of the bar stood a more moderate clutch of mainly newish members trying to attract the busy barmen's attention without appearing to be pushy. At the tables sat quiet members with their guests. They were quiet because they had realized that they were not able to introduce their guests to fellow-members because although they knew their fellow-members well, lunched with them, argued with them, bought them drinks, they had no idea what their names were. The far end of the bar was by custom propped up by the oldies; limpets, members of the House Committee and the Events Committee and any other member pushing eighty.

As William had hoped, at the end of the bar stood two members of the Events Committee, Sol Fish, transatlantic jokester, and Sir Archibald Alloway, Sporting Baronet and writer of illegible suggestions in the Suggestions Book. The baronet was wearing an old, baggy tweed suit about a quarter of an inch thick which had bits in it as though woven from marmalade; he looked as if he had dropped in for a drink after being released on bail on a charge of poaching.

William joined them and ordered a gin and tonic. He felt he had earned a large one.

'Have this one on me,' said Sol, 'as the actress said to the bishop.' He waved a ten-pound note at the barman.

'I say,' said Sir Archibald to William, 'has Chidding still got his full set of marbles?'

'As far, as I know, sir,' said William. 'Why, what's he done?'

'I arrived at the front door about half an hour ago and Chidding was standing outside on the pavement writing in a notebook with a pencil.'

'Perhaps he's writing his memoirs,' said Sol.

'Next to him,' went on Sir Archie, 'stood old Haydon Abercrombie the composer. He was holding a toy Minnie Mouse to Chidding's right ear. A little funny, wouldn't you say?'

'What you might call a Minnie Ha-ha!' said Sol Fish and chuckled away to himself for quite a long while.

'It's a little complicated to explain now,' said William,

'with all this noise going on, but it's part of a security operation to keep the Orange a secret from the outside world.'

The baronet nodded wisely. 'Mum's the word, what?'

'A nod's as good as a wink to a blind drunk,' said Sol, finishing his whisky. 'Must eat. At two o'clock I've gotta see a dog about a man. I'm travelling up the dread Northern Line with old Wick's golden retriever to consult a vet friend of mine in Bedfordshire. *Ciao!*' He left.

'Glad he's gone,' said Sir Archibald. 'No, no, didn't mean it like that. Salt of the earth if it wasn't for all those damned jokes. No, I mean I want to talk to you. In confidence. It's about the Orange.'

'I want to talk to *you* about that,' said William.

'That's all right then,' said the Sporting Baronet, 'as long as we don't both talk at the same time.' He gave a kind of wheezing bark which was the nearest he ever got to a human laugh.

'I need guidance, sir,' said William. 'I need to discuss, urgently, just what *entertainment* the committee wants me to provide for the Orange.'

'Yes, quite. Absolutely. It's what I wanted to talk to *you* about, matter of fact. The chaps, that is to say the other members of the Events Committee, the chaps have asked me to have a quiet word with you about a matter of some delicacy. Some of 'em are worried – very worried, some of 'em – and I must admit that I do see their point.'

William waited patiently for the point to emerge.

Sir Archibald fixed his watery, grey eyes on the head barman who instantly shot across and, without needing to be told, poured another large whisky into the baronet's glass. Sir Archie put down money and took a great gulp of whisky, his face puckering up as though he was downing some unusually repulsive medicine. He put his glass carefully down on the bar and settled into the stance in which he was most comfortable, his pigeon-shooting posture of left leg well forward, weight on right leg, back straight, eyes fixed on the distant horizon. He could stand like that for hours without even twitching.

'It's the ladies,' he said.

'Well,' said William, 'all I can say at this stage is that I will do my best to find some attractive ladies willing to participate.'

'You've hit the crux,' said the Sporting Baronet, his eyes staring unblinkingly over William's right shoulder to detect the first tiny, distant flutter of an oncoming wood-pigeon's wings.

William felt sorry for the surviving game-birds, if any, living within gunshot range of Alloway Hall, Leicestershire.

Sir Archibald went on, 'It's not how many ladies that's worrying the chaps. It's what the chaps will be expected to— er, to— er, well, to be involved in by way of participation, to use your word.' Drops of moisture were beginning to form on the baronet's forehead.

'The chaps,' went on Sir Archibald, 'for instance Sol Fish, Lord Wick, Brandy Jack, although I'm surprised at Brandy Jack's timidity considering what he keeps telling us about his private life, anyway the chaps are worried that they might be called upon to, how shall I put it, well, to perform physical exertions incommensurate with their advanced years and normally sedentary way of life. Doesn't bother *me*, of course, I still ride to hounds and go easy on the large brandies. My old father always used to say port and l'amour don't mix, he fought in France during the First World War, d'ye see, and tended to break into French to annoy my mother. But the chaps feel, and I must say that I tend to agree with them, that it might well be physically perilous for them to take part in, er, intimate activities involving the ladies. Do you catch my drift?'

'Indeed I do, sir. And I wouldn't dream of inflicting that sort of embarrassment on members. I had seen the ladies as performing – no, that's not the right word at all – as *fulfilling* a wholly decorative role.'

'Now that'd be perfectly all right!' said Sir Archibald cheerily, hugely relieved at surviving a hideously delicate conversation he had clearly been dreading for days. 'They could, for instance, trot about a bit in wispy clothing. Not falling out of it like they did at the dear old Windmill Theatre, bless its heart, but leaving their gear a bit loose about the *décolletage*, what? That sort of thing.'

'We think as one, sir,' said William. 'Now you really must excuse me, I have to grab Mr Fish before he leaves.'

As he made for the hall, William reflected that he was probably more relieved than Sir Archibald that ladies present at the Orange would be there on a look-but-don't-touch basis. It was an enormous weight off his mind for several reasons.

The small hall was crammed with a good twenty members milling about trying to get at the notice-board to put their names down for the Orange or one of the other celebrations and William felt both pleased and apprehensive, like an impresario who has sold most of the tickets for a play yet to be written.

Saying that he had to grab Sol Fish was only an excuse to escape from a silent lunch of cold, tough venison with Sir Archibald. After some months of eating at the Club William had observed that for some reason sporting gentlemen preferred their venison tough, in fact the tougher the better; perhaps, he thought, because the more difficult the meat was to chew, the more athletic and worthier an adversary the late deer would have been.

William really wanted to find Sergeant Chidding and learn what the good man had discovered about Tozer via Mickey and Minnie Mouse. But as he moved through the member-packed hall his arm was grabbed. It was Sol Fish.

'Gotta talk,' said Sol. 'It's the Orange, matter of some delicacy.' He pushed members aside and hauled William into the tiny lift which went up to the bedrooms. He left the gate slightly open and pushed buttons and the lift was effectively de-activated.

'It's about the dames,' said Sol. 'You gotta have dames in an orgy, right? Right. OK. Dames we have. But no hookers.'

'I never had any intention . . . ' William began.

'Well, mebbe not, but then again mebbe. All I'm saying is that most of my friends on the Events Committee have got it into their tiny little skulls that this whole joke might bounce right back at us and we'll be expected to climb into the sack with some bimbo. And in full view of the others, too. Well, that's what an orgy *is* in my book.'

'I can assure you . . . ' said William.

'The prospect don't bother *me*,' said Sol. 'Make no mistake there. I've been around. A coupla or five whiskies and some laffs and bring on the dancing girls, that's me; you're a long time dead. No, it's the others. Sir Archibald is petrified. So is Brandy Jack, and little Lord Wick will have nothing whatsoever to do with that kind of shenanigan.'

William closed the lift gate. 'Tell them they've nothing to worry about,' he said. 'During the Orange, members will be expected to remain seated at their tables at all times.'

'But hey!' said Sol, pushing buttons to get the lift back in service. 'We still gonna have girls! girls! girls! eh, Willy? Can't have a party without 'em, right?'

'Right,' said William, gloomily.

He found Chidders still outside on the pavement notebook in hand and the small, distinguished composer, mop of flyaway white hair blowing in the breeze, still standing on tiptoe holding Minnie Mouse to the sergeant's ear.

William took Minnie from the small composer and thanked him fulsomely for being so helpful in the cause of a very important Club security operation, details of which were a close secret which he, William, could only divulge in the presence of a magistrate.

'Any luck with Tozer?' William asked Chidders when the small composer had finally been persuaded to stop being helpful and go in to his lunch.

Chidders looked important and leafed through his notebook.

'At o twenty-one hours this morning . . . ' he read out, like a police constable giving evidence in an Agatha Christie.

'Hang on,' said William. 'There isn't an o twenty-one hours. There's a twenty-one hours which is nine at night on the twenty-four-hour clock, or there's o nine hours which is nine in the morning.'

Chidders looked aggrieved. Then he rallied and began again.

'This morning, halfway through my bacon sandwich, I heard Minnie give a burp and I heard Mr Tozer speak the following words: "Sod the Prime Minister". A minute or so later there was a crackling noise, like a house on fire, which I took to be the person under subvalliance folding his newspaper to a new page. He then said "Sod Sheffield Wednesday." During the next hour I took note of the following utterances uttered by Mr Tozer: "He's not in the Club yet, sir, try ringing later." "I've got Major Tuxford on the line, ducky. He wants to be connected to a Mrs Twyford. You've got a dirty mind, Muriel, I used 'connected to' in its British Telecom sense not in the meaning of plugging himself into Mrs Twyford, heh-heh-heh!" Then followed more sniggering and whispering, sir, and then Mr Tozer said, rather fervently I thought, sir,

"What colour knickers have you got on, Muriel, if you've got any on which would make a change?'"

'Is there much more of this?' asked William.

'About four pages, sir,' said the sergeant. 'In which Mr Tozer reveals himself as being, as if we didn't already know, what we in the Mule Section during the war in our rough way called a small, painful turd.'

'He didn't mention the Orange?' asked William. 'Didn't phone a newspaper offering information for money?'

'Not yet, sir.' Chidders riffled through his notebook again. 'Nearest, I suppose, is an outgoing call he made to the Club's newsagent at o eleven-hundred-and-thirty— er— at coffee-time. He said and I quote from my contemporary notes, "Hello, is that Mr Patel? Well, listen you. This is the managing-director of the Walpole Club speaking in actual person. I wish you forthwith to include in the Walpole Club's magazine order a weekly copy of the new magazine *Thighs*. And write on it, 'For the exclusive attention of Mr Tozer, Esq.' Thank you, my man."'

The sergeant closed his notebook. 'That's about the weight and width of it so far, sir. The reason I am out on the pavement here, sir, is that Minnie seems to work better out here. But I will proceed within now and continue normal subvalliance. I will report to you instantly when Mr Tozer becomes dangerous.' He added reassuringly, 'I've got me shovel handy.'

William thanked Chidders for his valuable help and hastened towards a latish piece of fish.

The long table in the dining-room had plenty of vacant seats as it was nearly two o'clock. William approached the table slowly. Slowly because the art of clubmanship was casually contriving to sit next to somebody to whom you enjoyed talking, or more importantly, listening. To his delight, with chairs empty on either side of him, sat Lord Wick.

'Good morning, William,' said Lord Wick. 'Do sit down.' He motioned vaguely towards the chair next to him.

William bowed slightly. 'Your servant, sir,' he said.

Lord Wick looked at William.

'Pity,' he said. 'I can't think of anything I need.'

William sat.

'The only thing is,' said His Lordship, pleasantly, 'you're not going to chat, are you? Y'know, chunter on about the political situation and the shameful lack of money for the National Health Service and the rise of crime amongst schoolchildren and the Common Market, issues which at my age are too trivial to waste time upon?'

'Scout's honour,' said William.

Lord Wick looked at William in pixie-like fashion over the top of his gold half-moon spectacles, the kind known to opticians as depressed clericals.

'Nor, I hope, are you going to assure me that during our Orange we will not be required to copulate with compliant females on the dining-room floor, a task which Sir Archibald and Sol Fish have assured you would present no problem to them personally but about which they are deeply worried on my behalf?'

William grinned. 'Cross my heart,' he said. 'I really want to talk to you about something much more interesting. After leaving you this morning I went out and bought this.'

He held up *A Feast of Orgies*. It was quite warm from being clutched to him for comfort during the several dramatic moments of the morning.

'My book!' said His Lordship, peering at it closely. 'Good Heavens! Haven't seen a copy for years! Where did you find it?'

'Where you told me I would find it,' said William. 'Burghley Court off the Charing Cross Road.'

'Extraordinary!' said His Lordship, taking the book and turning the pages slowly, eyes screwed up for a better focus. '*I* wrote this, you know. Good Lord! How did you know about it?'

William decided to let his side of the conversation lapse.

'Astonishing!' said His Lordship. 'I remember researching the whole thing in this Greek colonel chap's library in Crete. I was his prisoner of war, don't ye know. He was a university lecturer in civvy street, I believe. Crete's expert on growing olives.'

'What you didn't tell me,' said William, 'is that it's not a book about orgies, it's a collection of old recipes.'

'Ah, yes, but they're recipes for the meals eaten at orgies, d'ye see? It's all beginning to come back now. Memory goes in loops when you're over the age of twenty-eight, which I am. I can now remember clearly that villa where we were all held. It smelt of *retsina* wine and dubbin. Do you remember dubbin? We used it to soften our rugger boots at prep school.'

A waitress came to the table and William ordered fish pie, which could be eaten with a fork and thus was not a conversation stopper.

'Odd smell, dubbin,' said His Lordship, 'but it couldn't have been dubbin I was smelling because I don't think the average Cretan expert on growing olives played prep-school rugger. It was probably the smell of a permanent cook-up of hummus. Do you like hummus? Sort of paste made from ground up chickpeas. You find it all over the Middle East. Tasted good when we were hungry. I suppose it was being hungry most of the time that made me more interested in orgy food than in the orgy itself.'

'But in your research you must have got wind of what went on apart from the eating?'

'I got wind, all right. Couple of weeks of eating hummus every meal and we were blowing off like carthorses. But, yes I did learn quite a bit about orgies. And talking about the book seems to have brought some of it back.'

'I take it the original orgies were not like the modern version, a few lagers and a bit of wife-swapping in front of the telly?'

'Quite different. They began in Greece as secret, dramatic celebrations of religious rites. Pretty frightful goings-on but all quite official and holy. One of the gods they celebrated was Bacchus which meant that pious worshippers got plastered and dashed about the smaller mountainsides stark naked, dancing and feasting and generally behaving badly.'

'What about sex?'

'Lot of that. But more the result of getting pizzicato and finding themselves romping about a mountain with a lot of local girls with no clothes on than a beady-eyed bit of organized nastiness.'

'A bit more innocent than one might imagine?'

'Well, thing is they thought differently about these matters in those days. Greeks reckoned the human body was beautiful, especially the reproductive bits which were so useful as well, and the ancients thought that covering up the reproductive bits was a bad thing, made them out to be ugly and something to be ashamed of. So on all their religious and fun occasions, like wrestling, play-acting, orgies, the Olympic Games, Greeks liked to be naked and proud of it.'

'The Mediterranean climate must have helped,' said William. 'Would have been a bit trickier getting a good orgy going up the Cairngorms in January. So I can take it that the genuine, official orgies were not fundamentally sexual?'

'As I say, it was all thought of so differently. A good deal of riotous coupling was very much part of the goings-on but only in an incidental sort of way, as on a package holiday on the Costa Brava nowadays, or the firm's annual outing. To Greek peasants the main pleasures of an orgy were a lot of flute music and a tremendous amount of food and wine. Greeks tended not to be winos by nature and many of them only drank heavily at these festivals so they probably got pie-eyed very rapidly.'

'And the Roman version?'

'The Romans gave the orgy a bad name, as they seemed to do to everything Greek and life-enhancing. Roman orgies tended to be used by the rich and powerful to show just how rich and powerful they were. They threw conspicuously expensive orgies in their own houses and records exist of quite a few of 'em. Prostitutes by the dozen, boys, jugglers, dancers, acrobats, all naked, food delicacies from all over the world, which wasn't very big then, and fine and rare wines. Decadent extravagance at its most appalling.'

'Your book on orgy food is riveting,' said William. 'But appetites have changed a bit. I want to work out with Chef the kind of modern food we should offer. As well as bits and pieces from your book.'

'Anton'll have problems there,' said Lord Wick. 'I should think Tescos will want at least two weeks' notice for the peacock brains. Should you want me urgently, William, I'll be at Wick Castle tomorrow. As soon as I've collected my dog from Mr Fish's vet friend this afternoon I'll have to get the train up to Scotland. Bit of a crisis up there. How sound are you on cheese?'

'Cheese?' asked William.

'Yellowy stuff you have with a biscuit,' said His Lordship. 'Sometimes has varicose veins in it. Goes green and hairy by Tuesday if the weather's warm. Do you happen to know how to make the stuff?'

'No,' said William. 'I can say, hand on heart, that constructing a Brie is outside my experience.'

'Pity,' said Lord Wick. 'You are such a capable chap in most directions I thought you might know how to make cheese. You see, my eldest son, Alasdair, is full of ideas but has no brain to back them up. Strange things, chromosomes.'

'You don't get those in cheese, do you?' said William.

'I'm talking about my family. I am, I would claim, as knowledgeable and intellectually curious as any of my peers in the House of Lords, which is to say hardly at all. Yet even I am brighter than my son. He is more handsome than me, I suppose. Cuts a swathe through the Wee Marys at Country Dances and so on and yet he has this inert brain. My very dear wife is not only most beautiful but bright as a badger. Where did our chromosomes go wrong? Funny old world, isn't it, when the chips are down – whatever that means.'

'I would have thought that amateur cheese-making was fraught with perils,' said William, more as something to say on a subject about which he knew nothing than as a constructive comment. 'I mean. Don't you have to have the milk at a certain temperature, and clean out the pans with boiling water every five minutes or everything rots?'

'More or less,' said His Lordship. 'Alasdair's problem is that his whisky-flavoured cheese, so eagerly awaited in the sushi-bars of Tokyo so he tells me, simply doesn't taste of whisky. All it has so far is a remote, unpleasant hint of creosote.'

'Perhaps cheese might not be the right vehicle for the whisky,' said William. 'You probably farm salmon on your estate?'

'Oh, yes,' said His Lordship.

'Then how about experimenting with a few young salmon in a small tank? Gently, tot by tot, introduce a small quantity of cheap, local whisky into the water. After perhaps a generation or two of fish you could end up with

139

whisky-flavoured smoked salmon. Now *that* would sell!'

His Lordship gazed at William in awe. 'Brilliant!' he said. 'An absolutely brilliant idea!'

'It probably wouldn't work,' said William.

'Of course it wouldn't *work*,' said His Lordship. 'That's not the point, is it? Point is what fun it'd be to try. William, I think that you should have been my son. Is *your* wife beautiful?'

William was taken aback for a moment. To reply, 'Oh, extremely pretty,' would only trivialize how he regarded Milly, which was with inexpressibly deep affection. 'Yes,' he said.

'Good,' said Lord Wick. 'We are both blessed. And what does your beautiful wife think of our orgy, on which you are having to devote so much of your time and energies?'

'I haven't told her about it yet,' said William.

'Good God!' said His Lordship. He really did seem to William to be staggered. 'Why on earth not? When the going gets complicated a fellow *needs* his wife to sort him out. Wives are tremendously good at spotting points which we're too close to the problem to see. I've discussed the orgy with my wife. She told me it's a dangerous and dreadful folly and that I've really, at last, gone clean off my chump. Then she gave me a big hug. Unfathomable lady at times. Comes of being French, I suppose.'

'I couldn't tell Milly. I had a letter from the Master expressly forbidding me to discuss it with anybody, especially Milly. It has been miserable not being able to talk things over with Milly. Really bad.'

Little Lord Wick tutted and made little whistling noises and squirmed about on his chair, much disturbed. 'At times the Master seems to have the backbone of a damp Brussels sprout,' he said. 'That awful wife of his is behind this. He's terrified of her. Well, we're all a bit frightened of our good ladies when they go for us full throttle but the Master really has the moral strength of a paper cup of warm milk. His dictum is "anything for a quiet life". What a way to live!'

The little peer was positively popping.

'Do you think he's discussed the orgy with his Parthenope?' said William.

'She knew right from the start. He told me. That's what's so rotten about him stopping you telling *your* lady! And the ghastly Parthenope was dead against our little private orgy. Afraid it might get out, I suppose, and she'd have to resign from being Chairperson of the Berkshire League for the Supply of Water-Troughs to Egyptian Camels.'

'Pud?' said William.

'Just coffee, thank you,' said His Lordship. 'I rather overdid the roast lamb. Delicious.'

William mimed coffee to a distant waitress who brought Lord Wick a tray.

'My next move,' he said to His Lordship, 'is to catch Anton the Chef before he puts his feet up for his afternoon rest.'

'Where did you get hold of Anton?' asked His Lordship. 'Clubs simply can't afford to pay hotel wages and Anton does wonders.'

'It was a few summers ago,' said William. 'I had a job with a friend of mine selling encyclopedias, printed in Malaysia, from door to door. There were eight volumes so they weighed a ton to carry around. There should have been nine volumes but Volume 6 was missing in all of them so they were going cheap. There was no problem getting rid of them. Extraordinary thing was that nobody seemed to mind a volume being missing. The customers obviously had no intention of reading the books, they only bought them for their impressive bulk. Then Geoffrey, this chap I worked with, asked me to help him with a one-off job he'd just got which was giving him the trembles, planning the logistics of a steam traction-engine rally at Alton Towers on an August Bank Holiday.'

'The danger of being lynched by mile-long queues of bank-holiday motorists with steaming radiators?'

'I worked out a route for each rally entrant which had enough lay-byes *en route* to Alton Towers for the 4 mph steam tractors to pull in for ten minutes every ten minutes and let the swearing public pass by.'

'Pity the idea hasn't caught on.'

'When it was all over Geoffrey took me to his home for a scratch lunch cooked by his young brother, Anthony, Anton's real name, who had just left school and wanted to be a chef. A burly and surly lad with a mop of greasy hair hanging down his back. It was marvellous food, inventive and beautifully cooked, startlingly so for a schoolboy. A couple or three years later my friend wrote to say that Anthony was finishing his course at the Hounslow College of Catering and was looking for a job. So when I joined the Club and a chef was suddenly needed I asked Anthony to come for an interview. When he arrived and took off his silly beret he was a skinhead. And across his knuckles was tattooed S.O.U.P. and F.I.S.H.'

'Dear, oh dear!'

'Oh dear, indeed,' said William. 'I said to him, "We have a problem. A gentleman's club whose master is a Law Lord is not going to hire a chef who's a tattooed skinhead." "And what's wrong wiv being a skinhead?" demanded Anthony aggressively, putting his face too close to mine. "You wanna watch it mate. Me and my oppos at Hounslow Catering joined the party to reclaim Britain for the British. The foreigners are taking over, that's what. You try getting a job as a chef in a restaurant in bloody Southall or bloody Hounslow. All the jobs go to bloody Indians and Chinese." "But they're Indian and Chinese restaurants," I pointed out. "You don't want to spend your professional life stoking up tandoori ovens and defreezing packets of prawns do you?" "I think you're avoiding the real issue," said Anthony vaguely. "Well, here's what I'm offering you," I said and I read off the terms of service and then named the salary. Anthony gave a little whistle. "I'll take it!" he said swiftly, then added, "Just watch it, that's all." "Good," said I. "I'm really delighted. Now to make you look presentable." In spite of some bitter protests I covered the tattoos on Anthony's knuckles with strips of Elastoplast from Belkis's first-aid box and told him that his cover story was that the hatch of the service lift dropped suddenly and almost guillotined his fingers. Then I persuaded Anthony that until his hair grew back to an acceptable length, he would wear on duty his chef's hat, the traditional linen *bombe surprise*. And for Anthony's formal interview with the Master and for his general comings and goings around the Club, I borrowed from Milly the wig her father wore at school as Millamant. Anthony looked a little odd beneath its golden strands but reasonably human. The Master accepted him and Anthony became the Club's new chef.'

'Thank God, say we all!' said His Lordship.

'I must say,' said William, 'with Anton to cope with the food and your help with the basics of Orange-mounting, I am beginning to feel a little more hopeful, just a little bit more optimistic that things might now be beginning to go our way.'

William took a forkful of fish pie and suddenly found Sergeant Chidding standing at his elbow.

'Sorry to interrupt your dinner, sir,' said Chidders in a loud confidential whisper, 'but a minute or two ago this crusical message came out of Minnie's behind. I will hasten back to my listening post, sir, in order to observe any further development which might incur.' He put a page of his notebook down in front of William, seemed to salute without actually saluting and marched away.

William picked up the slip of paper, glanced through it and silently passed it over to His Lordship.

It read:

Mr Tozer's voice: ' *'ello? This is Mr Tozer esquire again. Will you kindly tell your Gossip Editor that I have valuable information at last on the shock horror goings-on about to be gone-on in the Walpole Club. And will he please ring me back to arrange for a cash payment. My information will enable your rag to strip the lurid veneer of civilization off of the denizens of the Walpole Club and reveal the secret lusts of a number of revered public figures including Lord Sidmonton. I have discovered from a paid informant in my pay that the Club is going to celebrate its 250th birthday, and this is my exclusive bombshell so listen carefully as I will only say it once – the Club members are going to celebrate its two-hundred-and-fiftieth birthday by going upstairs, locking the door of the dining-room behind them – and HOLDING AN ORANGE. 'ello? What you laughing at? 'ello . . . ? Well, listen you. Tell your boss on the Gossip Column that "Orange" is just a code-name for something nasty which is going to go on here and I expect to find out what "Orange" stands for any moment. If your boss wants said information I want a thousand quid now, deposit, in used fivers. Got that? As soon as I receive the money, I will reveal the Walpole Club's shameful secret. You have been listening to a Sidney Tozer world-exclusive phone-in scoop.*'
Sound of a phone being replaced.

'It's now a straightforward race,' said William. 'Can we discover which newspaper Tozer is phoning and step in smartly to block that problem, or will Tozer discover what "Orange" stands for first, blow the whole thing and collect his blood money?'

'If I were a betting man,' said His Lordship, 'which come to think of it I am, I'd have a fiver on Tozer; he must be the last mortal in this club not to know already what "Orange" stands for.' He got up.'In fact, I think I would make that a tenner.'

William looked so worried that His Lordship added cheerfully, 'Mind you, I'm a bit of a fool and usually get things entirely wrong!'

CHAPTER ELEVEN

ORANGE IN JEOPARDY

Lord Wick pottered off to collect his dog leaving William feeling bleak. He picked at his fish pie but it had cooled and lost its edge. Milly always said that some foods simply must be hot or went horrible. Other foods besides fish pie which Milly maintained must be consumed really hot or not at all were fried eggs, spaghetti, a cup of coffee, baked beans on toast and dumpling stew.

William had tried to add oxtail to the list but Millie argued that when she was a music student she had once eaten cold oxtail when the girls she shared with had eaten everything else in the flat and cold oxtail wasn't all that sick-making if you didn't think about it.

His first move was to trot downstairs to Sergeant Chidding's cubby-hole to check that all was well with Mickey and Minnie, the Club's vital allies in the Tozer Crisis.

All was not well.

'Minnie's going faint!' said the sergeant, in anguish.

'Probably only batteries,' said William, soothingly. 'Don't worry, I've got some spares in my desk. I'll fetch them right away. Has Tozer had his lunch yet?'

'No, sir. For the last hour he's bin on one of them telephone numbers where you listen to girls pretending to be saucy. All I can hear his end is nasal breathing and an occasional, "Then what did you do?". Must be costing the Club a fortune.'

'Does he usually eat in?'

'No, he always goes to the Eye-tie Expressive Coffee Bar up the arcade and has two cheese and tomato sandwiches and an Eccles cake.'

'If I get you the batteries do you think you can pop them into Mickey and Minnie as soon as Tozer goes to his lunch?'

'Leave it to me, sir. He has to pass me to get out either front or back door.'

'Wait a moment,' said William, 'what about *your* lunch? I'll take over while you grab something to eat.'

'Well, as it so happened, sir, I had a word with Mrs Bratby, you know, sir, Muriel, tables one to nine in the dining-room, and she smuggled me out some iron rations to keep me going.'

'A snack's not enough when you've got such important work to do. What did she give you?'

'Well, there was a plate of smoked salmon, then steak and kidney pudding, lovely, with gravy and new potatoes and hot veg, then two different colours of ice-cream with a dollop of real cream on top and a little triangular ripply biscuit thingy and then a wodge of Stilton cheese. And coffee.'

William sighed. Mostly in envy. 'Won't be long,' he said, making for the staircase and leaping lightly up the stairs two at a time.

At the top he was resting against the bannisters, heart thudding, trying to get his breath back, when Belkis floated out of her room carrying a bundle of papers. She was wearing the very fine billowy white job with the gold thread flirting in and out of the neckline and hem. William thought she looked ethereal.

'You all right, Willy?' she said anxiously in her caressing voice. 'You look pooped.'

'Just keeping fit,' William said, feeling better as the red mist in front of his eyes cleared. 'Are those papers for me to sign?' He followed her into his office, sat at his desk and rummaged through the drawers for his spare AA razor batteries. He found them.

'Thank God,' he said, holding them up thankfully.

'Now, Willy, tell me why you are excited about batteries,' said Belkis. 'You look so pale these days and you work so late in the evening. Is it the orgy which is being one damned problem for you?'

'Well, yes,' said William, 'you could say that. Actually the batteries are for Mickey and Minnie Mouse. The mice are our best hope of defeating the traitor Tozer and both their voices are going faint.'

Belkis perched on the edge of the word-processor table and shook her head in comic bewilderment.

William jumped up. 'Don't sit there!' he shouted.

Belkis stared at him with round eyes.

'It's your bottom I'm thinking of,' he said.

'Dear Willy,' said Belkis softly, 'do you think of my botty a lot?'

'No, no, no!' said William. 'Only in the course of duty. I'm just warning you from bitter experience, the sharp edge of that table could mark you for life. Sit here in comfort.' He urged her into his chair.

And then he explained everything about the battery-operated Mickey and Minnie, and Sergeant Chidding, and the need to listen in to Tozer's phonecalls to discover the name of his spymaster.

'My Malcolm!' said Belkis. 'Why do you not discuss these matters with me at their kindergarten stage instead of too latish? Mr Hardcastle is besotted about everything electronic and he will so happily lend you a little pocket recording-machine which only springs into action when somebody speaks. So you can rest it near Minnie Mouse and everything Mr Tozer speaks will be taped automatically! What a relief for the sergeant, eh?'

It occurred to William that the mini-recorder could be hidden in Tozer's room in which case there would be no need for Mickey and Minnie at all. But he realized what a blow this would be to Chidders who was so relishing his important MI5 role and the custody of Minnie. So he gratefully accepted Belkis's offer for a recorder to put in Chidders's office. At least from tomorrow all Tozer's calls would be monitored on tape.

'Surely the Master should be helping you?' said Belkis.

'It crossed my mind,' said William. 'But he's chosen to be away.'

Lord Sidmonton had gone to Edinburgh for a legal conference. This moot was supposed to decide whether or not judges and barristers wanted to be deprived of their Gilbert and Sullivan wigs and long red dresses and wear normal clothing in court, a lurch into modernity abhorred by most of the older lawyers who enjoyed being clad in medieval robes and wigs which they felt set them apart from, or rather above, the herd. These traditionalists argued that making lawyers wear lounge suits in court was equivalent to pawning the royal coach and requiring the royal family to pedal about on bikes.

The Master agreed whole-heartedly with the retain-our-robes lobby. But not publicly.

'And your dear Milly?' asked Belkis. 'Is she not worried that if you work so late every night you will be overdone?'

'Well, actually she's away, too,' said William.

Which is why he cycled back up the hills to an empty house every evening.

Milly and her Trio had been unexpectedly invited at a day's notice to play music during dinner at Durham University which during the summer recess and tourist season was holding an 'Eighteenth-Century Week'. The Baroque Trio was a replacement for another group of music-makers,

Wilf Greenstreet and His New Orleans All-Star Trad Jazz Threesome, who had the late offer of a more prestigious engagement at a Live Music Night in the local pub.

The Baroque Trio was prettily positioned in a deep grassy hollow outside the windows of the dining-hall. Although well-lit, the site was acoustically disastrous and only the Hon. Pippa's cello could be heard clearly. But the girls looked so attractive that enthusiastic reports in the local papers called them 'enchanting', 'fresh as daisies', 'champion lasses all three'.

To save money they stayed with Pippa's great-aunt, Lady Alice, who lived in an ancient Peel Tower, a tall, originally fortified stone house about eight miles from Durham and high up on softly rolling green hills.

Lady Alice was the oldest human being Milly had ever been close to. She was wrinkled and bent over at an angle of something like forty-five degrees, and as bright as a button.

Life in the house was complicated in that Lady Alice had so many dogs and cats milling about the place that it was almost impossible for the girls to take a step backwards or forwards without treading on a small furry something-or-other which then squealed or bit.

Great-aunt Alice was protective of animals. Her great-grandmother had been Jewish and when the Second World War broke out great-aunt Alice became convinced that Hitler would make her and her animals a target for his bombs. The only beast she was nurturing at that time was an obese and bad-tempered goat whose white coat stood out dangerously clearly against the green grass of the Durham hills. To prevent the goat being targeted by Hitler's Luftwaffe, great-aunt Alice bought a tin of matt brown paint and a tin of matt green paint and camouflaged it.

The Trio's first lunch was an enormous plateful of lettuce and other assorted boskage from the garden, dressed with a mixture of vinegar and sugar and topped with boiled eggs and sardines.

'Sit where you like,' said Lady Alice waving a tiny hand as brown and knobbly as a bunch of root ginger.

Pippa had briefed Milly and Estelle that great-aunt Alice would say grace before every meal, a traditional old text which the family had been using for over two hundred years. Lady Alice stood at the table, her white head bowed. 'Dear Lord, what we're about to receive has nowt to do wi' the Duke of Newcastle.'

The egg and sardine salad was delicious. It was followed by baked apples. The first time the girls had had white-hot baked apples since their schooldays. The baked apples alone were worth the journey. Great-aunt Alice waved aside their compliments. 'I grow the vegetables but that's all,' she said. 'My once-a-week daily is Mrs Owlglass from the village. For forty years she has come in and shifted the dust about a bit but she also cooks, and her innocently dirty mind is a perpetual feast.'

The girls were given a room high up in the house. On a table by their beds was a carafe of murky well-water, a china barrel of oatmeal biscuits and a bottle of malt whisky. The stone walls were so damp that small plants flourished in the gaps between the blocks. At breakfast Pippa said to Lady Alice, 'You know, great-aunty, when you have guests to stay I do think you should weed the bedroom.'

Lady Alice so much enjoyed having the girls that about forty years dropped away from her leaving her more mobile and about twenty degrees nearer the perpendicular.

When the girls arrived back from their evening's concert great-aunt Alice made them welcome in the drawing-room by batting animals off the sofas and chairs with the blockbuster novel she was currently reading and serving the girls a killer nightcap, the choice of a goblet of anonymous but powerful brownish wine from a grubby decanter, or a Gin-and-It, a fashionable drink in great-aunt Alice's younger days which, as mixed by great-aunt Alice, was a lethal half-tumbler of neat gin with a dash of Italian vermouth in it. The girls had never had a great-aunt Alice Gin-and-It before and after finishing their first, heads swimming, they fervently wished never to have another.

Great-aunt Alice's favourite of the Trio was Estelle. On the second evening she drew up her chair and examined Estelle's profile from four inches away with the huge magnifying glass she used to read *The Times*. 'You're beautiful,' she murmured. 'On the thin side but thoroughly beautiful.'

Pippa and Milly sat enjoying Estelle's embarrassment.

'What lovers you must have, my dear!' said great-aunt Alice chattily, massaging a malevolent-looking cat which had leapt onto her lap for a bit of attention.

'Er—' said Estelle.

'A stunning beauty like you – you *must* have lovers! Now admit it! Young sparks from the Brigade, eh? The cavalry? Now *they're* nice! Or they were when I was a gel!'

'I do have a sort of closeish friend,' said Estelle reluctantly, as though talking about him might make him disappear. 'His name is Foster and he was born on an island very near the one where I was born. Plays the trumpet in the evening with a brass ensemble. During the day he's a student at the London School of Economics.' She paused. 'He's coming up tomorrow by train to hear us play.'

'Then he must stay here,' said Lady Alice firmly. 'I'll put you both in the Otterburn room. I'll get Mrs Owlglass to weed it first thing in the morning.'

'Um—' said Estelle. 'Would it worry you very much if we didn't share a room?'

Milly and Pippa looked at each other, eyebrows raised.

'The thing is,' Estelle went on, 'we haven't got that far yet. Do you mind?'

'Of course not,' said great-aunt Alice briskly. 'He can have Otterburn and you can have Prestonpans. It's a bit dark in Prestonpans but it's above what used to be the moat so it's got its own privy. And if you change your mind in the night your friend's only a quick sprint down the corridor.'

Estelle's closeish friend the trumpeter and economics student Foster did indeed turn up by train next day, late afternoon, and Estelle went to pick him up at Durham station in Milly's 2CV.

Estelle introduced him neatly and proudly to Milly and Pippa and then took him up to unpack in Otterburn.

Pippa sagged against the wall. 'My God, he's dishy!' she said. 'Isn't he just dishy?'

'Tremendous charm,' said Milly. 'And good-looking, I suppose.'

'Well, don't be so grudging,' said Pippa.

'I must say you're a bit fickle,' said Milly. 'I thought my William was your Mr Wonderful.'

'Well, he was but Foster is quite something. And macho with it. Why are trumpeters usually the sexy ones? Trumpeters and drummers?'

'I think I'll stick to William,' said Milly. 'He's macho enough when he's in the mood. I'm missing him. And we've only been away three days.'

'I thought you'd been going a bit quiet,' said Pippa.

'I've got a strange feeling, a kind of presentiment, that I should be at home with William. Don't know why.'

'Only two more days and then you'll be with him again,' said Pippa. 'Funny, but I think this separation may have been just what you needed. Bring you to your senses a bit about what you've got in your Wonderful William.'

'I hope you're right,' said Milly.

Both girls were busy with their thoughts for a few moments. Then Pippa said, 'Do you think Foster's got a brother?'

William hurried down the stairs to the sergeant's cubby-hole clutching the batteries. The sergeant, face grave, met William at the door and handed William a sheet from his notebook. 'Not good news, sir, I'm very much afraid. I think that as far as Mr Tozer is concerned it might well be coming up to shovel time.'

William read: '*Sound of phone being lifted and dialling. Then voice: "This is Mr Tozer at the Walpole Club speaking. Please pass this message to your Gossip Editor toot de sweet. Quote. I have now found out everything about the so-called Walpole Club "Orange" and what I know is literally dynamite full-stop, comma. Send the money immediately, semi-colon. What d'you mean he's in New York? 'Ave 'im got back! What? I don't know that I can wait a week. Hello? Hello! Sod everybody." Sound of phone being replaced.*'

'Well,' said William, heart sinking. 'At least we've got a week to sort things out.'

'Tozer went off to lunch about five minutes ago so the coast's clear,' said Chidders. 'I'll get the batteries up the mice right away. I must hurry, my poor little Minnie's very faint and weak.'

'Mrs Hardcastle is lending you a little recording-machine so from tomorrow you won't have to write down the messages.'

'That'll be a relief,' said the sergeant. 'I don't mind admitting that handwriting things down by hand is not my fort, as the expression says.'

Chidders took the batteries and thudded off down the stairs to Tozer's lair and William moved through to the kitchens for a word with Anton. He was still clutching Lord Wick's book which seemed to have become permanently attached to him.

The kitchens hissed reassuringly and steam swirled around stainless steel and items of china were banged about as waiters and waitresses bore off puddings to late lunchers, and laid trays of coffee. Anton's tiny little private office was empty but one of the kitchen staff offered to find him and William sat down to wait, riffling through the pages of Lord Wick's orgy recipes to find a suitable passage.

'Ey-oop!' a voice sang out. William looked up to see what looked like a yeti dressed as a chef standing in front of him. A thick wad of lank blond hair escaped from beneath his chef's hat and dangled down like a greasy curtain in front of his face.

'Good God!' said William.

'Panic not,' said the yeti. He reached up to his hat and twisted it round in a semi-circle. The long blond hair went round with it and came to rest hanging down the back of his neck, revealing the rather red face of the chef. 'It's me, Anton.'

'That's my father-in-law's wig!' said William. 'What have you done to it, it's filthy! Look at it, all spattered with grease!'

'I've been frying parsley,' said Anton. 'You want to try frying parsley, mate. It's a right bugger, I can tell you. Spits at you like a cobra you've just trod on. I think I'll market this idea of wearing a wig back-to-front. Call it The Anton Patent Hot-fat Face-protector. Make a fortune out of those poncy foreign chefs on telly, they hate frying in hot fat on camera. Don't worry about the wig, a mate of mine runs a dry-cleaners.'

'You can't dry-clean a wig!' said William.

'You can try,' said Anton. 'Or I could get my girlfriend to wash it by hand. She's marvellous with my threads, she is. She could wash the grease out of a pound of butter and give you back a square of clean, dry paper with an anchor on it.'

'Thing is,' said William, 'I need your help with a pretty big problem that's come up.'

'You mean the orgy?'

Yet again a whiff of desolation swept over William. He closed his eyes. 'You're supposed to call it the "Orange",' he said. 'It's the code word.'

'Me and the staff did use the code for a few days,' said Anton, 'then we forgot the code word. So we used words which more or less sounded the same as "orgy", like "itchy" and "ugly". Then it all seemed a bit silly so we went back to saying "orgy".'

'The thing is, do you happen to know what actually takes place at an orgy?'

'Not really, no. Mind you, one of the lads in our class at Hounslow Catering claimed he actually took part in one just before he left school. Him and four of his mates paid his elder brother 50p each and their orgy turned out to be scoffing Mars Bars all one Saturday afternoon in a lock-up garage and muttering "Corrrr!" over old copies of *Knave*.'

'No girls?'

'Narr! Would have scared the daylights out of them.'

'I suppose the nude photographs in the magazines were the sexy element.'

'So the customers hoped but they found that the orgy organizer had cut out all the full-frontal filth to stick in his locker at the bus depot where he worked.'

'All in all the orgy doesn't seem to have been much fun.'

'Ah, that's where you're wrong, squire. My young mate always says that the orgy was the high point of his brief and unlovely existence. The afternoon, for him, held a touch of glamour and forbidden luxury which he's never been able to recapture since.'

'Squatting on a garage floor scoffing Mars Bars?'

'Yeah. Well, there wasn't much money hanging about where we lived and a Mars Bar, a whole bar not just a quick bite, was a kind of dream to a poor and more or less permanently hungry lad. Moreover it was forbidden fruit. Sweet things rot your teeth, we was warned all the time, so chocolate's bad for you. And toffee was supposed to be even worse. But at the orgy my friend could eat lovely, lovely Mars Bars until he was sick. Which of course he did. And was.'

A key aspect of this glimpse into the realities of orgy culture caused William furiously to think. Then he said to Anton, 'Now, food for the Orange. I've got a book of ancient recipes here by Lord Wick which I'll leave with you to go through for inspiration. It's strange stuff.'

'Like what?'

'Well. Here's a passage quoted by the Reverend Sydney Smith, who dearly loved his food, to the effect that food should be a pleasure to eat as well as being fuel. Which I would go along with. This is what he wrote.' William, who rather liked reading aloud, found his place and began: ' "Look at men when they are gathered round the eels of Syene, and the oysters of Lucrinus, and when the Lesbian and Chian wines descend through the limbec of the tongue and larynx; when they receive the juice of fishes, and the marrow of the laborious ox, and the tender lard of Apulian swine, and the condited stomach of the scarus – is this nothing but mere sensation? – or is it a proof that nature has infused in her original creations the power of gratifying that sense which distinguishes them, and to every atom of matter has added an atom of joy?"'

'Do what?' said Anton.

'I just wanted to give you a whiff of the extraordinary

and horrible things they ate in ancient days. And ask you what you think would be a reasonable substitute for, say, Lesbian wine?'

Anton's eyes were gleaming. 'I bet I could get hold of something similar,' he said. 'Let me have His Lordship's book to go through and I'll report back with some suggestions.'

'Look, Anthony . . .'

'Anton.'

'All right Anton. I don't think these weird old dishes are what we should go for. To start with you'll have a terrible problem getting hold of the semi-tropical shellfish and stuff.'

'Less of a problem than you think,' said Anton. 'Billingsgate Market up the East India Dock Road is the best fish market in the world. They can get you anything there, or the next best thing to anything.'

'Billingsgate?'

'Oh, deffinly.'

'We'd better have a planning meeting tomorrow then and between us agree the menu,' said William briskly. 'Here's Lord Wick's book. I warn you, if you read it now you'll only want a water-biscuit for dinner tonight.'

Anton took the book, began reading and fell into a fakir-like state of concentration, only his lips occasionally moving when the words got hard. William drifted away and made his way upstairs feeling a little lost without the book which during the day had become his worry-rag. He made a less sprightly ascent of the staircase and arrived at his office breathing almost normally.

Belkis was in there waiting for him. 'I have telephoned my Malcolm,' she said, 'and tomorrow morning in the early a.m. he will personally install the little recording-machine in Sergeant Chidders's cub-hole. There! Another of your problems done in!'

'You are being absolutely marvellous, Belkis,' said William, 'and I do appreciate it.'

'My dear Willy, when a girl is in love . . . ' Belkis breathed a small sigh, widened her soft brown eyes so that they gleamed at full wattage for a moment then closed them and seemed to swoon. Her soft and splendid bosom rose and fell hypnotically.

'Don't ring us, we'll ring you,' said William. 'Or rather, we won't ring you. Sweet Belkis, that over-the-top performance wouldn't get you a walk-on part in the Staines and Egham Operatic Society's production of *Salome*.'

'But I made you smile, Willy! I think it is the first time I have made you smile with my body-fun! And you so need relaxing.'

'You're a sweet and funny girl, Belkis, and I am truly grateful for your support and help. Particularly now that I understand your ways of going about things. Well, beginning to understand them. Actually things seem to be looking up as far as the Orange is concerned and I am feeling really hopeful. Can you do something for me?'

'Anything!' she breathed.

'Now stop that,' said William. 'Can you lend me Edgar to do some research on Club eating habits?'

Edgar was Belkis's clerk, a quiet, learned old man so narrow and fleshless as to be almost non-existent. He had worked in the Walpole office as long as anybody could remember. Nobody had ever seen him arrive at the Club, or depart, or eat, or sneeze or go to the lavatory. He just sat in his tiny office and kept the books in beautiful handwriting.

'Of course,' said Belkis. 'What is it you want to know?'

'Does he happen to keep records of the dishes on the menus and how many of each dish is ordered?'

'Oh yes, so that dining-room accounts can be itemized.'

'I want him to make me out a list of what were the

favourite main courses and puds ordered over, say, the last two months. Not interested in the hors d'oeuvre or cheeses, just main courses and puds.'

'Delighted to so do, Willy. If only to see Edgar burst faintly into life for a moment. You see, you're a male. Edgar doesn't approve of me because I'm a female and represent temptation.'

Belkis got up from the chair and undulating beautifully, moved to the door and yelled down the little corridor, 'EDGAR!'

They both listened. Tiny shuffling noises became audible and eventually Edgar appeared in the doorway. He stood there for a moment, perfectly still, looking like an unsuccessful applicant, too old, for the part of Ratty in *Toad of Toad Hall*.

William explained what information he wanted Edgar to provide.

As William was explaining, small sad whimpers like those uttered by a puppy who is on the wrong side of a door escaped from Edgar. When William had finished talking Edgar hung his head for a moment then nodded mournfully.

'Will tomorrow morning do you, sir?' he said. 'About eleven ten?'

And he shuffled slowly off back to his office.

The next morning William was in his office waiting for Edgar. At exactly ten minutes past eleven Edgar shuffled in and, with a glance of despair, gave William a sheet of paper on which was clearly laid out exactly what William wanted to know.

'This is a marvellous help to me, Edgar,' said William. 'Thank you so much.'

'If Mrs Hardcastle had given me warning of what you required, sir,' muttered Edgar, flashing a look of Old Testament loathing in the direction of Belkis, 'I would not have taken such an unconscionable time over it.' He left, gently.

William glanced through Edgar's figures. 'Great!' he said. 'Marvellous! Exactly what I'd hoped to find!'

'I am so glad for you,' said Belkis. 'At last you are really looking cheery again!'

'I now know what the food half of the Orange is going to be, and it's a bit surprising. All I have to do now is sort out the other half, some kind of suitable, semi-erotic cabaret.'

'Willy, I think I can help you over the females! I have had a big thought on that and a smashing idea has arisen!'

'I really am beginning to believe that the Orange will work, thanks so much to you, dear Belkis!' said William.

He grabbed her and whirled her round in his arms as they used to do in B-movies when the unknown young songwriter told his chorus-girl friend that his musical was going to be produced on Broadway.

Then, also just like a B-movie, the phone rang.

'Dammit!' said William, annoyed at his moment of euphoria being vandalized. He grabbed the phone, 'Yes?'

'This is the Master,' said the unmistakable voice of Uncle Sid. 'I want you to do something immediately.'

'Of course, sir,' said William. 'And what can I do for you?'

'Cancel the Orange.'

'*What?* I don't understand . . . !' said William.

'It's simple enough, surely. I am ordering you, repeat ordering you, Mr Secretary, to stop all preparations for the particular party you're planning. Send round memos to all committees concerned. I have decided that our Club birthday celebrations must take another form.'

'But, sir . . . !' said William. 'I can't cancel the Orange now. The members are greatly looking forward to it and speculate about it endlessly, the list for our surprise dinner is full, the food is planned, the – cabaret – well, that's being sorted out, security is holding. I'm sorry, sir, but if you insist on cancelling our Orange without some sort of discussion, it's clear that I'm not the right person to remain your Club Secretary . . . '

'Do as you're told,' said His Lordship. And hung up.

CHAPTER TWELVE

A HYMN AND AN OATH

William told Belkis that the Master had ordered him to cancel the Orange and great tears welled up in her eyes.

'After all your work, Willy!' she cried. 'Damned silly old bloody fool he is that man, stupid pillock! I don't know what "pillock" means but my Malcolm uses it a lot about people who annoy him, like our bald fishmonger who never has kippers when my Malcolm is at home. I *think* it means a small pill.'

'It means a lot stronger than that,' said William, 'I'm happy to say.' He was trying hard to think straight. 'I'd better ring Lord Wick, he's Chairman of the Events Committee and should be told first. He's also a great help. Do you happen to have his Castle Wick number handy?'

Belkis had.

The phone was answered by an elderly lady with a strong French accent, a sound as delightful to an Englishman as an Englishwoman speaking French with an English accent is agony to a Frenchman.

' 'Ello? This is Wick 2. Or it was. Now I 'ave to say, 'ello, this is 09552, which is so boring.'

'Lady Wick? I'm the Walpole Club Secretary. Would it be possible for me to speak to Lord Wick? I know I shouldn't be ringing him at home but something important has come up. Well, perhaps not all that important in the great scheme of world happenings, but urgent.'

'I will fetch Duncan. You must be William? I'm 'oping

to meet you during the birthday celebrations. Duncan keeps telling me about you.'

'I won't interrupt His Lordship if he's busy . . . '

'My dear, His Lordship's always busy! But doing what? Right now Duncan is down in the scullery composing 'is 'eem.'

' 'is 'eem?'

'There's an old 'armonium from the chapel down there and 'e's using that on which to compose 'is 'eem. The bellows are perished and 'e 'as to pedal like the Tour de France to get a note out of it but it keeps 'eem out of mischief. Please wait a moment.'

There was a thud as the phone was put down on a hard surface, a clatter of shoes and then William heard a far-off eldritch cry of 'DUNCAAAAAN! It's William from the Club on the telephone! WILLIAM'S ON THE PHOOOOONE!'

Feet approached and the phone was picked up again.

'Duncan won't be a moment,' said Lady Wick. 'I'm in the kitchen. The scullery is quite a way down the stone spiral staircase but Duncan won't be long. 'E is so tiny 'e's found that 'e can crouch in the old service lift and pull 'imself up by the rope.'

William waited. Remote, not easily recognizable sounds came through his earpiece, the background noises of a lived-in Scottish castle. A far-off baying sound which might have been a ghillie singing an old Highland lament for a dropped bottle of whisky, or the resident piper tuning the drone on the castle bagpipes, or an elderly stag farting in the stone corridor outside.

Then a rhythmic clanking which could have been a kitchen-maid pumping water up from the well into the kitchen sink or the washing-machine going into spin-dry mode.

Then there came a string of small bangs and bumps, a

cry of 'Oooo, my bloody head!' and a moment later Lord Wick came on the line.

'William!' he said. 'This *is* a pleasant surprise. Everything hunky-dory back at the ranch?'

'Well, no sir,' said William.

'I thought probably not,' said His Lordship.

'We have a crisis on our hands and I wanted to talk to you about it. I really am sorry to have to ring you at home . . . '

'That's all right,' said His Lordship, 'I'm delighted to be interrupted. That wretched harmonium in the scullery is so decrepit it's as tough to pedal as an exercise bike. And as boring. And the keys are so stained they look like a Bulgarian gypsy's teeth. But I need it to compose my hymns on.'

'Everything seemed to be going so well . . . ' William began.

'I know,' said His Lordship. 'I collected my dog from Sol Fish's vet and the vet gave me some magic pills which have worked a treat corking up old Madeleine. About a fiver a pill but she hasn't peed the carpet since I got her home!'

'Then we ran into trouble . . . '

'We certainly did. I was in the Underground on my way to collect Madeleine from the kennels when all the lights went out and the train came to a halt. We were becalmed. That's what gave me the idea, d'you see?'

'Lord Wick . . . '

'You remember? Cardinal Newman? When he was becalmed on a boat in the Straits of Bonifacio? Sat down and wrote the hymn "Lead Kindly Light". Inspired him, being becalmed. And there was I in the same situation, the only difference being that Newman was becalmed on a lugger between Corsica and Sardinia and I was becalmed in an Underground train between Finsbury Park and Cockfosters.'

'I really do need some help . . . '

'Don't we all, William. I know I do. You see, the Kirk's General Assembly is worried that some of the last century's good old Protestant hymns now sound a bit peculiar to modern ears. For instance, d'ye know this one?'

Lord Wick began to sing in a surprisingly clear and fervent baritone:

> *'Milk of the breast that cannot cloy*
> *He, like a nurse, will bring;*
> *And when we see His promise nigh,*
> *Oh how we'll suck and sing.*

'Well, I *ask* you! When I've set to music enough more suitable texts I'm thinking of publishing them as *Hymns Ancient and Post-Modern*. I'm making a start by setting to music some poems by Gerard Manley Hopkins. Our Minister is keen on us all sampling a whiff of fire and brimstone and there's a reasonable amount of that in old Hopkins. I'm having a go at the moment at his:

> *'All things counter, original, spare, strange;*
> *Whatever is fickle, freckled (who knows how?)*
> *With swift, slow; sweet, sour; adazzle, dim;*
> *He fathers-forth whose beauty is past change:*
> *Praise him.*

'I'll be frank with you, William, it's the very devil to set to music. I'm more used to the sort of poetry I learnt at school which went, tumpity-tumpity-tumpity-tump. "*I galloped, Dirck galloped, we galloped all three . . .* " You know where you are with that stuff. By the way, I've always wondered, what *was* the Good News they brought from Ghent to Aix?'

'Your Lordship . . . ' said William, a small vein beginning to throb in his forehead.

'*My* problem is that I never learnt music, but that's no drawback, as it happens. I cycle up a tune on the harmonium and play it back, if I haven't forgotten it, to the son of our village postman who's a staunch Puritan. He called his son God-Be-With-You and the lad is studying to play the electric piano-accordion. Goddy writes my tunes down for me, putting all those little tadpoles on the correct lines. Amazingly talented young man, do you know he can throw a salted peanut up in the air and . . . '

'Lord Wick!' said William in desperation. 'Shut up for a moment!'

'Yes, of course!' said Lord Wick cheerfully. 'I do tend to prattle on, don't I? Now what's *your* problem, William? As if I didn't know what your problem is.'

'How can you know?' said William.

'Ah. Through what I like to call the Ladies' Social Mafia, an intelligence-gathering network of wives and mothers not to be underestimated, William. I know, for instance, that your Milly and her Trio are even now being a huge success at Durham and look as beautiful as angels.'

'Really?' William glowed with pleasure.

'I know because the lady the Trio is staying with, old Alice, rang up earlier and told my wife. They are dear friends from many years back. When I brought my wife to Scotland as a young French-speaking bride, Lady Alice took her under her wing, cossetted her, helped her understand our North British ways of doing things. Bedded her in, as you might say. They still telephone each other with their bits of news and gossip.'

'Is Parthenope in this Ladies' Social Mafia?'

'She's not a member of the Wick chapter I'm happy to say but you can be sure she's in some Southern branch enjoying her particular kind of malicious intervention in other people's affairs. Parthenope is the archetypal social bum-sniffer.'

'The *what*?'

'You know the sort, meet 'em everywhere. Before they can take the first sip of their drink or spoonful of their soup they have to find out where the person next to them went to school, whether there might be a distant blood relationship, whether they are socially inferior and can be patronized or socially superior and need grovelling to . . .'

William recognized truth. 'My mother-in-law's one of those,' he said.

'Parthenope is also possessed of a loud and rattly voice, like pebbles being shaken about in a chamber pot. Above all the noise at a party you can hear her going about her sniffing: "Did your cousin marry into the Suffolk Dolt-Bumpkins or was it the poor-but-honest Lincoln branch? I do so hope it's the Suffolk side, I am an old friend of Fiona and hasn't she done wonders with the oast-house? Do remind me, before Lady Scott-Joplin married Hughie wasn't she a Butcher? Am I right in thinking that Lady Meriel, Gladys Temple as was, was once engaged to that druggy young viscount who now sells water filters?"'

'What does the Social Mafia tell you about the Orange crisis?'

'The latest report,' said Lord Wick, 'is that the Master, Lord Sidmonton, is on his way to Lady Alice's at this moment to talk to Milly on "a very serious matter". Put things together and it's fairly obvious that the ghastly Parthenope doesn't want our Orange to happen and has put the screws on Uncle Sid to get it cancelled, if necessary by getting at you through Milly. Am I right, do you think?'

'I'm afraid so, sir,' said William, worried but at the same time much fortified by this further glimpse of the shrewdness of Lord Wick's cunning mind. 'The Master telephoned a few minutes ago and ordered me to cancel the Orange.'

'Good Heavens! *Ordered* you? *Did* he now!'

'Yes. I said I thought it was wrong to destroy the Club's birthday party and if he insisted on cancellation without consultation it was a resigning matter as far as I was concerned. He said, "Do as you're told." So I rang you immediately.'

'To start with,' said Lord Wick, 'don't for Heaven's sake resign just like that. You mustn't – on principle. The principle is, if you must resign you do so in such a way that the Club has to pay you a large sum of money in compensation.'

'I don't want to resign but neither do I want to remain as the Master's lap-dog. Getting at me through Milly is a bit under-the-arm, isn't it, sir?'

'You can see his line of reasoning. Or more probably Parthenope's. As it was Milly who asked Uncle Sid to find you a job, Parthenope reckons that Milly owes Uncle Sid an undying debt of gratitude. The fact that Uncle Sid was desperate to find a Club Secretary and you're doing the job admirably and far beyond all reasonable expectancy *should* mean that you and Milly now don't owe the Master a damned thing, in fact he should owe *you*. But I'm afraid that this point of view wouldn't occur to our Lady Macbeth.'

'What do you think I should do about cancelling the Orange?'

'Nothing at all, my dear chap. Ignore that man.'

'But surely if the Master has issued an order . . . ?'

'The Master has no right to order *anything* more important than a whisky and soda. He can't cancel Club activities at a whim, he's not Vlad the Impaler, he's only the Club's Master, an honourable but only honorary part-time job like being Lord Rector of one of the better Scottish

Universities. He has lots of influence but no real power.'

'Then who can decide this kind of question? Who *does* have the real power?'

'The Events Committee, of course,' said Lord Wick. 'Chairman, me. I shall write to the members calling them to an emergency meeting to make the decision whether to accept the Master's request, note the word "request", or to go ahead with our Orange.'

'When are you proposing to hold the meeting, sir?'

'Remind me when the Orange is taking place.'

'Thursday week.'

'Then our meeting will be on Friday week. It can't possibly be sooner, Sol Fish is off to the States for a few days and Archie Alloway can't make it before Friday week. Without Archie we won't have a quorum and everything's got to be strictly legal at this meeting, eh? Archie's flying off to Norway tomorrow about some urgent forestry problem he's run into.'

'He didn't mention to me he was off to Norway,' said William.

'Well, he wouldn't, would he?' said Lord Wick. 'I haven't told him yet.'

William replaced the phone, still perturbed yet much cheered.

It was the Trio's last concert tomorrow so Milly would be home the following evening and he must tidy up the house because she would be knackered after driving down from Durham in the 2CV. And it might be a good idea to beg some chicken casserole or something from the kitchens so that getting supper would not be a problem.

It was time now to sort out the Orange menu with Anton before lunches were in full swing. With the food agreed upon there would be some minor details to worry about and then the only major problem left would be the 'cabaret'.

Belkis had slipped away while William had been on the phone to Castle Wick so William took his feet off the desk, rearranged the desktop to roughly how it had been before his feet had stirred everything about and made his way downstairs.

As William was passing the entrance hall Sergeant Chidding suddenly appeared. Chidders was holding Minnie in a noticeably different manner these days. Instead of clutching Minnie awkwardly, like a furry father in a David Attenborough programme who is not a good parent and trails his offspring about by its ear, Chidders now carried Minnie discreetly against his chest, his enormous hand protecting her.

The sergeant glanced upwards and to both sides looking for hidden cameras. Satisfied that security remained intact he leaned towards William. 'The latest news on Tozer, sir,' he whispered.

'What's that?'

'There isn't any. Thought you'd like to know, sir.'

William closed his eyes for a moment. He found himself doing this more frequently with Chidders as the difficulties of the Orange bit but any kind of reprimand was unworthy.

'Is Minnie working well with her fresh batteries?'

'Made a new woman of her, sir! I know she's not real, only made of tin and plastic and that but after I'd put the batteries in she seemed to have a new look in her eye. Silly but I could swear her whole being was somehow more cheerful. It could only have been gratitude for me giving her the new batteries, sir. Either that or because at the same time I gave her an all-over rub-up with Brasso.'

'We will probably never know, Chidders. Women are queer cattle.'

'*That's* not a very nice thing to say, sir!' said the sergeant.

'It's all right, Chidders,' said William. 'It's a quotation from an old play.'

'Glad to hear it, sir,' said Chidders, unmollified. He released Minnie's head to let her get a bit of fresh air.

'There was one tiny Tozer clue yesterday afternoon, now I come to remember,' Chidders went on. 'I noted it down in the logbook but I can't think where I put the book for the moment. I'll find it, sir, don't you fret. You can't lose a whole book, now can you?'

'You can,' said William. 'Don't you remember? Last year you lost the Bishop of Ickney and Mott's Bible.'

'Yes, but a Bible's not really a *book*, be honest, sir. It's a *Bible*. You don't sit down and treat it as a good read, like you do a Jackie Collins or *The Diary of a Chambermaid*. And it wasn't me what lost it. The Bishop left it on my counter in the hall, unbeknownst to me, reckoning to collect it later after he'd had his supper. But when he went back the Bible had gone, hadn't it? My personal theory is that somebody highly religious nicked it.'

William said, 'Tell me about your new Tozer clue.'

Chidders glanced about as usual before speaking.

'It was my Gwen who brought it up to my notice,' he said. 'We was sitting on the sofa watching an opera on television with the sound turned off and I was recounting my day's happenings as is my usual wont and I told her about a change in the way Tozer usually spoke on the phone.'

'Now this *is* interesting,' said William.

'Thank you, sir!' breathed Chidders, now mollified. 'Well, my Gwen said it was like that actor always said, the one who used to be on all channels at once, with white hair, always grumpy, oh, wassisname . . . ?'

'George Cole?'

'No, no, no! Took his wife for a six weeks' funny holiday in France and complained all the time . . . '

'That *was* George Cole, pretending to be an ex-fishmonger. Or do you mean John Thaw?'

'Who? Oh yes, that's the one, John Thaw! Well, my Gwen pointed out that when Mr Thaw used to work in Oxford hunting down murderers in his old red car with the wireless on loud, he always used to look for a change in a person's pattern of living. Then he would say to the police – there's your man what done it.'

'And Tozer's way of speaking has suddenly changed?'

'That's right. When he talks to that bloke who he's trying to get to send him money he's started swearing.'

'Oh, come on, Chidders, Tozer's always sworn on the phone! What about all that "Sod the Prime Minister" stuff?'

'Point is, sir, he's swearing *differently*. Yesterday afternoon he began to say "Gor blimey!" and "O Gor blimey!" and kept on saying it. If I was Mr Thaw I'd finish me pint of real ale in the Bodleian, back me old red motor out of the pub car park and get down to the copper-shop right away.'

'Chidders, I simply don't understand this. What is so significant about Tozer saying "Gor blimey"?'

'Well, sir, slang is local, even in a big place like London, and it keeps changing. You couldn't be expected to know about this because you went to a posh school I'm sure, sir, like Eton or Greyfriars, with a real asphalt playing-ground and free milk and blue-black ink and all that. But I come from the heaving underclasses, sir, and I can tell just from the way a bloke swears whether he's East End or South London, whether he's Bethnal Green or Bermondsey. Swearwords are a symblem of a man's background.'

'You're amazing, Chidders! Like Bernard Shaw's Professor Higgins in reverse.'

'It's not me, sir. It was my old dad made a lifelong study of it and passed his observations on to me just before he was snatched to Jesus, God rest his soul. Not that he was actually snatched, sir, like a tourist's handbag in Oxford Street. Actually on his seventy-second birthday he had a pint or two over the odds at lunchtime and fell off his crane into a ship's hold. But my Ma always liked to say he was snatched.'

A respectful silence in honour of The Departed held matters up for a moment or two.

Then William said, 'So what part of London does Tozer come from?'

'His whole speech is unmistakable, sir. He's a Bermondsey boy, that one is, through and through and out the other side, as you might say. Bermondsey like Tommy Steele, not Barking like Alf Garnett.'

'So if Tozer comes from Bermondsey, south of the river, from which area of London comes the phrase "Gor blimey"?'

'Well, "blimey" was used all over London, sir.'

William experienced yet again a feeling that getting information out of Chidders was like coaxing along an affectionate, anxious-to-please, but uncomprehending Great Dane.

'Do *you* say "blimey"?' asked William.

'Not on duty, sir. Only sometimes at home if I'm suddenly surprised by something, or impressed. My old dad used it a lot. While he was alive, of course. But he would. It was the slang of the old working men of London, the dockers, market porters, stall-holders. It was part of the old slang, that's the point. Young-uns don't use it no more, unless they're aping the old 'uns. You got old Alf Garnett coming out with "blimey!" and "Cor blimey!" and "Cor blimey O'Reilly!" and Tommy Steele showing how cockney the character he's playing is by saying the same. But real live youngish people, and Tozer must be in his early thirties, well, they talk stronger these days.'

'I'm beginning to understand,' said William.

'If that ship's hold had only been full of straw instead of iron sewage pipes and my old dad was still among us, he would have been able to explain to you in a flash. It's just that when I heard Tozer saying "Gor blimey" my old hackles rose. I dunno quite why, like I said, but I do know that it was somehow wrong for that man to keep saying "Gor blimey".'

'I'm really grateful, Chidders. It could be a very important clue. Perhaps the one which saves our whole Orange.'

'Thank you, sir,' purred Chidders. During his Alf Garnett impression he had inadvertently spat upon Minnie. He inverted her and, bowing his usual respectful quarter of an inch to William, marched majestically back to his cubicle, buffing-up the damp bit of Minnie's head on his lapel as he went.

Meanwhile in New York it was early evening and Osbert Gore-Bellamy was still in bed at the Algonquin hotel, where he had been all the afternoon with his research assistant, Alex McTuck.

Alex, whose name was really Alexandra but calling her 'Alex' saved Gore-Bellamy awkward questions from his fiancée and from the *Grass*'s accountant checking his expenses, lay starkers on the sheets in the New York heat. She was a tough, pretty girl, usually referred to by *Private Eye* as 'pouting hackette Alex' and she had that very Scottish kind of red hair which made it appear, as she lay there, that the main crevices of her body had caught fire.

'I think,' said Gore-Bellamy, leaning down and pouring himself the last of the champagne from the bottle on the carpet. 'I only think, mind you, but I am pretty certain, that I've got the bastard at last.'

'You're obsessed with getting your revenge on that old judge. It's eating into you,' said the pouting hackette, who really was pouting not having been offered any of the champagne. 'I mean what's the story? Not as though he was a royal or Michael Jackson.'

'It's front-page headlines all the way, Ally. THE GRASS REVEALS TOFFS' CLUB TO BE VENUE FOR VICE. APPEALS JUDGE CAUGHT WITH KNICKERS DOWN. INNOCENT GIRLS FORCED INTO SORDID ACTS BY CASH LURE FROM WEALTHY LAWYERS AND CELEBRITIES. SEE CENTRE PAGES FOR SENSATIONAL PICS.'

'Now listen well to me,' said Alex, removing his hand from her tummy, it was weighing on her like a kilo of warm veal. 'It's all supposition. You don't *know* all this. And suppose you're guessing wrong? The backlash'll kill you professionally. You're not exactly journalism's Cliff Richard as it is and if you get this story wrong the whole profession as well as the *Grass* board of directors'll have your guts for garters.'

'I know what I'm doing.'

'But what proof have you got? You're always telling me to check facts, check facts on every story again and again till you're absolutely sure of them. And *then* throw them away. Have you checked your facts about vice girls and all that?'

'I've got a mole,' he said.

She laughed. 'You've got seven,' she said. 'Eight if you count the little one on your . . .'

'Oh, ha-ha,' he said. 'I mean, as you well know, I've got this porter spying for me in the Walpole Club itself. Idiot by the name of Tozer. This birthday party the Club is going to hold is something secret and special. As soon as Tozer finds out what their code word for it means I can swoop. Get cameras all round the building – hide 'em if necessary in vans and windows opposite – photograph everything that moves. Then write it up. We can easily find out afterwards from Tozer what happened.'

'Can't you plant one of our investigative reporters inside to get the full story? Temporary waiter or something?'

'Tried that. They weren't taking on any new staff. No, I can wait until I get the word from Tozer and then I've got the managing editor's OK to surround the place with cameramen and reporters and do an FBI operation on the evening's fun. My God, what a shock that load of establishment creeps is going to get the next morning, eh?'

He smiled happily to himself.

Alex swung herself out of bed and stood up.

'Don't go yet,' said Gore-Bellamy. 'We've got time for a quicky.'

'You may have but I haven't,' she said. 'I've got to meet Debby in five minutes with the list she's selling us of Washington politicians who wear toupees.'

'She can cool her heels for half an hour,' said Gore-Bellamy.

'In half an hour I've got to go and see that Samuels woman who's got a list for sale of those Hollywood superstars who enjoy three-in-a-bed sex.'

Gore-Bellamy reached over and gave her bottom a quite vicious slap.

Alex closed her eyes. Always it's the rough trade I go for, she said to herself. Why in hell is it always the roughs? She got back on the bed.

'I hate you,' she said.

'Yeah, they all do,' he said, turning towards her.

Meanwhile, in Lady Alice's Peel Tower, Lord Sidmonton, Master of the Walpole Club, who had turned up in a rather large chauffeur-driven hire car, was welcomed, if that is the word, by Lady Alice.

'What a surprise, Hubert!' she said, ushering him into the drawing-room and smiling sweetly. 'I haven't been honoured with a visit from you since you and Parthenope stayed here for quite a few delightful weeks in 1984, I think it was. Do you remember? You had a case in Durham and Parthenope found the hotels a little expensive. And how *is* your dear Parthenope? Has that place on her face cleared up?'

'Now Alice that was a long time ago and you know perfectly well that it was just a small, temporary rash . . . '

'Of course, of course, rich foods . . . the thing about skin diseases, of course, is that you never die of them but they never get better! Oh, what fun it all is! But you've come to see Milly, not me. I'll fetch her.'

She tottered off and left Lord Sidmonton to glare disapprovingly at the room with its musty smell and higgledy-piggledy arrangement of an old lady's whims collected over the years from higgledy-piggledy travels. There were oriental engraved brass table-tops supported on fretwork legs, an enormous black lacquer screen with mother-of-pearl birds of paradise flying across it, an ordinary escritoire enlivened with uncommon marquetry.

He moved gingerly through the brass tables towards a huge old sofa which looked potentially comfortable.

There was a squeal and something bit him sharply on the ankle. He kicked out viciously but his shoe failed to connect with an animal and glanced off a brass table-top which rang like a temple gong.

Milly came in.

'Milly, my dear,' he said, in the loud yet mellifluous voice adopted by lawyers when bullying a witness, 'I need your help. More, I think I have the right to demand your help.'

He waved a hand graciously towards a chair near the sofa, in the manner of George III at Windsor Castle inviting Fanny Burney to sit down in his presence after she had been standing for a couple of hours.

'I'm having trouble with William,' he said. 'When you

begged me to find him work I had high hopes that appointing him our Club Secretary would prove beneficial to both parties. Alas, I was dangerously wrong.'

'What's happened?' asked Milly, intrigued as to why Uncle Sid was putting on this performance of being a sadly let-down benefactor.

'William's bent on doing something which is going seriously to upset our oldest and most important Club members, our distinguished actors and lawyers, our titled landowners, they are all very worried. I hoped at first that the fact that William didn't come from the same social and cultural background as us wouldn't matter but I'm afraid it's proved an insurmountable problem. Take for instance his appointing to the important job of club chef a complete oick . . . '

'A complete *what*?' said Milly.

'Oick! *Oick!* As I was saying, William's appointment of a complete oick was bound to lead to disaster sooner or later. You should see this oick. Long, greasy blond hair . . . '

'Uncle Sid,' said Milly. 'What *are* you going on about?'

'Your William, my dear, has completely lost the respect of the members because of his extraordinary behaviour and lack of judgement. I personally give no credence to the strong rumours that he has become romantically attached to Mrs Hardcastle our extremely attractive lady accountant; as you know I never listen to rumours but there is rarely smoke without some sort of fire. And now William's latest escapade is causing such wide concern that the members are asking me to remove him from office before he can seriously damage the Club.'

Milly was taken by surprise by all this. She realized that she'd not given much serious thought as to what William actually did at the Walpole. She had taken it for granted, when she thought about it at all, that being a club secretary meant that William did the sort of work normally done in an office by a secretary, answering the phone, writing letters, filing files, getting coffee. She was astonished that William was in a position to influence senior Club members strongly enough to cause Uncle Sid to put on such a histrionic display.

'Uncle Sid,' said Milly. 'I'm a big girl now. I think it's time you braced yourself and told me exactly what devilish deed William is about to do and why you think I should stop him doing it.'

'All right,' said Uncle Sid. 'A group of raffish members, all undesirables but difficult to get rid of under membership rules, have deceived ordinary decent members, including a distinguished clergyman, into accepting a grotesque and indeed indecent way of celebrating the Club's two hundred and fiftieth birthday.' He paused dramatically. 'On behalf of these ne'er-do-wells, your husband is organizing an orgy to take place on the dining-room floor.'

Milly's first reaction was to burst into peals of laughter at the thought of anything rude and passionate happening on the well-Ronuked and chill parquet floor of the Club dining-room, but this would be unhelpful. Her second thought was to wonder why William had got himself involved in such shabby fun and games. Was he in what Pippa would call 'a leg-over situation' with Mrs Hardcastle after all which would mean that she posed a real threat to Milly?

'Oh, bloody hell with ice and bloody lemon,' said Milly, half to herself.

'You simply must persuade William to give up this folly, Millamant, and to do what I tell him to do. I need hardly remind you that you owe this to Parthenope and me.'

'I think I'd better do what I can to help you,' she said to Uncle Sid after some thought. 'The whole thing sounds a bit offish, and William does seem to be behaving oddly. Why on earth didn't he tell me what he was getting involved in?'

'Indeed, indeed,' said Lord Sidmonton sadly. 'Such secretive behaviour. You see what I've been up against?'

'I'll have a good talk to him when I get home the day after tomorrow.'

'We're all relying on you,' said Lord Sidmonton.

When great-aunt Alice had finished listening at the dining-room window she went and sat on the lawn, in the sunshine, next to Estelle's Foster. She had drawn up her deckchair next to Foster and was examining his profile with her magnifying glass.

'So fine,' she breathed. 'Such masculinity. Fortunate, fortunate Estelle!'

Foster was doing the crossword in a two-day-old *Daily Telegraph* and did not notice. Or pretended not to notice.

They were joined by Estelle who dragged Foster from beneath the magnifying glass to show him, she told great-aunt Alice, the magnificent view from the upper windows of the tower.

'Off you go with him!' said Lady Alice, positively leering.

The young people made their way in a kind of dreamy silence up the five flights of narrow stairs to the tiny attic room with the magnificent view.

They did not look at the view.

'There is a legend', said Foster, 'that the longest screen kiss in the history of the cinema was in a wartime film with Jane Wyman. I think it was three and a half minutes. It's time the record was beaten.'

He held her and they kissed for ever.

Eventually: 'Will you marry me?' he said.

'Oh, my love,' she said. 'Oh, my love.'

'I don't quite know what we'll live on,' he said, 'but

until I get a degree and a job, neither of them all that easy to acquire, I have a bit coming in from the trumpet and any moment now your Trio is going to make steady money – it's a very good trio, you know.'

'Oh, my love,' she said. 'How soon can I have a baby?'

'Estelle!' he said. And they had another go at Jane Wyman's record.

When they told great-aunt Alice she let out a great shriek of pleasure.

'You must get married in Durham cathedral,' she ordered. 'I will arrange it all, the Dean is an old friend. And have your wedding-breakfast here. Mrs Owlglass is rotten at scrambled eggs but magnificent at cooking celebratory feasts. Oh, happy, happy day!'

When Estelle and Foster had drifted into the shrubbery not to look at more views, Lady Alice took herself to the phone and rang her good friend Lady Wick at Wick Castle.

'I couldn't help overhearing what that cunning old conniver Sidmonton was saying to Milly because I was listening,' she said. 'One advantage of being bent over like a starting handle is that I can stand under the drawing-room window and hear every word. And this is what he said. Do pass it all on to dear old Duncan immediately, won't you?'

And she recounted to Lady Wick everything Lord Sidmonton had said to Milly.

Half an hour after that William's phone rang in his office.

'William? This is Duncan Wick phoning from bonny Scotland. Actually it's not bonny at all, it's pissing with rain. However. Remember my telling you about the Ladies' Social Mafia and its powers as an intelligence-gathering organization? Well, my dear wife passed the word down the line that we wanted to know what any lady had on Lord Sidmonton and Parthenope and Milly and the Orange. Reports have been coming in and seem to me to be most helpful to our cause.'

'If Sidmonton has been bullying Milly, I'll . . . '

'No, no, he's been doing a pathetic act, imploring her help. Old Alice heard everything through the window and he's been lying like a trooper, saying that you're about to corrupt us all and we hate you and the chef is a disaster and an oick. What's an oick?'

'Originally, I think, one who spits.'

'Charming. Well, Milly is going to try to persuade you to drop the Orange when she arrives home the day after tomorrow. But there's been a development there. Gwen Farringdon-Trace-Farringdon says that it's Milly's parents' wedding anniversary the day after tomorrow. They'd forgotten all about it and suddenly decided to throw a small dinner party at their house in Fulham. Milly has been ordered to attend and you will get your orders tomorrow first post.'

'Oh, Gawd! What a time and place to have a row with Milly! Will the Master be there?'

'Happily no. Old Maude Tansey says that he and Parthenope are dining with her brother at Brougham. Minor royalty has accepted so the Sidmontons will *definitely* be there.'

'Anything more, sir? I am going down now to explain my food ideas to Anton. If he, please God, approves we are pretty well on course. I would very much like to involve you in our last problem, the female cabaret. I'll ring you tomorrow about that if I may. I have a clue, thanks to good old Chidders, which may lead us to discover who is paying Tozer and I have high hopes that we will win that battle. So that's the position down here.'

'Excellent. Chefs are highly unpredictable beings so good luck with Anton. And William . . . '

'Sir?'

'Very well done, so far.'

'Just one thing more, sir. Did the bush telegraph have anything on what mischief Parthenope has been stirring up?'

'Oh, didn't I tell you? She is the puppeteer pulling the strings in all this. And I'll tell you why . . . '

William descended to the chef's little office to persuade Anton to accept his ideas of what the menu should be, based upon a close study he had made of Edgar's breakdown of members' favourite main courses and puds.

As Anton, stirred by the challenge of serving up the alien bakemeats described in Lord Wick's book, enthused over the potential delights of such rare treats as parrot-fish stuffed with salmon and *veziga* – the dried spinal marrow of the sturgeon – and Middle-Eastern young goat roasted in olive oil, and some imaginative uses of fried locusts, William reflected on how much Anton had changed in the few months he had been at the Club. Matured by success? Or influenced to the good by his strong-minded girlfriend? Both?

Anton's hair had grown in so well that he no longer needed William's father-in-law's wig. This was returned to William washed by Anton's girl and beautifully clean but looking even more like a wig and even less like human hair than ever. Most surprising of all, perhaps, Anton had hired a new pastry chef whose name was Pipo.

'But I thought . . . ?' said William when Anton told him he had taken on a Mauritian creole as pastry chef.

'Don't you fret, mate,' said Anton. 'Jobs in white Britain should still go to white Britishers, I say. And that. But the way Pipo makes pastry . . . the instructors back at the Tech could learn a hell of a lot from Pipo just watching him rolling out. Those fingers, tough but capable of working so delicately. I tell you, never mind his fancy *petits fours* as light as angels' kisses or his sporting gents' golden game-pie crusts, I could flog his breakfast croissants any Sunday morning down Petticoat Lane for three quid a bleeding pair.'

And Anton had done his homework. He showed William his notebook of exotic game birds and fish which the wholesale dealers at Billingsgate could supply. He had found out how they should or could be served and he was raring to go.

'What do you reckon, squire?' he said. 'Shall we select a menu from this little lot? Or do you want me to seek out more alien flesh and fish to impress our members and give 'em the trots?'

William considered rapidly how to put his ideas to Anton without Anton reacting in a chef-like manner and either resigning in a welter of obscenities or coming at William with a meat axe.

'Terrific,' William said. 'But the food is such a vital part of the Orange that I've been giving it a lot of thought. It seems to me that we don't just want to put on a pretend orgy with the sort of food which the ancient Greeks and Romans enjoyed. We don't happen to *be* Greeks and Romans.'

'Praised be the Lord,' said Anton piously but warily, wondering what was coming.

'Something that Brandreth Jacques said about having luxuries to eat got me thinking. And then something *you* said clinched it in my mind. An orgy, in its day, was really an excess of pleasure. To the ancients it meant, as far as food and drink were concerned, a whole lot of the stuff which they loved to eat and drink but couldn't afford. To Mr Jacques this meant oysters. An admirable beginning to our Orange feast. I suggest to you – only suggest, it's up to you – that the first course should be great platefuls of oysters on all the tables, opened and lying in shaved ice, with thin brown bread and butter, slices of lemon, and so on. Also fat jars of caviare. That Greek journalist and professional rich man named Taki once wrote that you know you are rich when you put your spoon into the caviare jar and it doesn't touch bottom. Well, the Club's rich for just that one night. So let our night begin with loads of oysters and caviare and champagne.'

Anton seemed sunk in gloomy thought. 'Then what?' muttered Anton. 'After the oysters and caviare, then what?'

'I researched the favourite menu items ordered by members over the last two months and it set me thinking,' said William. 'I want you to work up two small but different menus.'

'Like a Chinese restaurant in Leeds?' said Anton. 'Canton on the left-hand page and pie and chips on the right?'

'A bit like that,' said William. 'I want you to give the members a choice of either a small selection of traditional English club food, a joint, a pheasant, a venison pie.' Like Charlie Chaplin's boot from *The Gold Rush* in pastry William thought of saying to lighten the mood of the meeting but wisely didn't. 'And the second menu, a sample selection of your foreign delicacies from Billingsgate, mainly, I gather, small edible fauna stuffed into larger edible fauna stuffed into even larger edible fauna. You could do your little nut over that part of the menu and really enjoy yourself.'

'And then?' muttered Anton, ominously.

'Lastly,' said William, 'for the triumphant finish to our dinner of guiltless self-indulgence we're going to offer our old gentlemen a further feast of the food which our records show they really enjoy. Good old-fashioned suet puddings, rice puddings, bread-and-butter puddings, the heavy puds they loved at boarding-school and in the army which no modern wife will have anything to do with and they can only get now at the Club.'

Anton seemed to have fallen asleep. His eyes were closed and he was breathing rather heavily. He suddenly sat up with a jerk, mind made up.

'I can relate to that,' he said. 'Bloody good thinking, guv. In fact, *bloody* good thinking!'

William immensely relieved, thought it a nice distinction.

'It's the Mars Bar syndrome, innit? That's what it's all about,' Anton said.

'Of course,' said William. 'For which, Anton, grateful thanks. We'll give our members the chance to feast on what they really like but aren't allowed to eat at home because it's fattening and unfashionable.'

'I'll do Figgy Duff!' said Anton in ringing tones. 'And I'll do 'em Marmalade Sponge, Spotted Dick . . . !'

He jumped up and wrung William's hand.

'You and me together!' he cried emotionally. 'Particularly me because the food's so important, we're gonna make this an Itchy . . . '

'Orange,' said William.

' . . . Orgy to remember!' said Anton.

CHAPTER THIRTEEN

WHIRLPOOL BATHS
AND TURKISH DELIGHTS

The following day was a difficult one for all concerned, with the exception perhaps of thin but radiant Estelle who seemed to be floating around about nine inches above the earth's surface.

'She won't be able to play a note this evening!' said Pippa. 'Just look at her. She hasn't been more than a cuff-link away from her Foster since breakfast.'

'It's a good feeling,' said Milly. 'No, it isn't, it's much more than that, being in love is a great feeling, the best there is. I remember it well.'

'I've known it,' said Pippa, 'in my time. Not a lot of it but enough to reduce me from a rational, semi-intelligent cellist to a grinning lump of goo. You still get a bit of it over your William, now don't you? Be honest.'

Milly was quiet for a moment. They both watched as Estelle and Foster drifted past them hand in hand. 'I can't read William at the moment,' said Milly. 'He's off into some area where I can't follow him.'

'Well, you'll be home tomorrow night. You must have it out with William there and then. Make him understand how miserable his odd behaviour has been making you. Really go for him.'

'Nothing's ever simple, is it?' said Milly. 'My parents have suddenly remembered that tomorrow is their wedding anniversary and William and I are bidden to dinner. Now *that's* a fine time and place to have a blazing row!'

'Nevertheless you've got to. What does William think he's doing? He's leaving you in the dark and behaving like The Phantom of the Walpole.'

'One good thing for the future of the Trio has come out of Estelle's romance,' said Milly. 'It seems that Estelle's grandmother is not too well and as Estelle's mother has never liked the cold of England, Papa is going to take her home for good. Estelle rang him this morning and Papa's delighted about Foster. Papa's been longing to return with Mama to their sunny island and they'll be off in a matter of weeks. He's leaving his property business for Foster to run, and Foster is London School of Economics, remember?'

'Papa's business? Papa's debts, you mean,' said Pippa.

'Incredible though it may sound, Estelle says that Papa has left his business in credit. Probably by about one pound fifty, but not in debt. Foster and Estelle are planning a wonderful Aunt Alice wedding up here in Durham sometime in September. And – this is interesting – as from now, Foster is going to be the Trio's agent and manager!'

'Well, well, well!' said the Hon. Pippa.

'Let's hope so,' said Milly.

It was a strange day for William, a day of suspended animation with not much to look forward to. The next evening Milly would arrive back dog-tired from the drive down from Durham and briefed by Uncle Sid would pitch into William at her parents' dinner party at the Parsons Green end of Fulham.

William's invitation from Milly's mother, more like a magistrate's summons than the offer of a fun evening, came in the first post and gave him no room for manoeuvre. 'We will be sitting down at eight p.m.,' his mother-in-law had written, 'so be there not later than seven thirty to help with the drinks. And do wear something tidy.'

The last command infuriated William with its

implication that unless instructed otherwise he would turn up for dinner dressed like the violinist Nigel Kennedy in mutinous mood. In fact William dressed tidily most of the time because the work he found himself doing usually called for it, and anyway it was not in his nature to be concerned with personal plumage. In the Club he usually wore his No. 2 suit, a thin, darkish, boring tweed, and for evening social occasions he changed into his other, No. 1 suit, the sincere grey worsted.

As he cycled to the Club he noticed a series of small but new squeaks and wobbles and realized that his bike was at last beginning to show symptoms of its great age. The teeth of the rear sprocket had worn down over the years and the chain now tended to slip, making him lurch forward over the handlebars. Sometimes it came off entirely which meant getting off, wherever he happened to be, up-ending the bike, removing the old-fashioned chain guard and fiddling the chain back on. Also the weld was beginning to come apart where the crossbar joined the front forks, and the coil springs were about to work their way through the leather of the saddle and bite the rider in painful places.

When he arrived at the Club he inspected the bike carefully before padlocking it to the kitchen-waste bin. It seemed safe enough for a few more journeys. Perhaps he would put it into The Shepherd's Bush Bikery for servicing at the weekend.

'*SAH!*' roared Chidders, saluting cheerfully and holding the door open. Then quietly, without moving his lips, 'Now you'ze arrised let day's lurk connence.'

'What?' said William.

'Nothing new to retort hron nister Tozer down delow,' said Chidders.

William guessed, correctly, that Chidders in his enthusiasm for his role as the Club's undercover agent had got hold of a *Teach Yourself Ventriloquism* manual and was putting in some heavy practice.

'Has he been in touch with the newspaper again? It's terribly important to find out which paper it is. As soon as possible,' said William.

'No, hir. Nododdy has telehoned hin since yesterday arsternoon. He honed out a cuttla tines dut only to gook tickets to the Codent Garden Otera and to hone hor a taxi to Taddington Station.'

'Brilliant, Chidders, but I think you could speak in your normal voice when there's just the two of us.'

'Hank you, hir,' said Chidders. 'It *is* a dit tiring.'

'It certainly is,' said William, 'but thank you for taking the trouble.' He made for the stairs.

'Nodadall,' said Chidders, managing a rather sinister, rigid-jawed grin. 'I do lot I can to helk, sir.'

William was hoping to see Belkis and hear her idea for the Orange's cabaret but she was not in her office so he went along to his own and put in an hour dictating replies to letters.

After that he turned to the Suggestions Book. Members were returning from holiday bronzed and rested or broke and exhausted but many of them were beginning to get into a party mood.

The first entry in the pages as yet unreplied to by William was from a hatchet-faced retired headmaster who had never been in a party mood in his life. He complained at least weekly about the way the Club was run.

As you must be aware, I am the last person to complain about how this club is run. But my hand is forced by circumstances. May I ask, and I have no doubt at all that I speak for a number of responsible and concerned members, on what authority the Bridge Club has been ejected from the Card Room on the

*night of the Birthday Celebrations? It is true that we
have been offered use of the library for that evening
but the library's atmosphere of semi-intellectual
hedonism is not at all right for serious players of
bridge. Rumour has it that our room has been hijacked
(a vulgar modernism but the right word in this context)
so that birthday diners may have somewhere to put
their coats! Can this possibly be true?*

H.B.L.Trowbridge MA

*It can and is. It was a democratic decision
arrived at by your elected Events Committee.
The alternative, suggested by the Chairman,
Lord Wick, was that diners hung their coats on
the spikes of the railings outside.*

W.G.

The next was what William deemed a routine entry:

*Anent Maurice Upglass's interesting comment on
Thomas à Becket's height, I rather think that when
Professor Upglass referred to E.M. Forster's love for
Bambi, he meant to say Forster's love for Bombay.*

Gerard Apsley Cunningham

Gratefully noted.

W.G.

The next three entries were from members trying, after
a good lunch, to be waggish about the roller-towel affair
and called for no comment.

The last entry came from a member called Emmanuel
Smallpiece, a quiet, elderly man who imported Chinese
powdered eggs for the bakery trade and whose surname
gave limitless amusement to the sort of member who wrote

unfunny post-luncheon remarks in the Suggestions Book about the roller-towel affair:

> *I wonder why our Club Birthday Dinner should*
> *be so shrouded in mystery? The two other functions*
> *on the Big Evening are frank and open about*
> *what is on offer to members – and what is offered*
> *is first-class and suitably eighteenth century in my*
> *opinion – that is to say, the whitebait dinner and a*
> *night gambling on the relative speed of greyhounds.*
> *But we are told nothing about the House Dinner.*
> *Are there reasons for this secrecy?*
>
> E. Smallpiece

> *Indeed there are. The Events Committee wants it*
> *to be a surprise evening. To retain this element of*
> *mystery the dinner has been given the code-name*
> *of 'Orange' and its menu and entertainment*
> *have been kept secret. As members fortunate*
> *enough to attend the Orange will become aware*
> *on the night, the rumours circulating the Club*
> *now as to what will happen during our Orange*
> *are hilariously wide of the mark.*
>
> W.G.

Well, thought William as he heaved the volume back on its shelf, that should give Tozer pause for thought. If he reads the Suggestions Book. But Tozer no doubt reads everything in the Club which is at all private.

William rang through to Belkis's office but there was still no reply so he thought he would have an early bite to eat and give himself a long afternoon, which would be useful if he had to go on a cabaret crawl.

He made for the bar.

William had quite early on realized that an essential technique in surviving as a club secretary was to avoid members as though they were chicken-pox positive when big issues were being debated among the membership. Club matters to aged members with all the time in the world on their hands were like politics to retired French postmen in cafés, to be discussed by all at little depth but loudly and at tremendous length. A good club secretary quickly works out routes of back-doubles, little-used corridors, staff staircases and unused rooms through which he can move invisibly, like a mouse behind the wainscoting.

This time it did not quite work. William went downstairs, into the laundry room and out of its back door into a small corridor which let the housekeeper and maids get at the tiny service lift which went up to the bedrooms. He got out at the top floor, went through Bedroom 4A, a vast and dusty old room which had been unused since before the war when a minor cabinet minister had been discovered in bed with his lover, who should have been back at Eton playing scrum-half in a needle Rugger match against Marlborough. The member was asked by the PM kindly to oblige the party by shooting himself, which, being a man of honour, he did.

William climbed through the window onto the fire escape, descended and climbed back into the building through the window of the morning-room, which had a door through to the bar.

But the morning-room was not empty and he was nabbed.

'My dear feller, a word?'

A bulky member rose from an armchair.

'If you're worrying why I climbed in through the window . . . ' said William.

'Oh, my dear feller, not at all. I presume you're cleaning

the windows. Have you quite closed them, by the way? These old sashes can often jam an eighth of an inch or even more and let in a dangerous draught.'

William tried to compose his face into an expression of charming concern, or failing that courteous anxiety but he had blundered into eye contact with H. Barrington Blessington, a vast, red-faced, ex-sports commentator, a rather irascible man who was the Club's number one hypochondriac.

'Wanted a word,' Blessington said. 'Can't be too careful, hey? Better to prevent than cure. Every time.'

William waited glumly. H.B.Blessington's previous move on the hygiene front was a demand for a supply of patent paper mats impregnated with germ-attacking chemicals which members could insert between themselves and the lavatory seat thus avoiding vile diseases. William found that these paper things were obtainable at ridiculous expense from those states in the USA which were prone to personal hygiene neuroses, which was nearly all of them. He arranged instead for the cleaner to be provided with a new mop.

Mr Blessington's redeeming virtue was that his hypochondria was not very organized and as soon as an exciting new danger to his health presented itself he completely forgot about the old one.

'Extremely worried, old boy,' he said. 'Discovered something. We in the Club are sitting on a time bomb. Just waiting to go off, then POUFFFF! Could destroy or severely damage all human life within the radius of at least a mile. Which includes, I need hardly say, St James's Palace.'

William pondered. 'Is your worry the wonky electric heater in Bedroom Four? It's got a fuse, you know.'

'No, it's not that. Though perhaps I should look into it. Wonky and electric, you say? Bedroom Four . . . ?'

William cursed himself for handing the man food for further worry.

'Perhaps you're concerned about the small crack that appeared last month in the billiard-room ceiling?' said William. 'A breeding-ground for killer ladybirds?'

'No, no, no,' said H.B.Blessington. 'What I'm concerned about is the bubbly bath in Bedroom Six.'

'Oh,' said William, relieved. 'Our dear old Jacuzzi. I wouldn't worry too much about that, it's a museum piece, a gift from a member who was high up in the sanitary porcelain trade. The only member to use it for the last ten years has been Lord Wick when bathing his dog.'

'I don't think you've got my drift,' said Mr Blessington. 'Actually, as a matter of actual fact, it *isn't* a Jacuzzi. "Jacuzzi" is a trade name which like "Hoover" has come to be used for all makes of the same sort of thing. Our fizzy bath is more properly a "whirlpool".'

'You seem to know a great deal about Jacuzzis and whirlpools, sir. Is it a professional interest?'

'Not at all. I just happen to belong to a kind of health club in Greek Street called The Whirlpool Club. Well, I thought it was a health club. It was recommended to me by an old friend Toothy Dent. Know Toothy? Jolly soul. Well, on old Toothy's sayso I paid a stiff subscription and joined this so-called health club in Greek Street. There was, for Soho, a largish room in which they had a couple of rusty exercise bikes that needed servicing and a machine for developing the pectoral muscles which didn't work, and a members-only bar with drinks at astronomical prices. But the main event, as they say at boxing-matches, was a stage at the end of the room which had four Whirlpool baths on it made of glass or plastic, anyway see-through and filled with hot water. Every hour, on the hour, a thug walked on stage and switched on the electric motors. The baths bubbled away and four prettyish girls in bikinis came on, got in, took off their bikini tops and cavorted in the bubbles for ten minutes while the punters ogled.'

'A little tame for Soho?'

'Yes, but it livened up a bit after a while. A gentleman originally from foreign parts, Malta I think, accompanied by a friend about ten feet tall and wide with it, came round with a bus conductor's satchel asking members for another tenner apiece. You either left at that point or coughed up. For those who stayed, the girls shed their bikini bottoms and re-cavorted in the bubbles, sticking their behinds out of the water and shrieking prettily as though they were schoolgirls having a terrific time in the local municipal swimming baths.'

William reflected, not for the first time, that garrulity seemed to go with hypochondria. 'I don't quite see, sir, as yet, where the time-bomb comes in. What sort of dreadful occurrence does a bubbly bath presage? Apart from eternal damnation for joining a squalid peepshow like the Whirlpool Club?'

H. Barrington Blessington gripped William's upper arm quite painfully and bent his head down towards William's ear. 'Legionnaires' disease!' he said.

'What about it?' said William, affecting ignorance. Always a useful ploy in moments like these.

'What about it? I'll tell you what about it, young man! It's mushrooming all over London and it kills! Don't you read your Thursday's *Daily Telegraph* Medical Section pullout? Legionnaires' disease is spread by a bacteria which breeds swiftly unless it's located and destroyed. And where does it breed? Where does this killer, this time bomb in our bosom, flourish? In warm and static water. Like, young man, the warm and static water which remains in the complex pipes of a whirlpool bath after the pump has been turned off! That's what about it!'

'Have you warned the Whirlpool Club about the danger?' asked William.

'I tried,' said Mr Blessington. 'The Maltese owner punched me in the abdomen. It was as high as he could reach. Didn't hurt much, and I can look after myself even at my age. I countered with a short left jab to his ribs and a right to the side of his head, bom-bom. Luckily it was the small Maltese, the big one had an appointment with his chiropodist that morning. This problem with whirlpool baths is well known, you know; there's special disinfectant stuff you can buy which you pour in and pump round the system after the bath's used. Have you done that to our time-bomb in Bedroom Six?'

'Well, no,' said William, 'but nobody's reported anything wrong. As I said, the only user of our whirlpool bath in the last few years has been Lord Wick's dog and she seems all right. Mind you she tends to pee the carpet. Is that a symptom?'

'I'm not sure you're taking this Club health crisis with quite the seriousness it demands.'

'I'm sorry to have given that impression, sir. In fact I am grateful for your information and will make sure that from now on our whirlpool is clean round its bends.'

With a bleak nod Mr Blessington strode past William and into the bar.

William gave up any thought of following him into the bar and nipped into the almost empty dining-room instead, ordering himself an omelette, chips and cheeses. And a quarter carafe of the house white wine – not that he particularly wanted it but he was blowed if he was going to let Blessington outmanoeuvre him and stop him having a drink.

It was a good, light lunch and enjoyable because he was joined at the table by the young publisher who was organizing the alternative birthday events. His preparations were going well and the two lists of members wanting to participate in the Greenwich Whitebait Feast and the Dog Racing Dinner were full and closed. Everybody was happy and enthusiastic. William could only report back, fingers crossed, that the old members' mystery birthday dinner was proceeding according to plan and he had high hopes of a memorable evening entirely suitable to the occasion.

The dining-room was beginning to fill with early lunchers and as William made his way out he was able to grin reassuringly at Sol Fish. In fact William grinned reassuringly at all those members and guests who seemed to be looking at him anxiously. In the doorway he bumped into the Sporting Baronet on his way in. Sir Archie nodded affably at William.

'Sir Archibald!' said William, in a sudden mischievous mood. 'What a surprise! Lord Wick told me you'd gone to Norway!'

Sir Archie fixed William with his watery gaze and said without the slightest pause, 'Didn't have to. Trouble turned out to be a sudden infestation of Dutch Spruce Fever-Beetle. It's the warm weather, you know. Rang the people in Norway and they told me what spray to use.'

'Diluted H.42, I imagine,' said William, countering.

'Only for the younger trees,' said Sir Archie, quite unperturbed by William's bit of invention. 'For the older growths it has to be Pheno-Filo-Paraquench, half a fluid ounce to a litre. Sven suggested spraying from a light aircraft.'

'If only you'd thought of telling Lord Wick that you'd cancelled your trip to Norway, the Events Committee's emergency meeting could have been held before Thursday after all,' said William, bowling a bumpy one.

'Telephoned him this morning,' said Sir Archie, easily stopping the ball dead with a straight bat. 'He wasn't in.'

'Odd,' said William. 'I spoke to him this morning.'

'Well, I didn't,' said Sir Archie. 'His wife said he was out walking his dog.'

Four-all, thought William, and no passes. He grinned amiably at Sir Archie who grinned his crooked grin back at William in perfect understanding and they went their ways.

Belkis was in her office this time, sitting at her desk juggling with lists and leaflets. She peered over the top of large reading-glasses at William.

'Belkis,' said William, 'for some reason you are looking spectacularly sexy at this moment.'

'I have arranged doings with my husband,' said Belkis. 'Mr Hardcastle will hire the sound equipment for us and install it himself in the dining-room on the afternoon of the Orange. This morning I went to a firm which builds exhibition stands and hired the platform for Mr Jacques to stand himself upon at the thin end of the dining-room. I have also arranged for lots of flowers to be supplied and arranged that afternoon.'

'Terrific!' said William. 'You really are coping beautifully.'

'If I may speak to you with solemnity,' said Belkis, removing her reading glasses and by so doing, thought William, reducing herself from being spectacularly sexy to being merely desirable. Not as sincerely desirable as Milly but sort of *theoretically* desirable.

'What's up?' said William.

'I am heavily worried about the effect putting on the Orange is having on you,' said Belkis. 'There are elephant-sized problems which your wife should be helping you with but she knows nothing about them. Because you don't talk to Milly about them, do you?'

'The last thing I want to do is burden my Milly with . . .'

'A husband's problems are not a burden, Willy. Sharing problems is the contact adhesive which binds a marriage together. You treat Milly as though she were a beautiful, fragile little harpsichordist, not a working partner. Marriage is struggling together through fat and skinny, Willy, and sharing everything, including worries. And respecting the other one, not just protecting them.'

'Is that how it works with you and Malcolm?'

'Not all the times because Malcolm likes to spend the evenings bent over his computer manuals and marking the table with his mini soldering-iron instead of reading aloud to me. But it's how it works when we run into any sort of crisis. Like now. He will be at home waiting to help me and nothing will be too bothersome for him, until our Orange is safely – oh, what's the word?'

'Squeezed?'

'That is a colourful and useful word, Willy, but what I had in mind was "over".'

'Belk,' said William, changing his tone of voice to indicate a change of subject. 'There are a couple of points I wanted to bring up. Clothes for Brandy Jack's compèring. I think we should hire him a decent set of white tie and tails, shirt and so on. He'll have to get them and we'll pay. OK? The other thing was the thought you had for the Orange cabaret. Is it the sort of thing I could investigate this afternoon or Monday? Time's getting so short.'

'Oh, yes, the girls give shows on most days. It was Mrs Addington who told me about this cabaret in which her daughter Trixie takes part. You know Mrs Addington, she Hoovers upstairs Mondays and Fridays? Well, she thought I might be interested in joining the show, earn a bit of pocket-money, but Malcolm would hit the sky if I took up that kind of thing.'

'What kind of thing?'

'Synchronized stripping.'

'Good God!' said William. 'What on earth's that?'

'You need not look so potty-faced, Willy. It is all quite innocent. Well, fairly innocent. The team of girls do a strip-tease in perfect unison. The act is owned and trained by a professional ex-Crazy Horse stripper named Bimbo Babyoil.'

'Good grief!' said William.

'They don't necessarily take *everything* off. Well, not to begin with. The trouble is, according to Mrs Addington's Trixie, the girls find it gets more exciting the more they take off and then they want to travel the whole hog. Six girls have been trained by Miss Babyoil – what a name of curiosity! – trained to a hairswidth to undress naked in perfect unison to a tape of Shirley Bassey singing "I Who Have Nothing". The troupe, known professionally as Six of the Bust, strip in clubs and pubs for a nice fee. Miss Babyoil takes half of the fee but that is life, is it not?'

William could think of absolutely nothing to say.

'Six of the Bust might be just the cabaret you are looking for, William, eh? Mrs Addington's Trixie assures her mother that the act is highly tasteful artistic-wise, the girls are all nice and don't touch the men or do depraved deeds. What do you think?'

'It's a possible,' said William. 'With only a week to go things are getting desperate. But Belk, tell me frankly, don't you think any kind of strip-tease, however nice the girls, is a just a bit *too* sleazy for the Club?'

Belkis pondered for a moment and then sighed. 'There's a smallish thing which worries me, Willy, and that is Mrs Addington's Trixie, whose opinions we are relying on. About six weeks ago Trixie put in for a job here as a summer temp waitress. Mrs Baxter interviewed her and her report said "Pretty girl but not for us: basically, I am afraid, a rather pert little slut." '

'Oh, dear!' said William. 'Oh, dear indeed!'

He went to his own office and felt yet another twinge of panic that the Orange was now only a week away. It was really time for quick action and bold decisions and he badly needed an ally to help him to decide. After a brief deliberation he rang Lord Wick.

The phone was answered by a Scottish maid with a Highland accent heavy enough to carve into a portrait bust of the poet Burns. After tactful repetition of his question William at last grasped that His Lordship was in London at his rooms in Albert Hall Mansions and was not expected back in Scotland for some days. She obligingly found the telephone number and gave it to William.

Lord Wick was at home at the flat and answered the phone.

'I hope I'm not interrupting anything important,' William said.

'It's all relative, really, isn't it?' said His Lordship. 'You see I'm having a training session of "lie down and die for your King and Country" with my dog. What I mean is, it's not all that important an activity for me but Madeleine absolutely loves it. The bit she likes best is the end when I roll over on my back and stick my arms and legs straight up in the air. She rushes over and licks my ears. To bring me back to life, I suppose. It's instinct, y'know.'

'Are you by any chance free this afternoon?'

' 'Fraid not. The reason I'm down here in the Great Wen is a board-meeting this afternoon. Bank of Scotland. What were you about to suggest?'

'I thought that if you happened to be free we could go together and investigate a potential cabaret for the Orange.'

'What sort of potential cabaret had you in mind?'

'I suppose we really have got to grasp the nettle and have a look at a girlie show in Soho. Mrs Addington, our upstairs cleaner, has recommended a strip-tease in which her daughter performs.'

There was a very long silence at Lord Wick's end. Then a little gentle whiffling sound grew and William realized that Lord Wick was laughing.

'O William, William!' he said. 'A board-meeting of the Bank of Scotland or a strip club! What a choice!'

'I can't manage tomorrow as Milly's coming home,' said William. 'Are you free perhaps on Monday afternoon?'

'I am indeed. My dear wife is meeting an old Parisian friend for tea and the two of them are going shopping. There is nothing I would like more than to be in your company and watch young ladies taking off their small-clothes for our delight. Does one cheer as bits come off?'

'I don't know, sir, I've never been to one of these performances.'

'Do these young ladies actually shed – you know – their bodices and all their other accoutrements?'

'To music I am told, sir. Shirley Bassey.'

'Oh, I like her!' said His Lordship. After a pause he went on, quietly and sincerely: 'I cannot express, William, how much I am looking forward to Monday afternoon. There is just one small thought bothering me.'

'Sir?'

'My wife frequently picks up the extension phone to check that the call is not for her. If my dear wife is listening to this conversation I'm a dead man.'

William made his way back down the stairs to the bar, hoping that the boring hypochondriac would by now be tearing into a nourishing carrot salad in the dining-room.

The bar was indeed without bore. And at the limpets' end stood, of all people, Brandy Jack.

'Mr Jacques!' said William with genuine pleasure. 'What a surprise. I didn't expect to see you here on a Thursday. I thought it was Fridays only.'

'No, once a year I come on a Thursday instead,' said

Branny, 'it's the day when Philly goes on his annual visit to Aldershot cemetery to tidy up his mother's grave.'

'Aldershot!'

'She used to live there. Did you think she was in the army? Old Philly trots off every year with his carrier-bag full of flowers and a clean jam-jar and a cheese sandwich for his lunch. And I come here. Same ritual every year. It's to commemorate his most happy anniversary.'

'Happy! The day his mother died!'

'No, no, no, no! Today is the anniversary of Philly's only win ever on the horses. He had a pound on a horse running at Sandown Park and it came in at forty to one. He bought his mother a gold-plated wristwatch, the only thing of any value she had ever owned and she loved it. She died on the following Boxing Day. A win worth commemorating, don't you think?'

'Absolutely. And to commemorate your visit this Thursday may I buy you a drink?'

'No you may not,' said Brandy Jack. 'You know perfectly well I never accept presents from strange men.'

'Am I a strange man?'

'Sometimes,' said Brandy Jack. 'But then,' and he grinned his famous lop-sided smile with the slightly raised left eyebrow, 'as you know perfectly well, so am I!

Once again William was awed by the easy manner in which these old men refused to react conventionally to having their various gaffes blown. William decided it was probably because at this stage of the game Brandy Jack couldn't be bothered to take anything too seriously any more.

'I've been talking to Belkis and we'd like you to pop along to Moss Bros and hire yourself a full set of compère's white tie and tails,' said William.

Brandy Jack looked at him, both eyebrows raised this time.

'And what makes you suppose that I don't own a perfectly good tail suit already?'

'Oh, sorry,' said William. 'It was just that Philly spoke of your "one good suit" and I took him to mean . . .'

'Philly was right in the sense that I only have one decent suit left, but he means a "suit" suit. Thing you stroll along the street in and wear in Albany,' William was treated to another of Brandy Jack's sly smiles. 'He didn't include, for instance, my suit of pyjamas, which are of black silk and were given to me by Gary Cooper after an early talkie I was in where I played his drunken English butler. It was a Western. Awful film, dreadful reviews, made a fortune for the studio. My tails are not a real suit to Philly, d'ye see. He calls my evening clothes "drag". He'll say, "You going to the party tonight in drag?" To Philly only "suit" suits are suits.'

'Do you think it might be a good idea for me to ask Philly along next Thursday to look after you?'

'You try keeping him away, he'd scream the place down. He'll be along at about seven o'clock Thursday morning clutching his green Harrods carrier bag – always Harrods – filled with his travelling electric iron and extension lead, clothes brush, bottle of water to spit out, mirror and comb, quarter bottle of Gordon's gin. No tonic. He just has a drop of water in his gin, the way admirals and Mrs Gamp used to like it.'

'All the same,' said William, 'this is a professional engagement for you and as you're not being paid the Club should at least look after you a bit. Isn't there something we could provide for you? We'll send transport to fetch you both, of course, but there must be something more we could do?'

Brandy Jack thought hard.

'I tell you what I *would* appreciate,' he said, rather hesitantly. 'If I could hire a set of the linen bits, y'know, boiled shirt, stiff collar, white tie and waistcoat. The suit is all right, built to last. It was my father's. Doesn't just *look* Edwardian, it *is* Edwardian. But the white stuff is another matter. Goes yellow with age. Philly has been at it with everything, "Dabitoff", paintbrush cleaner, petrol, breadcrumbs. One evening, in a fury, he tried brushing it with Dulux emulsion paint. It is now, alas, virtually unwearable.'

'Better still,' said William. 'Buy a new set of linen rather than hire it. It's the least the Club can do for you.' And before Brandy Jack could protest William swiftly diverted him with a new thought.

'What I want you to do is be Master of Ceremonies of the whole dinner,' William said, 'not just the cabaret. I want you to introduce Anton the chef, who will take a bow – richly deserved, wouldn't you agree? Then talk the diners through the menu.'

'You've decided what we're going to eat?'

'It was something you said which gave me the clue.'

'What did I say?'

'Roughly, give them what they really want and lots of it. Now the menu is a secret and please, please don't give it away, even to Philly. We're going to start with loads of oysters and caviare . . . '

'Good God!' said Branny, 'I say!'

'Then a choice of a simple English grill or some exotic bit of fancy stuff. Then the great treat – a choice of good old English suet puddings, rice puddings, bread-and-butter puddings, and so on. Introducing these could be quite fun. It's entirely up to you but there could be, for instance, a bit of nonsense describing the puds in the florid menu prose of bad restaurants. Like, "All our suet puddings are made from fresh, environmentally friendly young suets, dawn-gathered by local village maidens from beneath the ancient olive-trees of rural Windsor," and so on. Then comes the cabaret, and here I really need your professional advice. What sort of cabaret would you think suitable for the two hundred and fiftieth birthday of this Club? And remember it's supposed to be an orgy.'

'The rumours going round are that you're laying on some sort of strip-tease?'

'They are only rumours. But what's *your* thinking? You've got to introduce whatever it is.'

'My thinking is that it'd be a grave mistake to make the cabaret a display of sexual vulgarity. You happen to know, William, that a bunch of naked girls displaying their talents doesn't happen to be my personal cup of cocoa. But the idea doesn't revolt me, it's just that I think it would be quite wrong for the occasion.'

'But they all talk about the need to have girls, girls, girls . . . '

'And that's all it is, old love, talk. William, I'm an old hand at being a phoney and I can spot phonies a mile off. The old members are like adolescents, they talk big, macho talk about sex but really they're terrified that they might have to come face to face with it. Not one of the Events Committee really wants next Thursday to be within a mile of a naked girl.'

'But you all voted for an orgy . . . '

'We were being wilfully mindless and mischievous. An orgy sounded suitably wicked and we wanted to nail Canon Prout.'

'Having explained that you don't think that a parade of sleazy sex is the answer to the problem, then what do you suggest?'

Brandy Jack pulled a crumpled sheet of paper from his pocket. 'I think something along these lines might be what you're looking for,' he said. 'A cabaret both exotic and totally harmless. An evening of unfulfilled promise of delights. What the American advertising profession calls, "selling the sizzle, not the steak". It was our friend in the newsagents who told me about this group. They pin their leaflet on his small-ad board for 50p a week.'

'What group is it? What do they do?'

'Belly-dancing,' said Branny.

William's mind reeled.

'Oddly popular among young women nowadays,' said Branny. 'The fun of dressing-up in see-through pyjamas and bra and everything smothered in sequins. I think you should at least go and have a look at them.'

I wonder, thought William. A group of pretty, young belly-dancers? A touch of the mysterious East, well, Middle East. Sinuous movements of hips and bosoms, bare feet, slave bangles tinkling, exposed tummy-buttons winking, erotic music of a foreign nature warming up the senses, yes, could well be the sort of glamour the evening needs.

William eagerly reached for the leaflet.

It read:

THE GOLDEN HORN LADIES
BELLY-DANCING ENSEMBLE
CATFORD

Founder and Life-Presidentperson, Mrs Adelaide Gwendoline Beresford Dip. Acupuncture (Univ. of West Bromwich) 144 Linkfield Crescent, Catford

Display Team available (token fee negotiable) for Conservative Party Fund-Raising Fêtes, the quieter (mixed) Rotarian functions, selected Bar-Mitzvas and afternoon Wedding Receptions

Practice sessions and tea afterwards in the ex-Billiard Hall above what used to be Montagu Burton's gents' outfitters in the High Street (corner of Cathcart Road)

COME YE ALL AND SUPPORT CATFORD'S OWN MOVERS AND SHAKERS

CHAPTER FOURTEEN

A HINT OF EASTERN DISAPPOINTMENT

Belkis was in a protective, motherly mood and refused to let William go to Catford by public transport.

'You are supremely vital to the Club,' she said when William protested that he could find his way there by tube and bus. 'And you must travel on official business in a manner mirroring your distinction. Chidders will book a chauffeured car for you.'

She phoned down to Chidders and asked him to book William the most prestigious transport he could find. Chidders, delighted with the honour, searched the Yellow Pages Directory with a mighty forefinger, agonized over the choice and finally decided to confer the Club's patronage on a mini-cab company which he thought had the right air of distinction about it, *Mayfair Executive and Diplomatic Super-Cabs* (1993) Ltd.

'Pick-up in ten minutes' time exactly, if you please,' commanded Chidders briskly on the phone. 'Your driver will take our Club Secretary, in person, to Catford. Mr Grundwick has the precise address at whence you will drop him off of. Your driver will then wait and return Mr Grundwick back here to the Club so he can collect his bike and go home. Is that understood?'

'Yar,' said a voice.

The Mayfair Executive and Diplomatic Super-Cab was forty-eight minutes late arriving. It was a small yellow saloon car of some age with rust around its edges. The driver was a long, lean, louche, very young man with long, lean, greasy blond hair, incipient zits and a general air of insecurity. William trotted down the Club steps and looked at his luxury transport without enthusiasm.

'Well, get in, sir,' the driver called to William in a voice which managed to sound both aggressive and lacking in confidence.

William folded himself into the passenger seat. A difficult manoeuvre as the seat had a split in it which was beginning to ooze yellow plastic foam and was covered with a deep litter of the driver's personal detritus including several old copies of the *Evening Standard*, a battery-operated electric razor, a dirty and heavily used A–Z map of London, a can of Mobil oil, two tomatoes and a piece of cheese.

'Cheers,' said the driver. 'My name's Rollo Chad-Baxter. Hi. Mind if I smoke?' He was already smoking. He waved the cigarette at William as if to show William what a cigarette looked like.

'Go ahead,' said William amiably, putting the tin of engine oil on the floor and parking the tomatoes and cheese in his crutch, the only place he could think of where they wouldn't roll about, 'it's your cab.'

'As a matter of fact, it literally is,' said Rollo. 'It's the first of my Super-Cab fleet.'

'Apropos of nothing,' said William, struggling with his safety-belt which he found he could not plug in because Rollo Chad-Baxter had already plugged his own safety-belt into William's slot, so he had to find Rollo's slot and plug into that, 'over the years I have noticed a curious phenomenon: all yellow cars whatever their age are, to a greater or lesser extent, rusty.'

'What are you trying to say?' said the driver. He tossed his head angrily so that his mop of greasy golden hair swung backwards into place, and ran a none-too-clean hand through it. 'That my Super-Cab's rusty?'

'Well, no,' said William. 'It was just an amusing general observation. Yellow cars seem to go rusty very quickly, that's all. Shall we go?'

Rollo considered this, then switched on the starter. The engine just managed to turn over. It was making what William and Milly called 'sounds of woe'. 'Woe-woe' the engine went, turned over reluctantly and went 'woe-woe' again. This went on for three more 'woe-woe's, the process slowing up each time, then the ignition caught, a couple of modest explosions occurred in the car's lower colon and the engine came to uneven life.

'You had too much choke on,' said William. 'It's a warm day. You were flooding the carb. And there's not much life in your battery.'

'You can't blind me with science,' said Rollo amiably, 'I'm not a mechanic, you know. As it happens I'm chairman of the company.'

'Oh, sorry,' said William, by now intrigued by the chairman's accent, a wholly unconvincing go at an upper-class drawl.

Rollo carefully drew on driving gloves, skeletal affairs with ventilation holes punched in the thin black leather and the name Stirling Moss in large white letters on the backs.

'There you go,' said Rollo, easing the rusty yellow car away from the pavement and towards St James's Street with all the panache of Nigel Mansell making a getaway from the pits after a Grand Prix tyre-change.

'When I turn the right-hand corner coming up,' Rollo said casually to William, 'would you be so kind as to take a good grip on your door handle? The lock's a bit dodgy and it's been known to fly open halfway round a bend and centrifugal force can work like an ejector seat.'

William gripped the door handle tightly and the car,

heeling over strangely, went into the right-hand turn at a sedate but noisy 20 mph. They chugged and clattered up St James's Street, and eventually weaved into Tottenham Court Road.

'What make of car is this?' asked William politely and without any curiosity whatever.

Rollo shot him a glance. 'What's it matter?' he said. 'A good set of wheels is a good set of wheels, right?'

'Just wondered,' said William.

'Well, I'll tell you,' said Rollo, waving cheerily to disconcert an angry, middle-aged lady on a pedestrian crossing whom he had missed murdering by an inch. 'It was originally a Ford Cortina. One of the great cars of British engineering, wonderful engine.'

'The engine wasn't very wonderful a few minutes ago. It hardly started.'

'Yar, well. It's not a Cortina *engine*, as it happens. The car had a transplant a couple of weeks ago.'

'A *what?*'

'Human beings have a heart transplant, don't they? Well this car's had a change of engine. It came from a VW Golf. Very sporty motor. This one was nicked and used to ramraid a gents' outfitters and I bought the engine at a breaker's yard for peanuts. That's the way to your first fortune these days, my pa taught me. You can buy anything more cheaply if you go round the back door. Y'know, take a little risk.'

'What about the rest of the car?' said William.

'That's kosher,' said Rollo, letting his cigarette smoke drift through his front teeth like Humphrey Bogart. 'A boozing-pal put me on to it. The Cortina was underwater in a Devon lane for two weeks after a river burst its banks. It was an insurance write-off so it cost me next to nothing.'

'But car papers would be needed. Logbook. MOT certificate.'

'*They* cost a packet. There's this fellow Ronnie I was put on to in Camberwell. Pricey but just brilliant. He faked me a driving-licence as a birthday present; three months ago was my twenty-first birthday. A real artist, Ronnie. My pa always said that when you have to employ villains get good ones and pay them well.' He began to wind his window down but at the first turn of the handle the window dropped like a guillotine blade. He rested his elbow on the sill and gave a warm, crooked little smile, as smiled by Roger Moore being James Bond.

'A wise man in the ways of the world, my pa. I'll ever be grateful for his wisdom in sending me to a public school.'

'Which one?' asked William idly, hanging on to his door handle and hoping that the tomatoes had strong skins.

'Were you at Harrow?' asked Rollo.

'No,' said William.

'Know much about the place?' asked Rollo, casually.

'Hardly anything,' said William.

'I went to Harrow,' said Rollo.

As they drove up the Tottenham Court Road Rollo seemed to William to be twitching a lot at the steering wheel. Rollo noticed William looking at him.

'Track rods are a tiny bit worn,' he said. 'The car's quite all right going round corners. It's when the road's straight that she wobbles.'

'Rollo,' said William, after a near-miss in Swiss Cottage with a parked lorry delivering yoghurt, 'do you, or your shrewd pa, sincerely believe that you can build up a whole fleet of cars from the profits of this one wreck?'

'Ex-wreck,' said Rollo. 'It's been rebuilt by hand from top to bottom by Alexander and Damien in Stockwell. The finest rebuilders of condemned cars in the trade. And in two months' time I'll be looking for an upmarket, low-mileage Japanese Mazda. My dad always told me to expand, expand. It's the quickest way to a fortune.'

'But how on earth does your dad reckon you'll be able to buy a Mazda from the hundred or so quid you'll earn with this reconstructed wreck?'

'Use the risk factor to your advantage, my dad taught me. To accumulate you've got to speculate. Go for the big money.'

'And how does your father suggest you do that?'

'Save up the profits from this car and put the lot on a horse.'

That killed the art of conversation for a few miles. The pleasant silence was broken by Rollo.

'You're probably wondering', he said, 'how an ex-public school man like me got involved in this plebeian area of merchant adventuring?'

'No, I wasn't,' said William. 'I was wondering why we're travelling north when Catford's south.'

'Catford? I thought the bloke on the phone said Watford,' said Rollo.

'Catford,' said William.

'Shit!' said Rollo.

He managed to stop suddenly without anything hitting them and backed the car into a side-street, parking half on the narrow pavement and half on double yellow lines. William handed him the A–Z and Rollo examined it anxiously, muttering quietly to himself. Eventually – 'Got it,' he said, handed the A–Z to William and turned the car back down the Finchley Road. 'Trafalgar Square,' he recited to himself, 'Parliament Square – over Westminster Bridge – Kennington Road – have another shufti at the map . . . '

William found that closing his eyes rendered his ride in a recently drowned Cortina driven by a loopy, over-ambitious, apprentice con man faintly less stressful. The noise the car made sounded as though at any moment the Cortina would reject its transplanted VW engine but it held together and they bumped and banged their way across Westminster Bridge. At least having to concentrate on remembering the route stopped Rollo chatting to William, a great relief because when Rollo talked he turned to face William and the car swerved all over the road.

There was a traffic jam at the roundabout on the south side of Westminster Bridge which gave Rollo the chance for another little talk.

'When I get the Mazda,' he said, facing William, 'I'll be the one who drives it, of course, which means I'll need to hire somebody to drive this thing. If you know of a likely lad who'll do what he's told and keep his mouth shut, give me a bell at the office, would you?' He handed William the firm's business card, a spectacular production of green ink on silver card. 'Don't forget my name, Rollo Chad-Buxton.'

'Baxter,' said William.

'Oh yar . . . Chad-Baxter . . . cheers.'

'What's the best time to ring you?'

'Any old time, I'm the only one there. I'll get an answering machine as soon as the business grows but at the moment I spend most of my time sitting in the office – well, it's my bedsit really – reading the financial columns in the newspapers. Which reminds me, I need to see my pa soon. Couple of money investments I want to check out with him. We're a sort of business partnership.'

The traffic jam thinned out. Rollo grabbed the A–Z and murmured his new mantra, 'The Oval – Camberwell – Deptford – Catford . . . ' He found a gear and the Cortina lurched into motion.

On they went. The shops, blocks of flats and pubs of South London began to give way to suburbia, tight little between-the-wars housing estates with well-kept privet hedges, and stained-glass galleons under full sail in the front doors.

William realized they had left the granite pavements of true London for the more leafy outskirts when the Cortina hit a small plane tree growing on the pavement. It was only a glancing blow and a piece of bark wedged in the front bumper was the only damage.

'Where's your father to be found these days?' asked William, trying very hard to be matey. 'Fleet Street? The City?'

'Ford Open Prison,' said Rollo. 'Seven years.'

'Ah,' said William.

'All right,' said Rollo. 'I grant you Kensington Palace wasn't his to sell but the little Japanese he sold it to was so rich that the hundred grand in cash he handed to my pa as deposit was like a waiter's tip to him. Yet they called it fraud! Fraud! A travesty of justice. Oval – Camberwell – Deptford . . . '

William closed his eyes again and dozed off.

He was woken by a small, intermittent stabbing pain in his reproductory parts. He sat up and passed a hand between his trousers and the car seat. One of the coiled springs in the car seat had come adrift from its moorings, pierced the upholstery and the sharp point of the spring was probing William's fundaments. He reached down and made a kind of armoured pad out of the old *Evening Standard*s which he eased into place between the needle-sharp spring and himself. The agony abated a little.

'I should have sat at the back,' he said gloomily.

'Well, not necessarily,' said Rollo. 'That Devon river water corroded the locating lugs on the back seat and it tends to shoot forward when I brake. Yesterday I had to stop quickly at a traffic light and my lady client hit her nose on the back of my seat and bled for an hour. I charged her a fiver extra for cleaning it off so I didn't lose by it. I managed to scrape off a bit of the blood this morning but it's a horrible job so I left most of it where it is. It'll wear off in time.'

'I'll stay where I am,' said William.

'Yar, I would,' said Rollo. 'The water got at the seat springs at the back and they're poking through the upholstery.'

'Not only at the back,' said William.

'Eh?' said Rollo, not really listening. He never really listened. 'I'll get it all fixed soon. Teething problems, that's all. Every fleet of luxury cars has to mature, like wine.'

This nonsensical piece of philosophy deepened the gloom into which William, normally a striking example of non-gloom, was beginning to descend. The journey was getting a bit much. The driving was dangerously incompetent and the inside of the Super-Cab was not only painfully uncomfortable but, it had now been revealed, enriched with dollops of a customer's dried blood.

William tried to rally his spirits by re-reading the leaflet put out by the Belly-Dancing Ensemble, hoping to find some hint of veiled naughtiness, a clue as to the sinuous eroticism performed by the group, perhaps coded because the leaflet was meant to be pinned up on local newsagents' boards alongside postcards announcing humble items like SMALL MOTOR-MOWER FOR SALE – LACKS GRASSBOX AND STARTING-HANDLE OTHERWISE SOUND. He found nothing which even hinted at the possibility of the Ensemble's performance being in any way, shape, or form, sexy.

He peered out of his window. The houses were now changing style slightly, moving towards older, Edwardian semi-detached villas with small but solidly built bay windows and their front gardens concreted over for the family car to be parked off the road. The rows of houses and shops rambled about in a higgledy-piggledy kind of way and there was a decent incidence of Wesleyan chapels and Pentecostal missions.

William was hoping wistfully that he might glimpse a small opium den to cheer him up but instead the car rattled its way past such lesser stews of iniquity as 'THE TUDOR CAFE – Afternoon Tea's with Gatteaux' and 'FRUIT OF THE SHEEP – Prop: Mr Wilfred (Wilf) Gutteridge, Specialist In All Makes of Wool, also Fishing Tackle'.

A sign above a post office told him that against all odds they had actually arrived in Catford. He grabbed the A–Z and sought Linkfield Crescent. Belkis had promised to phone ahead and warn Mrs Beresford that he was on his way to discuss her troupe. The crescent was easy to spot on the map as it was crescent-shaped but navigating Rollo there was less simple. The car seemed to be driving him rather than the other way round. 'Left at the ironmongers,' William would sing out. 'OK, Batman!' Rollo would reply in his Robin voice and sail on past the turning. As usual he was not really listening. He would then have to turn up another side-street and reverse amid angry hooting from endangered fellow drivers and make a right turn back the way they had come, then there was only a hair-raising U-turn in the main road and they were poised to have another go at the turning.

But they got there. The last bit of the journey, from passing Catford Post Office to arriving at No. 144 Linkfield Crescent took them, by William's watch, just over thirty-five minutes.

'There it is! There! Number 144!' William shouted. 'Stop!'

Rollo, who was accelerating up the slight hill at the time, stood on the brakes. The rear seat shot forward and struck them in the small of the back but the car stopped. 'Great little car!' said Rollo.

He gave a strong, triumphal pull on the handbrake. There was a loud ratchet sound and the handle came away in his hand. The car began to roll backwards. Rollo trod on the footbrake and the car halted. 'Would you nip out and find a brick?' he said to William. 'Shove it under the back wheel?'

'No,' said William. 'No, I bloody well won't. Find your own brick. I'm pissed off with both you and your rotten car.' William's rare swear, which he instantly regretted, was an indication of the depth of his pissed-offendness.

'OK, I'll go and find one,' said Rollo, unperturbed. 'Would you mind pressing hard down on the footbrake?' He got out and went loping off down the slope, whistling cheerfully and regarding his bald suede shoes. He seemed to have forgotten that he was on an urgent quest for a brick.

Meanwhile, back in the car all was not well. William was unable to slide across to Rollo's seat to get his foot on the brake pedal because of his safety-belt which had jammed itself in Rollo's socket, and also because of the killer prong which jabbed at him as soon as he slid away from the protection of the *Evening Standard*s beneath him. The car began to roll backwards, slowly at first but gathering speed. William, now in a state approaching quiet panic, swung like an acrobat upside down in his safety-belt so that his shins rested on the top of his seat, his forehead touched the carpet and he could reach down and press the brake pedal with both hands. He had to fight a strong spring and just pressing the pedal slowed the car but did not stop it. Then suddenly the car stopped dead.

'Hello, within!' cried a forceful female voice. 'Doctor Grundwick, I presume!' This was followed by a jolly bellow of laughter. The driver's door opened and William was able to turn his head sufficiently to see, inverted though he was, a beefy lady peering down at him and grinning cheerfully. William rapidly put two and two together. 'Mrs Beresford?' said William. 'Delighted to meet you. Excuse me if I don't get up.'

'Don't worry about the car,' cried Mrs Beresford. 'I've got hold of the blighter!' William tentatively took pressure off the brake pedal and sure enough the car stayed still.

'It can't move!' cried Mrs Beresford. 'I've jammed my foot under a wheel.'

'You'll be run over!' cried William.

'Rubbish!' cried his fair rescuer. 'My metatarsals are as safe as the Bank of England. No vehicle has enough energy to climb up somebody's foot unaided, from a state of rest, on a slight slope. Simple dynamics. Be different if the car was moving, of course. Anyway, I'm also hanging on to the door handle.'

'I'll give you a hand,' said William.

He managed to turn himself right side up and extricate himself from the safety-belt. He joined Mrs Beresford in holding on to the car, which had been trying to drift downhill but now seemed docile and willing to comply with orders from Mrs Beresford's left hand and right foot.

'I was on the lookout for you,' said Mrs Beresford. 'A lady called Mrs Hardcastle telephoned to say you were on your way to inspect my little group of "sirens". I never use the word "houris", it makes the girls titter. Unfortunately the word "sirens" also makes them titter. Not all of them, only those who went through the last war but that includes most of 'em.' She swept the road with a gaze as piercing as that of a hawk circling at a thousand feet on the lookout for a baby lizard for lunch. There was no sign of Rollo.

William realized that Mrs Beresford was undoubtedly going to go on chattering until Rollo arrived and they could let go of the Super-Cab. And then she would go on chattering while Rollo drove them to the Ensemble's practice hall where she would chat William through the rehearsal and then chat to him afterwards. On the other hand it was enjoyable chat.

'Tell me, what made you create the Golden Horn Ensemble?' he asked politely, hanging on gamely to the nearside door handle which was beginning to hurt his hand. It was a safe question to ask as she was bound to tell him about that before long.

'I was just going to tell you about that,' said Mrs Beresford loudly across the car's roof. 'It was about fifteen years ago, soon after my husband, Sydney, was taken from me.'

'I'm so sorry,' said William. 'Was it unexpected?'

'How do you mean?'

'Had your husband been ill? Was it an accident?'

'When I said Sydney was taken from me I meant he was taken from me by Elspeth Potter, his secretary at the Gas Showrooms, but Sydney was no great loss. One Sunday morning in the kitchen he was cutting the Xs in the bottom of the Brussels sprouts as per usual and he suddenly put his knife down and said, "Adelaide, there's something I've been meaning to mention. For the last fourteen and a half months, Mrs Elspeth Potter at the office and I have been having a liaison. We have been having a liaison every Tuesday evening, sometimes twice, in a luxury rented room above the Oxfam Shop in Venables Road." "You told me you were at night school taking Carbon-Fuel Engineering," I said. "Well, I wasn't, was I?" he said. "I have become attached to Elspeth and her little ways and she has consented to become my wife." "But you're married to *me*!" I cried. "Don't think I don't know that!" he exclaimed, rather bitterly for such a short man. "As soon as we have legally disconnected ourselves from our spouses, Mrs Potter and I plan to wed and begin a new harmonious life. I've done the sprouts."

'With which Sydney went upstairs, packed his necessaries and disappeared from my life, slamming the front door behind him. Not that slamming the door was significant. You had to slam the front door or it wouldn't shut. He always promised to Surform a slice off it but what with creosoting the garden shed at weekends and liaising Mrs Potter on Tuesday evenings he seemed to have run out of puff.'

Rollo suddenly appeared bearing a brick. He rammed it against one of the rear tyres and they all got into the Super-Cab. William spread the newspapers over the rear seat trying not to look at the congealed bloodstains all over the carpet and upholstery. He braced his knees against the seat in front so that the back seat would not slide about when Rollo braked.

'Up the hill and third on the right!' commanded Mrs Beresford briskly. 'Then second right. Down the hill. Turn right at the bottom and you're in the High Street. Cathcart Road is first left. Got that?'

There was no reply. Rollo was off into one of his reveries, no doubt concerning money and easy ways of getting hold of lots of it.

'HAVE YOU GOT THAT?' bellowed Mrs Beresford directly into his ear. Rollo elevated about three inches from his seat and woke up.

'OK, Batman!' he said brightly.

'*What* did you call me?' asked Mrs Beresford with quiet menace.

Fortunately, at that moment the car in front braked suddenly and Rollo ran into the back of it. However, the driver in front was not the owner and there was obviously something dodgy about him driving the car at all. The two drivers eyed each other warily for a moment then, recognizing a kindred spirit, bribed each other with a fiver apiece to forget the whole thing.

'So you founded the Ensemble when you were a sweet young bride newly deserted by your husband?' said William with elephantine tact as they continued on their journey.

'No, no, no!' said Mrs Beresford. 'It was years later. I managed to force a reasonable settlement out of Sydney, not difficult with a worm like him, and the house had always been in my name for his tax purposes, so I was all right financially. But I was starved of intellectual challenges. Before beginning the belly-dancing I found solace in preaching the gospel of Alternative Personal Hygiene. I lectured on the Open University once and gave many a talk to Townswomen's Guilds and Women's Institutes. I was invited to address the Isle of Wight but I sat on my prescription sun-glasses and missed the ferry.'

'I don't think I know anything about Alternative Personal Hygiene,' said William.

'What do you know about green movements?'

'Don't geese have them?' said William, after some thought.

'I use "green movements" in the sense of ecological, human, group activities,' said Mrs Beresford severely. 'Let me go straight to the nub. Do you ever pause to consider the damage that continual washing with soap does to your skin?'

'Well, no,' said William, 'actually—'

'The human body was not designed to be washed regularly.'

'I think mine was, because—'

'Think of your skin as a Fair Isle jumper.'

William pondered. At certain times it had undoubtedly gone a bit blotchy with reddish bits in a kind of pattern. And in a bad light . . . 'I see what you mean,' he said.

'Don't think of your skin as a kind of waterproof plastic mackintosh, rather think of it as a perfectly fitting Fair Isle woollen body-stocking which keeps your muscles and bones in place and stops your lungs and other vital internal organs from dropping out onto the floor. It has neat edging around the lips to stop your mouth from fraying and holes for your eyes like a Balaclava helmet has as we know from *News at Ten*.'

'I'm with you,' said William, eyes closed to give the impression that he was concentrating on her every word.

'Good egg,' said Mrs Beresford. 'Now, like a Fair Isle jumper your skin is a living, breathing thing, full of natural oils which preserve it and keep it supple. Are you still with me?'

'Marching shoulder to shoulder,' murmured William, almost asleep. It had been a mistake to close his eyes.

'Now imagine the consequences of treating a Fair Isle woolly as you treat your skin, soaking it frequently in hot water and rubbing it all over with a chemical substance made from rancid grease boiled up with caustic soda? The result would be that the natural protective oils were washed away leading to shrinkage and eventually—'

'Rusty ribs?' suggested William helpfully.

'This is a serious problem,' said Mrs Beresford.

William, reprimanded, sat up straight and met her eyeball to eyeball as though following her every syllable attentively. 'Then do tell me, Mrs Beresford, what exactly *is* your Alternative Plan for Personal Hygiene?'

'It's simplicity itself and entirely in accord with nature,' said Mrs Beresford. She was now into her lecture which she knew backwards and was on automatic pilot, her voice going into a rather didactic and monotonous drone. 'Once a week, or whenever your habit of hygiene commands, stand naked in the bath, if you'll pardon my frankness, and dab yourself lightly all over with a ball of cotton-wool soaked in rainwater. On no account use tap water which has chemicals and impurities added to make it taste nicer. A useful tip is to keep an old bucket handy and stick it under the downpipe of a gutter when it comes on to rain. In that way you will always have a supply of soft rainwater standing by for usage, especially in the winter and Manchester. If areas of your person are besmirched with dried mud, grease, paint, tar or similar, the dirty bits should be attacked boldly with a loofah. Not a wet loofah which is flabby but a dry loofah which is hard and scratchy. Scrub away at the offensive matter until either it comes off or you begin to draw blood. The final treatment is to towel off and then rub yourself all over with half a loaf of stale bread, using a circular motion. Don't use sliced white bread as this rolls itself into damp pellets; for your health's sake it's better to stick to Hovis. Bread has the property of absorbing any water or grease lurking in your crevices and, of course, it erases any pencil marks you might have made for some reason on your person. And that's the big job done. Your body is pure and fragrant again using only organic, natural means!'

'Have you done, Missus?' said Rollo. 'We're there.'

The car had stopped and William could see through his window, just, that on one side of the road there was a sign halfway up the wall saying CATHCART ROAD and on the other corner was a Burton shop. He and Mrs Beresford climbed out.

'You'll probably be an hour or two,' said Rollo to William, 'so I thought I'd pop along to the railway station, it's quite near, and see if I can pick up a couple of quick fares. OK?'

'No, it's not OK,' said William. 'You stay here and wait for us as you're booked to do. Right?' He turned towards Burton's side entrance.

'****,' mumbled Rollo.

'*What* did you say?' said William, turning back.

'I said, "Can't." I'm parked on double yellow lines, aren't I? Can't stay parked here, can I?'

'Any experienced chauffeur will tell you that you'll be all right if you stay in the car. If a warden or a copper comes up you just circle the block a couple of times and return.'

'It'd be easier for me if I knew how long you'll be. Give me a rough estimate.'

William looked Rollo in the eye and said, softly but clearly, 'Can't.' Feeling much better, he crossed the road and joined Mrs Beresford.

'. . . and then, eleven years ago, I founded The Golden Horn Belly-Dancing Ensemble,' Mrs Beresford was saying. 'It was somewhere the married girls could go to once a week and get away from the telly. All their husbands wanted to do in the evenings was watch *Miss World*, football, snooker, fishing and Jim Davidson, not really what their wives were interested in. My little club gave the wives a night out, a bit of music and dancing, a giggle amongst themselves, exercise and a chance to cheer up people less fortunate than themselves. Furthermore . . .'

The ex-billiard room above what used to be Montagu Burton's was vast and cool. There was a stage at the far end which had been painted pale green and shocking pink some years previously and was encumbered with an ancient drum-kit with *The Whizzbangs* picked out in tinsel on the bass drum. This was the property of the ballroom-dancing school which hired the room every Friday evening after the Ensemble for their weekly practice dance. This was a popular function run by a couple of local celebrities, Alf and Conny Ryman (aka Alfredo and Conchita Raymonde, runners-up in the *Bertoli Sunflower Frying-Oil* South-Eastern Counties Latin-American semi-finals, 1979).

Dark bentwood chairs were put out against the walls. William and Mrs Beresford sat in the middle of the row of chairs at the far end of the room so that the Ensemble would not hear what was being said about them.

'Sorry for the hiatus,' said Mrs Beresford, 'but we're a bit early and the girls are still changing. While we're waiting, I wonder if you would care to tell me what sort of function you want my little troupe for? One cannot be too careful these turbulent times and I vet everybody who is interested in renting my ladies. I even vetted the Reverend John Boddy when he wanted to book the girls for his Grande Wynter Solstice Fayre in St Mary's parish hall, and he was Sydney's first cousin. Completely harmless job, of course.'

'Well, Mrs Beresford,' said William, any hopes he had left of finding an exciting cabaret dispersed like joss-stick smoke in a howling English gale, 'I am interested in hiring your Ensemble to perform their cabaret at a gentlemen's club in London. I can supply you with impeccable references, of course. The problem for me is, I wonder whether your troupe puts on the kind of rhythmic, orient-inspired, deeply *feminine* kind of dance programme which my function requires.'

Mrs Beresford thought deeply. She said, 'I think you may have the wrong impression of what the girls actually perform in their performance.'

'Well, according to your leaflet—'

'Those blinking leaflets keep coming home to roost!' said Mrs Beresford with some heat. 'They were distributed when the Golden Horn Ensemble was started all those years ago. Things have changed since then but the leaflets haven't. I stopped paying the newsagents to display them years ago but you know what people are like, it's less effort to leave them up than take them down.'

'What things have changed?' asked William.

'Well, for a start, let's admit that we now place less emphasis on belly-dancing. To be honest we don't place any emphasis at *all* on belly-dancing, in fact only one of the ladies can still do it. They all carry on wearing their costumes because the dressing-up is so much part of their fun but they're eleven years older now and belly-dancing can be off-putting when your muscles have stretched and your tummy droops.'

'But one of the girls still performs a belly-dance?'

'Phyllis Fuller. She's *supposed* to be quite pretty. The girls call her The Fuller Figure and Glamourknickers, but I don't know, I find her a little obvious. Phyllis is a physical type, good teeth and hair and a good mover in spite of five children. She's always performed what I call the Glamour Solo. We put "In a Persian Market" on the hi-fi and Phyllis shimmies out, false eyelashes jutting out like flue-brushes, a ruby shining in her navel.'

'A ruby?'

'Well, actually it's the red reflector that fell off the back of her little son's mini mountain-bike. She glues it in her tummy-button with Copydex. Phyllis spoils that boy, he only has to say he wants a mountain-bike and she's scanning the postal bargain catalogues. She also wears a diamond on one nostril. Well, it's really a big crystal of washing soda attached to the side of her nose with a pellet of Blu-Tack. The trouble is, it keeps dropping off mid-performance. It's the heat from the dancing, you know.'

'I suppose glueing bits on is a problem if a lady tends to "glow".'

'Mrs Fuller doesn't "glow". She's a big woman and it's good, honest sweat. On a hot summer night Phyllis has been known to sweat her way through a quarter of a pound of Tesco washing soda.'

A kind of sadness settled over William.

He said to her, 'A little while ago you mentioned something about the girls "cheering up people less fortunate than themselves". What did you mean?'

'The group now mostly puts on its little show in hospital

wards, nursing homes, OAP sheltered accommodation, places like that. We've even appeared at Ford Open Prison, are you familiar with it?'

'Not yet,' said William.

A thunderous scratching and banging noise came through the speakers. Mrs Beresford leant towards William and said knowledgeably, 'Testing. The sound, you know. Mrs Hackett's always been in charge of the electrics. Her son's in the RAF.'

William was sorting out the logic behind Mrs Hackett's appointment when the speakers crackled into life, happily with the sound level modified, and a tape of 'That's Entertainment' filled the hall with bouncy, happy music. From the wings appeared The Golden Horn Ensemble, eight ladies of assorted weights and sizes in a line, arms round each other's shoulders, legs kicking quite high and in good unison in a dance routine lifted intact from The Tiller Girls.

They each wore dangling gold earrings, a muslin veil hanging down from the bridge of the nose, an outer and upper garment covered in sequins which seemed to be a cross between a blouse torn in half in front and a cheesecloth waistcoat, and baggy muslin trousers through which could be glimpsed peach-coloured knickers of a generous cut.

The chorus line medium-high kicked their way offstage and peace reigned for a few minutes. Then two of the ladies re-entered. They had removed their veils and earrings, reddened their noses and wore bowler hats and rough scarves.

'Mrs Bradstowe and Mrs Welkes,' whispered Mrs Beresford. 'They're *awfully* good. They're supposed to be pantomime villains.'

A piano off-stage struck up a melody and the two ladies went into their ancient comic song:

Do you want any dirty work done, any dirty work
    today?
Here we are, ready and willin',
To murder your mother-in-law for a shillin',
We'll wring your landlord's bloomin'—
Bell, and run away,
Do you want any dirty work done, any dirty work
    today?

William applauded them noisily. The simple, ancient, music-hall humour of the song was oddly good fun and it was done well.

The next item was a bit nearer the Middle East. It was a copy of Wilson, Keppel and Betty's famous Egyptian sand-dancing act. Two ladies had put on a fez apiece and a moustache and striped nightshirt to represent Wilson and Keppel, and Mrs Brollie, William was told by Mrs Beresford, was impersonating Betty, the voluptuous lady dancer of the act. William thought that Mrs Brollie, though obviously dead keen and smothered in make-up, could not in honesty be termed voluptuous. She was not only thin and bony but 'twixt sequinned waistcoat and see-through pyjama trousers there was no exciting glimpse of tummy but a stretch of heavy-duty, thermal vest. It seemed that she was nursing a chill on the stomach and the hall was draughty. But the trio did the funny sand-dance to the music of the *Egyptian Ballet* very well and William found himself again clapping loudly.

After that came the Star Turn: Phyllis Fuller, mother of five, checkout cashier at Sainsburys and exotic dancer, the last of the Catford belly-dancers to belly-dance. Mrs Hackett put on 'In a Persian Market' and on came Phyllis. Now *she's* voluptuous, thought William to himself, in a genuine Middle Eastern kind of way, feminine shape, good eyes, bit of a tum, bit of a bum.

Mrs Fuller undulated very well but more than that, William realized, she was also gently sending the whole thing up. She was giving a fond parody of the cliché Hoolahoop twists and sidles as danced in early Hollywood thrillers set in Cairo nightclubs.

William applauded her at length.

There were other bits and pieces danced and sung and an old and brief sketch by Gertrude Jennings which ended in the notable exchange, 'Where, then, is the body of my husband?' 'It's down in the kitching 'aving its breakfast.'

For the finale all the ladies returned and sang 'There's No Business Like Show Business', including the bit where they all kneel and whisper the chorus.

William was moved. The ladies tried so hard and enjoyed themselves so much. And performing their homely material dressed as houris gave a fine surreal air to the whole thing. But it was not a cabaret for the Orange. There was a pay-phone in the corridor and William rang Belkis.

'It's not on,' he said. 'It's not a belly-dancing group now, it's an old-fashioned end-of-the-pier concert party.'

Mrs Beresford escorted William back to the car, still chattering cheerfully. 'I must get those misleading leaflets taken down,' she said. 'You've had a wasted journey and it was all my fault. I'm so sorry.'

'I enjoyed the show very much,' said William, honestly. 'It's so sad that it's simply not for us.'

He got into the passenger seat. 'What's the smell?' he asked Rollo.

'Eh? Oh, nothing really. I backed over the kerb and a piece of the exhaust system fell off. I don't think there's enough carbon monoxide to injure you but I'd leave a bit of window open just in case.'

He turned the starter key and the sounds of 'woe' began. The engine gave no sign of starting. Ever again.

There was a great thump on the roof and Mrs Beresford's face appeared at the windscreen.

'Open the bonnet!' she commanded.

'There's no need,' Rollo said. 'It's only—'

There was an even more tremendous thump on the roof.

'OPEN THE BONNET!'

Rollo bent down and wrestled with the release lever. The bonnet sprang up an inch. Mrs Beresford put her fingers in the slot, twiddled and raised the bonnet.

William watched as she bent over the engine, unscrewed a small piece of something with her fingers and blew down it. She screwed it back and leant into Rollo's window. Her fingers and lips were marked with black oil. Work for the loofah there, thought William.

'Don't pump the accelerator!' she said to Rollo. 'Take your foot right off it. The automatic choke has jammed on.' She took a small screwdriver out of her handbag and bent again over the engine. 'Pay attention!' she shouted to Rollo. 'Put your foot back on the accelerator and press it down to the floor and turn the engine over twice.'

Rollo did so. 'Woe— woe—' went the engine.

'Now take your foot right off the accelerator and try again,' she shouted.

'Woe— woe—' went the engine, then it fired and purred happily into life. Mrs Beresford dropped the bonnet into place and wiped her hands on a tissue.

'Thank you so much, Mrs Beresford,' said William through his window. 'Incredible piece of luck for me that you know about engines.'

Rollo, afraid of the engine stopping, put the car into gear and it began to move forward.

'Only too pleased to be of assistance,' Mrs Beresford shouted, jogging alongside. The car was accelerating and Mrs Beresford began to flag.

'Again, thank you!' shouted William, waving out of the window as she fell behind.

The last he heard of Mrs Adelaide Beresford, the unsinkable polymath of Catford, was her voice, fading as the car drew away, 'I also do origami and bereavement-counselling . . . '

CHAPTER FIFTEEN

MILLY CONFRONTS WILLIAM AT
A JOLLY WEDDING-ANNIVERSARY PARTY

As they used to say in adventure yarns, William slept but fitfully that night.

On being returned to the Club late afternoon by Rollo, after several navigational crises on the way back – William had spotted that Rollo was driving him at speed down the Commercial Road towards Essex – William sought Belkis and made his sad report on the unsuitability of the Golden Horn Belly-Dancing Ensemble to be the Orange's cabaret. Belkis already knew this from William's phone call and was more distressed by William's account of the perils of his luxury drive with *Mayfair Executive and Diplomatic Super-Cabs*.

'I will not pay their perfidious account!' she cried, bosom heaving (William noted that it was the saffron sari with the heavy, silver-thread lotus flowers bobbing about).

'But you must,' said William. 'They fulfilled their part of the contract; they got me there and brought me back. The deal said nothing about providing a car which was not a dangerous wreck driven by an incompetent, embryonic criminal. All we do is never use them again.'

Belkis fumed and muttered. 'You let people walk all over you!' she said. 'Yes, you do, I'm telling you you do.'

'Don't worry,' said William cheerfully. 'It's Friday tomorrow, then only six days to blast off!'

'There are important, secret things I must arrange,' said Belkis darkly. 'I will see you, perhaps, tomorrow?'

'Let's meet in the morning,' said William. 'I want your advice about decorating the dining-room for the supper. And there's the question of what we do about giving the staff some sort of celebration. See you about ten?'

William went to his office and began tidying his desk but the phone rang. It was Lord Wick.

'William?'

William checked that Tozer was not also on the line. It was possible to detect when Tozer was listening in because Tozer's nasal wheezing could be heard and there was also a slight echo. 'Lord Wick? I'm glad you phoned. A few small things to report, mostly gloomy.'

'Oh, good. My dear wife and I are still in London and I've been feeling much too cheerful for my own good.'

'Is Madeleine better?'

'In great form. She only had one pee indoors today but it was a beauty. My wife had some craggy old Scottish ladies in for a cup of tea and shortbread and Madeleine peed in Lady MacDee's handbag. Well, silly old trout shouldn't have left it open on the floor. Old Florence had to empty her bag out on to *The Times* to dry it and all sorts of things plopped out including spare dentures, quite a few of the shortbread biscuits from tea and a near-empty quarter bottle of gin, which was worrying. She's rich enough to buy Gordon's Distillery so why should she mess about with horrid little quarter bottles like salesmen's samples?'

Before Lord Wick could launch into another wee anecdote William dived in and told His Lordship the story of his dangerous journey to Catford to audition the homely belly-dancers, and the disappointing result.

'Be philosophical about it, William,' said Lord Wick sympathetically. 'You know what they say: when one door shuts another fails to open!' Chuckling pleasantly, he rang off.

William's phone rang again almost immediately.

'William?' came the voice of Lord Wick. 'I really am getting old, I forgot to tell you what I rang up to say! By the way, our visit on Monday to see the you-know-what is still on, I trust?'

'The what?' said William, momentarily lost.

'I'm speaking in code for personal security reasons,' said His Lordship. 'Are we still going to see the young thingummies taking off all their whatchermacallits and leaping about in the Call My Buff?' Light dawned on William. 'Oh, yes indeed,' he said, 'it's terribly important – our last chance of finding a cabaret. I thought we might have lunch together here and then proceed to Soho. As soon as I can I'll arrange things with Miss Babyoil.'

'Splendid,' said His Lordship. 'I look forward to Monday with keen anticipation. Incidentally, if you see Mrs Fuller, the large lady in Catford you were telling me about who still belly-dances, you might recommend her to have a rivet put in her nose rather than glueing on washing soda. My game-keeper's middle son Rufus turned hippy in the Sixties and had a rivet put in his nose at Macaulays, you know, the ironmongers in Thurso High Street? He said it was a bit painful and there was a fair bit of blood-letting but worse things happen when you're a beater to an Italian pheasant-shooting party. Young Rufus now works in the Royal Bank of Scotland and wears a corn plaster over the hole in his nose but at parties he takes the plaster off and wears a drop earring or a Celtic Supporter's badge. Well, must get on. Nice to talk to you.'

'Lord Wick!' yelled William into the phone.

'Hello?'

'What was it you rang up to tell me?'

'When? Oh, yes. Well, yesterday I phoned our dear friend, Lord Sidmonton, and told him the facts of life as regards his unimportant role in important Club matters. There was a very great deal of huffing and puffing at my deflation of the bogus importance he'd built up for himself over the years. He was really quite annoyed. And in the background I could hear dear Parthenope telling him what to say, like the prompter in a provincial rep company.'

'Where does this leave us?'

'Well, the Master now knows that we're ignoring his order to cancel the Orange and we're going full steam ahead with it. So he and his good lady's only hope of sabotage is to persuade Milly to get at you tomorrow.'

'I understand he's dining tomorrow with Minor Royalty so he won't be with us, which is a blessing.'

'I hope so but I hear from my Ladies' Social Mafia that the dinner's had to be postponed until Saturday night, their Royal Highnesses are stuck up an Alp in a storm and now can't get a flight from Lyons until Saturday, though what they are doing up an Alp in midsummer is a good question. The great thing, William, is *not to worry*, it gives you varicose veins. Now, must go. I promised I'd put Florence MacDee's peed-on dentures through our washing-up machine; she's having supper tonight with the Secretary of State for Scotland. Goodbye for now.'

The phone went dead. A moment later it rang again.

'William? Guess who. Thing is, I've just remembered the important matter I rang up to tell you in the first place. Through my dear wife I briefed the Ladies' Social Mafia to gather what intelligence they could about Canon Prout. They came up trumps.'

'Are they reliable?' asked William.

'Totally,' said Lord Wick. 'Gossipy, yes. A bit too interested in sexual misdemeanours – aren't we all? But I've never known their information be other than accurate. I suppose it has to be, there'd be no fun in it if they all lied to each other, would there? It seems that the pompous and unacceptably boring Canon Prout is not only a dog-kicker and a waiter-baiter in restaurants but he also ejected his local Boy Scouts from the hut he had promised to lend them for ever so that his wife could make money breeding deep-litter turkeys, which I don't think anybody has ever succeeded in doing profitably heh! heh! – eh? Furthermore, a vital fact emerged. We now know the unacceptably trivial reason why Parthenope and the Master are so keen on forcing us to drop the Orange.'

He told William the reason.

William, deep in thought, tidied his office and then drifted down for a drink in the bar, which turned out to be a bad idea as boisterous members kept asking him questions like were videos of the Orange going to be on sale in Soho sex-shops and was it true that Mrs Hardcastle was going to de-sari and Reveal All.

Luckily for William, Sol Fish was back from the States and was a great comfort, acting as William's press officer by fielding the questions and diverting them with his one-liners. They went in to an early supper together as Sol was going to the opera. Sol explained, 'It's that stuff where a guy's stabbed and instead of bleeding he sings,' and William, relaxing, realized how anxious and taut he had become. He refused coffee so as to get home early and by seven-thirty was on the steps, waving good night to Sol.

Outside, the weather had gone peculiar. This was the first warning of the oncoming thunderstorms which were ravaging the Continent so severely that French farmers were burning down motorway service-stations in protest. In London the early dusting of light rain had strengthened into a steady downpour, the sort which bounced up from the pavement and soaked the ankles. And the sky was slate-grey with a lot of mean, narrow little clouds scudding about like celestial sardines, warning that beastly winds were on their way.

William decided that trying to get home on his wobbly

bike was unwise and went back inside the Club to get Chidders to phone for a cab, if possible a genuine, black, London taxi, driven by a trustworthy driver with a name like Dave.

It was a busy time for Chidders as members streamed in for dinner or streamed out to find their way home in the rain. 'Yes, milord,' he was saying on his phone. 'I will chase up what's happened to your taxi but it's the rain. Piccadilly is blocked as solid as a constipated camel, if you'll pardon the expression. I'll do what I can, milord.' The phone rang again. 'Porter's lodge,' said Chidders, juggling the receiver.

A small member came in and thrust a largish, wet suitcase towards Chidders. 'Will you carry this up to my woom, please?' he said. 'At once.' It was a command, not a request.

'If you'll kindly leave it round the back here, sir,' said Chidders, 'I'll take it up when I have a mo. I've only got two pairs of hands. Hello?' Chidders saw William and put the phone down. 'Anything I can do, sir?'

'Chidders,' said William. 'I need a cab to get me home but so does the rest of the world. Don't worry, I can wait till the rain slackens off a bit.'

Chidders put his finger against the side of his nose in a gesture of complicity and dialled a number. 'Reg?' he said. 'Well, switch *off* the television. I want you to pop round the Club and drive a friend of mine home to Notting Hill. What? Look, Reg, never mind hairy Mexican spiders having it off. Video it if it's that exciting, David Attenborough'll never know. I'll expect you in seven minutes.' He put the phone down. 'My brother-in-law, Reg,' he said to William. 'He's as lazy a sod as Stanley Tozer but at least he's got a car.'

'Chidders, you're a marvel,' said William, sincerely. 'Is nothing beyond your talents?'

Chidders' brow corrugated in thought. 'Flower-arranging,' he decided at last. 'My favourite flowers is leaves.'

William was dropped at his front door in Peel Street by Reg. Reg did not give William his views on the political situation nor have a radio playing pop and his driving was disgruntled but safe. William's tiny glow of pleasure at this was increased by the thought that this was probably his last night at home on his own.

As usual when Milly was away, the house smelled slightly differently and was a little chillier than normal. William vacuumed and tidied, and battled with a sinkful of used saucepans until the state of the happy home was neat enough to win home Brownie points from Milly for househusbandry.

He went up to the bedroom to sort out what he needed for the following night's dinner-party with his in-laws. He knew what to expect of the party. There would be another two or three couples there, the men either something important in politics or the City or both and his mother-in-law, looking very slim from her diet of bananas and hot water, would talk in a shrill voice and twitch with nerves having just given up smoking.

His mother-in-law did not cook so she would have hired in a debby student from an expensive cookery college in Surrey and the menu would be the sort of exciting dinner-party food which photographs beautifully but which nobody can be bothered to enjoy while they're talking.

From a bottom drawer William drew out his black corduroy evening shoes with his initials embroidered upon the toes in gilt, a present from Milly which he had never liked but he knew she would be pleased to see him wearing. And he took from the wardrobe his

Number One suit, the sincere grey worsted, to check it for moth-holes and hitherto unperceived mud and gravy. Only the jacket emerged. The trousers lay in a sullen, crumpled heap at the bottom of the wardrobe. William picked up the trousers and shook them out. During the time they had lain there, a month or so, they had acquired a pattern of creases and looked like a dark grey face tissue which had been scrunched up and flung into the wastepaper basket.

In bed he lay for a long time, dozing. He considered what options he had left in providing a suitable Orange for the Club, yet protecting his old men from gossip and scandal. Then he thought of Milly with a longing sharpened by the days of separation. Not a longing for her thighs, well not primarily, but for her presence. The knowledge that she was in the house, even when she was practising her music in another room, warmed his world. What would happen tomorrow evening at their confrontation over the Orange was a dismal thought he did not at that moment want to contemplate.

Wide awake still, he dragged himself out of bed and searched the kitchen cupboards and shelves for alcohol to drug himself to sleep. He took to bed a glass containing every drop of booze in the house, namely a millimetre of duty-free whisky left over from last year's holiday, a tenth of an inch of vodka which had remained unconsumed because it was virtually invisible unless the bottle was shaken, a few dregs of sherry so dry it would have stripped marine varnish, the remains of some sticky fluid in a jar labelled 'Peaches in Brandy' and a slug of Fernet-Branca, a dark and bitter Italian liqueur which, on the advice of her father, Milly had bought as a sovereign remedy for post-Christmas diarrhoea.

William got back into bed, drank off his sleep-inducing

cocktail which was subtly and profoundly horrible and lay for the next two hours bright-eyed as a bird, staring up at the ceiling.

Up in Co. Durham, Milly was also wide awake. Rain had leaked onto Pippa's bed and onto Pippa, so she had bunked in with Milly. The ceiling had then begun to leak onto Milly's bed so the girls took turns in holding up the Trio's freebie umbrella, a large red, blue and green affair proclaiming in elegant lettering OXFORD DICTIONARY.

'I have an uncle', said Pippa, 'who believes that adult education shouldn't mean teaching the young how to wire a 13 amp plug or the contribution of the Lake Poets to the Romantic Revival. It should mean warning young people of the unpleasant truths they'll have to face when they grow up. Like: "However princely and charming your young man seems to you now, all husbands fart in bed." '

'Truth is beauty, as the poet put it,' said Milly. 'What other old saws is your uncle putting about?'

'More aptly, he says: all flat roofs leak. Some are bone-dry for years, he says, some can be easily repaired and made waterproof, but sooner or later – all flat roofs leak.'

'What a wise man your uncle is,' said Milly.

'He also says never eat vol-au-vents at a drinks party if you've got hay-fever. That thing over there growing out of the wall – is it a tulip?'

'No, it's a weed of the daisy family. Pippa, are you happy about Foster's plans for the Trio?'

'What does a tulip look like, then?'

'It's the one like a coloured wineglass.'

'*Is* it? I always thought that was an iris. Foster? I'm very happy with the arrival of our Foster. Up to now we've been just a cosy little group of girls enjoying ourselves and now we're being made to think more professionally.'

'What about him telling us to work up a programme of Victorian Palm Court music?' asked Milly. 'Are you sure we want to do that?'

'Very good idea, seems to me,' said Pippa. 'It's the sort of stuff which'll get us more conference work. You know, Foster is so musicianly and intelligent and creative it's extraordinary that it was our lovely but just a little bit dim Estelle who found him.' Pippa handed across the umbrella. 'It's your turn. Now Milly don't worry, just think of tomorrow. In the evening you're going to be reunited with your own loving William, and you're going to give him hell.'

Pippa burrowed into the bedclothes and drifted into the arms of Morpheus.

Milly lay there clutching the umbrella, miserably turning things over in her mind and realizing that there was no possibility whatever of her getting any beauty sleep that night. And there was the long and tiring drive south the next day.

The drips of water were building up and then running down the panels of the umbrella onto the bedclothes. Milly wedged the umbrella handle between Pippa's pretty knees and, on a thought, went groping in the dark for the big sheet of plastic which the trio spread over their instruments when they needed protection. She found the plastic and spread it over the bed, using the brolly as a tent pole. She snuggled down in the bed, a night of helpless insomnia stretching out remorselessly ahead of her, and listened to the loud 'plop', 'plop' of the rain as it dripped steadily onto the plastic.

At the third 'plop', Milly was asleep.

Next morning William had intended to leap out of bed early and throw himself eagerly into what he knew was going to be a problem day but he did not hear the alarm and woke up an hour later than usual with a small but vicious hangover, the effect on his digestion and nervous system of the ill-judged nightcap of distilled grain, varnish-stripper, raw Russian alcohol, Italian emetic and the lees of the jar of Christmas present Peaches in Brandy. When he told Sol Fish about the Peaches, Sol said piously, 'It's not the gift that matters, William, it's the spirit in which it's given.'

It was still raining and William had to walk what seemed like halfway to the Club before he found a cab. During the slow journey the driver gave William a critique of every quiz show on television and had his radio tuned to Radio 1, pop music at full volume.

'SAH!' bellowed the sergeant at the front door and William's head seemed to twang like a tuning-fork. Chidders leant down and picked up William's suitcase of dinner-party clothes. 'I'll carry this up for you, sir. You look a little deleterious this morning if I might say so. Did you, as Shakespeare put it, hang one on last night?'

'In a sad sort of way,' said William.

Helped by Chidders, he unpacked in his office. By some miracle it was all there, clean shirt, sprightly hand-painted tie – another present from Milly who thought William's suits desperately dull – his velvet pumps, clean hanky, brush and comb, neatly folded jacket and heavily creased-up trousers. 'There's a 24-Hour Valeting Service which members use, isn't there?' he asked Chidders. 'How long would they take to press my trousers?'

'They're very good, sir,' said Chidders. 'If you take the stuff in before eight-thirty in the morning the 24-Hour Service will rush it back to you in a couple of days. But if I take it round now they'll take four working days, so excluding the weekend, you're looking at next Wednesday or Thursday.'

'But I need them this evening. Look, Chidders, grateful thanks for your help, as ever, but you'd better get back to your cubicle. Any fresh news on Tozer, by the way?'

'Not a sausage,' said Chidders. 'I've been listening carefully to the tape and he hasn't contacted the tabloid rag for a long time now. My own personal, private theory is that the bloke he's trying to touch for money is abroad but due back any day now. Then things should liven up.'

Chidders reached into his pocket, dragged out Belkis's Malcolm's tiny recording-machine and put it on the desk in front of William. 'My advice to you, sir, is to play the tape over and over again and study every word the little bugger says. I'm only a simple old soldier, sir, but you're officer material with educational degrees I wouldn't be surprised, and you might well spot some small clue I've missed, though I doubt it.'

'What do I do to make it play back?' asked William, focusing with difficulty on the tiny lettering under the machine's operating buttons.

'It won't play back,' said Chidders. 'The batteries are flat.'

William closed his eyes for a moment, which was so calming that he wished he could leave them closed for a fortnight.

'Just leave it with me, Chidders,' said William. 'I've got spare batteries.'

'Righto, sir. Excuse me mentioning it, sir, but would you like me to lend you my squeezy thing of eye-lotion? The whites of your eyes are all pink like a pig's bum.'

'No, I'm fine, Chidders. Thanks for your concern.'

William closed his eyes again to give them a treat and to formulate a plan for pressing his trousers. He heard Chidders leaving.

An idea occurred. William sprang up, winced, and moving more slowly, laid his trousers flat on the carpet, twitching them and smoothing them into shape. Then he took down the heavy volumes of his encyclopedia and carefully laid them, like flagstones, on the trousers. Then he stretched himself out supine on top to add more weight and set about composing his thoughts.

About fifty years later he was awoken by the voice of Belkis, 'Willy, what the blazes are you doing down there, eh?'

'It's called lateral thinking,' murmured William.

William got up stiffly, hoisted the encyclopedias back onto their shelf, picked up his best trousers from the carpet and examined the creasing. It seemed, if anything, faintly worse.

'Are those the trousers you are hoping to clad yourself in for your in-laws' dinner-party tonight?' asked Belkis.

'Yes,' said William. Then, apportioning the blame firmly on the trousers, 'They slid off their hanger.'

'Oh, Willy, Willy,' said Belkis, 'you mustn't try to do everything yourself. You must learn to accept help from others, you really must.'

'Meaning?'

'Give me your tousled trousers.'

'What are you proposing to do with them?' asked William, handing them over reluctantly. 'I happen to know the dry-cleaners will take much too long.'

'And I happen to know that the housekeeper downstairs has an electric iron and she'll deliver your trousers back to you, beautifully pressed, in about ten minutes.'

'Ah,' said William. 'Yes. Point taken. I hadn't thought of asking the housekeeper. Good thinking, Belkis.'

'Willy, you are looking very tired and also upwardly-tight and that is not a good thing. You are the chief boss, right? Your job is to do the brainwork and decide what needs to be done. But all the doing doesn't have to be done by you, now does it? That's where we others enter. You are the leader of a team, Willy, not a one-man orchestra.'

William looked at Belkis for quite a while and then leant over and kissed her gently on the forehead.

'I'll tell Milly you did that!' said Belkis. 'It's about time *somebody* told that poor girl something of what's happening.'

'Be fair,' said William. 'You know I've been forbidden to discuss the Orange with Milly.'

'Yes, but forbidden by whom? The Master. I swear, Willy, if you don't tell Milly everything about the Orange at your dinner party tonight I will get my Malcolm to fist-fight you tomorrow and he's very fit and agile at the moment, I am so happy to tell you.'

As the day progressed, William's frail state of health improved rapidly. The faint headache cleared, the pink disappeared from the whites of his eyes and reappeared in his cheeks and by lunchtime he had acquired enough of an appetite to order a small piece of Anton's rough pâté and a slice of toast. Then some mussels. Then a few more mussels because they were particularly light and fresh and Anton's white wine sauce was irresistible. Then some cold roast beef and potato salad. Then cheese-on-toast and coffee.

In the afternoon he established an open-ended Orange planning conference in his office. Heedful of Belkis's point about the need for delegation he asked all the time for suggestions and opinions. He and Belkis had a long session with Edgar, the Sylvester Stallone of double-entry bookkeeping as Belkis called him, and worked out the maximum the Club could afford to give the staff as a birthday present. This turned out to be a week's extra wages plus a bonus based on the number of years each member of staff had worked for the Club. As most of the staff seemed to have worked at the Club since birth it was going to be a happy group come Orange day.

William also arranged with the restaurant manager to

give his waiters and waitresses the night off on Thursday and to replace them from the list of reliable temporary waiters he hired for special Club occasions.

Then there was the question of who was to be responsible for decorating the dining-room. Eventually it was William who suggested that the best plan would be to hand the problem over to the Club's great international star of stage and silver screen, Mr Brandreth Jacques, MBE.

This made a lot of sense to the others and the suggestion was accepted warmly. William made a note to get Brandy Jack's Walthamstow phone number from The Albany's head porter and ring him. The meeting also agreed that Mr Jacques should be asked to investigate the possibility of hiring the turn-of-the-century American waiters' costumes worn by the agile young male dancers in the stage musical *Hello, Dolly!* in order to add a touch of glamour to the Club's temporary waiters, most of whom were elderly Cypriots with huge, painful feet.

The housekeeper had laid out William's newly pressed trousers along with the rest of his clothes on the bed in Bedroom 4A so that he could change there. The weather had cheered up in an unreliable kind of way. It had stopped raining and there were occasional shafts of sunshine but a brisk breeze kept the clouds scudding. About six o'clock William took a look out of the front door and decided to risk going to Fulham by bike rather than try to find a taxi in the rush hour.

'I wish you a joyful weekend, sir,' said Chidders, emerging from his cubicle in his street clothes. 'And I'll wish myself one, too, while I'm at it.' He donned an enormous ex-cavalry mac and a small, squarish bowler hat.

'Chidders,' said William.

'Sah!'

'Just between ourselves, what did your little unit in the war actually use your mules *for*?'

'Mules? What mules, sir?'

'You've always talked about your unit being concerned with mules, and many of us have wondered . . . '

'Not mules, sir. My unit wasn't never concerned with mules, sir. Not mules as such.'

'What, then?'

'Meals.'

'*Meals?*'

'Yessir, meals. I was a cook in the Army Catering Corps. Sah.' Chidders saluted smartly and marched, head held high, out into the sloppy civilian world.

William went up and had a leisurely, Jacuzzi-type bath in 4A, dressed carefully and was awheel in good time, his office clothes in a carrier bag on the handlebars. The rain had held off for the time being.

Sir Garnett and Lady Bracewell always referred to their little house in Parsons Green as 'our London *pied-à-terre*' although it was bigger and more expensively furnished than the accommodation they chose to call 'our little place in the country', a post-war flat above an Abbey National Building Society office in Norwich.

William hid his bike under the privet hedge black with soot and pollution, chained his front wheel to the railings, pocketed his bicycle clips and then went through the welcoming routine he always went through when Milly was home again after playing away. He rattled the letter-box in a fierce tattoo then put his mouth to the slot and yodelled very loudly, 'YOO-EEE-OOO-EEE-OOO! IT'S YOUR FANCY BOY!'

From then on the evening went steadily downhill.

The door was opened by Lady Bracewell. 'Oh, shut up!' she cried. 'I've got enough of a headache as it is.'

'Where's Milly?' asked William, following his mother-in-law into the house.

'Not back yet. Trust her to let me down. And why on earth are you dressed like that? I hope you're going to change.' She grabbed a cigarette from the packet she was cuddling and lit it. She sucked on it so hard that William thought smoke might come out of her ears.

'You said you'd given up the fags,' said William. She gave him a withering look. 'I've got the Onslows arriving at any minute and Hughie and Marsha are coming on from a cocker's p, and that stupid little deb I hired as a party cook is trying to grill a brace of pheasants. It would take all night. You can't grill a fucking pheasant!' Her face had almost disappeared in the clouds of cigarette smoke she was producing.

'Just sit down and listen to me for a minute,' said William soothingly.

'You? You don't know how to boil a bloody egg,' said his mother-in-law.

'My advice is to forget pheasant for tonight,' William began.

'What do we dine on? After-Eight Mints?'

'No, listen. Get Sir Garnett to drive along to the King's Road—'

'Sir Garnett can't drive anywhere at the moment because he's taking a shower. He's always doing something somewhere else when he's needed. When that crucial vote of confidence in the Government was taken in the Commons, where was the Right Honourable Sir Garnett? He was in Trumpers having his hair cut.'

'He hasn't got any hair.'

'I know, he goes once a month for fifteen quidsworth of chat and to be seen going in.'

'Then *I'll* go, on my bike.'

'Go where?'

'There's a very good Chinese Take-Away, Fu Wong's,

just off the King's Road. Milly and I've used it often. I'll get along there right away and bring back Chinese food for, let me see, eight?'

'For Heaven's sake be as quick as you can.'

'Now relax and get your deb going on the pud. Grilled ice-cream? Perhaps she can do card tricks to keep your guests amused. I should be about half an hour.'

And off William pedalled. He failed to find the Fu Wong Chinese Take-Away at first which was alarming but after cycling past where it used to be a few times he realized that it had undergone a change of nationality and was now The Purple Pagoda Thai Take-Away, which looked from the outside like a run-down betting-shop in Limehouse. There was nothing he could padlock his bike to so he padlocked it to itself, which meant it could not be ridden but could easily be stolen, so for forty minutes he waited for his order to be de-tinned, de-frozen, microwaved and spooned into foil cartons, with one foot keeping the shop door ajar and one eye on his bike.

The Thai menu was a mystery to William. When ordering Chinese he knew to avoid dishes with descriptions like 'A Sizzling Platter of the Harvest of the Seas', in fact to avoid anything described on the menu as 'Sizzling Dishes (watch out, here they come!)' because all Chinese take-away food was, by the very circumstance of it being taken away, tepid and flabby when got home. But the Thai menu was strange territory, with mysterious exotic offerings like Tales of the Sea, Royal Orchid Platter and Thai Tom Yum Kung Soup. William thought his safest move was to order two of the Set Gourmet Thai Feasts For Four, with a mental reservation that anything on a Far-Eastern menu described as 'gourmet' usually turned out to be too small and tongue-numbingly seasoned.

It began to rain again as William carefully slung the four small, warm, brown-paper carrier-bags over his handlebars and began to pedal back. All seemed to be going well when drama struck. The road had been dug up recently and the hole had only been roughly filled in, leaving a four-inch step for William's front wheel to negotiate. Without thinking of the state of his bike, William reacted as he had done since a small boy and heaved upwards on the handlebars to jump the front-wheel over the obstruction. The handlebars came off in his hands.

William was not going fast and managed to crash land against the side of a parked coach without falling off.

The coach was taking a party of old-age pensioners from Salisbury to the musical at the Victoria Palace theatre and in a moment he was surrounded by retired mechanics and engineers who knew more about machinery and old bikes than William would ever know. In a trice they had fitted the handlebars back in the bike frame and tightened the retaining bolt, checked the brake cable and three-speed gear and launched William on his way with a shout of 'One, two – six!' and an enormous, corporate heave.

Five minutes later William was back at the Fulham *pied-a-terre*, bike again under the hedge manacled to the railings and his precious cargo of warm carrier-bags held carefully in his left hand. As he pressed the bell-push he became aware that the rain had soaked his Number One suit and his hair was tousled and stuck to his face, not at all how he was hoping to greet Milly.

Moreover his left foot had become wetter and warmer than the right foot. He looked down and saw that his velvet evening slipper was shiny with a viscous substance, and steaming slightly.

'Oh, God,' he thought, 'the *Thai Tom Yum Tum* soup.'

A glance at his carrier-bags confirmed the worst. His bang against the coach had displaced the lid on the container of soup and the liquid had made a hole through the damp brown-paper carrier-bag and leaked downwards.

He had half a pint of clear broth, plus the odd prawn, soaking into his left velvet slipper.

The front door had opened and Milly stood there, looking even more beautiful and fragile than ever.

'You never did like those velvet slippers, did you?' she said, tears beginning to form.

'Darling!' cried William. 'I wanted to be here to greet you but your mother had a food crisis.' He made to kiss her but Milly slid back.

'I'm deadly tired,' Milly said. 'Sorry. I didn't get much sleep last night. Woke at one o'clock and the journey down from Durham in the rain was a pig.'

'I've got to talk,' said William. 'It's very important for us.'

'I know. There's an awful lot I must sort out with you. But when? The humidity's loosened all my harpsichord strings and I'll take hours to tune it and Foster wants us to rehearse tomorrow and Sunday at his place for our new programme. We've simply got to talk tonight.'

'Oh!' said William. 'You're going away again!'

With a heavy heart William took off his left slipper and tipped it up. A brace of prawns fell off and a trickle of *Thai Tom Yum Tum* oozed out onto the doorstep.

There was suddenly an eddy of white smoke, a cough, and like the Wicked Fairy in pantomime Lady Bracewell appeared behind Milly.

'*You* took your time!' she said to William, reaching forward and grabbing the carrier-bags. 'It would be nice if one of these days just one member of my family did *something* to help me. But no, it's take, take, take . . . they're all in the drawing-room. For Heaven's sake go and make yourself useful and help Garnett with the drinks.'

She disappeared down the narrow stairs to the kitchen and Milly touched William's arm lightly, the implicit message being, whatever problems we have to iron out thank you for not kicking mummy in the teeth.

'I must say she does get a bit het up when she's got people coming to dinner,' said William, holding Milly's arm tightly and steering her towards the drawing-room. He had the feeling that if he let go her arm she would spiral down to the carpet and fall asleep.

The two male guests and Sir Garnett, looking like triplets with identically bald heads and comfortably rotund figures, were standing by the fireplace clutching glasses of whisky. They were in dinner jackets.

William glanced down at his wet lounge suit and tried to smooth out a crease or two, without success.

The two ladies were sitting on the sofa quietly swapping two or three hundred photographs of their grandchildren.

'Congratulations on your anniversary, sir,' said William.

'What?' said Sir Garnett. 'Oh, I see. Yes, most kind. Thank you – er – thank you. Jim, may I introduce – er – my son-in-law – er—'

'William,' said Milly.

'What? Oh, yes. William. William, my two oldest friends Jim Rice-Burroughs, Concrete, and Arthur Baverstock, Airports Authority.'

Concrete – or Airports – waved his glass cheerily at William. 'So you're the famous William,' he said. 'Correct me if I'm talking balls as usual but didn't Garnett tell me you'd become a member of the Walpole Club?'

'Not quite,' said William politely. 'I'm a paid member of staff there.'

A silence fell. Whisky glasses rose and fell.

And so the ghastly evening went on. Dinner was not too bad because the Thai food was unexpectedly pleasing, tepid and soggy but with sharp and bright flavours from much cunning use of chillis, and William did a smart musical-chairs manoeuvre so that he could sit next to Milly and keep her awake by talking to her, like an explorer stranded on an ice floe keeping a colleague from freezing to death.

'Look,' he whispered to Milly, 'about the Club's birthday party.'

'What the hell do you think you're doing getting mixed up in an orgy?' demanded Milly in a fierce but rather loud whisper.

'It's part of my job,' hissed William back.

'So you're quite happy to let down poor Uncle Sid, after all he's done for you? Do you know what anguish your behaviour is causing him and poor Parthenope?'

'Yes, I do. None at all. I'm sorry, my darling, but the truth is that poor Parthenope has turned out to be a shabby snob and dear old Uncle Sid is an opportunist and a liar.'

'How can you slag them off like that? What proof have you got?'

Unhappily William and Milly had to put their debate on hold at this interesting point because they were drawn into the general conversation by their hostess who, maddeningly for her, was sitting slightly too far away to make out what Milly and William were saying. The general conversation was concerned with the relative good looks of the TV weather girls.

The student-cook from Surrey, Fiona, an ample girl, appeared and trudged round the table, red-eyed from weeping. She collected up the plates, smiling bravely, and brought in her exam-passing pud, a complicated and unlikely liaison of slices of home-made brown and white bread soaked in various liqueurs and festooned with slices of anonymous foreign fruit and blue ice-cream.

'And the stories about you having a leg-over with Mrs Hardcastle,' whispered Milly to William, smiling happily to fool her mother. 'Uncle Sid said it's the talk of the Club.'

'A hopeless lie,' said William, 'we're both far too happily married.'

'And bringing in a skinhead friend as chef, which has proved a disaster?'

'Another porky,' said William. 'Anton's a huge success.' They both pushed their helpings of pudding around their plates, too unhappy to eat.

'But you do admit you're arranging an orgy for your dirty old men?'

'Once again, they are not dirty old men, and secondly do you know what's going to happen at our orgy?'

'How could I know? It's your deceit that gets me down, William. Why couldn't you have told me about the orgy? Uncle Sid was astonished that you hadn't discussed it with me from the very start. He couldn't understand how you could be so secretive with me.'

'I was specifically ordered not to mention the orgy to anyone, particularly you.'

'Ordered? By whom, may I ask?'

William took Uncle Sid's original letter out of his pocket, smoothed it carefully on the tablecloth and passed it to Milly.

'Line three,' he said, 'and signature at the bottom.'

Milly read. Then she slid the letter back to William and held on tightly to his hand.

'Bloody hell,' she said. 'What a hypocritical bastard!'

'To begin with,' said William, 'he was as keen as everybody else on our Orange, that's our code name for the orgy. It began as a ruse by some frisky old members to embarrass a nasty clergyman, Canon Prout, and then like Topsy it just growed. The reason that Uncle Sid suddenly went off our Orange is simple. Parthenope ordered him to. When she found out about it she remembered that Canon Prout's wife had gone to school with Parthenope's cousin so it was unthinkable that Parthenope could allow her husband's club to make mock of the canon.'

'I've misjudged the Sidmontons,' said Milly. 'They're rubbish, aren't they?'

'Oh, yes,' said William. 'Not nice people one little bit.'

'I can't get over how rottenly they've treated you. And it's all my fault for asking him to find you a job! Oh, William, I'm seething. You must get your own back, we simply can't let them get away with it.'

'OK, darling, I'll think of something.'

'But *will* you? You know what you're like, you always turn the other cheek, let everybody walk over you.'

'That's funny, that's the second time I've been told that today.'

'Well, it's true and this time you're not going to. I, your wife, demand that you pour retribution on the nasty Sidmontons from a great height! I'm sorry, darling, I'm beginning to shout. I really am so tired . . .'

William stood up and pulled her gently to her feet beside him. 'Come on, my love,' he said, 'I'm driving you home.' He picked her up gently and hugged her to his chest. She was very light. 'Thanks for a lovely party!' he called out cheerily to his in-laws. 'We must all do this again some time!'

The hosts and their friends stared at William, mouths sagging, unmoving, like a group caught in an early flash-light photograph.

'But you haven't had coffee!' cried Milly's mother in an incredulous voice.

'We're trying to give it up,' said William from the door.

William carried Milly out to her 2CV parked in the road outside and fed her carefully into the passenger seat.

'Why are we leaving the party?' she murmured drowsily. 'Was it something I said?'

'Sort of,' William said.

'Was I funny?' asked Milly anxiously. And fell asleep as though pole-axed.

CHAPTER SIXTEEN

MASTERLY RETRIBUTION
AND GIRLS, GIRLS, GIRLS

Next morning William took Milly her breakfast in bed. With the resilience of the young she woke at eight bright as a button, fully recovered from her damp Durham night and her dangerously wet motorway drive followed by the dread dinner.

William found sleep more elusive and was awake and up at half-past six. As a surprise for Milly he tuned her harpsichord for her. He had made it portable a long time ago by modifying the legs so that Milly could unscrew them and lower the instrument through the 2CV's roof, and he was able to carry the instrument through to the kitchen table where he could tune it without waking up Milly. The harpsichord, like all harpsichords in damp weather, was painfully off-note but William was good at tuning, it was the kind of job needing precision and patience which he enjoyed. He saw Milly off to her rehearsal at Foster's digs, caught a cab to his in-laws and managed to retrieve his bike from under their hedge without being spotted. Cycling to his office on a sunny Saturday morning with a quarter of London's car-drivers away sunbathing on the Algarve was pleasant indeed.

His first priority was to talk to Brandy Jack about dressing up the dining-room for the Orange. Mr Dymchurch, the head porter in The Albany, was instantly helpful and William got Brandy Jack on the phone in Walthamstow just as Branny and Philly were on their way out to their Saturday morning trawl of the supermarket wine shelves. Brandy Jack, after checking *sotto voce* with Philly, assured William that both of them were delighted and honoured to be given the job of, in Philly's words, 'poncing up the dining-room'. They would begin planning immediately by phoning round their old scene-designer friends and finding out what stored-away film and theatre props and curtains and stuff could be borrowed or hired or nicked for use on Thursday.

William's next problem was to arrange for himself and Lord Wick to audition the Synchronized Strip-teasers on Monday afternoon. Belkis had helped by leaving a note on his desk giving Miss Bimbo Babyoil's address and telephone number which, Belkis explained in the note, she had obtained from Trixie's mother, Mrs Addington. Miss Babyoil lived in Eaton Square.

The number was engaged for quite a while which gave William, feet up on his desk, the opportunity to muse on what revenge would be most satisfying to inflict upon those tatty manipulators now referred to by Milly as The Sodding Sidmontons, which made them sound like a variety act sub-titled The Thames-side Unicyclists.

A painful, ringing but unlethal blow on the back of the head from Chidders' shovel was an attractive thought as come-uppance for His Honour the Judge but less suitable perhaps for Parthenope, although she was probably the tattier and the soddier of the pair of them. William let his fancies float. If he could find out what make of shampoo Parthenope used and replace the contents with indelible mauve dye? Too complicated, would mean renting a burglar. Put a notice in *The Times* from Parthenope announcing that she would no longer be responsible for her husband's debts? An obvious hoax which the newspaper would probably refuse to print. Also a feeble idea. Drive away His Lordship's car, the ancient sit-up-and-beg

Rolls-Royce which the Master cherished as a status symbol, and return it sprayed with psychedelic daisies as per John Lennon's car in the Sixties? Not possible as William happened to know that the Rolls was away in Derby having something fundamental done to its cylinder block. Balance a bucket of whitewash over their bedroom door?

William's diminishing spiral of creative ideas for revenge was interrupted by the sound of the number he had dialled giving a ringing tone at last. A feminine voice purred 'Hello? Mrs Hume-Vansittart. Who is this?'

William restrained an impulse to say, 'You've just told me: you are Mrs Hume-Vansittart,' and said instead, 'At this end it's William Grundwick, secretary of the Walpole Club. I am trying to contact Miss Bimbo Babyoil on a professional matter.'

Mrs Hume-Vansittart had a hybrid accent, William noticed. An overlay of soft, home-counties vowels almost obscuring, but not quite, an American half-strangled twang, resulting in a voice which was a cross between Dame Barbara Cartland and Madonna.

'Mr Grundwick, I am going to put you on hold while I go through to my bureau.' She pronounced it 'bur*EAU*'. 'Please forgive my rudeness but Ed my husband and business partner has a finance concept meeting in five minutes with Belgian Porno-Video's bankers. It's like it's Grand Central Station in my lounge on a busy day and you better believe it!'

The line went dead and an old, badly stretched tape of Kiri Te Kanawa singing 'Smoke Gets in Your Eyes' came on for quite a while. Then Mrs Hume-Vansittart returned. Being in her own bur*EAU* obviously encouraged her to revert to being Bimbo Babyoil, ex-Crazy Horse Saloon Stripper. Her voice lost most of its Dame Barbara Cartland upper middle-class throb and went back to being almost wholly screechy Madonna. 'Hi!' she cried. 'Sorry about the delay, honey. Wanna tell me your problem?'

'Well, Miss Babyoil—' William began.

'None of that crap,' said the lady. 'Will you call me by my real name? Will you do that? I'm Fawn.'

'Fawn,' said William. 'Righto. Well, Fawn – hello – my name is William.'

'That's great,' said Fawn.

' . . . and I'm secretary of a gentlemen's club and we want to have a bit of excitement after dinner on our two hundred and fiftieth birthday and the troupe known as Six of the Bust was recommended. I believe you train them.'

'Listen, honey, I don't just train 'em, I *own* 'em. Tits, wigs, routines, they're all my legal property and you apply to me for everything, OK?'

'Yes, yes, of course. Good. Well done. Point is, time is of the essence this end and my Chairman of Committee and I want to audition the act on Monday afternoon.'

'No way, darling.'

'Oh. Well, we'll have to think of something else then, won't we? Thank you for sparing me your time—'

'Hold on a minute now, easy does it. There might be a way.'

'But you said "no way".'

'Look, don't you know any damn thing about negotiating?'

'No, not really. Only that at this moment I seem to be one point ahead.'

There was a bit of breathing the other end and then Fawn said, 'You'll have to pay the girls and hire the venue for the afternoon.'

'No,' said William. 'I will not pay the girls, it's an audition and should they get the job they will then be adequately paid. It's a most improper and unprofessional suggestion that the client should pay for an audition.'

More deep breathing from Eaton Square.

'But I'm willing to meet you on the cost of hiring a hall,' said William affably. 'We'll pay half if you cough up the other half.'

Even deeper breathing.

'Can't we hire an hour at that club in Greek Street with the transparent Jacuzzis?' said William. 'Or do they bubble away all day?'

'The Whirlpool? They lost their licence last week,' said Miss Babyoil with what seemed to be quiet satisfaction. 'Westminster Council Health Officer labelled it a health hazard. Said in court that the Whirlpool baths were the kind of warm water installation that could well breed Legionnaire's disease.'

William felt a touch of sadness that his boring, garrulous, hypochondriac club member had been right.

'But the room can still be hired?' asked William.

'It sure can, honey,' said Miss Babyoil. 'The Maltese heavies who own the lease can't sell it because the rents are so high that only some Tsar of Vice can afford to buy it. And Tsars of Vice have since moved into easier ways of laundering Mafia money, like marketing pirate videos and backing ethnic restaurants.'

'The Purple Pagoda Thai Take-Away, Chelsea?'

'Yep. That's one of 'em.'

'Fawn,' said William, 'book the Whirlpool Club for three until four on Monday afternoon. Right?'

'OK. But do you only want to see Six of the Bust? I got groups and single acts spread out all over the country; Nudiegrams, French Maids, nude Coronation Street look-alikes, whaddyafancy? You name it, I'll supply it.'

'Madame,' William used the word deliberately, 'I can only reiterate in the strongest terms that all I am looking for is an innocently unusual cabaret to entertain some old and rather distinguished Club members after dinner.'

'Try Salome Sammi,' said Miss Babyoil. 'She shimmies

all her veils off and you know what? She's a feller! It's a great laff!'

'Madame—'

'A bit of The Love Whom Dareth Not Speak Thy Name? I strongly recommend Veronica and Vera, they do a fan-dance and then roll all over each other, groaning. They're really big in the Lincolnshire area. It's all that fox-hunting, I guess.'

'Madame,' said William firmly, 'my committee chairman and I will be at the Greek Street address at three p.m. when we will expect your Six of the Bust to audition for us. Thank you so much for your time, goodbye.'

William put the phone down feeling grubby, as though he had been delving through somebody's dustbin. But the hall and the act were booked for Monday afternoon.

William began to write out a report for Belkis on what he had achieved and what there was left to do. This was because Belkis, he had realized rather late, was adept at quietly sorting out Orange problems on her own and easing the strain on William. Phone numbers he needed seemed miraculously to appear on his phone-pad without being asked for, as did the addresses and full names of people he was going to see. Little yellow Post-its saying, 'Ring Lord Wick', 'You said you were going to speak to Anton', 'Check parking with police for Thursday?' appeared, stuck to the edge of his desk.

The process of writing the report caused William to simplify the problems still facing him. There were still three main concerns. There was the matter of the retribution he must somehow arrange to fall about the ears of the Sodding Sidmontons – and he had given his word not only to Milly and Belkis but also to Lord and Lady Wick that he *would* cause severe retribution to descend. There was the problem of finding an unusual cabaret acceptable to the Club members, most of whom did not know their own minds on the subject. And looming ever larger was the problem of security. Tozer's paymasters had still to be identified and somehow prevented from printing what would obviously be an immensely printable story for any tabloid, providing come-on quotes like 'Toff's orgy in London's West End', 'Peer of the Realm and stripper . . . ', 'Behind the door was discovered His Honour Judge . . . ', 'Television personality's wife says she will stand by him this one last time . . . ', 'Famous Sunday newspaper editor caught with his . . . '

William groaned.

But then the phone rang and it was Milly.

'Darling!' he really yelled into the phone in surprise and delight.

'You're very ducky tuning the harpsichord. Very thoughtful and a lovely surprise, thanks.'

'How are things in Ealing?' said William.

'Bags of room to rehearse here in Foster's digs. Big old Edwardian house. Normally full of music students but blissfully empty as it's holidays. Rehearsals are going a treat. Fossy is brilliant and really pulling our playing together and we've started work already on our new programme.'

'Marvellous. Oh, Mil, it is good to hear your voice!'

'Now for the wonderful news. Pippa had a phonecall late last night. It was Catriona. Willy, she's come home! Flew back on the red eye last night!'

'What happened? Hadn't she and Trev joined some heavy sect which preaches that inanimate objects have souls like the rest of us?'

'That's right. Run by a Los Angeles nut named Tarquin Cohen. Tarquin's credo is that a lump of wood might well have a nervous system which we don't know about yet so we should give all inanimate objects the benefit of the doubt until we *do* know and treat them as equals.'

'Wonderful California.'

'It was just the kind of mumbo-jumbo that Trev could relate to. He got so keen on the Movement that Tarquin Cohen appointed him Vice-President.'

'It couldn't happen to a nicer idiot. I'm so glad that Catriona had the sense to jack it all in and come home.'

'She had to, really. Trev got married yesterday.'

'*What*? He ditched poor Catriona for somebody else? Well, I dunno, that was quick! Where was the wedding – Las Vegas?'

'To get publicity for the movement Trev's simply wonderful marriage took place in a Beverly Hills furniture shop. The ceremony was transmitted live on afternoon television.'

'Who was the bride? Presumably an old flame.'

'There wasn't a bride.'

'Surely every marriage has a bride?'

'Trev married his guitar.'

There was silence at William's end.

'Catriona's getting over it, she's really happy playing music again,' Milly went on. 'Estelle has only to look at Foster and her bow drops from her nerveless hand but Catriona's in terrific form, strong and sure and making lovely sounds. The Trio's transformed. I'm really happy with it.'

'What sort of honeymoon can Trev be having, wrestling with a guitar?' said William pensively.

'Now don't brood on it, William, you've got a lot you really need to worry about.'

'Can a guitar give grounds for divorce?'

'William, stop it!'

'There's a warning to Trev somewhere in Shakespeare. "Untune that string and hear what discord follows . . . " '

'William, *listen*! With Catriona home we've got some solid rehearsing to do and we're all going to bunk down here in Ealing for a couple of days. Sorry, darling, but Foster has got us an audition at Wednesday lunchtime for a City Livery dinner and we're not nearly up to it yet. I'll be back on Wednesday evening. Here's the Ealing address and phone number in case you need me.'

William carefully and silently copied down Milly's details.

'OK, darling?' said Milly, a little anxiously.

'Well, I must say there is one slight thing bothering me,' said William, hesitantly.

'And that is?'

'What if the guitar wants children?'

'Silly bugger!' said Milly affectionately and gently put the phone down.

Once again William's thoughts turned to the urgent problem of how to humble the snobby, selfish Sidmontons. And the more he thought about it the more he became convinced that inflicting physical discomfort on them was not the answer. The punishment must fit the crime, or rather the criminals. It had to be demeaning within the Sidmontons' own code of conduct, some sort of social humiliation would be far more distasteful to them than being pushed off a cliff.

But what?

Brooding on it, William strolled past Belkis's empty office and was just descending the stairs for a quick bite of lunch when he heard his phone ringing again. He belted back up and snatched up the phone as it was beginning its sixth ring, about the maximum number in William's experience before the average caller gave up.

'William?' It was Lord Wick.

'Sir,' said William.

'Why are you breathing hard? Have you got Mrs Hardcastle in there with you?'

'I will treat that remark, milord, as an unwelcome sexist

reference to a valuable member of staff, and unfortunately no she's not in here squashed up against me. I was halfway down the stairs and dashed back up again to answer the phone.'

'I didn't really want you, I wanted Chidders.'

'It's his Saturday off.'

'I know that now. But *you* might do. Have you got a Rolls-Royce?'

'Not on me, sir, no.'

'Och, we are in skittish mood this morning! I take it you've made it up with your Milly. William, the Master has just been on to me asking for help. He had a message from Their Royal Highnesses' secretary to say that they'll be landing at Stansted airport about six this afternoon and would the Master kindly meet the plane with his Rolls and convey the royals on to Maude Tansey's postponed dinner-party at Brougham.'

'But the Master hasn't got his Rolls. Isn't it away being welded or something?'

'Yes, and therein lies the problem. He rang me asking me whether I had a Rolls. But I haven't. I had an old one once but I didn't get on with it so I gave it to the shepherd who uses it to cart pregnant ewes about in the back. The Master's afraid he might have to let the royals down which, extremely minor royals though the royals undoubtedly are, goes against every fibre of the Sidmontons' social pretensions.'

'What did you want Chidders to do? Hire a rickshaw and pedal them to dinner?'

'Of course not, it would take him too long. And the duke's too mean to tip him. No, I thought Chidders could ring round and lay on a hired Rolls with chauffeur, but as Chidders is off-duty perhaps you wouldn't mind doing it.' He gave William the plane's flight number and estimated time of arrival.

'It's terribly tempting to do nothing and let the royals wait there,' said William, 'as revenge on the Master and Parthenope.'

'What a nasty idea. It was my first thought, too,' said Lord Wick cheerfully, 'but it wouldn't do, would it? It would be such an easy, tatty victory. And the Duke and Duchess could always hire a taxi outside the airport and hang the expense. Not that either of them is likely ever to hang any expense, they're boringly careful with their money, and also boringly status-conscious, as only very minor royalty seem to enjoy being.'

'Status-conscious, eh?' mused William. Then he had his beautiful, golden, poetic, thoroughly reprehensible idea.

'Leave everything to me, sir,' said William briskly. 'I will make the arrangements and ring you back to report, if I may, about six o'clock this evening.'

'I'll be here,' said Lord Wick. 'My dog and I quite enjoy watching *Star Trek* on the telly at six. At least I do. Madeleine goes to sleep and snores through the exciting bits but she likes some of the music.'

William laid his plans with his usual thoroughness, what Milly during a tiff one day defensively called his 'nit-picking attention to unimportant details'. The tiff was caused by Milly parking the phone bill in the bread bin so as not to lose it and accidentally toasting it stuck to a slice of bread.

Planning completed in his head, William got to work. Happily, and not very surprisingly, Rollo Chad-Baxter, Chairman of the Board of *Mayfair Executive and Diplomatic Super-Cabs* was not out on a job but dozing in his group head office/bedsit. After five rings Rollo answered the phone, still half asleep. William explained that he was phoning on behalf of Lord and Lady Sidmonton, who wanted Rollo to pick up Their Royal Highnesses the Duke and Duchess of Westmorland at Stansted Airport at 18.10 hrs and convey them with all speed to Brougham, Lord Tansey's estate in Gloucestershire. William instructed Rollo to scan the passengers pouring through Customs with their wobbly trolleys, spot the royals and wave at them a large cardboard sign saying LORD SIDMONTON'S TRANSPORT FOR YOUR HIGHNESSES. Rollo was to parry any complaints about the car, if there were any which was laughably unlikely, by reiterating that the vehicle had been arranged personally by Lord and Lady Sidmonton. Rollo was now fully awake and tense with excitement, anxious to start work on the sign he was to hold up in Arrivals, which he saw with his entrepreneurial flair as being in the firm's colours, green ink on silver card. 'Tell you what,' he said to William, 'how about if I pick out the words with stuck-on sequins? It'd give the sign a suitable touch of royal class.'

William spent the afternoon on desk-work, which had been somewhat neglected amidst the week's greater excitements. There was a reference he had to write for a fired waiter, not an easy thing to do fairly as the waiter had been the laziest, most foul-mouthed and dishonest employee the Club had ever endured. A little double-speak was called for. After chewing the end of a Biro until he struck ink, William wrote:

> When working for this club Mr Xerxes proved
> to be a waiter of rare skills and even rarer
> enthusiasm for his work. Despite being constantly
> provoked by diners complaining of the service
> it must stand to his credit that he never once
> struck a member. His interests include reading,
> particularly fiction, a fact which is reflected
> in his interesting C.V. Employers who are
> looking for skilled, reliable staff should lose no
> time in interviewing Mr Xerxes.

Then William turned to the Suggestions Book. There was little new except an interesting entry from a nice old member who always signed himself Thos Thorogood so was known to his many Club friends as old Thos.

Thos was a very gentle person, slightly surprised by everything about him. Even turning a corner in the corridor he would start back a little at the exciting prints of London on the wall. He had been starting back a little at them for forty years. Thos had written, very, very neatly:

When I arrived this morning there was a stranger in the hall reading the notices on the notice-board and peering about in a suspicious manner. He was short, stooping, and uncouth about the face; an ill-preserved forty years of age I would suppose. 'Can I help you?' I asked. 'No,' he said, busy copying something down from the notice-board into a notebook. 'I'm afraid you are on private premises,' I said to him. 'May I know who you are?' 'I'm the Archbishop of Canterbury,' he said. For some reason warning bells tinkled. He was wearing pink socks and had four or five ball-point pens sticking out of his breast pocket. 'Can you prove you're the Archbishop of Canterbury?' I asked him. His reply was 'Piss off' so I still don't know whether he was the Archbishop or not. Discussing the matter later with a friend who is a rural dean we decided the man could well have been an imposter. I thought I should record this disturbing occurrence. Might somebody be spying on the Club?

Thos Thorogood

You did very well to report it. Almost certainly the Club is being spied on by a tabloid newspaper anxious to fabricate scandal stories

*about our Orange. I do urge members not to
discuss the Orange with anybody suspicious;
secrecy is absolutely vital over the next few days.
If you spot a stranger on the premises please
report it to me or seek Sergeant Chidding's help.
Should the stranger become violent, Chidders has
a shovel. But care is urged; the Archbishop of
Canterbury really is a guest sometimes.*

W.G.

At six o'clock William rang Lord Wick.

'Yes, a good moment,' said His Lordship. '*Star Trek* is
a repeat and Madeleine has gone to sleep. How goes the
struggle?'

'My three problems are now reduced to two. How do
we finish off our Orange with some suitable entertainment
– and the keyword is suitable – and how do we spike the
press's guns?'

'I presume that the third problem was how to wreak
revenge on the Master and his Madam for being so
deceitful, and so horrible to your wife?' said Lord Wick.
'Do I take it that revenge has been wreaked – racked –
wrecked?'

'I have the honour to report, sir, that on instructions
passed on to me from Lord and Lady Sidmonton I booked
a suitable vehicle to transport their royal highnesses from
Stansted to the dinner-party at Brougham. The vehicle I
arranged as from the Sidmontons was the car operated by
Mayfair Executive and Diplomatic Super-Cabs.'

'Oh, William! You mean that wreck you went in to
Catford?'

'Yes.'

'Just let me savour the situation.'

'Any moment now the Duke and Duchess will be

ushered swiftly through Stansted Customs to be faced with Rollo holding a large green and silver sign, picked out in sequins, saying that Lord and Lady Sidmonton have sent him to collect them.'

'Green and silver and sequins? Wonderful!'

'The inside of the car lacks charm,' William went on. 'There's the dried blood over the carpet and part of the back seat.'

'Dried blood,' repeated His Lordship, happily.

'Sharp springs poke up through the seats.'

'Doesn't one of the doors have to be hung on to or it flies open?'

'At least one.'

'And the steering wobbles?'

'And carbon monoxide fumes could be a medical problem.'

'You know, William, chances are that one look at the car and the royals will hire a taxi.'

'I sincerely hope so,' said William. 'We don't want to cause *them* woe.'

'All the same, I don't fancy the Master and Parthenope's chances of being invited to the Royal Box at Ascot next year,' said Lord Wick, 'but come to think of it, I don't suppose the Duke and Duchess get invited all that frequently.'

'Are we not being over-beastly to the Master and Parthenope?' asked William. 'I have a niggly feeling that there's something a touch shabby about revenge.'

'Not a bit of it,' said Lord Wick. 'Remember what Francis Bacon wrote? "Revenge is a kind of wild justice." The Sidmontons of this world almost always get away with it, but you've brought about a little wild justice and that's nothing at all to be sorry about. I refer to Francis Bacon the dead essayist, not the late painter. I think the old Francis

Bacon's full title was Lord Vera Lynn of St Albans but my memory is a bit dodgy on names. Well done, William. We meet for lunch Monday?'

At lunchtime on Monday, William made his way down to the bar and Lord Wick was there waiting for him. William had vaguely wondered what a Scottish peer would wear to go striptease-fancying. In the event Lord Wick was sporting a pair of mangy corduroy trousers worn down to the canvas at the knees, a Viyella checked shirt with a frayed collar, a vaguely military striped tie, and a very long tweed jacket, hairy as an army blanket, which had strange oblique pockets to hold dead hares and small deer.

It was good to see some of the other doddery funsters also there at the end of the bar, though it was no great surprise as they were always in the bar at lunchtime, notably the Sporting Baronet, eyes watering as usual from gulping his whisky, and Sol Fish.

'William, I've ordered you a large gin,' said Sir Archie. 'You're looking a bit cream-crackered, if you don't mind me so saying. If you're over-worrying about the Orange you really mustn't, it's really only our bit of fun. An excuse for a party, what?'

'*Ici, ici,*' said Sol Fish. 'For the insular British amongst us that's French for "Here, here."'

'No worries,' said William, 'it's all coming together beautifully.' He uncrossed his fingers, knocked back his gin and tonic and he and Lord Wick escaped to the dining-room to enjoy a leisurely cutlet and to check whether Anton had run into problems for Thursday's food, which to William was the real heart of the Orange.

But Anton had everything well in hand. Billingsgate dealers had responded to his call for rare items and everything was organized from the huge order for fresh

Colchester oysters down to Pipo the Mauritian pastrycook's little bowls of *gateaux piments* for each table.

William and Lord Wick walked along Piccadilly to Soho. An odd experience for William as Lord Wick chattered away the whole time in his normal speaking voice making no allowance for passing traffic or general hubbub. As his head was at the level of William's waist, his comments were borne off by the wind. Also, for a small man he had a remarkable turn of speed, twinkling along on his tiny legs and vigorously manipulating his sawn-off walking-stick with a stabbing, corkscrew action. He enjoyed walking, as he seemed to enjoy everything.

He stopped and jabbed his stick at a narrow alley next to the Burlington Arcade. 'Up there,' he said, looking up at William and therefore becoming audible, 'up there's Albany.' He gave a cackle. 'As you'll have found out by now, that's where Brandy Jack doesn't live!' He twinkled off towards Piccadilly Circus at speed. William almost had to run to catch him up and bring him to a halt.

'You *know* about Brandy Jack?' he asked, amazed.

'Of course I do. We *all* know about Branny and Philly and Walthamstow. Branny's a kind old thing and we're all very fond of him. I think we'd probably assassinate anybody who tried to put it about that Branny was not what he seemed.'

Soho had changed considerably since the brief period when William had worked there watering hanging baskets and window-boxes at night for a contract nursery. As he and Lord Wick worked their way up Brewer Street, trying not to be run over by motorcycle couriers doing 30 mph clutching reels of video tape, he hardly recognized it. Most of the tatty sex shops and shows had been cleared away and were only creeping back slowly. HOLLYWOOD NUDES PEEP-SHOW above which he had once watered a sad row of geraniums was now a brilliantly lit shop selling discount electric duvets and smoke alarms, STRIPORAMA had become a travel agency specializing in cultural tours of the Greek islands, ADULT BOOKS sold carving knives and copper saucepans and THREE IN A BED – LIVE! was a fish shop.

William and Lord Wick had some difficulty finding THE GREEK STREET WHIRLPOOL HEALTH AND NATURIST CLUB as it was not in Greek Street but in a narrow alley off Greek Street. A huge, dark-haired lady sat at a tiny desk inside the door knitting and chewing. 'Ite-a pun,' she said without looking up. 'Ite-a pun hitch.'

There was a sign above her head reading: UNDER NEW MANAGEMENT – INTERNATIONAL STRIPATHON – non-stop 10.30 a.m. to midnight – seats £5.00 – Members Only (membership £3) – no cameras, no binoculars, no camcorders, no macs.

'Good afternoon, madam,' said Lord Wick with charm. 'I take it from your accent that you are from that most heroic of islands, Malta?'

'Nyah,' said madam, knitting on, 'I am Maltese. My son is boss man 'ere so dun try on nuthin', you unnerstan me? It's ite-a pun hitch.'

William stepped forward. 'Good afternoon, madam,' he said firmly. 'My name is Grundwick and my colleague and I are a little early but we've hired the theatre from three o'clock to audition a group of girls belonging to Miss Babyoil, so *we* are your bosses for the afternoon and we've no intention whatever of paying you eight pounds each.'

The fat lady put down her knitting and gazed up at William with respect. 'You know Miss Babyoil? Ah, she a queen that woman. So rich! She not work hard, oh dear, like we poor people but she make money from here and there all day, y'know that? Everybody she meets pays her money for something and she now grand lady, ain't it!'

She shook her head in wonder at such business acumen, consulted a scrap of paper on her desk and waved William and Lord Wick down the stairs with a dentist's nightmare of a smile.

The stairs were steep and narrow and the walls all the way down were decorated with framed pictures of young ladies wearing little or nothing. They were not photographs but colour centrefolds ripped from newsagents' top-shelf girlie magazines of some years ago and the colours were beginning to fade with age, but Lord Wick glanced at them all curiously. 'I wonder where the girls are now?' he said to William. 'Married? Three children at school? They look happy enough posing but unexcited, wouldn't you say? And on the whole therefore, unexciting. I suppose it paid better than stacking packets of biscuits in a supermarket. More fun, too.'

When William and His Lordship had first entered the premises a far-off drum was rhythmically thumping away below as though delivering a lengthy and tedious jungle message. As they descended the stairs the noise grew louder and more pulsating and revealed itself to be an amplified recording of disco dance music.

The noise was ear-splitting when they arrived in the room which was the club's theatre. The tiny stage at the far end was lit with a spotlight in which a beefy girl writhed, dressed solely in a guardsman's bearskin. She had her back to the small audience and was waving her bare bottom about in time to the music.

'Well, really!' said His Lordship.

They were starting to grope their way in the gloom to seats when the girl with the guardsman's hat, at a key point in the music, turned round and faced the room, striking a pose. For a millionth of a second, giving the punters no time to focus, she stood revealing her extraordinarily uninteresting all and then the lights went out.

Through the darkness could be heard a scraping noise and a crash and a muffled oath, and a female voice hissed, 'Who left that sodding chair there?' And another female voice hissed, 'They're my props, you stupid cow.'

Another deafening piece of music began and the lights went up on the minute stage to reveal a plump young bride in her wedding dress holding a large snake which in private life was clearly a linen draught-excluder.

The bride drifted about the stage nearly in time with the music, uttering little erotic sighs for no clear reason and running her free hand over her prominences. She trailed the snake along behind her like a fat dog-lead lacking an attached dog. She suddenly stopped drifting, presented her back to the audience and began undoing the many buttons on the back of her dress. The audience, such as it was, went quiet. When the dress was unbuttoned she shucked it off and turned round facing the punters, clutching the dress to shield her frontage. She was not wearing a bra, just a minute pair of briefs, the elastic of which had dug a weal in her generous waist. She was sliding sinuously sideways towards the wings to the music when she stopped in front of a gentleman in the front row.

'You still 'ere?' she said. 'Bloody 'ell, you bin 'ere since 'alf-past ten this morning!'

'I'm entitled,' he replied, hurt, 'I've paid, 'aven't I? Get on with it, ducky. Get 'em off!'

'Charming!' she said.

She arrived at the side of the stage and at the right moment in the music turned her back on the audience, held out the dress in her right hand, dropped it into the wings, turned and thrust out her considerable breasts at the audience. She clearly enjoyed this moment and posed there breathing heavily, and effectively, for a pleasant moment or two.

'Good Heavens!' whispered His Lordship to William.

'Little Annie MacDougall from Campbells the bakers!'

'You've recognized her?' said William, deeply impressed at the secret life of the Scottish nobility.

'No, no,' said His Lordship. 'This girl's face reminded me of someone back home and I couldn't remember whom.'

The bride then stuck her tummy out at the audience and drew the snake slowly between her legs, uttering little fake whimpers as though it was the sexiest thing in the world. But her facial expressions suggested that the linen draught excluder, far from giving her pleasure, was in fact rough in texture and rather raspy and altogether an unfortunate requirement of her act which she could have done without.

Her big finish was routine. Knickers stripped off and held in front of her until music arrived at a loud end, then, with lustful abandon, modesty-retaining knickers hurled towards audience with just enough force for them to drop to the edge of the stage for easy retrieval later. Pose. QUICK BLACKOUT.

The lights came on in the auditorium. It was lightly peopled. There were five rows of old and tatty tip-up cinema seats, upholstered in plush with a tapestry design, which must have been rescued from a condemned Electric Kinema under demolition. William and His Lordship slipped into seats in the third row, behind a pair of large visitors down from the North who kept falling asleep. Just behind them was a party of assorted Japanese who spent the whole time chattily trying to load a film into a complicated camera so they could take home a photograph of Carnaby Street. Six or seven lone souls were slumped about the place, some of them sipping carefully at glasses in the manner of customers who have paid a large amount of money for very small drinks.

The speakers crackled and a recorded voice of Mediterranean origin announced, 'The management of the Greek

Street Whirlpool Health and Naturist Club is 'appy to announce its international star attraction. For the first time ever in London, England, direct from Paris, France, we proudly present the famous Olympic Gold-Medal team of synchronized strip-teasers – Miss Babyoil's Six of the Bust!'

Loud music crashed out of the speakers and on came the girls, pretty and well trained, dancing in unison, all of the same height and all dressed as traffic wardens complete with peaked caps over their long blond wigs. William's hopes rose that he had found his cabaret. The hopes did not stay risen long.

The music segued into 'Hey Big Spender' and the girls marched to the strong beat. Suddenly they reached up with their left hands to the left epaulettes of their uniforms, yanked in unison and a square of their uniform tore away on velcro, opening up like a trapdoor and revealing a bare breast which bobbed about as its owner danced.

The music changed to Shirley Bassey's 'I Who Have Nothing', a moodier and slinkier piece altogether. The six breasts settled down to a sway and the girls turned and writhed upstage. On arriving at the back of the stage each girl felt behind her, gripped the back of her tunic jacket and, again in perfect unison, pulled. The skirts of the uniform jackets ripped off leaving each girl wearing the sort of short jacket known as a bum-freezer. A bit more rhythmic writhing and sighing and some erotic stroking of the behind and then each girl reached back with her right hand, grasped the top of her dark-blue skirt and, on the right note of music, heaved. Velcro ripped, a square of the right-hand side of the skirt opened like another trapdoor and one buttock per girl sprang into view, flour-white and semi-glossy. The girls lolloped round the stage on a kind of lap of honour; as William later described them to Milly, single-breasted and half-assed. The girls went off to a little slightly stunned applause and the lights came on.

The performance was summed up by Lord Wick to his wife as *un mauvais quart d'heure*. To William it was hopelessly, drenchingly vulgar, with a pointlessness about it which made the young bride and her snake draught-excluder seem like a little gem of folk-theatre.

Lord Wick could not see the stage over the heads of the huge Northerners slumbering in front of him so he had let his seat spring back and William helped him up to perch on the top edge of it. This worked to begin with but as the girls began to reveal their bits he became agitated with the ugliness of it all and kept falling off, pulling the seat forward a little and letting it spring back with a bang. The Japanese hissed and whispered loudly, 'Shhhh, please, thank you!' Nobody else was bothered by the bangs, least of all the artistes.

His Lordship looked at William and shook his head sadly, and fell off his seat again. The seat banged back and the Japanese went 'Ssssh!' so he pulled the seat down and sat on it in the normal way.

'Not obscene,' said His Lordship to William, 'much too boring for that. Nor erotic. Just silly and unbelievably tacky. Utterly wrong for our cabaret, surely?'

'Unthinkable,' said William. 'What a waste of an afternoon.'

Then slowly the realization crept over William that he was now in real trouble. The Orange was just three days away . . .

'When a piece of wood has become warped through damp,' said Lord Wick, 'carpenters bend the piece of wood in a vice so that it's bent twice as much the other way. It comes out of the vice straight. They call the process putting the wood "in purgatory". After such a shabby afternoon I think we deserve a touch of purgatory ourselves.'

'And how do you suggest we bend ourselves the other way?' said William.

'My darling wife allowed me ten pounds spending money for the afternoon. Let's go and wallow in a pot of tea and an assorted French pastry at the Ritz, shall we?'

CHAPTER SEVENTEEN

COUNTDOWN

On Tuesday morning two thin but bright rays of hope shone for William. He had arrived rather early at his office but Chidders rang up from his cubicle to report that a lady had tried even earlier to ring William about the cabaret on Thursday. To avoid Tozer trouble, Chidders had given the lady the number of William's direct line. A short while later William's direct line rang on his desk.

'Hi, William!' came the voice of Dame Barbara Cartland/ Madonna. 'It's Fawn! Look, honey, I was hoping to tempt you to Eaton Square for a working breakfast but I guess it's too late now – it's nearly half after eight.'

'Yes, lunchtime looms,' said William agreeably.

'Gotta talk to you right away,' said Fawn. 'Can I come up?'

'Where are you phoning from?'

'Outside the front door. I'm in a cab.'

'A cab!'

'I have a mobile phone, sweetheart.'

'Yes, yes, of course, hasn't everybody? Do come up and join me for a working chat.'

Chidders ushered Mrs Hume-Vansittart into William's office with a mixture of professional unction and personal distaste. Fawn was a semi-striking blonde with an aggressive smile, excellent sinewy dancer's legs and a good figure to which a dress of patterned silk clung. She had survived an indeterminate number of summers and looked to William like a successful hooker who had recently retired and gone into management, which was probably, William decided, not unadjacent to the truth. Chidders described her to his wife that evening as a brassy-looking bint ponging of scent.

Fawn looked round William's tiny, cluttered office with wide-eyed delight. 'Love it!' she said. 'Everything you need in a small space! Why spend more?'

William handed her into his one chair and leant up against the wall rather than sit on the wounding edge of the plastic table.

Fawn rummaged in her handbag, pulled out some of the bulkier items like the mobile phone and a hairbrush and a wallet, and found what she was hunting for, a scarlet leather diary with corners bound in gold, and a gold Cartier ballpoint.

'OK, honey,' she said, pen poised over diary page. 'Thursday evening, right? Six of the Bust? The performance runs about twenny minutes and they'll need a dressing-room and a good cassette sound system. I'll have to ask you to sign a paper which will be your legal commitment, right? The troupe's fee for the engagement is eight hundred pounds, half upfront on signing the contract. OK?'

'I'm not booking your girls,' said William. 'The act was cheap and nasty and disastrously wrong for our purposes. If you remember, I briefed you exactly on what we required.'

Fawn waved her pen around slowly in the air, in the moody, resentful way that a cat swishes its tail when peeved. 'Ah, c'mon, honey, relax!' she said. 'Don't be so *negative*, right? Have fun! Get a life!' Then Fawn snapped her diary shut and flashed towards William the sunniest of smiles.

'OK, OK! You win!' she cried, raising her hands in mock surrender. 'You didn't like the act, William. That's

OK, why should you? It was the crummy act the girls perform for daytime Soho punters. I wanted you to see the girls working, that's all, show how pretty they are. "Sexy, yet subtle" is my credo. But, listen, honey, I've choreographed the girls in an entirely different, upmarket act for the conference circuit and, William, it's *just right* for you! No sleaze, nothing crude, goddam artistic all the way, and you can trust me, baby!' Her eyes shone with innocent, girlish enthusiasm.

'What do the girls get up to?' asked William, with a sinking feeling that he was in the presence of a high pressure, highly trained, New World salesperson.

'You know Manny's day-journey sewer lurb?'

'Not intimately,' said William, cautiously. 'Tell me more about it – him - them.'

'It's a world-famous painting by the superstar French painter Edward Manny. It shows a picnic on the grass in a woodland glade in the Boyda Belong in Paris, France. It caused a scandal at the time because one of the girls at the picnic was in the nude while both the men were fully clothed.'

'Yes, I know the painting,' said William.

'I reproduce it on the stage as a beautiful tablow veevon,' said Fawn. 'I dress the stage with shrubs in tubs, and plaster tree trunks, and grass mats. The men are in frock coats and velvet trousers. It starts as a lookalike of the painting. The nude girl is looking at the audience, the guys are lounging back on the grass on their elbows and the girl at the back in a see-through muslin dress is cleaning her toes. Then another girl and guy come on carrying a portable gramophone and a bottle of champagne. They all drink, laughing happily, the men put on a gramophone record of Maurice Chevalier singing "Thank Heaven for Little Girls" and the girls entertain the men with a cute little strip-tease dance. Nothing gross, William. Bouncing young bosoms, the occasional flash of a nipple, all very British, a class act. And for the big finish the music changes to Offen-what's-the-guy's-name? and all six in the cast dance the cancan, ending with a chase round the bushes and all tumbling in a heap mid-stage, giggling and laughing like the carefree young lovers they are. Superb entertainment, William. Gracefully erotic whilst being in the best of taste.'

I wonder, thought William. He was wondering how far, if at all, he could trust entrepreneur Fawn to deliver the product as described by her. It all seemed innocuous enough, just about the degree of oo-la-la the Sporting Baronet said would be welcomed, and yet – the Traffic Warden act in Greek Street had been so dire. On the other hand the Orange was only two days away now. *Two days*.

'If you can assure me that the act will be exactly as you've described it . . . ' he said.

'Money back if you're not fully satisfied, sir,' said Fawn, 'except for the deposit, of course. If you'd be so kind as to make me out a cheque for the £500 deposit, your Thursday night's booking is confirmed.' Like magic, an invoice appeared in her hand and she handed it to William. The cheque was to be made out to *The Hume-Vansittart Adult Leisure-Pleasure Group Inc. plc.* William made out the cheque.

Fawn left swiftly and William sat wondering whether he had behaved in a criminally foolish manner in booking her strip-tease group. Not least because she had left his office with an expression on her face like that of a cat licking cream off its whiskers.

Elation should have been coursing through William's veins. If the strip-tease came up to the relatively tasteful scene described by Fawn he had overcome the biggest of his three major problems. He had already set up the

Sodding Sidmontons for a grievous experience so he was left now only with how to prevent Tozer from blabbing. But elation refused to course; the solutions to his problems were too fragile.

William finished his report to Belkis by telling her that after much internal debate he had booked the Hume-Vansittart Group to provide the cabaret. Their girls would perform a *tableau vivant* strip-tease and dance the cancan in the setting of *Le Déjeuner sur l'herbe*. £500 deposit, non-returnable.

He dropped the report in Belkis's IN tray and went downstairs to find out what news Chidders had on Tozer.

When William approached Chidders by the front door Chidders grabbed his arm and made little silent jerking movements of his head towards his cubicle. Once inside he peered out into the hall for suspicious strangers but there was only an ancient member trying to read the lunch menu on the notice-board without his glasses. Chidders opened his drawer and took out a small cardboard suitcase. This he unlocked and drew forth a tea-cosy, a rather jolly tartan affair with 'Gang aisy wi' the tea' embroidered on it. From this he pulled an old khaki army sock, unrolled it and drew out Belkis's Malcolm's tiny recording-machine.

'Can't be too careful,' Chidders whispered breathily into William's ear, causing it to itch.

'Is this amount of security vital?' asked William, rubbing his itch vigorously.

'Who knows?' whispered Chidders. 'The depths to which a cunning little machine like this can get up to is a scientific enema. If you ask me, this little box of tricks is a bit too clever for its own good. Do you know it starts up all on its own as soon as anybody starts talking near it? Well, that's not natural, is it?'

'It's what it's *supposed* to do,' said William. 'Switch it off if you're worried by it.'

'Oh, I do, sir. And I take the batteries out an' all, but I still don't trust it. And when all's said and done the recorder only repeats what Minnie tells it; it's Minnie who's our good and faithful servant in the words of the Holy Bible. Moreover, she doesn't start up whenever she feels like it, she waits for me to turn her on. As a "for instance", it was my Minnie not the recorder who warned me on Friday that things were beginning to hot up on the Tozer front.'

'Eh? What sort of things?'

'Tozer telephoned that newspaper of his on and off all day Friday. From what I can make out, his contact has just got back from America and Tozer's trying to get the money out of him in return for telling everything he knows about the Orange. Tozer's already phoned through and read out the list of members who'll be at the dinner. Everybody, from the Master down.'

'Has he, now. It's touch and go, Chidders. If only we knew the name of the newspaper . . .'

'I know you don't really approve of my rough military methods, sir, but the way to keep Tozer out of harm's way is for me to lock him in the stationery store next to your office until it's all over.'

'There's no ventilation in there.'

'True, there's not a lot of air but it's only for a couple of days and he's such a scrawny little sod he probably doesn't need to breathe all that much. Like fish. Anyway, I could bore some holes top and bottom of the door. But the other gobbet of intelligence I have to report is that Tozer's old-fashioned "Gor blimey" swearing has increased. But only when he's talking to that newspaper.'

'Very odd, isn't it?'

''Ave a listen to what I recorded this morning.' said Chidders, switching the little recording-machine to PLAY. A Scottish girl's voice was saying ' . . . well, I'm sorry

Mr Tozer but he's not here, he's just back from America and dead busy. I'm his P.A. Why don't you give me your information and I'll pass it to him when he comes in? Surely that's sensible?' 'Listen, missus,' came Tozer's unmistakable nasal whine, 'when I've got important information for the engine-driver, I don't talk to the oil-rag.' There was a small gasp the other end. 'This is sensational Gor-Blimey material, missus, and worth a pile of dosh. If he don't ring me back soon I'll take it to *The Times* or the *Sun*, so tell 'im to shift 'is arse. Inform 'im that I now have a good idea as to what Lord Sidmonton and the other bleedin' toffs are going to get up to at the Walpole Club on Thursday evening and I tell you it's dyna-bloody-mite.'

Chidders switched off the recording-machine.

'What does he mean by "Gor-Blimey" material?' William asked.

'It's an expression sometimes used to decribe cockney clothing, like in that song a few years back sung by wassername – Leonie Donegal, was it? ". . . my old man's a dustman, 'e wears a dustman's hat, 'e wears 'Gor-Blimey' trousers and 'e lives in a council flat . . . "'

'Lonny Donnegan,' said William.

'Whatever 'er name was,' said Chidders, 'you can't describe our distinguished club members as wearing "Gor-Blimey trousers", now can you?'

'I don't know,' said William, 'what about Lord Wick mid-week?'

'Oh, yes, milord of course,' said Chidders, 'but apart from 'im?'

Wednesday. O-Day minus one. William arrived at the Club early again as there was a tremendous lot to get through.

He had to arrange a temporary change in members' eating-habits, about as simple to arrange as persuading cats to walk backwards, but Brandy Jack and Philly had to have time and space to decorate the dining-room and the sound equipment had to be installed by Belkis's husband Malcolm. So William had the huge, old disused Smoking-Room on the third floor unlocked and the dining-room furniture carried up there.

Anton was prepared to wrench himself away from his Orange preparations to provide the Smoking-Room with a simple service of cold meals. As the Orange banquet took shape, William was interested to note the effect on Anton. The old Hounslow Catering gritty, rebel, all-lads-together-against-the-world attitude had gradually given way to the more professional, chef-like behaviour of pleasant, cheerful co-operation tempered by short explosions of malignant fury.

Lots of humping and shifting of furniture had become necessary. William had arranged for the Club waiters and waitresses to have both Wednesday and Thursday off as part of the birthday celebration and the corps of temporary waiters had been hired for both days. These patient, gentle East Mediterraneans with the defeated feet had little to do as lunch and dinner in the Smoking-Room were only scratch meals and few members would bother, so the old waiters were available, in theory, as casual labour.

William realized that arranging bonuses for those willing to help was about as much as he could manage; getting this potential labour force into useful shape and directing their activities was wildly beyond his abilities.

But help was at hand. The Chairman of the House Committee was Brigadier-General Sir Humphrey Finch-Finch, a red-faced, white-moustached ex-Indian Army officer who had spent most of his army life quick-marching up and down the Hindu Kush in between playing bridge and terrifying subalterns. In retirement the Brig had become immensely kind and helpful and had volunteered to organize the temporary waiters.

On the way down the stairs to talk to Chidders, William became aware of a low, vaguely melodic noise coming up. He leant over the bannisters and saw below him a procession winding slowly, *Aida*-like, up the staircase towards the Smoking-Room. It was a column of elderly temporary waiters, each with a heavy dining-room chair inverted on his head. Ahead of them all climbed the Brig with the heaviest item on his head, a huge and pretentiously carved oak armchair reserved for the Master. The Brig was leading the column in a work-song version of *Ol' Man River*.

Chidders was standing in his glass cubby-hole with Minnie on a shelf an inch away from his ear when William arrived. 'Sweet Football Association so far, sir,' he reported. He consulted his pad. 'Tozer's only phone call today was to a Mrs Frenchy Bidmead pleading with her to reconsider. He said the very memory of her lying starkers on the candlewick bedspread at the B and B in Croydon clipping her big toenail was still enough to send him *non compost mentis*. He then explained that his suggestion that she paid half the hotel bill for their forthcoming weekend's slap and tickle at Birchington was meant to be a sally of rapier wit not a request for money and would she please stop buggering him about and agree to be there.'

'Any reports from the Petherbridge Court Irregulars?'

William had persuaded Chidders to organize his behind-the-scenes maintenance staff into a part-time Early Warning Group, commanding-officer Sergeant Chidding, to observe and record anybody in the road outside who was observing and recording the Club.

'Not a sausage,' said Chidders. 'Everything's normal out there. It's as quiet as a dormouse.'

William thanked Chidders, urged further vigilance and went to inspect the dining-room. It was now empty of furniture and strewn with huge heaps of material, quite a lot of it white cheesecloth, waiting to be hung up. A dozen huge plaster pillars, detritus from some film drama, lay propped up against the wall. Several large loudspeakers and other chunks of sound equipment were piled in a corner. Brandy Jack, dressed in an ancient pale blue safari suit and a flowing foulard stock, was wandering about looking keenly at corners of the ceiling and making sweeping movements with a riding crop, indicative of a man lost in creative thought. Philly was trotting about near him carrying his Harrods carrier bag and mumbling. Philly saw William and came over. 'Look at 'im,' Philly snorted, "'e's thinking of smothering the room in white tulle. It'll look like a fairy's armpit.'

'Could you spare me a moment, my good chap?' asked Sir John Gielgud from behind William. William turned round and seeing not Sir John Gielgud but a tall, shambly young man with a great mop of hair which shot out from his head sideways. He was wearing gold specs and behind his ear was parked a small screwdriver, as spare cigarettes were once parked.

'Mr Hardcastle?' asked William.

'Belkis's Malcolm,' said the large young man, with a small, embarrassed smile. 'I've come here to, you know, start setting up the sound equipment, if you don't mind.' He looked down at his toecaps for a while.

'Please do,' said William. 'I'm most grateful for all your help.'

'Sure thing. Ya. Brilliant.'

'Who was that?'

'Cliff Richard.'

'Of course. Very good.'

'Waller, gwaller, gwaller, war, war,' said Malcolm.

'Don't tell me,' said William. 'The Right Honourable Selwyn Gummer, MP?'

'No, a turkey,' said Malcolm. 'I'm teaching myself some animal impressions. Well, I'd better be getting— um—' Malcolm looked down at his trainer toecaps again and then silently slid sideways towards the loudspeakers.

That evening, toying with an early sandwich in the Smoking-Room, William began for the first time to feel seriously nervous. He simply had to break into the Tozer conspiracy but at the moment had absolutely nothing to act upon. He reluctantly decided that he would have to stay at the Club overnight in case of shock developments.

He had rung earlier and arranged to borrow a dinner-jacket the following morning. William did not own a dinner-jacket but knew a man who did, a friend who was what might be termed a professional dinner-jacket wearer, not the leader of a symphony orchestra or a member of an escort service but a cinema manager. Tim ran a tiny, expensive but quite beautiful cinema in Mayfair which ran screenings of delicately sexy Italian films for stick-like Mayfair dowagers and divorcées, the last social group in Britain still to chain-smoke and wear a mink coat to the pictures. Tim was a good friend, not overly burdened with a questing mind and blissfully happy in a career requiring him to charm old ladies and watch the same mildly erotic film all day for weeks. He was exactly the same size as William and had four splendid dinner suits any of which he was happy to lend.

William then rang Milly at Foster's number in Ealing, hoping to get her before she left to drive home. 'Darling, darling . . .' he said in a muffled kind of way. He was so glad to hear her voice that he nearly burst into tears.

'You all right, Will?' said Milly anxiously. 'You sound a bit het up.'

'How did the audition go?' William managed to ask in a more controlled tone.

'Terrific. Foster is a breath of brilliant fresh air. He's reorganized our basic programme and given us confidence as a group and taught us how to walk on stage and get off. And he's shown Pippa how to carry her cello gracefully, a small miracle. She was in love with him from the start as she was with you, you know what she's like with our menfolk. Now she thinks the sun shines out of his—'

'So you've got the booking?'

'Could be the first of many. Foster says all livery clubs like a bit of music.'

'That's marvellous, really good news. Look, Mill, I'm terribly sorry but I won't be home tonight. I simply must stay at the Club in case something breaks.'

'Don't overdo it, Will, you know what you're like, you just plug on and on and you've worked so hard already. I'd no idea how deeply involved you were, responsible for the whole thing. If only you could have told me all about it. Bloody Uncle Sid. Will, why don't you cancel the Orange? Seriously, though. Some snoopy newspaper could make the Club members look a load of cheap and nasty old men, you know that. Is it worth the risk? I mean – *is* it?'

'Well, yes, I think it is. You see, Mill, they're not rich layabouts or dreary piss-artists, they're decent old jossers enjoying a late flowering of mild wickedness. A last flowering for most of them; I doubt whether any of them'll still be here to celebrate the Club's next big anniversary. They fiddled through an orgy as the birthday party because it seemed dashing, it was an embarrassment for the obnoxious Canon Prout and they were pretty sure it would turn out to be, one way or other, a bit of fun. The old boys don't want to go gentle into that good night. And, my love, I'm completely and utterly on their side.'

'Oh, Will! I should be there trying to help you, not sitting here tuning my bloody harpsichord yet again. Even

Belkis's husband is there putting up the sound equipment while I'm miles away just—'

'Just a minute!' said William. 'How do you *know* Belkis's husband is putting up the sound equipment?'

'Belkis told me,' Milly said. 'She's here with me.'

'*Belkis?* In Ealing? Well, I'm blowed!' said William. 'What's she doing there?'

'Came to tell me what's been going on, all about the troubles you've been coping with, and about Rollo the lethal mini-cab tycoon and the non-belly-dancers of Catford and the strip-tease ladies. Isn't Belkis great? So beautiful and *funny*, particularly on the subject of shy English men.'

'I don't wish to know about that. Hang on a sec darling, Chidders's come in, might be important. Don't go away.' William put the phone down on the desk. 'Chidders,' he said. 'Something up?'

'It's Ted, sir, maintenance staff,' he said. 'Light bulb replacementing, winding clocks and mattress-turning.'

'Ah, yes, of course, taciturn Ted,' said William. 'Ear-disadvantaged, has an on and off meaningful relationship with Gwen-on-coffee. What about Ted?'

'He's a warrant officer in my Petherbridge Court Irregulars, sir. His territory is the North-West Passage.'

'Eh?'

'The top-floor passage between bedrooms 4A and 16, sir. A little while ago Ted was routinely looking out of the window checking the street below for suspiciousness, as instructed by me, when he saw a man come out of the block of flats opposite in a furtive manner. Ted reported the matter to me by bedroom telephone and I immediately strolled out of the front door, affecting nonchalance, and took a keen butcher's at this stranger. He was youngish and a bit scruffy and I surmised that he was a photographer.'

'What led you to surmise that?'

'He was holding a camera. One of those big 'uns with a zoom lens like the barrel of a howitzer and a flash on top and a tripod sprouting out of its bum.'

'Not good news, Chidders. Not good news at all. Almost certainly a press photographer.'

'You were on the phone so I couldn't get further orders. I'm very sorry, sir, I do hope you won't take it the wrong way, but I'm afraid I used my initiative.'

'Chidders!' said William. 'What did you do?'

'What I did was, I got Maintenance Ted to tell Gwen-on-coffee that I said she could have the rest of the day off if she'd do a bit of spying for the Club. She agreed that she'd change into Ted's favourite pretty white blouse which she could undo a few of the buttons of, take a large whisky out to the photographer and then wheedle out of him who he was working for.'

'Did it work?'

'Like a dream. He's taking her to a candlelit dinner at an Indian restaurant off the Marylebone Road.'

'I mean, what's he doing here with his camera?'

'Dunno yet, sir, Gwen wants to Mata Hari him tonight and lure him into revealing all to her.'

'Very well done both of you. Deeply grateful.'

William picked up the phone. 'Did you hear any of that, darling?'

'All of it. It sounds as though somebody's on to you.'

'I don't think it matters much if they are. The evening as planned is respectable enough and they can't hurt us by publishing a few pictures of judges and notables arriving at the front door. The cabaret is a dance version of *Le Déjeuner sur l'herbe*. Where's the shock horror story?'

'I don't know but I'm dead worried all the same. Does the newspaper know something you don't know it knows?'

'I don't think they know anything much. We've monitored Tozer on the phone and he's been promising some newspaper to tell all but he's actually delivered very little. He's convinced them that something vile is going to happen tomorrow evening at the Club but so far he hasn't the faintest idea what.'

'I do hope you're right. Look, darling, if you're going to stay at the Club tonight I might as well remain here and carry on rehearsing. The others want to. Ring me tomorrow and *do* be watchful, my love.'

William made warm noises of love and reluctantly put down the phone. It rang again almost immediately.

'Hi, Mr Ziegfeld!' It was Miss Babyoil. The diction being 95 per cent Madonna and only 5 per cent Dame Barbara Cartland indicated to William that it was a business call. 'May I please know what time you want my girls to start their show tomorrow?'

'Oh, hello. Ah – about nine-thirty, if you please.'

'You got it. We'll be there at nine to put the scenery up. Doesn't take a moment. Stay cool. Bon-soir, Wilhelm. Miss you.' She rang off.

William lay back in his chair, put his feet up on his desk and applied his mind once again to his problems. Underestimating the strain he was experiencing, he closed his eyes to encourage deeper concentration and descended almost immediately into soft, merciful oblivion.

CHAPTER EIGHTEEN

THE WALPOLE ORANGE

An urgent banging on his office door woke William. The sun was shining. He was lying in the same position in which he had fallen asleep, feet up on desk, head lolling back on the chair. He realized with a little shock that it was Thursday and the Day of the Orange at last.

Happy 250th birthday, Walpole Club!

William tried to leap up but his muscles had locked into a knot; at the slightest movement the stringy bits behind his knees twanged in agony and any movement at all of his head produced sharp pains and grinding noises in his neck as though somebody had topped up the gaps in his vertebrae with gravel.

More knocking.

'Come in,' he called, weakly.

Chidders bustled in bearing a small tray.

'Thought you might like a cup of early morning char, sir,' he said, putting a steaming mug on the desk.

'What time is it?' said William, weakly.

'Just gone a quarter to twelve!' said Chidders. He grinned at William's look of shocked horror.

William noticed that Chidders was not in his uniform but was wearing a pair of working dungarees and the sounds coming up the stairs were not the normal muffled Club morning noises but the sounds of voices and banging and movement.

'What's going on downstairs?' William asked, sipping gratefully at his tea.

'Nothing for you to get up for, sir, everything's working like a well-oiled charm. Mr Brandreth Jacques and his funny little friend are transforming the dining-room helped by some old actors and volunteer students from the Camberwell College of Art and the kitchens are going full blast, steaming like the boiler-room of the old *Mauretania*.'

'I really must get down there,' said William. 'Ouch!'

'Lord Wick, Mr Sol Fish, Sir Archibald and the Brig have formed a small breakaway work force which they call The Flying Pick-at-its, and they're doing the fill-in jobs which nobody else can be bothered with, like feeding everybody hot bacon sandwiches and lugging rubbish down to the skip.'

'Now, very important this, Chidders – any word from Gwen-on-coffee and the photographer? Did he let on to her who he's working for?'

'I don't want you to pass animosities on Gwen-on-coffee, sir, particularly after what you know about her regular kindnesses to Ted-on-maintenance. The Christian facts are that Gwen is a generously affectionate young lady who got married much too young to a not very affectionate Leyton Orient supporter. What I'm working round to saying, sir, is that Gwen rang at eight o'clock this morning, not from her home but from the young photographer's luxury bedsit in North Kilburn.'

'Good luck to her in her pursuit of the elusive bluebird of happiness, Chidders, but did the photographer happen to mention which newspaper he's working for?'

'No, he's freelance and he doesn't know himself, does 'e? Gwen says his work's doled out to him by his agency which just tells him where to go and what to snap and how much he'll get if his snap comes out.'

'Oh, hell! What's the latest on Tozer?'

'I'm watching him closely, sir,' said Chidders. 'He's been creeping around the place, upstairs and downstairs, all morning. The general impression I've arrived at is that the little bastard desperately needs to find out our exact programme for tonight so he can collect his blood-money.'

William thought hard. 'One good thing is, he *can't* know yet about the strippers, it's not possible. I've told nobody so there's no way he could . . . Oh, my God!'

'You 'ave told somebody, sir?'

'Has Mrs Hardcastle been in?'

'Not yet, sir, no.'

William creaked painfully to his feet and made for the door. 'I left a progress report in Mrs Harcastle's IN tray and it describes everything. Come on, and pray Heaven it's still there!'

But it was not still there. The contents of Belkis's IN tray consisted solely of three forms giving staff PAYE code numbers and half a packet of Fox's Glacier Mints.

'Right, Chidders,' said William. 'The cat's out of the bag at last. We're in deep trouble. Somehow we've got to stop Tozer passing on what he knows.'

'If I could insert a suggestion in your ear, sir. Might it be shovel time?'

'Battering Tozer into a pulp is a sweet thought, Chidders, but English justice is quite strict on murderers. You'd find yourself behind bars with restricted television viewing, only worn old snooker tables to play on and no chance of regaining your freedom for at least two or three years.'

Chidders fell silent.

'Your other idea's better, locking Tozer in the stationery store until tomorrow morning. There's no phone in there so he can't pass on his information. There's no window so he can't escape or throw messages out. We'll lure Tozer in there right away; chances are that editors of gossip columns don't get into their office until it's liquid lunchtime so we should be all right if we nab him swiftly. He won't die in there overnight, will he?'

'Not a hope. Unluckily the door doesn't fit and there's a gap through which air can freely transpose in and out under.'

'Then I'd better get downstairs and order Tozer up to draw out some stationery. You hide in my office until you hear him through the wall and then nip out and lock him in. OK?'

'Sah!' said Chidders. 'Just one thing, sir, you can order Tozer to come up here but 'e'll smell a rat as sure as eggs is eggs, 'e's as cunning as a cucumber.'

William considered. 'Well, you stay up here and wait anyway and I'll nip down and find some excuse to send him up, OK?'

He made his way slowly and painfully downstairs. He found that he could take the strain off his knotted hamstrings by sagging low at the knees and loping along like Groucho Marx, and the grinding noises in the back of his neck lessened if he worked his head continuously round and round. In this fashion he walked into the bar downstairs.

The Flying Pick-at-its were serving themselves behind the bar. Lord Wick's forehead was just visible above the mahogany; the Sporting Baronet was leaning against the shelves of bottles playing with the optics and pouring himself a sextuple Johnny Walker Black Label whisky; Sol Fish, in a borrowed, skittish pinafore, was drying glasses vigorously and putting them back on the wrong shelves.

Lord Wick found a case of wine to stand on so that his face rose above the bar. 'Why are you so bent, William?' he asked, anxiously.

'I fell asleep in my chair in the office,' said William. 'Slept like that all night.'

'My God, I did that once!' said the Sporting Baronet. 'Bloody agony!'

'And I've got to get myself to Ladbroke Grove some time and collect a dinner-jacket.'

A unanimous cry of disapproval rang out from the Flying Pick-at-its.

'No, no, no, you don't!'

'Name and address of the jacket, please,' said Sol Fish. 'I'll go and collect it right now by taxi.'

William gave Sol the details thankfully, then went on: 'And it's vital that Mr Tozer be locked up immediately out of harm's way in the stationery store next to my office. Question is, he's suspicious so how do we lure him up there?'

They had been joined at the bar by the Chairman of the House Committee, the burly Brig, who asked Lord Wick if he would kindly pour a fellow picketeer a Campari.

'No,' said Lord Wick, 'I don't know where the Campari is. You can only have what's within my reach, which is either a bottle of vintage Veuve Cliquot, a can of piss-poor foreign lager or a snort of, what's this stuff? – peach-flavoured schnapps. Now *there's* a tart's drink.'

'Charming service,' said the Brig. 'I'll have a piss-poor lager, please, barman. William, I heard what you were saying about luring Tozer upstairs into captivity. Leave him to me, if you like, I'll get him up there one way or another.'

'I'd be hugely grateful,' said William. The Brig went off immediately, even eagerly. After a while he returned to the bar and picked up his glass of lager and drank deeply.

'All done,' said the Brig. 'I instructed Tozer to go up to the stationery store and report to the sergeant but he wished to stay and discuss my order so I picked him up and carried him up the stairs.'

'We didn't hear any shouting or squealing or anything,' said the Sporting Baronet, who had discovered how to jam the optic's automatic tap so that it would pour until the bottle was empty, and was hugely enjoying himself filling a great number of glasses. 'It wasn't in Tozer's interests to make a noise,' said the Brig. 'I carried him upside-down. By his ankles.'

'It's a wonder that he didn't at least yell "put me down!" ' said William.

'He was hardly likely to yell that,' said the Brig. 'I was dangling him over the far side of the bannisters. Odd thing, human nature. Several of the Cypriot temp waiters passed me going up and down the staircase carrying tablecloths and cutlery and stuff and none of them looked at me twice, and I was dangling somebody by their ankles over the stairwell. Funny home-lives Cypriot waiters must lead. Well, William, you can relax now. The terrible Tozer is safely under lock and key. And here's the key.' He gave it to William.

Some half an hour later Chidders came in looking worried. He spotted William and came hurrying over.

'Don't tell me Tozer's done a Houdini,' said William.

'No, no, sir, he's still locked up in the stationery cupboard.'

'Then we're still safe.'

'I do hope so, sir. But it's that lady who come in early on Tuesday morning to see you, the one with the scent and the legs.'

'Miss Babyoil?'

'She just phoned up. She left her mobile phone on your desk this morning and could she collect it when she comes this evening.'

William's heart sank. 'I remember,' he said, 'she took

303

the phone out of her handbag when she was looking for her diary and put it down on my desk. Quick!' he said to Chidders, 'Bring a wineglass,' and ran out of the bar and up the stairs.

He saw the smart little phone in his mind's eye, small, dark-grey, lying on his desk beside the framed picture of Milly.

Horribly out of breath, he staggered into his office. There was no mobile phone on the desk.

Chidders wheezed in and William grabbed the wineglass, held it against the wall and put his ear to the base.

He could just hear Tozer talking but very indistinctly. William concentrated and began to make out some of Tozer's words, 'scandalous behaviour of the dirty-minded nob classes' he heard, and 'naked romps with lascivious dancing-girls' and 'starts nine-thirty' and 'calls herself Miss Babyoil'.

William handed the wineglass back to Chidders. 'Tozer's phoning the newspaper on Miss Babyoil's portable phone which he must have nicked from my desk and had in his pocket when he was locked in the stationery store. He also nicked my report from Mrs Hardcastle's desk so he is at the moment revealing to the scandal sheet exactly what we're doing tonight. And it's all my fault, I just didn't think ahead. I left the phone and the report where they could be nicked by Tozer, and nick them he did.'

'Don't worry, sir,' said Chidders. 'It'll all work out in the wash. Would a glass of whisky help? I could bring you up a few of Sir Archie's. Oh, I forgot. I was a bit overexcited at nabbing Tozer and hoping that I might be allowed to accidentally punch him on the nose and I forgot that Mrs Addington and her daughter Trixie are downstairs waiting to see you. They're helping decorate the dining-room so there's no great hurry.'

'Can you wheel them up here? I've got some swift thinking to do otherwise I'd come down.'

'Will do, Sah!' said Chidders crisply, and went.

William swiftly thought, and then Mrs Addington and her Trixie arrived. He recognized Trixie from the Whirlpool Club as the young bride with the draught-excluder.

'Oh, hello!' said William. 'I saw your dance with the snake last Monday. Well done.'

'I had to bring our Trixie in, Sir, when I heard what was being planned,' said Mrs Addington. 'I knew our gentlemen wouldn't like it.'

William's heart sank. 'Why, whatever's the matter? Is it the new show?' he managed to ask lightly.

'She's 'orrible woman, sir. Evil,' said Trixie. 'I've 'ad enough. More than.'

'She means Miss Babyoil, sir,' said Mrs Addington. 'That woman's got most of the exotic dancers in Soho working for her and she and her company are buying up all the Soho properties as they come on the market. It's not healthy.'

'I won't go,' said Trixie. 'Not if she doubles the wages, I won't.'

'Where aren't you going?' asked William.

'Brussels,' said Trixie, 'or some German place which sounds like *mazeltov*.'

'Düsseldorf?'

'Yeah, that's it,' said Trixie. 'Madam wants six girls to go out to some nightclubs she's opened there to work as nudes and hostesses, live-in, along with some Russian girls. My friend Gail and me don't like the sound of it but Madam says we've got to go as we're under contract to 'er, but we ain't. Gail's dad says Madam's tricking us into working as prostitutes but Gail's mum wants the money Gail'll send home; Gail's parents are 'aving almighty punch-ups over it. Oh, she's dead frightening is Madam.' Trixie began to sniff, quietly and miserably like a small girl.

'I'm a widow,' said Mrs Addington, apologetically.

'Trixie, listen to me,' said William. 'You've got absolutely nothing to be afraid of. You don't have to do anything you don't want to. I'm here for you to talk to and lean on and we've got barristers and solicitors and judges in the Club who'll look after any legal problems. But just tell me, what's the matter with the show?'

'It's not nice,' said Trixie. 'Not just naughty but *yuk*!'

'Surely it's just a framed picture with a cancan and a bit of strip-tease in the bushes?'

'That's not how Madam works, sir. The show starts peaceful but when one of the boys opens the fake champagne he spills it on the girl's dress, so she takes it off and she ain't got nuffin' else on, 'as she? That's me. So he pours the champagne over me, laughing, like it was a shower-bath and I 'ave to wriggle about and pretend to soap meself all over. The strip-tease to the Maurice Chevalier record is down to the skin, and then if you please, Madam now wants us to dance the cancan starkers. The *cancan*! Can you imagine it?'

'I don't think I will at the moment, thank you,' said William.

'Tell him about the big finish,' said Mrs Addington.

'Is the big finish where you all collapse in a jolly heap?' asked William.

'Well, we're in a heap all right but us girls are in the buff and we have to pretend that the boys are at us. What they call "stimulated sex".'

'Tell him what Madam wants now,' said Mrs Addington.

Trixie began to sniff quietly again. Then she rallied and said, 'Madam says that stimulated sex is so commonplace these days that why don't we go the whole hog and do the real thing, as they do in arty films? She says she'll pay us a bonus of a hundred pounds for each complete performance.'

'Trixie, listen to me,' said William. 'You really are in some danger. Do not, under any circumstances, accept that offer. And don't do the show.'

William had no doubt that Mrs Addington's Trixie was fashioned by nature to find happiness and fulfilment in being a half-naked Kissogram or a strip-tease bride manipulating a draught-excluder, but fortunately Trixie had a personal cut-off point of conscience beyond which she simply could not bring herself to go. She was a survivor.

'Ta so much for your helpful help, Mr Grundwick!' Trixie breathed huskily as she and her mother left. She touched William's sleeve and gave him a cute, intimate little smile.

William stared bleakly at the wall. It wasn't just the carpet that had suddenly been dragged from under him but also the floorboards, joists and the ceiling of the room below. He had won a Pyrrhic defeat.

The tabloid – identity unknown – was now in full possession of the facts and would surround the Club with reporters to button-hole the Members and trap them into indiscretions as they arrived. Worst of all, the cabaret was Soho porn at its tackiest. And there was nothing whatever William could think of to do to save the evening.

'A bit of luck! *Please!*' he shouted at the ceiling. 'I promise I'll finish my greens and be nicer to—'

The phone rang.

'William,' said a familiar voice. 'It's me, Pippa.'

'Pippa!' said William with pleasure. 'Where are you?'

'Just about to leave Ealing for home. Milly thought I should ring you first. You know Belkis has been here? Well she told us about your troubles and I can tell you which tabloid newspaper is gunning for you.'

'Oh, Pippa, that'd be terrifically helpful!'

'It's a horrible gossip columnist who's got it in for your Lord Sidmonton. A revenge thing, I'm afraid. His name's Gore-Bellamy.'

'Gore-Bellamy,' repeated William, savouring the sound. Of course! '"O" by any chance? As in "O Gor-Blimey"?'

'Yes. O for Osbert,' said Pippa. 'His paper is that illiterate cesspool of showgirls and lies called the *Grass*. Osbert's column is titled *The Grasser*. If you could in some manner kick O Gore-Blimey in the groin you would earn the eternal gratitude of a spinster cellist. Any hope?'

William's mind was racing.

'William?'

'Oh, sorry. I'll do what I can and a thousand thanks, Pippa. This information is exactly what I've been praying for, bless you.'

'Have a nice evening!'

William pondered a moment longer and then dialled Madam Babyoil. She was in.

'Hi, William,' she said. 'Anything I can do to give you pleasure within the bounds of reasonable good taste?'

'I'm very sorry,' said William, 'but there's been a change of arrangements. The Club committee has decided that the dining-room must stay the dining-room for this evening, so the after-dinner entertainment needs to take place elsewhere. It's very short notice but rather than cancel the engagement could you possibly put your show on at the Whirlpool Club in Greek Street, where I first saw the girls working?'

'It's possible,' said Miss Babyoil. 'It'll cost you.'

'I don't see why,' said William. 'You own the place, don't you?'

Silence the other end. Then: 'Who told you? One of those dumb Maltese?'

'Nobody told me. I guessed.'

'No big deal, anyway,' said Madam after another thought-ful pause. 'I already own nine other Soho venues.'

'The requirement is now as follows,' said William. 'Nine-thirty this evening your girls perform *Le Déjeuner sur l'herbe* at your Greek Street premises. And may I add this. My committee has decided that as the performance is now off the premises it can be as raunchy as you care to make it.'

'You really mean that?'

'No holds barred,' said William. He rang off and galloped down the stairs, all aches and pains forgotten, to borrow the recording-machine from Chidders who was only too glad to get rid of the devilish device. William then had to gallop up the stairs again because Belkis's Malcolm was having a late beef sandwich in the Smoking-Room. William put the little recording-machine down in front of Malcolm.

'Sorry to interrupt lunch, Malcolm, but very urgent and dreadfully important,' William said. 'Your machine here has been used to record the voice of an awful little club traitor named Tozer. I'll explain all about it later but what I want you to do, right now if poss, is to play back Tozer's voice over and over to yourself until you're satisfied you can imitate his voice on the phone.'

'Good Lord!' said Malcolm.

'I honestly don't think it'll be that difficult,' said William. 'It's an odd voice. Listen.' He switched on the machine and Tozer's voice emerged in full whine.

'See what you mean,' said Malcolm. 'Leave it with me. When I'm ready to have a go I'll come and find you.'

'Excellent,' said William, and galloped down the stairs again to the Flying Pick-at-its in the bar. He glanced at his watch. Ten minutes to four. Time was fleeting all right.

'Gentlemen,' he said with some urgency in his voice. 'Anybody know an important policeman? Preferably Vice Squad?'

'Trouble?' asked Lord Wick.

'Sort of.' said William. 'Owing to a silly bit of carelessness on my part, Tozer has been able to tip off a tabloid called the *Grass* which is now dead set on exposing Club members tonight as privileged Upper-Class sex-perverts – particularly, it seems, the Master. Is the Master coming, by the way?'

'Unfortunately, yes,' said Lord Wick. 'I put out a three-line whip to the Ladies' Social Mafia for information. They reported that the Master and Parthenope are being shunned by the County for sending that dreadful mini-cab to collect the royals from the airport. The County look upon it as the worst kind of suburban, Communist-inspired, *lèse-majesté* practical joke. The Master and Parthenope have decided to rent a property in the Dordogne for a year until the incident's been forgotten. So Lord Sidmonton's coming tonight to resign as Master.'

'*I'm* not a sex-pervert!' said the Sporting Baronet. 'At least, I don't think I am. What do you have to do to be one?'

'I know what you have to do,' said Sol Fish. 'Might have given it a whirl when I was younger but I've left it too late. Can't qualify any more.'

'You don't count, Sol,' said Lord Wick, 'so you'll get no sympathy from us. You're not Upper Class, you're classless, a humble colonial.'

'God bless you, milord,' said Sol, tugging his forelock.

'I know a policeman,' said the Brig. ' "Chummy" Cholmondeley. I was at Winchester with him. Fine shot. His father kept a kestrel named Disraeli, I've always remembered that. Chummy's a Deputy something-or-other at Scotland Yard. Shall I give him a tinkle and tell him you'll be ringing him?'

'I'd be most grateful,' said William.

Upstairs in his office he was put through swiftly.

'How may I help you, sir?' asked Deputy Chummy.

'It's a Vice Squad matter really, I suppose,' said William. 'There's a lady named Mrs Hume-Vansittart who used to be a stripper trading under the name of Bimbo Babyoil.'

'And she wants to join the Walpole Club?'

'I think it'd probably be beneath her, sir. No, the daughter of a lady on our staff works for Madam Babyoil and she's told us some disquieting things about Madam's activities. Madam and her husband have been systematically buying up Soho property.'

'Oh, dear, here we go again,' sighed Chummy.

'They also own similar basement-theatre properties in Brussels and Düsseldorf. Madam Babyoil is operating a stable of strip-tease girls in Soho and she's trying to persuade them into a little light prostitution. She also seems to be pushing the limits of Soho strip-tease shows over the edge of acceptable licence.'

'Well!' said Deputy Chummy. 'This new little murky development in London's sex scene merits investigation.'

'Tonight at nine-thirty Madam Babyoil is secretly mounting a new strip-tease show at the Whirlpool Club in Greek Street. I suggest that some plain-clothes officers should attend. Also perhaps some licence-granting members of Westminster Council. The show will be quite an eye-opener to them, almost certainly Soho's shape of porn to come if not quickly nipped in the bud.'

'I am most grateful to you, Mr Grundwick. Action will be considered immediately.'

William hurried upstairs to his office to collect a writing pad and then, seemingly for about the fortieth time that day, rushed downstairs again to the bar and sat down at a corner table to prepare a script for Malcolm.

Malcolm arrived just after five o'clock. He padded silently up behind William's chair and whined: 'It's bleedin' airless in that storeroom, Mr Smartass Secretary!'

William leapt an inch or so in the air.

'Tozer! – how'd you get out?' he yelled, and then saw it was Malcolm. He sank back again. 'Excellent, Malcolm,' William said, 'pretty nearly perfect Tozer. Now here's a rough script of what to say to Mr Gore-Bellamy. Let's go down to the basement where our switchboard is then I can prompt your answers.'

Malcolm, in his bashful, timid way, was brilliant. He wrapped his handkerchief round the microphone end of the handset to muffle and slightly distort his voice and after a few practice runs, and clutching his script, he dialled the *Grass* and, to William's great relief, got through to Gore-Bellamy first time.

'Stop hounding me, Tozer,' said Gore-Bellamy. 'We pay informants when the story's printed and not before.'

'I will jog your memory button, Mr Gore-Bellamy,' whined Malcolm, 'and remind you that this is not just a common tip-off, it's an international, nationwide exclusive scandal from the only contact you've got who's *persona au gratin* in the watering-holes of the nobility.'

'Oh, piss off.'

'All right. It's only this. I think you've got the name of the venue wrong for tonight. You're all going to turn up at the wrong place and look very, very silly.'

'Waddya mean? Waddya talking about? You've told me over and over again, it's the Walpole Club!'

'No, it ain't. You've got mixed up. It's the Walpole Club's birthday but they're not going to hold an orgy on the Club premises now are they? Use your loaf.'

'You said clearly over the phone, "the rude bits will begin at nine-thirty sharp at the Walpole Club".'

'No, I never! What I said *was*, "will begin at nine-thirty sharp at the *Whirlpool* Club". Not the *Walpole*, the *Whirlpool*. It's in Greek Street.'

'I know where it is! Oh, sod it. You're sure of this?'

'Course I'm sure. Ring the Whirlpool Club and check. Nine-thirty tonight. You'd probably 'ad a couple when I rang, your speech was a bit slurred, and "Walpole" and "Whirlpool" sound much the similar same.'

'Oh, hell! I'll have to switch our whole operation to Greek Street.'

'Yeah, but you can book seats at the Whirlpool Club and they allow anybody in. Take plenty of photographers because the show's hard porn and a lot of young Walpole members'll be there, good gossip-column names. Rough 'em up a bit and take their photos, they hate that sort of publicity.'

'OK. Good thinking. Now get off the line, Tozer, I've got a lot of phoning round to do.' He rang off.

William clutched Malcolm. 'You've done it!' he said. 'I can't be more grateful, Malcolm! A superb piece of work!' He wrung Malcolm's hand. Malcolm flushed with pleasure, gave a modest little cough and got up. 'Must – er – bit of wiring to tidy up and – er – if you'll – er—' He left.

William, glowing with relief that he had, by the skin of his teeth, avoided single-handedly sullying the good name of the Club and its members with a vice scandal, made his way upstairs to his office, this time at his own speed. Now that Tozer was no longer a menace William began to feel a little sorry for him, one of life's fully paid-up losers. He would have to sack Tozer, of course, but William wondered whether he should write to Rollo and ask him to take Tozer on as his new driver. For a moment this Christian thought made William feel a better person, but then he reached the door of the stationery store and heard a groan within. He paused, ear to door panel.

'Gimme air,' gasped the voice of Tozer, piteously. 'I can't breeve. Air, for mercy's sake or I'm a goner!'

William hurriedly found the stationery store key in his pocket and flung the door open. It was dark in there but there was enough light for William to see that there was nobody gasping on the floor.

'Tozer?' he called anxiously.

'Right be'ind yer, sucker!' came the voice of Tozer and something not all that hard but very heavy thumped William on the back of the head. That was the last thing he remembered for a while.

He came to lying face downwards on his own desk with Chidders dabbing at the sore part at the back of his head with a handful of wet loo paper.

'What happened?' said William, feeling decidedly groggy as well as having an aching skull.

'Tozer lured you in so he could make 'is escape, sir. 'E was waiting behind the door and bopped you on the back of the bonce with a box of fax-paper rolls. They're 'eavy, those Fax-paper rolls,' said Chidders.

'I'm aware of that,' said William.

'Fax-paper rolls are specially coated with shiny chemicals, sir, that's why they're so heavy,' said Chidders, dabbing William's wound more carefully now that his patient was awake. 'Sorry about this bog paper, sir, couldn't find a cloth.'

'What's happened to Tozer?'

' 'E got clean away. Dashed past me in the 'all, stuck up two fingers at me in a gesture of mock, shouted "To 'ell wiv the bloody lot of you, I'm off to collect a fortune!" and went out the front door. By the time I'd broken free from a waiter telling me about his teeth and given chase to Tozer he was riding off round the corner towards St James's Street. And I'm very much afraid, sir, that the thieving little swine was riding your bike. 'E must have nicked it from round the back.'

'That might have been his big mistake, Chidders. I

314

don't think he's got enough time to get to the *Grass* before Gore-Bellamy leaves for the Whirlpool Club, but anyway the bike's beginning to fall apart and it really is getting a danger to the rider's life and limb. It should slow him up quite a bit.'

'Now that *is* good news, sir, quite cheered me up! Now, sir, don't think me bossy but you must have yourself a bit of a kip before this evening and you've got well over an hour before you need show your face. The housekeeper's laid out your evening kit in 4A. Have a wobble-bobble bath and a lie-down and I'll come up and wake you when it's time.'

William was in no state to argue. Chidders rolled up the wad of damp loo paper into a ball and aimed it at the wastepaper basket. It missed. He made a move to retrieve it and have another go but decided not to bother. A knock on the door and the Flying Pick-at-its filed in silently and took up positions round William, forming a tableau resembling Rembrandt's painting, *The Anatomy Lesson*, thought William dazedly . . .

'In case we get pissed this evening and forget,' said the Sporting Baronet, 'we wanted to tell you that we're aware of the terrific efforts you've put in to make our foolish orgy jape work.'

'*Ici, ici,*' said Sol. 'No, I've done that one before.'

'You've done 'em all before,' said the Brig cheerfully.

'It's really just to say thank you, William,' said Lord Wick. 'Everything's going well downstairs, no problems have arisen. All's serene, as we used to say. You've had a hell of a day so do have a bit of a zizz now so you can enjoy our birthday party with us.'

'There's no cabaret,' said William. 'I haven't got a cabaret for you. I had to lose the cabaret.'

'It won't be missed,' said Lord Wick. 'You've organized us a splendid evening of over-eating and over-drinking and the opportunity for everybody to talk themselves hoarse. Who's going to want such bliss interrupted?'

An hour later William, woken with some difficulty by Chidders from a brief but profound and probably unwise sleep, bathed, immaculately dressed in his borrowed midnight-blue wild silk dinner-jacket, and with a throbbing headache, tottered downstairs.

He clung to the banister and descended slowly and carefully because his eyes were not giving him very accurate information as to how far away from his foot the next stair was. A hum of conversation rose from below.

In the hall below, Belkis was being the Club's hostess, greeting members as they arrived and putting them into party mood with an enchanting smile and a glass of Dom Perignon. She was in her special party sari which was alarmingly diaphanous, of a subtle beige hue and encrusted with fine, wavy gold thread. She held a barely visible wisp of something delicately flame-coloured which she floated about with negligent Oriental chiffon-craft.

'You look absolutely terrific,' William said to her. 'Lucky young Malcolm.'

'Willy!' cried Belkis, hugging him. 'You look so pale and done in.'

'It's been quite a day,' said William. 'But there'll be no scandal; I've diverted the strippers to Soho and sent the press off chasing them there so the Master and all our distinguished old boys are safe.'

'Brilliant, William! Your Milly is so proud of what you are achieving. And so am I!'

'But we've got no after-dinner entertainment. If only I could – wait! A thought. Your Malcolm! His impersonation of Tozer was so good that he fooled the newspaper. He's here working the sound equipment and the lighting; couldn't he do us his impressionist act after dinner? You suggested it a few days ago, remember?'

'Oh, Willy, I was just joking. Malcolm is a mass of shyness. He could never, ever stand up in front of people and perform; he'd topple to the floor with a nervous collapse! His facsimile voices are just a hobby-horse!'

'Then – another thought–' said William. 'I'll ask Sol Fisher to give us a show. He's our resident jokester and he'd have no problem leaping on to the stage in front of an audience. The problem'd probably be to get him off.'

'Not a good idea, Willy. Well, it is in a way but the snag is that Mr Fisher has been giving the Club his stand-up comedy act for years. The act is always the same and the members are now as familiar with it as he is. The last time he did it was after our Derby Day dinner: the members knew each joke so well they shouted out the punch line with him.'

'What sort of jokes are they?'

'He always starts with "Sorry I'm late but I've just flown in from New York - doesn't it make your arms tired?"'

'I see what you mean,' said William. 'We should surely be able to rustle up something more suitable for a 250th birthday party. I've just got to think of something a little more—'

'Now, Willy, you listen to me. I'm going to talk to you like a Dutch aunt. You're in no condition to think of anything. You're knackered from worrying about tonight and being hit on the head with a packet of stationery and you mustn't knack yourself furthermore. I've put you with the committee on table one in the dining-room. Take your chair now before the crush starts, settle down and enjoy the party.'

William, feeling not at all robust, realized the sense of this and sipped down his champagne, enjoying for a moment the bustling scene in the entrance hall. Chidders was very busy exercising his front-doormanship. He was a massive and impressive figure in a well-pressed and spotless uniform, his chest twinkling and clinking with enough campaign gongs to give him medal-fatigue.

There was fiesta in the air. Members arrived chattering and laughing. Many oldies wore full evening dress of ancient cut, and very splendid they looked, William thought. Some of the suits were so old that they were going rusty and the white waistcoats were turning a pale tobacco colour around the edges and the button-holes, and some of the very old members wore their white tie in such a peculiar knot that they were clearly of that multitude of husbands who had never learnt how to tie a bow-tie, and their wives had forgotten.

There was a back way into the dining-room which led, through a corridor and a door, on to the permanent platform. William found the corridor had been made the 'backstage'. Malcolm was there plugging in wiring and tweaking at his electrical equipment and Philly was steam-ironing a pair of black trousers on top of a quite rare inlaid eighteenth-century library table.

'I'm getting the "Hello Dolly!" costumes ready one by one,' said Philly, 'but they're running to fat, your temp waiters, and I've had to let out most of the seams. It's been bloody go all day.'

There were three doors off to the right. William reflected that builders in earlier centuries were very good at including what they called 'closets' off other rooms, which came in most useful in later years for promoting such activities as voyeurism in literary works like *Fanny Hill*, and high speed dashing-about in theatrical farces.

The first door was open and through it William could see Brandy Jack in his vest applying make-up with the help of a mirror propped on a card-table.

'All well?' he called through the door.

'Hello, William!' Branny called back. 'All serene! Well, it is now. That old fool Philly, the malignant dwarf on

318

the other end of that electric-iron flex, wanted me to compère the evening dressed as Aristophanes. I tried on the costume he found me. It was like wearing a lambswool raincoat over a woolly Y-front.'

William felt Philly tugging at his arm. 'Don't you believe a word the silly sod tells you,' he whispered. ''E looked bonny, all lovely and classical in 'is little nappy!' A vagrant tear tried to work its way down Philly's mottled and bumpy cheek. 'Chuck a bucket of whitewash over 'im and you could've stood 'im on a plinth in the British Museum.'

'What's he dressed as now?'

'Well, I had a pick through Monty Berman's and found him something he likes, all boots and breeches and baggy silk shirt. 'E looks a bit like Dennis Price as *The Bad Lord Byron* but in point of actual fact it's the costume Harry Welchman wore in the original London production of *The Desert Song* in 1926. Branny and Harry were always the same size. Small but neat.'

William moved to open the next door along.

'*Don't go in there!*' shouted Philly.

William froze. 'Why on earth not?' he said. 'What's in there?'

'Never you mind,' said Philly. 'Stop poking about.' He opened the third door and held it open. 'Off you go,' said Philly. 'Follow the noise for the auditorium.'

The noise was easy to follow. There was a small queue at the door waiting to get in because those who had got in were standing still in amazement. Branny and his team's transformation of the dining-room was an extraordinary achievement; the room no longer even looked like a room. The permanent platform at the end had been raised and plaster pillars, a fringe and hanging curtains had made it into a kind of stage. Huge, shallow rostrums both round and square had been carried in and arranged so that they formed mounting curves, like wide steps, facing the stage.

Each rostrum carried a table for six, most of which were now full, and a separate table with a splendid arrangement of flowers and ornate and heavy silver dishes – of paté, oysters, pots of caviare and tiny flasks of vodka on crushed ice. A waiter stood by each table with a knife and handcloth to open the oysters and serve whatever was asked for. Every member could see every other member present, there was room to walk about, conversation with anybody was possible and the noise was rapidly approaching the deafening.

William looked up at the ceiling. This no longer looked anything like a ceiling but more like the roof of a 'closet' on Parnassus. Huge clouds of white material camouflaged the cornices and billowed out over the diners, and through the fine cheesecloth material, little electric stars of various colours, not at all unlike the Club's Christmas Tree decorations, could be detected twinkling against a dark blue paper sky. In the centre of the sky hung not the moon but a huge orange.

William began to feel a little dizzy.

A baying noise caught his ear and he saw the Sporting Baronet waving at him and calling his name. William joined the Events Committee – aka The Flying Pick-at-its – at table one, picking up one of the flasks of vodka and a dab of caviare en route. He sat down thankfully next to Lord Wick and had a restorative swig of vodka. Almost immediately he felt even dizzier.

'Do you think the party's mixing?' yelled Lord Wick. 'I wish somebody would start talking to somebody!'

'What?' yelled William, so loudly that his sullen head-ache returned.

The closet on Parnassus filled up. Members had now had a good look around, found their seats and sat down clutching their fishy luxuries or their liver paste. The elderly, traditionally trained Continental waiters circulated busily, pouring champagne with one white-gloved hand behind the back and the other hand with a thumb up the bump in the bottom of the bottle.

The curtains parted and to tremendous, partly ironic, cheers Brandy Jack bounced onstage, laughing healthily like Douglas Fairbanks Senior, the epitome of macho, pleasure-seeking, sexual magnetism.

'Don't go to sleep yet, Willy!' urged Belkis, who was now sitting on his other side. William cleared his head with a shake and watched Branny welcoming everybody to the party with wit and tremendous charm. Then Branny's tone of voice changed. 'But, alas, a sad note must now intrude upon our revels,' he went on. 'As Beerbohm Tree might well have remarked after one of his amorous weekends, "Life ain't all beer and Skindles", and now I must ask our Master, Lord Sidmonton, to come forward to make a melancholy announcement.'

From the back of the stage Lord Sidmonton emerged into the light. He was leaning heavily on a stick and biting back the grimaces of pain which the act of walking was evidently causing him. He arrived at the microphone and waved his free hand graciously to acknowledge the great surge of welcoming applause and cheering which he had apparently anticipated. There was no surge of anything, so after a moment he lowered his hand.

'Fellow Walpoleans . . . ' he began. He glanced down at the stick in his hand and smiling wryly at it, hurled it heroically to the back of the stage. He paused a moment, arm still upraised, in case there was a burst of applause at this *coup de théâtre* but nothing at all happened so he carried on: 'My days as Master of the Walpole Club are over as from midnight tonight. A number of circumstances have forced resignation upon me. A fragment of metal still in my leg, an inheritance from my days as an over-zealous company commander in Burma, is playing me up and I simply cannot continue with my many social engagements, however pressing my friends are for me to stay and guide County affairs. My wife, such a tireless worker for the underprivileged, will be joining me in a leafy part of France for a well-earned retirement, though knowing her I have no doubt that she will soon be working for the good of the deserving peasantry of the Dordogne as valiantly as she did for the good yeomanry of Goring-on-Thames . . . '

Lord Wick leant towards William's ear. 'I didn't realize the old fraud was such good value,' he whispered rather loudly, 'what a loss to British justice! Any hope one of our rich young members is recording this on one of those video camera thingies?'

'Sssssh!' said William.

The Master was continuing: '. . . some consolation in the thought that I have exerted a beneficent influence during my all-too-brief reign. I need only mention having Anton appointed as our new chef . . .'

'Oh, *really*!' said William.

'Ssssssh!' said Lord Wick.

'. . . and most of all being, so my friends claim, the co-instigator and planner; or as they rather embarrassingly say, the mind and dynamic energy behind the preparation of our Birthday Celebration tonight – the Walpole Orange!'

'Rubbish!' said Lord Wick.

'Ssssssh!' said William.

A plump Queen's Counsel with a pink face jumped to his feet and waving his arms, began singing 'For He's a Jolly Good Fellow—'

'NO, HE ISN'T!' said Lord Wick very loudly.

The pink QC sat down. The Master, visibly seething with fury, disabling hunk of Japanese shell in leg forgotten, strode smartly off the stage and into expatriate oblivion.

Malcolm pulled cords backstage and the curtains closed smoothly.

'Where's the Brig?' asked William, peering about.

'Greek Street,' said Lord Wick. 'He's gone to monitor and report back to us what happens when the gutter press and the plain-clothes police collide in the Whirlpool Club.'

'Excellent,' said William, and went back to his snooze.

'Wake up!' said Belkis in his ear a little later. 'You've missed the cold ham and tongue.'

It seems that Anton had become anxious that diners, not realizing what delights were awaiting them in the way of puds, would top up as they usually did with the main course and not want a pud at all. So he decided at the last moment to offer only the choice of a sliver of ham and tongue or a slice of game pie, with a wicked fried chip or two as company on the plate.

Branny came through the stage curtains holding a huge gong and a padded hammer, and Malcolm lit him with a spotlight.

'Every few hundred years or so,' said Branny in his beautiful, unforced but penetrating actor's voice, 'civilized man has invented something to make his eating more exciting or cheaper or more fun. Round about the sixteenth century the Italians instituted the use of forks, valuable not only to twirl spaghetti but to disturb the itching insects in the diner's hair. Then the wooden trencher was replaced by the china plate which couldn't be thrown at the cook if the roast carp was overdone. Well, not more than once. Then the invention of such modern epicene refinements as tomato ketchup and the gas-fired barbecue on wheels. Tonight, dear friends, our own chef Anton joins the Immortals. He has rewritten the world's banquet menus to provide the perfectly balanced celebratory dinner for the mature male, a menu orchestrated around the pride and strength of Old England, the Boiled Suet Pud. Sit back, my masters, and contemplate well Anton's delights before making your choice. Here be Treasures!'

He banged his gong once and the curtains behind him parted revealing five waiters lined up bearing covered silver dishes on bent-back wrists.

Another bang on the gong and the first waiter removed his lid.

'Pudding One,' announced Branny. 'Bread and Butter Pudding!'

Polite applause.

'A steaming cauldron of mushy bread and milk and butter all bubbling away.' Groans.

'Pudding Two,' said Branny. 'Rice Pudding!'

Wild but erratic applause.

'A new species of rice pudding created for us for tonight by Anton: creamy rice baked in very shallow dishes so that 90 per cent of it consists of crispy, burnt edges.'

Loud, greedy cheers.

Gong. Lid lifted. 'Pudding Three – Spotted Dick!'

Spontaneous applause burst out around the room.

'The finest suet, from deep within pedigree cows corn-fed by unmarried ex-beauty queens on the Isle of Wight, blended with the finest flour milled from contented corn, producing a matchless pudding crust at the same time both light and crisp, the whole studded with squashed flies.'

Cheers rang out.

Gong. Lid off. 'Pudding Four – Figgy Duff!'

Incredulous gasps.

'The Sailors' Favourite!' Cheers.

'An inch slice weighs a pound and a half which is why Figgy Duff was much in demand in Admiral Nelson's fleet as emergency ballast, even fashioned into spheres and fed into the guns when the cannon-balls ran out. Naval tradition has it that at Trafalgar it was a six-pounder ball of Figgy Duff that finally crippled the *Bucentaure*.'

Patriotic cheers from retired high-ranking Naval personnel.

Branny banged his gong again. The fifth waiter removed the lid from his dish revealing something not unlike a huge, smooth, shiny, greyish sausage.

'Pudding Five,' said Branny. 'Boiled Baby!'

Wild applause.

'A heavy, densely textured suet pudding rolled up in a cloth and plunged into rapidly boiling water for quite a long time. The genuine article can be detected from the fake because the real thing comes to a point at either end. A characteristic of this neglected delicacy is its soft coat, known to *aficionados* as "the slime" [cheers], which has to be scraped off before the hot syrup is poured on. Even then each spoonful has to be chased around the plate before it will give itself up.'

'So there's your birthday treat, my masters!' said Brandy Jack. 'Order your favourite from your waiter, or just ask for the Anton Extravaganza; a bit of each – WITH CUSTARD! The House Committee has asked me to announce that members have permission to undo such of their mid-area buttons as is compatible with the retention of dignity.'

Branny bowed low to prolonged applause. Before backing through the gap in the curtains he added: 'Or you could have a yoghurt.'

'Wake up!' said Belkis in William's ear. William emerged from his snooze with difficulty. The room was now alive with talk and laughter and the clattering of spoons and forks on plates. Waiters wove in and out of the tables and up and down the rostrums bearing trays of loaded and empty pudding plates.

'I've brought you some ham and tongue,' said Belkis. 'You've got to eat or you won't last. And the Brig has just arrived back from Greek Street.'

William pulled himself together and urged his chair sideways to make room for the Brig. 'Anything happening there?' he asked.

'Oh, yes!' said the Brig, sinking William's glass of champagne. 'All most satisfactory. As far as I can gather, a batch of plain-clothes Vice Squad lads and Council inspectors bought tickets for the show at the Whirlpool Club and sat down pretending to be ordinary punters, then a contingent of young journalists from the *Grass* did the same. When the show got really dirty a fat man gave a signal and half the reporters produced cameras from bags and cases and began photographing the girls and everybody in the audience. The plain-clothes cops did not like this at all and tried to stop them. A fight broke out and many arrests were made. My friend Chummy was punched on the side of the head by the fat man . . . '

'Gore-Bellamy!' said William.

'. . . and took him into custody. As they were squeezing him into the back of the Squad Car a big, heavy bicycle, out of control with no brakes, careered into the side of the police car, scratching and denting the door panel.'

'Tozer!' cried William.

'Indeed, Tozer,' said the Brig, with quiet satisfaction. 'He was shouting, "Take me to Gore-Bellamy, I want my money!" Chummy said, "With pleasure, sir, you're under arrest," and flung Tozer in the back of the Squad Car with the fat man.'

William finished his ham and tongue, took a swig of Lord Wick's Chablis and was back snoozing in a trice.

But this time it was a troubled, sad snooze. It was excellent news that he had protected the Club by out-manoeuvring Gore-Bellamy, and perhaps saved Tozer's soul from the nether regions by making Tozer realize that Malpractice Does Not Pay If You Are a Bit Thick. But they were negative achievements. It was plain that members expected some kind of suitable entertainment after their splendid and original dinner: the entertainment should have been the high spot of the Orange. And William had failed to provide what was wanted, failed miserably and completely.

'Wake up!' said Belkis. 'It's cabaret time!'

William struggled to clear his head. He had been fast asleep during which time the tables had been cleared, coffee and potent drinks served, cigars offered, and the diners, replete, were sagging down comfortably in their chairs.

Through the gap in the curtains sprang Brandy Jack, teeth a-gleam. 'And so,' he proclaimed, 'our Orange reaches its grand climax! Heads were broken in thought as to what this entertainment should be. Wild rumours have been circulating for months, the wildest being that the conclusion of our evening would involve naked ladies, clothes off and every man for himself. I hope that not too many of you will be unhappy when I say that our birthday celebration does not include nakedness.'

A sigh of relief, like a great gust of wind, swept through the tables.

'It seemed to your Events Committee that what an orgy *really* means is simply a brief excess of personal pleasure. In ancient times this meant promiscuous sex, all together, all over the place, but we're not Greek peasants nor Roman decadents and our ideas of what constitutes a bit of fun have changed over the centuries. And a most important factor is that ours is a birthday celebration. We are raising a glass to those gentlemen who founded our Club two hundred and fifty years ago and it seemed right that we should find a way in which our celebration would, for an hour, bridge that gap between the years. So we decided to do this with music. The music that our founders might well have listened to after their inaugural dinner.'

A patter of appreciative applause grew quickly into a good solid round.

'Because it's not just a party but an Orange, feminine beauty very much has its place, as you will observe as I now hand over the rest of our memorable evening to – The Millamant Baroque String Trio!'

'Good God!' said William, sitting up straight.

The curtains parted. The stage was dressed with four bentwood chairs, three skeletal music-stands and Milly's harpsichord.

'Bloody hell!' said William. He turned to Belkis. 'This is your doing!' he said. 'That's why you went to Ealing!'

'I only asked them to stand by', Belkis said, 'in case your cabaret turned nasty on you, which it did. And the girls happily stood in for you.'

'Well, I'm damned!' said William. 'Good Heavens!'

The Millamant Trio – all four of them – drifted on, smiling, half dancing, holding their instruments casually and affectionately. Pippa was swinging her cello by its neck and twirling it round as though it were a novel form of sunshade. They were all differently and beautifully dressed.

Belkis said, 'I brought their measurements back with me and Philly spent hours this morning sorting out dresses for them at Bermans and then ironing them. Milly's comes from *The Importance of Being Earnest*.'

Welcoming applause was loud and prolonged as the girls sorted themselves out on their chairs. Milly came to the front of the stage, looking to William delicate and vulnerable and utterly beautiful. Malcolm lowered a tiny microphone over her.

'We're going to start', said Milly, 'by playing you a Trio Sonata by Johann Hummel. This is a bit of a cheat because it was written in the late eighteenth century rather than the middle but there are good reasons for playing it. For one thing Johann Hummel had a most interesting career, working and living for a while with the young Mozart. There are other interesting things about his career but for the moment I've forgotten what they are. Another powerful reason for playing this sonata is that Johann Hummel had a wonderful middle name – "Nepomuk". What more distinctive way of celebrating a birthday than by listening to music written by somebody called Johann "Nepomuk" Hummel? The third reason is that all four of us love playing it.' Milly gave a little nervous smile, turned and sat at her harpsichord, and said to the Trio, 'Right all? Then let battle commence!'

Bows hit strings and away they went. William sat in a daze. He had never realized quite how good the Trio really was, nor how skilfully professional Milly was in introducing the items apparently so casually. Foster's influence was visible all along the line. The Trio's originally rather narrow repertoire had been widened and a new atmosphere of unpompous fun had crept into the presentation, giving their performance added charm. They played Handel and Bach and Telemann and the Walpole Club loved them. Then Foster, with a wonderfully clean, crisp tone, played a cadenza from Hummel's Trumpet Concerto.

The greyhound-racing contingent arrived back and, attracted by the music, crept in and sat on the floor wherever they could. A while later they were joined by the whitebait party home early from Greenwich. The room was jam-packed.

The Trio changed style and became an Edwardian Palm Court orchestra for a while, playing light melodies like 'In a Persian Market', and gems from *The Merry Widow*. And Catriona played Monti's Csardas as a solo, standing sideways, and a sigh like the sirocco swept through the room. And then the singing began, trembling baritone solos to begin with – seven quite old gentlemen wanted to give their *On the Road to Mandalay* – and then some very noisy community singing verging on, but not quite reaching, the emotional intensity of *You'll Never Walk Alone*.

Lord Wick leant over to William during a brief moment of comparative quiet. 'Well,' he said, 'you, with Milly's help, have done it, the almost impossible. What a birthday party! What an evening! William, on behalf of the whole Club I want to say that wholly due to your persistence and applied intelligence, we have tonight . . . William, wake up! . . . William! . . . '

* * *

'I gather,' said William, 'from your veiled hints from the concert platform, that if we have a baby next spring you intend to give it the middle name of Nepomuk.'

'Oh, Fie, sir! Next spring?' said Milly, wriggling. 'Such talk! I am not, as yet, *enceinte*.'

'The night is, as yet, a pup,' leered William, rather pointlessly as his face was buried in her hair.

The party was over and Milly was curled up in William's lap in his office. The Orange had ended on a high and noisy note. There was a good deal of mildly alcoholic cheering, and impromptu speeches thanking almost everybody for something or other. The Events Committee had arranged some presentations: Chidders was given a stainless steel shovel engraved with his name. He gave a short speech of thanks, made briefer by emotion. Belkis was presented with an enormous arrangement of flowers which delighted her. The tremendously helpful Malcolm received a voucher for electronic goods which made him grin most happily, and Milly and the Trio, because there was no time to

330

arrange anything else, were presented with a cheque, which made Milly go pale when she unfolded it and took a look. Anton was also given a cheque and was cheered to the echo. 'Roll on the 500th,' he said, waving the cheque. 'Cheers, mates!'

'I take it you won't stay at the Club now that all the excitement's over,' Milly said. 'What next?'

'Well,' said William, 'once we've got Nepomuk's education out of the way . . . '

Milly reached up and tweaked his hair quite painfully. 'Don't tease me,' she said. 'Nepomuk's important to me. Oh, darling, did I pull a bit hard?'

'What does a little agony matter when you're in love?' said William, through clenched teeth. 'But what next indeed? I think tonight Foster had enough enquiries for the Trio's services for us both to be kept men for a couple of years. How about it? I'll stay at home and change Nepomuk's nappies while you OWWWWWWW! That really did hurt!'

'I bet Lord Wick will offer you something when we have dinner with him to meet Lady Wick . . . '

'And his dog, Madeleine . . . '

'And Madeleine, tomorrow night.'

'He's already spoken. He wants both of us to move to Castle Wick and get the whisky-flavoured smoked-salmon farm going. And a friend of mine wants us to set up a Margate International Arts Festival.'

'Margate!'

'Why not? It's got one of the oldest Georgian theatres in the country, plenty of bookshops and concert halls.'

'But surely a successful Margate International Arts Festival's an impossibility?'

'Oh, yes, absolutely. Attractive, isn't it?' William smiled, and the smile turned into a huge yawn.

'You go to sleep at this stage of the game and so help me I'll swing for you!' said Milly.

'You've changed, you know, Mil,' said William. 'In the last few weeks you've become – I don't know what it is. But different. We've become immeasurably closer.'

'I'll tell you what it is,' said Milly. 'I liked you very much to begin with, but – I'm sorry about this, Willy – I married you to get away from my parents.'

'But so does everybody, don't they? To some degree or other?'

'What I mean is, I didn't really know you, not really, only superficially. The last few weeks have been different. I've seen you under stress, under temptation – and who but a block of wood could stay untempted by the wonderful Belkis in mischievous mood—'

'I could,' said William.

'Liar,' said Milly. 'Belkis told me you kissed her. She only told me because she finds you very attractive but in a totally unsexy way—'

'Thank you, Belkis.'

'—and she and I get on. The weird fact is, William, for the first time in my life I'm in love, *really* in love, and you're right, it's changed me.'

William was trying hard to think straight. 'It's not unusual for semi-happily married women to fall in love,' he said tentatively, 'is it?'

'I think it's unusual for a wife to fall deeply in love with her husband,' Milly said.

The message finally penetrated the mists of William's tired brain. He made a quiet, whinnying noise and hugged Milly until she could not breathe and the huge cameo brooch on her costume had impressed itself painfully in her breast like a signet-ring in wax. He released her and touched her hair and her lip and held her again more gently.

Milly nibbled his ear for a moment and then she whispered: 'My place or yours?'

William's grip tightened in a galvanic twitch.

'Oh, both!' he whispered. 'At the same time!'

And so, arms around each other, William and Milly walked out of the Walpole Club, through the archway and on towards St James's Street and a taxi. Progress was slow because they had to stop every few steps to kiss.

'There's only one thought that worries me on this perfect night,' said Milly during one of the stops, 'and that's that it is a perfect night. Belkis warned me about the danger of attracting the Evil Eye.'

'What's the Evil Eye's problem?' said William, increasingly anxious to get home.

'We're so happy that a malevolent onlooker with magical powers would spot this and "cast the Eye" upon us. Do us mischief. Make something fall on us.'

William hugged her for a while. 'Did Belkis say what we could do to protect ourselves?' he said.

'There are various counter-charms we could use like wearing blue beads or being spat upon. The main thing is that our happiness must be halted for a moment, we have suddenly to become figures of acute distress and then the marauding Eye will stop envying us.'

'Fat chance of that,' said William. 'Tonight is simply not our night for being distressed.'

They stood on the kerb of St James's Street, William's hand uplifted with finger pointed high to indicate to cabbies that he was wishing to hire. But it was that awkward hour when the daytime cabbies had all gone home to Essex and the night shift had yet to arrive. There were many late revellers strung along Clubland with finger up but no roving cabs at all.

Suddenly a car, going quite fast, pulled into the kerb with a screech and the rear door was flung open.

'It's illegal for me to pick up in the street so would you mind hopping in quick, squire,' said the driver.

William handed Milly in and swiftly joined her in the back.

'The Evil Eye has been thwarted!' he whispered to Milly. 'Nepomuk is going to be a *beautiful* child!'

'What do you mean?' said Milly. 'We're still to be envied, we're the only ones on the street who've managed to get a cab!'

'I know,' said William, 'but look who our driver is.'

It was Rollo.

THE END

THE COVER ARTIST
Paul Micou

'OUTRAGEOUS FARCE IS TEMPERED BY A GENTLE WHIMSY AND THE CHARACTERIZATION AND PLOT CONSTANTLY SURPRISE AND DELIGHT'
Sunday Telegraph

'MICOU MANAGES TO HIT MANY TARGETS WITHOUT LOSING THE GENTLE FRESHNESS OF THE SATIRE'
Sunday Times

'MICOU'S GIFT IS FOR FUSING OUTRAGEOUS ELEMENTS INTO REFINED FARCE'
David Hughes, *Mail on Sunday*

Oscar Lemoine's artistic medium is the celebrity nude caricature; his ageing black labrador, Elizabeth, is a late-blooming exponent of Canine Expressionism. The minor notoriety of Oscar's covers for the New York based *Lowdown* magazine sends master and dog into exile in the South of France, where Oscar hopes to improve his primitive social skills – and to do what he can to develop Elizabeth's budding artistic talent. Oscar finds romance in Val d'Argent; Elizabeth paints a series of masterpieces.

Paul Micou's critically acclaimed novel *The Music Programme* introduced an exciting new writer; *The Cover Artist*, the story of a man's social myopia and his dog's artistic triumph, emphatically confirms that remarkable début.

'IT'S QUICK, BRIGHT, CONSISTENT, AND PROBABLY HAS SOME SECRET INGREDIENT TO KEEP YOU COMING BACK FOR MORE'
Saul Frampton, *Time Out*

'*THE COVER ARTIST* IS AN EFFORTLESS READ, OF THE SORT THAT IS FAR FROM EASY TO WRITE'
David Honigmann, *Listener*

0 552 99408 1

A SELECTED LIST OF FINE NOVELS
AVAILABLE FROM CORGI BOOKS AND BLACK SWAN

THE PRICES SHOWN BELOW WERE CORRECT AT THE TIME OF GOING TO PRESS.
HOWEVER TRANSWORLD PUBLISHERS RESERVE THE RIGHT TO SHOW NEW
RETAIL PRICES ON COVERS WHICH MAY DIFFER FROM THOSE PREVIOUSLY
ADVERTISED IN THE TEXT OR ELSEWHERE.

☐	99348 4	**SUCKING SHERBET LEMONS**	Michael Carson	£5.99
☐	99465 0	**STRIPPING PENGUINS BARE**	Michael Carson	£6.99
☐	13947 5	**SUNDAY MORNING**	Ray Connolly	£4.99
☐	13827 4	**SPOILS OF WAR**	Peter Driscoll	£4.99
☐	99599 1	**SEPARATION**	Dan Franck	£5.99
☐	13598 4	**MAESTRO**	John Gardner	£5.99
☐	13282 9	**PAINTING THE DARKNESS**	Robert Goddard	£5.99
☐	13144 X	**PAST CARING**	Robert Goddard	£4.99
☐	13839 8	**HAND IN GLOVE**	Robert Goddard	£4.99
☐	13840 1	**CLOSED CIRCLE**	Robert Goddard	£4.99
☐	99466 9	**A SMOKING DOT IN THE DISTANCE**	Ivor Gould	£6.99
☐	13695 6	**IN HIGH PLACES**	Arthur Hailey	£4.99
☐	99467 7	**MONSIEUR DE BRILLANCOURT**	Clare Harkness	£4.99
☐	99169 4	**GOD KNOWS**	Joseph Heller	£7.99
☐	99538 X	**GOOD AS GOLD**	Joseph Heller	£6.99
☐	99369 7	**A PRAYER FOR OWEN MEANY**	John Irving	£6.99
☐	99206 2	**SETTING FREE THE BEARS**	John Irving	£6.99
☐	99204 6	**THE CIDER HOUSE RULES**	John Irving	£6.99
☐	99209 7	**THE HOTEL NEW HAMPSHIRE**	John Irving	£6.99
☐	99567 3	**SAILOR SONG**	Ken Kesey	£6.99
☐	14249 2	**VIRGINS AND MARTYRS**	Simon Maginn	£4.99
☐	99384 0	**TALES OF THE CITY**	Armistead Maupin	£5.99
☐	99569 X	**MAYBE THE MOON**	Armistead Maupin	£5.99
☐	99408 1	**THE COVER ARTIST**	Paul Micou	£4.99
☐	99381 6	**THE MUSIC PROGRAMME**	Paul Micou	£4.99
☐	99597 5	**COYOTE BLUE**	Christopher Moore	£5.99
☐	14145 3	**MANCHESTER BLUE**	Eddy Shah	£4.99
☐	99122 8	**THE HOUSE OF GOD**	Samuel Shem	£6.99
☐	14143 7	**A SIMPLE PLAN**	Scott Smith	£4.99
☐	99546 0	**THE BRIDGWATER SALE**	Freddie Stockdale	£5.99